Praise for Christopher Golden

DEAD RINGERS

"Golden's chilling tale will have you shivering the next time you glance at your reflection. Is it really always you looking back?" —*Washington Post*

"Deeply disturbing and studded with ghastly imagery, this beautifully written narrative will inspire shudders with every turn of the page." —*Publishers Weekly*

"*Dead Ringers* rises above the standard horror-novel clichés with style . . . A supernatural horror novel that seems all too plausible thanks to its fast pace, adept characterization, and fine sense of place."
—*Shelf Awareness*

"A book with the momentum of a thriller, but it's driven by character . . . [Golden] excels at character development and is one of the few writers working today who plays in the same league as Stephen King."
—*Slush Pile Heroes*

"Reminiscent of Jack Finney's *The Body Snatchers* (without the aliens) . . . [Golden] delivers enough chills to satisfy." —*Library Journal*

SNOWBLIND

Also by Christopher Golden

DEAD RINGERS

CHRISTOPHER GOLDEN

St. Martin's Paperbacks

This is a work of fiction. All of the characters, organizations, and events portrayed in this novel are either products of the author's imagination or are used fictitiously.

DEAD RINGERS

Copyright © 2015 by Christopher Golden.

All rights reserved.

For information address St. Martin's Press, 175 Fifth Avenue, New York, NY 10010.

ISBN: 978-1-250-09725-5

Our books may be purchased in bulk for promotional, educational, or business use. Please contact your local bookseller or the Macmillan Corporate and Premium Sales Department at 1-800-221-7945, extension 5442, or by e-mail at MacmillanSpecialMarkets@macmillan.com.

Printed in the United States of America

St. Martin's Press hardcover edition / November 2015
St. Martin's Paperbacks edition / December 2016

St. Martin's Paperbacks are published by St. Martin's Press, 175 Fifth Avenue, New York, NY 10010.

10 9 8 7 6 5 4 3 2 1

For the lost ones, the happy ones,
the broken ones, the sad ones, the hopeful ones . . .
the ones with their minds on fire. For my friends.
I love you all.

ACKNOWLEDGMENTS

Profound thanks to my editor, Michael Homler, my agent, Howard Morhaim, and my manager, Pete Donaldson, for their faith and enthusiasm. Thanks to everyone at St. Martin's Press for your efforts on my behalf. A special thank you to those who served as early readers on this novel and whose feedback proved invaluable: Leah Zander, Amy Young, Jim Moore, and the inimitable Tom Sniegoski.

Finally, much love and gratitude to Connie and our children, may they be near or far. Forever, my darlings.

All my favorite people are broken.

—*Over the Rhine*

MONDAY

Frank Lindbergh had managed to escape his childhood home for a handful of ambitious years before death and fate conspired to bring him back. The house on Hammersmith Street was a faded, peeling memory with a sagging front porch that propped up an equally sagging second-floor deck. The two-story colonial duplex sat among a dozen other houses that were nearly identical except for the age and hue of the paint job. This was the street where he'd ridden his bike and chased the ice-cream man. Back in those days, the front porch would have been full of people drinking Budweiser and listening to the last Red Sox game of the season on the radio. The grill in the side yard would have been billowing clouds from a sausage grease fire, smoke whirling off into the sky with the first autumn leaves on a late-September breeze.

Twenty years was a long time.

Growing up, Frank had promised himself he'd get out of this neighborhood. His dad had done painting and plastering and his mom had been a school lunch lady, taking in seamstress work on the side to make ends meet, and all the happy blue-collar horseshit he heard up and down Hammersmith Street made him want to scream. He'd never wanted that life for himself.

Frank didn't like to think about his childhood, mainly because it all seemed so trite to him. Drunk old man, funny after four beers, mean after eight, violent if he turned to whiskey. Frank had a cap on an upper incisor that he'd only gotten fixed when he graduated from college and was on the hunt for a job—prior to that he'd liked seeing it in the mirror, would smile at himself every day just to catch a glimpse. His father had torn up his knuckles on that broken tooth one night and had vivid white scars there until the day they'd closed his coffin lid.

Frank had scars, too.

He'd moved out three days after high school graduation, worked three jobs to pay for UMass Boston and a spot on a friend's couch. All the time—hell, from seventh grade on up—he'd been laser-focused on becoming a newspaper reporter. A *journalist,* he'd told anyone who'd listen. When he hit the streets after college, he landed a job at the *Boston Phoenix,* which had been the craigslist of local rags before it went under. From there he'd moved to the *Boston Herald,* pretended he believed at least half the crap they printed, and dedicated himself to the dream he'd promised to his thirteen-year-old self: becoming a crime reporter.

Six months after coming on staff, Frank had gotten his wish. Crime beat.

Seven weeks later he received his pink slip, and

things had gone to hell from there. He'd lost the latest in a string of girlfriends, lost his apartment in Somerville, and had to move back in with his mother, Ruth. *Just* his mother, because his dad had fallen off a ladder the year before, broken his neck, and been dead before the paint bucket hit the ground. Living back on Hammersmith Street, Frank gave the same answer whenever anyone asked what had happened with his journalism career—the Internet was killing print journalism, but he planned to start his own Boston news Web site as soon as he finished raising the funds.

Dad had been drunk the day he died. He had fallen from the ladder, yeah, but it was alcohol that killed him. Frank and his mother never talked about it, just like they didn't talk about his own drinking once he had moved back into the house. Ruth stayed silent and picked up the bottles Frank left around, just as she'd done for his father for nearly forty years. She cleaned up after her son until the moment the cancer made her too weak to get out of bed.

Lymphoma. It had killed her ten months ago, a week before Thanksgiving. Ever since, Frank walked around the house with a trash bag twice a week picking up his empties and quietly apologizing to her ghost for the mess.

Most nights he sat in front of the television, the laugh tracks of old sitcoms a temporary respite from the yawning silence inside the house at night. Sometimes, though, he turned the TV off and sat in the wan light from the floor lamp, just listening to the ticking clock on the wall and the groaning beams up in the attic. It would be worse this winter, he knew. The baseboard heat would pop and hiss and somehow he'd feel even more alone.

Tonight he felt himself nodding off, licked his lips, and sat up straighter in his chair. Last time he'd been to the fridge he had retrieved two beers to save himself another trip. Now he drained the dregs of one and used the opener on his key ring to pop the cap on the other. He stared at the darkened television screen for a few seconds.

"My kind of party," he whispered to himself.

Nights like this, when he sat and drank beer without even the company of those old sitcoms . . . those were the nights he worried. He found comfort in the idea that worrying about himself must be healthy, that he had not hit rock bottom as long as his behavior concerned him. But that reassurance always came cloaked in the blur of drunken logic, and in the mornings he remembered that noticing your car was headed for a tree was not the same as swerving to avoid it.

"Enough of this shit," he whispered to himself. He rested the bottle of Heineken on his thigh and stared at the label. "Tomorrow, this is all gonna change."

A week ago, he'd run into Bobby Suarez, a friend from the neighborhood who'd moved a total of six blocks from his parents' house and was now assistant principal at Doherty Middle School. The eighth-grade English teacher was going out on maternity leave and they needed a long-term substitute starting in mid-October and going through the end of the school year.

You keep your shit together, come in for an interview, I can probably hook you up, Suarez had told him, following the words with a smile just a hair shy of condescending. *Could be they'll even let you start up a student newspaper or something, inspire the next generation of future journalists.*

Suarez's tone made clear how useful he thought journalists were. Frank told him to fuck off, in the way friends did, especially in this part of town. He half meant it, but only half. Suarez was doing him a solid and if he could get himself cleaned up in the morning, go in and give a decent performance at the interview, he promised himself he would track down an AA meeting on the way home.

He'd made empty promises to himself before and had learned to recognize them, so he sat up a bit straighter in the chair and took a breath.

"You're going," he told himself.

Frank had been in AA for nearly a month last summer. He used his mother's death as the reason for falling off the wagon, but in truth he'd started drinking again weeks before she'd passed. Not this time, though.

He glanced around the living room with its faded photos on the walls and threadbare furniture . . . and the ghosts of all the times he'd vowed to leave and never return. If he didn't seize the reins of his life, he would end up nothing more than a drunk old man and die right here in this house. His ugliest demon was the knowledge that his life had no purpose, but the spark of hope and ambition that hadn't been completely extinguished in him reminded him that he could still *find* purpose. Choose a path.

"Tomorrow," he rasped in the gloom of that dingy floor lamp.

The Heineken bottle felt warm in his hand, but he

tipped it back and drained two-thirds of it without taking a breath. Lowering the bottle, he stifled a belch, then brought the bottle to his lips again and sucked back the last gulp of beer before setting the empty on the little table beside his chair.

Dead soldier, he thought. *The last one.*

Late-night promises were like Schrödinger's cat, existing in a state of flux, full of the potential to be kept or broken. Only in the morning would he know if the cat was alive or dead.

Frank pushed himself up out of his chair, unsteady on his feet. The dark, silent television screen seemed to mock him, reflecting a fun house–mirror image of him as he stumbled and caught himself on the back of the chair. He shook his head to clear it, chiding himself for letting six beers have such an impact on him. *Should've finished your dinner,* he thought.

Making his way to the stairs, he heard a thump from the back hall. His thoughts were swollen and wrapped in gauze, but he stopped and frowned as he peered toward the back of the house. A long, low creak came from the kitchen, something shifting its weight on the old flooring back there.

A knot formed in his gut and he felt an icy tickle at the back of his brain. His skin prickled with the impossible certainty that he was not in the house alone, and he held his breath. Even as he stepped along the hall, shoving himself away from the stairs, he knew he ought to head up to his bedroom—to the cell phone charging on his nightstand. *Call 911,* he thought, but instead he listed toward the kitchen, heedless of the warning an intruder might receive from the creaking of his foot-steps on the floor.

Frank put a hand on the kitchen door, felt the cold, chipped paint. An image swam into his head of his father, rooting around for a midnight snack. The few times Frank had come down during the night—frightened by a nightmare or coming down with a flu—and discovered him there, his father had barked at him and sent him back to bed. All but once. That one time, Frank Sr. had made his boy a mug of hot chocolate and told him, in a rare moment of introspection, that people made their own monsters . . . that half the time, they *were* their own monsters.

The memory froze him. He hadn't thought of that night in years. His resentment had no room for the memory of the kindness and sadness in his father's eyes as they'd talked over their steaming hot chocolate.

Inside the kitchen, something shifted. The floor creaked once, and then again.

"Anybody home?" a voice called softly from behind the door.

Frank stared at the chipped paint, at his hand upon it. The voice sounded vaguely familiar, but not enough so that his heart stopped racing. It was nearly midnight, after all. Visitors didn't drop by this late at night, and they certainly didn't let themselves in.

"Who the hell is in there?" he demanded.

A soft chuckle, a rasp of movement, a creak on the floor. "Come and see."

He yanked his hand back as if the cold paint had seared his fingertips. Wetting his lips, heart thundering in his ears, he tried to clear the alcoholic fog from his thoughts. He remembered his cell phone again, charging on the nightstand upstairs, and took several stumbling steps back toward the front of the house.

Come and see.

No thanks.

His hand grabbed the newel post at the bottom of the stairs, managed to get a foot onto the first step, but then he heard the squeal of hinges as the kitchen door swung open. Frank couldn't help but stare at the dark silhouette emerging from the kitchen, a tall man who started along the short hall toward him.

The wan light from the floor lamp in the living room cast a gloomy yellow pall into the hallway. The man stepped into the light.

Frank narrowed his eyes, tried to blink away the beer goggles.

"What the hell?" he whispered.

The man walked toward him with a familiar smile. Drunk and stunned, Frank shook his head, trying to force the world to make sense. Only when the man was three paces from him did he see the malice in those eyes.

His own eyes. His own smile. His own face.

"Hold on," he said, trying to wave the guy away. "Just back up a second and—"

The intruder had quick hands. The first blow crashed into Frank's left temple and he slammed against the faded wallpaper at the bottom of the steps, sagging, knees already weak. Anger rushed through him, a righteous fury that made him spring off the wall and swing wildly at that familiar face—a face he hated every time he saw it in the mirror.

The intruder batted his punch away, stepped in and slammed a fist into Frank's gut, shoved him hard so that he slammed into the wall again, and followed up with a barrage of punches to the jaw and throat and abdomen. Lost in pain and the buzzing fog of half a dozen beers, he tried to muster up some words of protest.

The best he could manage was a single syllable. "Stop."

The smile had vanished from the intruder's face. His eyes were wide with a kind of dread all his own, and with sorrow.

"I can't," he said.

He grabbed a fistful of Frank's hair—hair so entirely like his own—tugged and twisted, and drove Frank headfirst into the newel post. Pain exploded in Frank's skull and then a sea of blackness swept in, blanketing his thoughts, suffocating them. He felt himself falling toward the floor, but then the darkness swallowed him whole.

The intruder with Frank's face made himself at home.

THURSDAY

ONE

When Tess Devlin spotted her ex-husband, Nick, standing at the intersection of Oliver and High Street in the shadow of the curved, glassy towers of International Place, her first thought was that he must have gotten a raise. His suit had the right cut, crisp lines, and a subtle pattern that suggested surprising confidence. It had been two months since she'd last seen him and in that time he'd apparently shed ten pounds and decided to tame his sometimes unruly hair. If she didn't know better, she'd have guessed he was one of the attorneys at Barr and Crowe, the massive law firm inside One International Place.

But she did know better. Nick taught archaeology at Boston University and couldn't have afforded this beautifully tailored suit on his best day. Their daughter, six-year-old Maddie, had seen him every other weekend but Tess and Nick had avoided each other during the handoffs, staring in their respective cars, pulling into driveways and beeping horns as if they were engaging in some kind of late-night drug deal instead of co-parenting their beautiful little girl.

Now Nick waited at the crosswalk for the light to change. Tess thought about hanging back, avoiding contact, but she was a big girl. They hadn't ended well, but they had tried to put any animosity behind them for Maddie's sake. Tess stepped up beside him, smiling at him even though he kept his gaze straight-ahead.

"Nice suit," she said. "You come into a fortune you didn't tell me about or were you hiding it all along?"

Several other people gathered at the curb, but the DON'T WALK signal remained lit. Nick took out his cell phone and glanced at it, perhaps checking for text messages, either ignoring her completely or just profoundly distracted. He'd always had a touch of what had once been called Asperger's Syndrome and sometimes would just get lost in himself. In small doses, his difficulty with socialization and with reading people's facial and verbal cues was easily overlooked, but the little, unintentional hurts built up over time and had contributed to the ruin of their marriage.

"Yo, Devlin," she said, tapping his arm.

Nick flinched away from her, holding his phone off to the left as if he thought she might try to steal it. He gave her a down-the-nose, slightly askance look that made her feel like some kind of freak, but he said not a word. The old scars on her flesh burned for a moment before the memory of them faded, but the pain in her left shoulder and her spine . . . that never faded. It lingered all day, every day, so familiar that sometimes she even forgot to feel the hurt of those old injuries. Nick had not caused the accident that left her with chronic pain, but he had never understood how it had taken up residence within her. Pain was the ghost that haunted her every waking moment. He wasn't really capable of empathy, but this?

"Seriously?" Tess whispered. Nick might be her ex-husband, but even at their worst, he'd never given her this cold a shoulder. "What the hell is wrong with you?"

For the first time, he swiveled his head to meet her gaze, brow knitted in a deep frown. "I'm not sure what your story is, but could you maybe go psycho on somebody else?"

Tess gave a hollow laugh, hating the way her gut turned to stone. This shouldn't hurt so much, but it did. Goddamn him, it did.

"Nick, come on," she said. "Why are you—"

His frown deepened and his mouth twisted in a cynical huff. "I get it now. Nick, is it? Sorry to break it to you, but you need your eyes checked. The name's Theo. Whoever Nick is, I wish him luck."

Tess stared, mouth open in a round little moue of shock. She appraised him again, the chin and jawline, the ears, the cast of his vivid blue eyes, even the pattern of late-day shadow that his razor would have to combat in the morning. Thinner, yes, and maybe the circles under his eyes had vanished and he had a better haircut, but . . . was it possible?

"Well, damn," she said quietly. "I think you may have a twin brother you've never met."

The man who was not Nick Devlin blinked, gave her a small scowl, and then turned to march away from her. The WALK signal had lit and the cluster of end-of-the-workday refugees spilled onto the crosswalk, striding quickly toward wherever their Thursday night would bring them. Tess stood frozen on the curb, the stream of people flowing around her, and stared at the rear of Not-Nick's head.

He glanced back at her, and something about that glance made her wince. His expression held a flicker of fear and his eyes hid *something,* and suddenly she felt like a fool. The son of a bitch had almost pulled one over on her—what an idiot she'd been to buy his spin for even a second.

"You little shit," she muttered, tugging out her own cell phone.

Turning from the street, she began to pace along the sidewalk, anger making her forget the pain in her back. Her foot caught an empty fast-food drink cup and it skittered on ahead of her. The wind picked up, bringing in the cold air off Boston Harbor, and she shivered as she searched her contacts for her ex-husband's name. The late-afternoon sun had fallen so low that the buildings cast long gray shadows, enveloping much of the city in a premature dusk. Normally she loved the crisp chill of the autumn air, but not today. Not right now.

She tapped the screen and put the phone to her ear. It rang twice before he picked up.

"Hello, Tess," Nick said, his voice warm but curious. "To what do I owe the pleasure?"

The kindness in his tone only made her angrier.

"You can be a real prick sometimes," she said, stuffing her free hand into the pocket of her coat and turning away from a pair of well-dressed women striding past.

"Yeah," he agreed warily. "You said as much when you were divorcing me. What's this about?"

Tess looked across the street, searching the pedestrian crowd for him, but he'd either blended in with the herd or turned a corner already.

"Were you trying to be funny, or did you want to make a fool of me?" The phone felt clammy in her hand.

"Y'know, I don't appreciate . . ." Nick began, but she heard him falter. "No. I'm not gonna fight with you, Tessa. I can hear in your voice how pissed you are right now, but I don't have the first clue what I've done to set you off, so maybe you want to elaborate?"

She pressed her eyes shut. Felt the chill breeze run up her dress and whip her hair around in front of her face. A shudder went up her back, like someone had just walked over her grave. Her mother had always used that expression but Tess realized she had never really understood it till now.

Your face, she wanted to say. *Even your voice.*

But he sounded so sincere.

"If you're playing some kind of game—"

"Tess. Explain."

She exhaled, once again searching the sidewalk on the opposite side of the intersection. In all the time she'd known him, she'd never seen Nick in a suit that nice, never known him to be willing to spend that kind of money on anything, or to have that kind of money to spend. Not even on his daughter, whom he professed to love.

"Where are you?" she asked.

"Just got back from a hike. Where are you?"

"You're hiking?"

"Up in the White Mountains, staying at the Notchland, but right now we're just having coffee at that little place across from the train station in North Conway. You remember it?"

Her thoughts raced. She turned to stare at the spot on the corner where she'd encountered Not-Nick—because he really had been Not-Nick, hadn't he?

Tess felt her cheeks flush with heat. She lowered her head. "With Kyrie."

"What . . ." He trailed off for a moment before replying. "Of course with Kyrie. You know . . ." Nick broke off again and she heard his muffled voice as he explained that it was his ex-wife calling. "Sorry, I'm back."

"I'm the one who's sorry. Go and enjoy your time off with your girlfriend. Take her to that little Irish pub for the late-night music." Tess shook her head, feeling foolish now that all of the anger had bled out of her. Of course Nick—her Nick, with that touch of Asperger's—would not consider that telling her he was taking his girlfriend to the places they used to enjoy together might hurt her. They had loved to hike, back before . . .

Stop, she told herself.

"Call me when you get back," she said. "I have a wicked stupid story to tell you."

"You sure you're okay?" he asked.

Over at the crosswalk, the WALK signal lit up. She started toward it, laughing softly as she rejoined the post-workday exodus.

"Right as rain," she said, trying not to imagine Nick and his new mate riding the North Conway Scenic

Railroad. Were they staying in the same room at the Notchland that she and Nick had always booked, the red-walled one with its drafty windows, creaky four-poster bed, and enormous fireplace? If there'd been one thing Nick had never failed to do properly, it was build a fire.

"I'm right as rain," she said again. "I'll give Maddie your love."

Tess heard him say her name as she hit the button to end the call, trying to remember Not-Nick's exact features. Had she overestimated how much the stranger looked like her ex? That seemed far more likely than him having a secret twin brother that his parents had never told him about. Didn't they say everyone had a double somewhere?

Weird, she thought. *So damn weird.*

She hurried across the intersection, phone still clutched in her hand. As she stepped up onto the opposite curb, she glanced again at her contact list and tapped the screen to call her best friend Lili. The line crackled as it rang three times, then a fourth and fifth, and when she was about to give up, Lili answered.

"Hey, lady," her friend said. "Did you get that babysitter? We still on for drinks tonight?"

"Oh, yes," Tess replied, the autumn chill caressing her legs and racing up her back. "A thousand times, yes."

TWO

Tess had met Lilandra Pillai in a drama class back in their bad old days at Tufts University, just a few miles outside of Boston. Lili had been double-majoring in archaeology and history, Tess in history and political science, but they both had a not-so-secret love of the theater and simultaneous terror of the stage. There would be no auditions for them, no performances outside of the soliloquies and scenes required within the relative safety of the classroom, but from that point on, they hit Boston's theater district on a regular basis, scoring tickets at student discounts and waiting at stage doors to effuse over the actors together. Each had other friends, but between their history majors and the live-theater fanaticism, they enjoyed a rapport others couldn't touch.

They had shared the best of times, and Tess had been with Lili through the worst of times as well, after Lili had woken up in a pile of dirty laundry in the basement of a frat house with her pants around her ankles and her underwear lost forever. Lili had shown up at

Tess's dorm room that morning, numb with rage, and they had gone to the infirmary together. When Lili had reported the assault, the university's investigation had concluded that since Lili could not identify her attackers or provide any evidence to support the idea that someone from the fraternity was responsible for whatever drugs had been in her drink, no punishment would be forthcoming. The administration had seemed relieved to have a rationale that allowed them to avoid pursuing it any further.

In the years since they had rarely spoken of it, but Tess knew they both still shared a simmering rage at the injustice. It had taught them to rely on each other, that maybe they could rely *only* on each other. Tess had always admired Lili's resilience. Years later, after the accident, the pain, the kiss, and finally her divorce, it was Lili's example that made it easier for Tess to cope. They'd both had their lives torn apart and found a way to put them back together again.

And they went on helping each other heal as only the best of friends ever could. Their work brought them together occasionally, as with the dig at the Clough House, a documentary about abandoned subway stations, and the bodies discovered in the renovation of the Otis Harrison House. And, of course, they kept visiting the Playwright Tavern, which they'd discovered in their college days.

A block from the Charles Playhouse in the theater district, the Playwright was like a low-rent Sardi's, the walls hung with photos of the famous and semi-famous and no-longer-famous people who'd come into the bar over the years, along with *Playbill*s that stretched back into Boston theater antiquity. They'd seen Mandy Patinkin having dinner the first time they'd gone into the Playwright and waited until he'd been walking out before stopping him to say hello. By silent agreement—that almost telepathic connection they shared—they didn't ask for a photo or autograph, just for hugs. Mandy obliged, held them each by the hand for a moment, as kind and warm as your favorite uncle, and then went on his way.

From that point on, the Playwright had become their favorite hangout. The quality of the food had improved, then fallen off steeply, and then improved again as the theater scene in Boston had undergone a resurgence, but for the most part, they went for the ambience and the memory. As time passed—and especially once Tess became a wife and then a mother—it had been more expedient and sometimes more desirable for them to meet at other bars or restaurants or cafés, but at least a couple of times a year, they found their way back to the Playwright.

Tonight Tess arrived early, about a quarter after six, and sat down at the corner of the bar, putting her thin, green fall jacket on the next stool to save it for Lili. She didn't recognize the bartender, which saddened her, reminding her how infrequently they made a point of visiting their old stomping grounds. Then she pictured Maddie's smiling face and suddenly nostalgia faded. Instead she felt the twinge of guilt that struck her every time she did anything that required an evening babysitter. Her world revolved around her daughter, Madeline, who had her mother's coffee-brown skin and her father's blue eyes.

"What can I get you?" the bartender asked, barely paying attention as he wiped his hands on a small towel and put a coaster on the mahogany bar in front of her.

"That depends," she said.

He glanced up, really looking at her for the first time, and broke out into a smile. The wattage turned down an instant later, as if he'd suddenly become self-conscious, but she'd seen his reaction and it delighted her. Between her work for the Bostonian Society and being a mom, she'd nearly forgotten what it felt like to share a moment with someone, that mutual frisson that had an electricity all its own. His dark, smooth skin and broad shoulders didn't hurt, but it had been more than just finding him attractive.

"Sorry. I was preoccupied," he said after a moment. " 'Depends' on what?"

"Whether you still have Newcastle on tap."

"Ah, so you're the one."

"Sorry?"

"The one who drinks it."

Tess smiled and tucked a lock of her hair behind her ear, then chided herself for such trite body language. Her shoulder throbbed and she sat up straighter, not to draw attention to her breasts but to ease the burden on the pins in her spine.

"So, you're telling me it's been sitting there for months," she said, "which means it's gone stale by now."

The bartender grabbed a glass and then reached for the tap. "Nah. People drink it, but I always tell the owner there are a hundred beers we could have on tap that would sell better. Maybe he thinks it gives the place a certain verisimilitude."

He poured a perfect pint, paused to make sure, and then returned to the end of the bar and set it on the coaster in front of her. Tess touched the glass and found it cool but not cold, perfect for Newcastle.

"Thanks so much," she said.

"My pleasure. I'm Alonso, by the way."

He'd spoken while she had the beer glass halfway to her lips, so she took a sip before setting it down again, and then she put out her hand.

"Tess," she said. "Well met, Alonso."

He chuckled softly at her archaic choice of words and then shook her hand. "Well met, Tess. Waiting for someone?"

She glanced at the stool where she'd placed her jacket. "I'm meeting a friend. But if you guys still do that hummus appetizer, I'd love that while I'm waiting for her."

"Coming up," he replied. "And two menus."

Alonso went off to order her hummus and pita chips. Tess wondered if she was imagining the relief she'd seen in his eyes when she'd identified her dinner partner as female. *What are you doing flirting with a bartender?* she thought.

Yet as she waited for Lili, eating hummus on pita chips, she couldn't help wondering what else Alonso might be. What did he do when he wasn't tending bar? Did he have other jobs? Passions? She couldn't hold on to any real interest in a guy with no passions. Really, she knew nothing about this guy except that he could pour a perfect pint and he had just about the most beautiful skin she had ever seen—skin that made her want to touch him. But there had been that moment when they'd first locked eyes, that instant recognition that said, *hey, you don't know me, but I see something in you,* like some invisible thread connected them.

Tess regretted the hummus. Every time the bartender spoke to her in the half hour she spent waiting for Lili to show up, she could think of nothing but garlic breath so strong she feared it would melt his face off. *Hummus,* she thought. *Idiot.*

Alonso was such a pleasant distraction, in fact, that by the time Lili arrived, harried and flushed and looking in total disarray—as she always did—Tess had stopped thinking about her ex-husband's double almost entirely. The pain in her shoulder had subsided and the ache in her spine felt distant, as if it belonged to someone else. She chalked that up to the Newcastle more than to the handsome man serving it.

"Hello, sweetheart," Lili said, slipping off her rust-colored peacoat. "Sorry I'm late."

"You're not, really. I was early." Tess retrieved her jacket and folded it across her knees as Lili sat down.

"Of course you were." She picked up the menu, glanced at it for several seconds, and then set it down. "They still have that black bean burger. I nearly broke off my romance with it after the last time, but I'll give it the benefit of the doubt. Everyone has an off night."

Her thick black hair was a mad, shoulder-length tangle, her bone-white blouse wrinkled, and her muted, dark teal skirt twisted slightly around, as if she'd come from a torrid sexual encounter or a very long, fully-clothed nap. With Lili, either was possible but the latter more likely.

The bartender glided over. "Well, hello—" he began.

"Hello yourself," Lili said pleasantly. "You're new."

"Lili, this is Alonso," Tess said.

"He certainly is," Lili observed.

Tess shot her a look that said, *What the hell are you talking about?* Lili replied with an amused glance and a shrug, as she always did.

"I'm Lilandra," she went on. "Lovely to meet you. I'll have a black bean burger and a pint of Newcastle."

Alonso shook his head. "I see. So there are two of you."

Lili arched a curious eyebrow.

"Apparently nobody drinks the Newcastle but us," Tess explained.

"Not nobody," Alonso corrected. "But I'm starting to think the boss only keeps it on tap to bring the pretty girls in."

"Well," Lili said, batting her eyelashes ironically, "it's clearly working."

Alonso arched an amused eyebrow at Tess. "Okay, one black bean burger, and you?"

"Anything but more hummus," she replied. "Though I'm thinking the blackened mahimahi sounds good."

Alonso vanished into the kitchen to put in their order and by the time he emerged a trio of scruffy college guys had roosted at the end of the bar, summoning him with a wave. Tess took a sip of beer and glanced over to find Lili studying her.

"What?"

"He likes you."

"The bartender?"

"Alonnnsssso," Lili said, leaning over to bump Tess

with a shoulder. "Is my Tess finally gonna get back on the horse that threw her?"

A shiver went up Tess's aching spine. "Nick."

Lili put her pinky into the hummus and licked it off. "Not Nick. Ew. You should never get on *that* horse again. I mean romance, dummy."

"It's just flirting, Lilandra."

"Well, that's a start anyway," Lili said. "Now what were you so excited about when you called me earlier?"

The noise in the Playwright had been a familiar tapestry of sound until that moment. Abruptly it seemed too loud, the laughter and clinking of glasses rising to envelop them so completely that Tess felt almost claustrophobic. She took another long sip of her Newcastle, then finished what was left at the bottom of the glass and immediately wished for another.

Lili touched her forearm. "Hey. What's going on?"

Tess took her hand and squeezed. The noise in the bar receded again and she felt the tension in her shoulders relax. Even after the accident, she had never had a full-on anxiety attack, but she had felt herself on the verge a hundred times.

"It's a freaky thing," she said.

Lili smiled. "My favorite things are freaky things."

Tess saw Alonso watching her and lifted her empty pint glass. He nodded to acknowledge her as he served a couple who'd come in together, gave a little wave to let her know he'd be along momentarily.

"I saw Nick earlier."

"Define 'saw,'" Lili replied.

"Funny you should say that, but no, I did not engage in ex sex. Thing is, Nick's up in North Conway with his girlfriend, whose name always seems to flee my mind the moment he reminds me."

Lili had moved her glass and taken to shredding the damp cardboard coaster that had been under it. Now she looked up sharply. "What were you doing in North Conway? Tell me you're not stalking him or something. I thought you were—"

"Fine. I'm fine. Remember, I'm the one who wanted out of the marriage and I feel zero temptation to go back." A cold little stone formed in her gut. She'd told herself everyone had a doppelgänger somewhere, that most people looked like *someone* else, and that this guy maybe hadn't looked as exactly like Nick as she'd imagined. But now she felt a little frisson of uneasiness that made the skin prickle at the back of her neck. "And I wasn't in North Conway."

"I'm confused," Lili said.

Alonso approached along the bar, smiling pleasantly, drying his hands on his bar towel again. The spark that had been jumping between them had apparently been extinguished, because suddenly she didn't want him to stand so near. Conversation about Nick and especially about today's weirdness needed to stay far away from the life of the Tess who flirted with handsome bartenders and worried about her garlic breath. Two worlds, with a wall between them.

"Another Newcastle?" he asked.

"Please."

Alonso must have sensed that their conversation was not meant to be shared, because the moment he set the Newcastle down, he moved quickly down the bar.

"You want to start over?" Lili asked.

Tess turned on the stool to face her directly. "I was outside International Place today and I saw this guy. . . . I saw Nick. Only it wasn't Nick. I mean, okay, Nick in a really nice suit but he looked so much like Nick that I went up to talk to him and got totally pissed off when he ignored me and then acted like he didn't know me—"

"Oh, my God," Lili said. "That's embarrassing."

"It was. But I was so angry that I called Nick's cell and at first I didn't really believe that he was in New Hampshire because—"

"Because you'd just seen him."

"Yes!" Talking about it made the little ball of ice inside her start to melt. Tess exhaled and found herself laughing. Her face flushed a bit, both from the beer and the embarrassing memory. "The guy must've thought I was a total wackjob."

"Crazy," Lili said.

But there was something in her tone that brought Tess up short, an airy quality that seemed like something more than just commentary on the run-in with Nick.

"You've got that look on your face," Tess said.

"What look?"

"I know all your looks. This is the I-just-remembered-something-I'd-rather-forget look."

Alonso interrupted them again, this time with their dinner. He warned Tess that her plate was hot and again seemed to realize it was best to leave them to their conversation.

Lili picked up a French fry and pointed it at Tess. "Like three weeks ago, one of my students told me she had been to this art gallery opening in the Back Bay and one of the artists looked exactly like me."

Tess frowned. "That sort of thing . . . I mean, lots of people—"

"Since then, at least four other people have mentioned going to this gallery and seeing this artist who's apparently my double, right down to my voice. At first I chalked it up to most non-Indians being unable to tell one Indian woman from another, but after the fourth person, I did start to wonder."

Splitting fish with her fork, Tess glanced up at her. "It's a little creepy, right?"

Lili gave a half shrug. "Actually, I thought it was sort of cool until you told me *your* story. Now it's definitely on the freaky-deaky side. I was going to swing by the gallery this weekend, but—"

"Let's go tonight," Tess said, lifting a hand to hide the fact that she was talking with her mouth full.

"Tonight?"

"I've got the sitter till midnight. Is the place open Thursdays, do you think?"

Lili pulled out her cell. "Plenty of foot traffic on Newbury Street in September, so I'd guess yes, but it's easy enough to find out," she said, typing away at the phone. "Problem is, it'll be at least eight thirty before we can get there, maybe closer to nine even if we skip coffee. . . ." She hesitated, reading something off the little screen. "Okay, they're open until nine o'clock on Thursdays and Fridays."

Tess had just forked another bite of blackened mahi into her mouth. She washed it down with a gulp of Newcastle, enjoying the burn of the spices and the cool earthiness of the ale. Now she raised a hand to wave Alonso over.

"Let's try to make it. I'm intrigued. And my back is stiff as hell. I need to walk more."

"Why not?" Lili said good-naturedly. "We haven't been on an adventure in a while."

Alonso came over and put his hands on his hips. "Another round, ladies?"

"Actually, can we get the check?" Tess asked. "Turns out we have to be somewhere."

"Oh, sure," Alonso replied. "I'll get you squared away."

He frowned a moment, then returned to his cash register to print up their bill.

"That was pretty adorable," Lili said quietly, rooting in her purse for something.

"What was?"

Lili pulled out a pen and a business card and began scribbling on the back. "You really didn't notice? Handsome Alonso is very disappointed that you're in a rush to leave."

Tess shushed her as Alonso came back with the bill. She'd already slipped out her American Express card and she handed it to him without looking at the total.

"What are you doing?" Lili asked.

"Finishing my dinner," Tess replied, digging into what remained of her dinner.

"I'm pretty sure it's my turn to pay," Lili argued.

"You're paying for the cab over to the gallery. We don't have time to take the T and you know I never have cash for anything more than coffee."

Lili raised her eyebrows. "True enough," she said,

and went back to her black bean burger. She would never have eaten more than two-thirds of it anyway, so Tess didn't feel too badly about hurrying things along.

Alonso brought back her Amex card and the receipt for her signature. She smiled at him but while she was signing, Lili held out a business card to him.

"Her number's on the back," Lili said. "You should call her."

Alonso blinked in surprise and his brilliant smile returned. "That's not how this usually works . . . getting a woman's phone number, I mean."

"Call it divine intervention," Lili replied, lifting her chin. "You didn't look like you were going to ask and she's too preoccupied to offer. You'd both regret it later, and that would be a shame, don't you think?"

Tess had gone rigid on the barstool as the blood drained from her face. Caught between horror and amusement, she could only stare at Lili and then at Alonso, and then she laughed softly, shaking her head.

"It would be a shame," Alonso said. "But I guess that depends on what Tess thinks."

Tess thought about her scars and how they looked when she studied them in the bathroom mirror, thought about how long it had been since she had been naked with a man. Somehow she managed to affect an air of nonchalance. "Tess wouldn't be averse."

Lili rolled her eyes. "She doesn't usually talk about herself in the third person."

"Well," Tess replied, "she figures since we're all talking about her as if she isn't here . . ."

A customer called to him from farther along the bar

and Alonso put up a finger to indicate he'd be right there.

"Alonso doesn't mind a little third person," he said, studying her closely. "He thinks we could all use a little shift in perspective now and then."

Saluting Lili with the sneaky business card, he slipped the rectangle of cardboard into his front pocket before turning to Tess one last time. "He will be calling. And he hopes she'll answer."

He went off down the bar and they watched him go.

"I like him," Lili said.

"He does seem to have his charms," Tess agreed, but really she wanted to hurry out of the bar, to hide and pretend the flirtation had never happened. She could feel the way her bra strap always slid and tugged against the smooth, opalescent scar tissue on her shoulder and the strange numbness of the remaining muscle around her diminished left breast, where the surgeon's repairs had left an odd indent in her flesh.

"No," Lili said. "I mean I like him. If you don't want him, send him my way."

Tess glanced at her. "You're welcome to him, but you have a boyfriend, Lilandra. Just, y'know, in case you forgot."

"I didn't forget," Lili said with a sniff and a tightening around her mouth. "But Steven did. Several times, according to the nurse he's been sleeping with. She works at the Jimmy Fund Clinic, though, so how can I hate her, right? She treats kids with cancer. In the movie of my life, she's got to be the protagonist, right? Which must make me the evil bitch."

Lili slid her plate away from her, clearly no longer hungry.

"Oh, shit, Lil," Tess began. "Steven's such an idiot."

"I'm fine," Lili said. "I waited to tell you in person so we could be drinking at the time. She showed up at my apartment on Saturday morning. Cute girl. Twenty-five. She had zero interest in being anybody's 'other woman,' and it turns out, neither did I."

Tess felt deflated. Ever since she'd spotted Not-Nick on the street, her brain and body had been operating in some kind of heightened state that gave a surreal quality to the world around her. Something about that encounter had set her off-balance. It had just felt wrong—off-kilter—and with Lili's story about her art gallery double, she'd felt like she had stepped through the looking glass into a place that looked the same as the world she knew but contained subtle and sinister differences.

All of that had been pure fantasy, and this cold splash of reality had brought that home.

"Damn it, Lili, I'm sorry," she said, taking her friend's hand. "Maybe we should just order another drink. It doesn't have to be here. We can—"

"Screw that," Lili said, standing up and pulling on her jacket. "We can drink anywhere. I've gotta see if this chick really does have my face."

Tess drained the last of her pint. She nearly dropped her jacket as Lili took her hand and tugged her toward the door, though she did spare a glance at Alonso as she left. Today had been filled with thoughts of her past and she liked the idea of thinking about the future.

On the sidewalk, she and Lili linked arms and waved

madly at the first taxi they saw. The girls out on the town. Though they were hardly *girls* anymore.

As they piled into the backseat, Lili giving the driver instructions, Tess had the urge to blurt out a different address—anywhere but this Newbury Street art gallery. Meeting Not-Nick had been weird enough. If the artist at the gallery really turned out to be a perfect double for Lili . . . Tess thought she might rather not know.

But they were on their way. The taxi's engine rumbled and the chilly night air blew through the half-open windows as the storefronts and human sidewalk traffic blurred by in a familiar rhythm. During the day, the city was so familiar—she thought she knew every brick and turn. At night, though, it seemed almost like another place entirely. A place where anything might happen.

THREE

Frank had no idea where the guy had gotten handcuffs, but he knew where the handgun had come from. A nine millimeter SIG Sauer, it had rested in a shoe box on the top shelf of the closet in his parents' bedroom for at least a decade. Had the man with his face found the gun just by searching, or had he already known where he ought to look? Did having Frank's face mean he knew what Frank knew?

Don't be an idiot, he thought. *That's just stupid.*

But was it? How much more outrageous was that idea than the reality of this guy having his face? Frank had been handcuffed to the round, pitted metal iron support column in his own basement for three days, and theories that had seemed ridiculous on Monday somehow did not seem quite as absurd as Thursday wound to a close. Not when he was naked from the waist down in a cold basement, surrounded by concrete and boxes of old tax files and rusting tools from the days when his father would actually visit the workbench down here.

The cuffs might be stolen from somewhere, or purchased from some law enforcement surplus or online vendor. Frank had tested them enough to know they weren't chintzy sex shop handcuffs. He'd used his weight and leveraged himself against the pole, trying to break the chain between the cuffs. Kept at it until his wrists bled and even then he had tried to use the blood as a lubricant to slide his hands out. They weren't coming off, and he couldn't risk further injury, or an infection.

Unless the fucker decided to let him go—which didn't seem likely—the best he could hope for was that his captor would make a mistake that would allow Frank to get the drop on him. He had this fantasy that his double would leave a fork behind and he could bend all but one of the tines, using that last one to pick the lock on the cuffs, but the logistics were impossible. Even if he could hide a fork and have the guy forget about it, and even if he had the skill to pick the handcuff lock, his hands were behind him and the pole made it impossible for him to maneuver so that he could see them. If he was a fucking ninja or something, or Batman, he could pull it off.

But he wasn't Batman. Or a ninja.

Exhaling, he slumped back against the pole. The blanket under his bare ass provided little protection from the chill of the hard concrete floor. He'd given up being ashamed of his nakedness on the second day, realizing that the guy holding him prisoner probably had exactly the same junk as he had. But the humiliation stayed, burning inside him, keeping him angry. He thought anger would come in handy when *the moment* arrived.

The moment. The very idea of it had weight and heft. Concept as weapon. Despite being fed, inactivity was taking its toll, weakening him. With no way to escape the cuffs, he had to act during one of the times—early morning, dinnertime, and late at night—when his double came down to bring him food. He would descend the stairs with a tray of food in one hand and Frank's father's gun in the other. Setting the tray down, he would toss Frank the key to the cuffs. Frank would unlock the cuffs while the guy stood eight feet away with the gun barrel pointed at his chest.

Near the washer and dryer was a big plastic bucket that was all Frank had for a toilet. At gunpoint, he relieved himself into the bucket, wiped himself with toilet paper that had been there when he'd first regained consciousness, and then he ate whatever the bastard had brought down on the tray. The food was never much—cereal in milk, a peanut butter sandwich—but it would keep him alive. The man allowed Frank five minutes to eat, then forced him to cuff his own hands behind the pole again. Gun in hand, he'd come over and tighten them, make sure there was no wiggle room.

Every time his double came into the room, Frank watched his gun hand, knowing his only chance was to lunge, try to grab his wrist, and fight him for the gun.

Every time his double came into the room, Frank felt himself grow a little weaker, and he knew that eventually he would be too weak to have any chance of wrestling that gun away. His fear of that imminent weakness kept increasing, and soon it would be stronger than his fear of the gun. That would be *the moment* . . . the now-

or-never moment when he had to act, or all hope would be lost.

Frank leaned his head back against the post. A little too hard. Did it a second time because the pain and shock of it made him strangely alert. The ringing in his head, the radiating pain, made him grit his teeth. He inhaled deeply, remembering too late the stink in the cellar. His double emptied the bucket and rinsed it out during his second visit of the day, but the smell of shit and piss permeated the concrete by now, and Frank's own body odor didn't help. Days without shaving or bathing had him so gritty and stale that his skin crawled if he let himself think about it.

He missed bathing even more than he missed the softness of his bed and the smell of fresh air and the warmth of clothing—clean clothing especially.

It surprised him, really. When he'd first woken up chained to the support column, he'd been sure it would be the booze he missed most. He'd figured going without it would unravel him. In some ways it had—the need had been gut deep, and as painful as true grief, and he'd had the sweats all through Tuesday night and Wednesday—but he hadn't puked and he hadn't tried to sell his soul to the devil. Part of him thought the reason he hadn't gone for the bastard's gun yet was not hope for an easier option but relief. Imprisoned, all choice had been taken away from him. The option to get drunk was not on the table. Maybe he was a little bit grateful.

The creak of movement came from upstairs. Frank exhaled loudly and rested his aching head against the metal column, staring at the bottom of the steps. The footfalls overhead were loud squeaks and he could trace the bastard's progress through the living room and into the kitchen.

The door at the top of the stairs clicked open. As his double descended into the cellar, Frank caught a different smell on the air and his stomach growled.

The bastard stepped into the pool of light thrown by the caged bulb on the basement ceiling. He wore a gray suit—the one Frank had bought to wear to his mother's funeral—and had managed to match it with the same tie as well, a red and yellow disaster that his mother had loved.

The man held the gun in his right hand and a greasy brown paper bag in his left.

"You're early," Frank said. He wouldn't say a word about the funeral suit. Wouldn't give the bastard the satisfaction.

"I've got to be up early tomorrow," the man said.

Frank could not get used to looking at his own face but he was glad that his own voice sounded different in his head than it did to those around him. If he could have recognized this man's voice as his own, he might really have gone insane.

"I had a job interview yesterday," his double went on. "Went out for drinks and Chinese food with the editor tonight—a follow-up, but really a formality. I'm supposed to go in bright and early to meet with the HR director, fill out some paperwork. If my references check out, they figure I can start middle of next week."

Frank swallowed hard. His head was still ringing

from smashing it against the column and now he wanted to bang it again. Wanted to scream.

"Editor?" he asked softly.

The bastard gave him an apologetic sort of smile. "Yeah, about that. When I say my references, I mean your references, of course. You'd already made contact with the Web site, started the ball rolling . . . I figured I'd send some of your portfolio articles over and call to follow up. They're adding staff, so the timing was perfect."

Frank closed his eyes, stomach roiling with nausea. Bile surged up the back of his throat but he choked it back. If detoxing himself hadn't made him throw up, he wasn't going to puke now.

"You can't do this," he whispered.

"Oh, Frank," the bastard said, almost sadly, "it's the only thing I *can* do."

He walked over and dropped the greasy paper bag onto the floor. Frank could have kicked out with his legs, but what would the point have been? He couldn't defeat the son of a bitch with just his feet.

"Leftover Chinese food. Figured it was better than another bowl of Cheerios. Some of it might still be warm."

Frank glared at him, lip curled in fury. He hocked up a gob of phlegm and spat it onto the front of the suit coat. His double tried to twist out of the way but the yellow phlegm hit the fabric and clung there.

Gun gripped tightly in his right hand, he kicked Frank in the ribs. Hard. Frank huffed in pain, grunted the air out of his lungs, and a fresh burst of pain went through him, but he didn't think his ribs had cracked.

"Shit!" his double hissed, seemingly in regret.

It made Frank wonder. Why would the bastard not want to hurt him? If he meant to take Frank's place, why not just kill him?

"Why are you doing this?" Frank said, steadying his nerves. "And how. Damn, man, how can you look exactly like me?"

The man narrowed his eyes. "I don't look like you, Frank. I *am* you." He glanced around and shuddered lightly. "Cold down here. I'll give you another blanket in the morning and over the weekend I'll pick up a space heater. Next couple of months it'll be freezing in here."

Frank's mouth dropped open. He blinked as a numb dread spread through him and for a few seconds all he could remember to do was breathe. Then he shook his head slowly.

"You can't . . . I mean, *months*?" He strained against the cuffs, hurled himself forward, felt the heat of rage burning in his face. "*Months!* What the hell do you want from me? Why are you here?"

A haunting sympathy passed across the double's face, but then it hardened with resolve. He tossed the handcuff key onto the floor and it skipped on the concrete and struck the paper bag.

"Eat your Chinese food." He lifted the gun, took aim, just in case.

Frank thrashed against the column, tugged against the cuffs, causing the blood to run along his arms again. Pain seared his wrists.

"Fuck the Chinese food!" he screamed. "Fuck . . ."

The strength went out of him in an instant. Rage had been undercut by despair.

He slumped against the column. Rested his skull gently against it. Tears welled in his eyes and slid down his cheeks.

"Fuck you and your fucking leftovers."

His double hesitated, seemed about to argue, and then walked over and retrieved the handcuff key, gun pointed at Frank's head. He pocketed the key and stepped back, studying Frank with an expression that had gone hard and cold.

"Have it your way."

The man with Frank's face strode across the cellar and up the stairs. The door clicked open and then closed and Frank heard the footsteps crossing back toward the living room, then the creak as the bastard ascended to the second story, likely to sleep in Frank's own bed.

Only then did Frank remember his bladder and bowels. The bucket sat empty over by the washing machine, useless to him at this distance. He'd never be able to make it through until morning without pissing, at the very least.

He slumped again, and squeezed his eyes closed.

The smell of Chinese food filled his nostrils. The bag was right beside him. He could twist around and maybe get his hands on it, but even then he would be unable to bring the food to his mouth.

The long night stretched ahead.

FOUR

First Light Gallery took up the first floor of a row house on Newbury Street, a tourist-magnet neighborhood full of trendy boutiques and high-end shops. Lili paused on the sidewalk, staring up at the soft white light of the gallery windows. The few paintings that were visible through the glass were startling in their beauty, but otherwise the shop seemed sterile and unwelcoming. On the upper floors were the offices of some kind of elite auction company, and a small set of steps with an iron railing led down to the sunken entrance to the gourmet chocolatier on the bottom floor.

"We could just get chocolate," Lili suggested.

Tess gave her a nudge. "Or we could go inside. Why is this freaking you out?"

Lili laughed nervously. "The whole cab ride over all I could think about was your run-in with your ex-husband's doppelgänger. It's just—"

"You wanted an adventure," Tess reminded her. "Besides, the guy probably didn't look as much like Nick as I thought."

Lili put a hand to one cheek, glancing at Tess. "I'm being stupid."

"Yes. Yes, you are."

Lili whacked her arm. "You don't have to agree with me."

"But I do," Tess said, snatching her wrist and tugging her up the four steps to the art gallery's entrance.

The white lights seemed cold instead of warm, like the bright misty glow inside a freezer.

A strong wind kicked up and Lili held the front of her jacket closed as Tess reached the gallery's door and pushed inside. Lili followed her in, a bell ringing above their heads, and when the door had swung shut she felt an almost-claustrophobic warmth envelop her. The place looked chilly from the outside, but the heat was on inside and the air was suffocatingly close. *Weird,* she thought. All she knew about art was what she had learned as an archaeologist, how to identify things and preserve them. She didn't know quality and certainly couldn't identify one modern artist from another, but she felt sure it must be inadvisable to keep a gallery so warm. Couldn't be good for the paintings.

An old woman cleared her throat. Lili glanced over and saw that the woman stood with an old man, her husband or companion, and both were perusing the paintings on the walls with the air of people who believed a certain amount of gravitas was necessary for the appreciation of expensive art. The only other noise in the gallery was a man's assured voice talking low at the back of the shop.

"Did any of the people who mentioned this place to you get the name of this woman?" Tess asked.

"Devon something," Lili said, navigating her way around a half wall. The gallery had a number of them, thrusting out at angles like the room had jagged teeth. White lights and white walls made the whole thing seem like Heaven's waiting room.

They came around another of those walls and the voice at the back of the gallery grew louder. It belonged to a thin, bespectacled man of about fifty, his silken silver hair combed neatly to one side. He wore artfully faded blue jeans, distressed leather shoes, and a shirt that Lili thought had to have cost at least a week's worth of her salary. The fortysomething woman he'd been addressing wore a tailored suit, the skirt long enough for the executive boardroom but short enough to show how much work she put into making sure her legs didn't reveal her age.

Both of them glanced over when Lili and Tess came around the corner. The executive cast them a snooty look that Lili tried to tell herself had nothing to do with two brown women walking into the whitest room on Earth. But the silver-haired guy brightened immediately, a huge smile spreading across his face.

"And here she is now!" the man said, delighted, and made a beeline toward Lili. He took her hands in his and began to lead her back toward the executive. "Dev, this is Laura Niswander. Laura, this is Devani Kanda, the artist of the piece you were just on the verge of buying."

Lili went cold. The man's delight seemed to bleed into the executive, who began to smile and babble something about the beauty of her paintings. The art itself had nothing overtly remarkable about it— cityscapes of Boston from an earlier era, painted in a style that allowed the thick gobs of paint to look crude up close but to take on an almost elegant beauty the farther away from it one stood.

The man—maybe the owner or manager—narrowed his eyes. "Dev, say something, honey. Are you okay?"

The executive woman's gaze turned cold and she shrank back an inch or two, clearly feeling snubbed by the lack of a proper greeting. Lili smiled and shook her head.

"I'm sorry. I'm not her," she told the proprietor.

"What?" He cast a worried glance at the executive. "She's being funny."

Tess moved closer to Lili. "She's not, actually. Not being funny and not the artist. Just looks a lot like her, apparently."

The silver-haired man sneered at Tess as if he'd been wearing a mask of amiability before and now it had slipped. "What are you talking about?" He glared at Lili. "I know you say when you're off the clock you're off the clock, but this is taking it too far. This woman is a patron of the arts. She's been admiring your work and is interested in—"

"Actually, Peter," the executive said, "it's getting late and I should go. Perhaps I'll come in again and you can show me the work of an artist who appreciates her good fortune and might be less rude to those who can afford to support her efforts."

"Laura, please, you misunderstand," the proprietor said.

"Do I?" the woman asked, staring at Lili and Tess a moment before she sniffed and strode away.

Lili knew she ought to attempt to stop the woman,

but she was too stunned to do anything but watch her march off in a huff. Moments later they heard the sound of the bell over the gallery's front door as the woman departed.

Peter stared at her, obviously furious. "What's gotten into you? You know what can happen for an artist when a woman like that becomes passionate about your work. Word spreads. There are more sales. Prices go up. What were you thinking?"

Lili bristled, staring at him. "I was thinking that I'm not this Devani person."

Something in her tone made him blink and tilt his head, evaluating her more closely. He stared at her clothes for a second, then narrowed his eyes as he seemed to notice other differences. For a moment he seemed to consider the possibility, but then he searched her features and scowled.

"Dev—"

Tess put up a hand to stop him. "Stop. You're not getting this. Her name is Lili Pillai. We heard there was an artist being shown here who looked a lot like her and got curious. We meant no harm and certainly didn't want to piss off your customers, but she's really not the woman you think she is."

The older couple from the front of the gallery had come around one of the angled half walls and they were stealing glances in their direction while they pretended to contemplate some of the paintings. Some people would have been driven away by the raised voices and the angry spectacle, but not this couple. They seemed as intrigued by the unfolding drama as they were by the art on the walls.

Peter frowned, dubious. "You're serious?"

Lili threw up her hands as if in surrender. "Completely. I've never been inside this gallery before."

He pushed one hand through his silver hair and paused, head cocked as he stared at her. "You don't just look a lot like her. I went to high school with two sets of 'identical' twins, but you and Dev look more alike than they ever did. You've got to be sisters."

Not that I know of, Lili wanted to say. But that wouldn't be putting it strongly enough. She'd grown up an only child and, nontraditional as they might be, there was no way her parents would have given a baby up for adoption—especially a twin. No way.

"This is just too bizarre," she said, glancing at Tess. Thinking about her run-in with her ex-husband's doppelgänger.

"Getting more bizarre by the second," Tess replied.

Lili turned to Peter. "Do you have a picture of her? Devani Kanda?"

Still studying her with the sort of unsettled fascination that might have greeted a revelation of Martian birth, the gallery's owner slipped a thin, gleaming, white smartphone from his pocket, tapped the screen a few times, and then turned it for them both to see. Lili heard Tess make a tiny gasping noise, but she herself could not even draw a breath. The woman in the photo on Peter's phone had shorter hair, courtesy of a doubtless expensive stylist, and her daring, glittering red dress would have made Lili blush, but she bore a shocking resemblance.

No. Not a resemblance at all, Lili thought. *She's me.* Right down to the mischievous twinkle in her eyes.

"Holy shit," Tess muttered.

The man lowered his hand, tapping his phone before returning it to his pocket. "Now you see why I—"

"Her phone number," Lili said.

Peter frowned. "I'm sorry?"

"Can you give me her number? Or tell me where she lives?"

"Lili—" Tess began warily.

"I have to meet her."

The gallery owner shook his head. "I can't do that. She has a right to her privacy. But we're having another little reception tomorrow night at seven o'clock, if you really want to meet her. I'm sure she'll be just as astonished as you are."

Lili thought of the confident, stylish woman she'd seen in that photograph and wondered if such a woman could ever be astonished by anything.

Tess took her arm. "Thanks so much, and sorry about the mix-up," she said. "We'll see you tomorrow night."

Then they were turning together and striding back across the suffocatingly warm, sterile gallery. When Tess pushed open the door that bell chimed overhead and it seemed to snap Lili out of the trance she'd been in. They went down the few steps and the chilly ocean wind kicked up again, making her shiver as she turned to Tess.

"How much like Nick did he look, really?" she asked. "The guy you saw today?"

Tess kept her arm looped through Lili's and steered them both along the sidewalk.

"This isn't ordinary, right?" Tess said. "This is—"

"Surreal."

"—creepy."

They exchanged a glance as they hurried away from the gallery, neither of them wanting to look back.

When Lili shivered again, it wasn't from the cold.

FIVE

Nick Devlin lay in the huge, creaky, four-poster bed and listened to the sound of the shower running. On the nightstand on Kyrie's side of the bed, a single lamp glowed dimly. The antique glass globe had been hand-painted with roses, the whole thing tinted pink, and it was that pink hue that threw odd shadows into the corners of the otherwise darkened room. Nick had loved the Notchland Inn since his first visit all the way back in college, more than a dozen years before. Every time he came—first with his college girlfriend, then with Tess, and now with Kyrie—he stayed in the Franconia Room. Nick did not do well with change and he appreciated the fact that the room never changed, even when the current owners had taken over. When they repainted, they used the same shade. It was a comfort to him. Even so, no matter how many times he'd stayed here or how comfortable the familiarity of the place was, he could never get used to how completely black the nights were.

The Notchland sat between peaks in the midst of

White Mountain National Forest, a beautiful, mid-nineteenth-century stone mansion with only a handful of rooms in the main building. Thousands of acres of woodland surrounded the place and the Saco River flowed nearby, offering some of the loveliest trails Nick had ever hiked. By daylight, the inn's setting seemed like it must have changed not at all since the house had been built, and by night it felt like civilization retreated entirely. Half the allure of the place was the complete absence of televisions and cell towers. The owners had bowed to modern demands and offered free Wi-Fi, but anyone wanting to reach a guest at the Notchland by something other than e-mail had to phone the inn's main desk. At ten P.M. the owners turned out the lights, locked the doors, and went to bed. Without the outdoor lighting, the entire valley went pitch-black, with only the moon and stars for light.

Outside, standing on the lawn with the forest behind and below, Nick could always find a peace and solitude available nowhere else he had ever been. In the bed in the Franconia Room, he could lie still and listen to the creak and moan of the old building. Though Kyrie had decided it was a bit too early in the season to build a fire, Nick had been tempted. It would have completed the evening for him, this return to settings and experiences that he had always found so comforting. They'd gone down to North Conway to wander the shops and admire the old train station, then had dinner at May Kelly's Cottage and listened to the two old men playing Irish music in the bar. Now they were here, in the peaceful darkness, with just that old rose lamp casting the same light that had no doubt illuminated the nights of a thousand lovers over the years, not to mention the pages of a thousand books.

A perfect day and a perfect night.

So why are you so out of sorts? he thought.

Kyrie had noticed how unsettled he had become after the phone call from Tess. She had naturally assumed he felt guilty for bringing her here, for sharing with "the new girlfriend" some of the things that he and Tess had cherished together. Nick had firmly denied this, and truthfully. He had loved this place since before Tess had come into his life, had cherished it all for himself, and so he did not feel it any sort of betrayal to share it with Kyrie now. But Tess—and Maddie—were very much on his mind, and he struggled to banish them, at least for the night. It seemed horribly unfair to Kyrie to be too distracted by thoughts of his ex-wife and their daughter to be able to give her the attention she deserved.

All his life, all he had ever wanted to be was a better version of himself.

With a squeal of old water pipes, the shower turned off.

Nick took a deep breath and let it out. He picked up his phone from the nightstand, tapped the screen, and saw that he'd received five new e-mails. Half wishing for the days before the Notchland had Wi-Fi, he put the phone aside. Whatever those e-mails were, they would have to wait.

The bathroom door opened, the old, heavy wood sticking for a second before being dragged wide. A halo of steam surrounded Kyrie as she stepped over the threshold with a thick white towel wrapped around her; she dried her hair with another.

"Brrrr," she said, smiling. "I'm starting to think a fire would have been a good idea."

"I can turn the heat up," Nick told her. He whipped back the covers on her side of the bed. "Or you can just come here."

Kyrie wrapped the towel around her head, rubbing her wild red hair dry so fiercely that when she lowered her arms she looked like a beautiful Medusa. Twenty-four years old to his thirty-three and formidable despite her petite, almost spritelike appearance, her presence in his life had invited a barrage of comments about professor-student relationships from friends and colleagues on both sides. But Kyrie was working toward her master's in medieval literature and Nick had never been her professor.

To hell with them, she'd said over and over.

In the seven months since they'd begun dating, they'd made it their mantra.

Now she laughed and raced for the bed, slipped off the towel, and dove in beside him, burrowing immediately under the covers as she snuggled against him.

Nick kissed her head. "Don't worry. I'll keep you warm."

But she knew him too well. His tone gave him away and she looked at him with those piercing eyes whose intelligence was like a laser, searching his face.

"Hey," Kyrie whispered. "I'm naked here. Skin still warm from the shower. Slightly drunk on whiskey and high on the music from tonight. It's quiet and dark and it's just you and me—"

"I know. I'm sorry I—"

"—but I love you," she said, putting her hand on his

chest. "A romantic night doesn't have to mean a room full of antiques in a mountain inn. There's more to us than soft skin and pretty pictures."

Nick smiled. "I love the way you talk."

She smacked him. "Hush. I agree I'm pretty excellent. Now what's on your mind? Still thinking about Tess?"

"Not Tess," he said quietly. "Maddie."

"She can come with us," Kyrie said, eyes bright in the darkness, skin luminous in the rose hue of the bedside lamp. Her smile turned shy. "With you, I mean . . ."

"With us. I'm going with you."

"Maddie can come, too—"

"Tess will never go along with it. Letting her daughter spend two years in London? Even if I brought her home in the summer and at Christmastime . . . she'll never go for it."

Kyrie twined her fingers in his. "It's not too late to change your mind."

Nick wondered if she meant it. The plan had come together almost accidentally. Just two months after they'd started seeing each other, Kyrie had told him that she intended to do her Ph.D. at Oxford and he had mentioned that he had always dreamed of living in England for at least part of his life. She had kissed him and invited him along, flirty and half kidding. He'd also been half kidding when he had agreed, but it had niggled at him until he had started putting feelers out and learned there might be an adjunct faculty position there for him if he wanted it.

"I'll understand," Kyrie said, nestling into the crook of his arm. "This has been fast, you and me and England. Even if you travel to see Maddie, even if Tess lets her come out and stay with us for the holidays and part of the summer, it's not even close to the same as seeing her as often as you do now. It's a big decision—"

"It was," he said, a calm coming over him. "But I've made it. We're talking about two years, with lots of visits in between. I'll make it work."

"*We'll* make it work," Kyrie promised.

It was the right thing—Nick was certain of that—he just hoped that somehow Maddie would understand when he explained it all to her on Tuesday. He had always had difficulty reading other people's emotions, but never with interpreting his own. Tonight he felt sadness and regret mixed with the excitement of anticipation and the contentment of being with Kyrie. Normal, ordinary emotions. But as always he wished he could understand the emotions of others as easily.

It had been the loose string in his marriage, the thing that had begun the unraveling. Tess had claimed to understand the hints of Asperger's in his personality and to accept them, but she never had. Not really. Nick himself had never really understood, had met people much more deeply afflicted with the altered perceptions of human behavior that came with this particular brand of autism. From his perspective, relying on it as an excuse was tantamount to a person who needed reading glasses claiming to be blind.

Still, it had been enough to create a hairline fracture in his marriage. When Tess had been recovering from her accident, Nick had tried to be attentive and sympathetic, but knew his efforts came off as stiff and awkward. The rift between them had grown wider, resentment breeding in the newly opened space. Then Tess had kissed another man. Nick had assumed it had been to get his attention. Furious, he'd told her she'd gotten what she'd wanted, but he'd been wrong about her motivations. Too much wine had been part of it, but it all circled around the fallout from the accident, her pain and her scars and the fact that she couldn't get past the assumption that he would be repulsed by the damage done to her body.

That was when he'd fully understood that neither of them had ever really understood the other. A marriage couldn't survive that sort of epiphany, and theirs had been over just a few weeks later.

"Hey," Kyrie whispered, leaning in and kissing his neck, cleaving her body to his in a soft, stark reminder of her nakedness. "There's nothing you can do about London and Maddie tonight. Come back to now."

Nick exhaled, released her hand, and reached over to trace his fingers along the curve of her hip.

"I'm here," he said in a quiet rasp.

She kissed him and all of his concerns fled. Kyrie seemed to understand him, worked at it, and he did the same for her. Made a conscious effort. In the peaceful, rose-hued isolation of that room, they made love without sparing a single thought for the noise of the squeaky antique bed or their own exhortations. The rest of the world retreated and nothing mattered but that chilly room and the heat that passed between them.

Later, Nick would remember the hours they had spent in that room and wish they had never left.

FRIDAY

ONE

Early Friday morning, under gray skies threatening rain, Nick and Kyrie drove south. She sat in the passenger seat, wrapped in the green knit sweater she'd bought the day before, and searched satellite radio stations for the silliest, frothiest pop songs she could find. On blue-sky days she liked to listen to stark folk music and bands like The National, which Nick thought of as mourning rock, but when the clouds rolled in and the rain began to fall, Kyrie always wanted something bouncy and fun. She found an all-'70s channel and started singing along to a one-hit wonder Nick himself was too young to know the words to. How Kyrie knew the song so well, he had no idea, but he couldn't stop himself from grinning.

When his cell phone buzzed, it took him a couple of seconds to recognize the sound. His first instinct was to peer out through the windshield and then into the rearview mirror. They'd only come a mile and a half or so from the Notchland, but apparently just far enough to move in range of a cell tower.

"Check that for me, would you, love?"

Kyrie picked up his phone from the cup holder where he'd placed it. "Voice mail from Derek Wheeler. Isn't that—"

"The Realtor, yeah."

Wheeler had been preparing the listing on Nick's apartment in Somerville. Kyrie tapped the phone screen twice and the radio cut off as the message began to play through the car speakers.

"Hey, it's Derek. I know you said not to bother calling, but I can't just let it go."

Nick sat up a bit straighter. The Realtor sounded angry.

"I'm not gonna swear at you or anything," the message continued. "I'm a professional. But I've rarely been so tempted to throw professionalism aside. I have no idea what I could've done to piss you off so much. We've barely started this process. You didn't even give me the opportunity to really try to sell your place. If you want to go with someone else, that's fine, but you didn't have to be so rude about it. That's all I wanted to say, I guess. You won't hear from me again."

The message ended and '70s pop started streaming through the car speakers again. Brows knitted, Nick turned to stare at Kyrie.

"What the hell was that about?" he said. "He's talking like I fired him."

"You didn't?"

"Of course not."

"Well," Kyrie said with an amused shrug, "someone did."

TWO

Tess emerged from the conference room with a cup of cold coffee. She'd barely taken a sip during the meeting and now she just wanted to dump it in the sink and start over. Her skirt had been riding up—maybe because she'd been fidgeting in her chair—and she needed a few minutes in her office to adjust it and just exhale. All through the meeting, the rain had pattered the windows and streamed down the glass, distracting her. She stretched now, arching her back for a count of thirty before holding her left arm across her chest to give the shoulder some relief.

"Hey, Tess, got a minute?"

It took her a second to realize she was being addressed. Smoothing her skirt, aware that the zipper was out of alignment and irritated by it, she turned to face Eli Pinsky. At sixty-three, he continued to defy those who thought he ought to step down from the management of the Bostonian Society, a nonprofit association whose staff worked with museums, architects, local government, and the historical society to research, promote, and preserve the city's rich history. They hosted parties, lobbied politicians, recruited corporate and wealthy individual sponsors, and marketed Boston to the media, but the staff put just as much effort into research, sometimes hands-on. That was the stuff that intrigued Tess the most—exploring abandoned T stations and leafing through centuries-old blueprints—and she knew it was the part Eli Pinsky enjoyed the best as well. The short, portly man with his walrus mustache and round spectacles still had the passion for all aspects of his job, and she was glad he hadn't bent to pressure.

"What can I do for you, Eli?" she asked.

Her boss glanced around to make sure that the others departing the meeting moved on to their offices or wherever else they were headed.

"Just wanted to check on you," he said.

Tess frowned. "Check on . . . ?"

Eli fixed her with a fatherly gaze. "You weren't in the meeting."

"I was two seats away from you."

"That's not what I meant, Tess. Your head's not in the game today. I'm not saying you were falling asleep, but all I could think about every time I looked at you was what it felt like to be sitting in the back of my high school geometry class while the teacher droned on. I didn't think I was as boring as that guy, but today I sure felt like I was about the least exciting orator on the planet."

Flushing, feeling guilty, she smiled apologetically. "You're not boring, Eli. It's a rainy Friday and I didn't get a lot of sleep last night. Plus my back's acting up. But I swear I wasn't ignoring you."

"I'm not offended," he assured her, "and I'm as susceptible to rainy Fridays as the next guy. I just wanted to make sure you were all right. You're not usually one to space out, so I wondered if something might be wrong. Something more than the usual aches and pains, I mean."

Tess felt a pang in her heart at the man's sweetness. From someone else, the approach might have been some kind of passive-aggressive management technique, but she'd known him long enough to see his sincerity.

"I'm fine," she promised. "Maddie, too."

The urge to kiss his rough cheek came over her, but she resisted. It would have been entirely inappropriate in the office. Instead, she grasped his arm. "You're a kind man, Eli."

"This isn't a job for me," he said, and she knew that words would follow, just as they always did. "It's a calling."

"Me, too. Except on rainy Fridays. Then it feels like work."

They both laughed and Eli glanced around to make sure they weren't being overheard.

"If you want to knock off early, I won't tell the boss," he said.

"Thanks," she whispered theatrically, "but I don't want to risk it. That guy's an ogre."

Eli stroked his mustache, enjoying their playacting, and wished her a fruitful afternoon—the sort of sentiment that would sound silly coming from anyone but him. He headed for his office, though she knew he would stop in the staff galley and make himself a cup of tea on the way, maybe grab a couple of Milano cookies. They were his greatest weakness.

It occurred to her that she loved the balding, gray-haired little man, and she marveled at how fortunate she was to have a boss who inspired such feelings. Suddenly, rainy or not, Friday didn't seem quite so depressing.

The morning had not started well. She'd slept less than five hours and woken at half past four, shoulder hurting so much that she was unable to fall back to sleep. When Maddie had dragged her sleepy self into the kitchen two hours later and Tess had told her that she'd have a babysitter again that night, the little girl had sulked over her waffles. Tess had offered her a choice of three different juices to go with her breakfast and her daughter had huffily replied that she didn't care, didn't like juice, and didn't like Erika, the babysitter she had always adored beyond all reason. In retrospect, Tess knew there were a dozen things she ought to have said to reassure the girl, and to remind her that she loved spending time with Erika. Exhausted as she was, she'd let impatience get the best of her.

"Honey," she'd said, "it's important."

Her little girl, not yet seven years old, had cocked her head, tossed her hair to one side to give her mother a searing glance, and said, "*I* used to be important."

The memory cut at Tess's heart. She walked to her office window and stared out at the rain-veiled city and the sea of black umbrellas on the sidewalk below. Maddie's remark had led to a stream of further reassurances and eventually she had gotten the girl to smile and later to laugh. Erika would entertain her, and Tess knew Maddie would eat better for the babysitter than she ever did for her mother. Still, the words had hurt. How had her baby girl become so smart, so fast? Attitude and sass were going to become a part of their daily ritual— Tess could see it coming—but that was all right. Mothers and daughters sparred all the time. It was perfectly natural.

Still, she had considered canceling on Lili a dozen times. Going out two nights in a row made her feel neglectful.

Yes, you're such a bad mom, she thought.

Maddie knew Tess loved her. She'd been four at the time her parents divorced and barely remembered what life had been like before it. Tess knew her daughter's irritation stemmed from how much she hated to be left out of anything, to feel like she might be missing something fun. But it was their weekend together, and she had promised to make up for it, to devise some adventure for them to share, and Maddie's ire had been mostly extinguished.

It'll return, Tess thought. *Just wait till she's twelve or so.*

Oh, boy.

Her cell phone buzzed and she glanced at it, not recognizing the number. A shudder went through her, a lingering uneasiness. Her modus operandi was to let unknown calls go to voice mail—ninety-nine percent of them were scams, surveys, or sales—but cold curiosity prodded her and she answered.

"Hello?"

"Too early for a Newcastle?" asked a male voice.

Tess's tension evaporated. A small laugh bubbled up from inside her. "Alonso?"

"You remembered my name."

"You only served me two beers," she said. "I don't start forgetting guys' names until at least the third pint." *God, what are you saying?* "Which isn't to say I do a lot of drinking, or meet a lot of guys whose names I want to remember."

Now she was babbling. Tess slumped against her desk, closed her eyes, and promised herself she'd remember that he'd called, even though he wasn't likely ever to make that mistake again.

"So . . . you wanted to remember me," Alonso said.

Tess perked up. "Apparently."

"Sometimes women flirt with the bartender and then they remember that he's just a bartender."

She heard the edge of resignation in his voice. Alonso seemed like a generally confident, good-natured man, but she reminded herself that nearly everyone had their demons of doubt. The only people she'd ever met who weren't sometimes crippled with self-doubt were the same assholes whose certainty invariably led to disaster for those around them, if not for themselves.

"I'm glad you called, Alonso."

"Since your friend Lainie gave me the number—"

"Lili," Tess corrected, privately ecstatic that he'd remembered her name and not Lilandra's. The opposite had so often been true.

"—I wasn't sure I should call."

"Tuesday," she said before she could stop herself, privately terrified.

"Sorry?"

The pain in her back flared and she felt the scars on her chest and shoulder tingling and aching as if they were far more recent than they were. More than two years had passed since the accident. She wanted to hide in her closet, certainly had no intention of letting a strange man see her naked. So why did the thought make her want to smile?

"My ex takes my daughter on Tuesday night. If you want to have dinner or get drinks or something, and you're not working, that's the next time I'm free."

Alonso chuckled softly. "You asking me on a date, Tess?"

"I'm at work right now, so I thought I'd hurry things along."

"If you like Thai, I know a place."

Tess forced herself to breathe, forced away all the ugly scenarios that she imagined when she thought about anyone seeing her without her clothes on. "I love Thai. Seven o'clock?"

It had been a very long time. She wasn't ready to have sex, but she told herself she was being a presumptuous fool. Alonso might spend ten minutes with her and want to run for the hills. Even if he liked her, who was to say she would do more than kiss him?

Your vibrator says so, she thought, and stifled a laugh. Guys had hit on her plenty of times in the past two years, but they had almost universally been swaggering asshats, or just flirting to pass the time. Reflex flirting, married men keeping in practice.

"I'll text you the address and I'll see you there on Tuesday," Alonso said.

"Sounds good," she replied. "I'm glad you called."

"So am I."

He hung up without the sort of awkward, diminishing

farewell small talk most people indulged in. Tess liked that. Thus far, there were a lot of things about Alonso she liked. Suddenly her rainy Friday didn't seem quite so dismal.

Until she remembered Lili, and the plans they'd made for after work.

The butterfly of anxiety in her chest began to beat its wings again.

THREE

It was midafternoon before Nick could get Derek Wheeler to call him back. He'd left three messages on the drive home from North Conway, dropped Kyrie off in Allston, where she shared a place with two other Boston University grad students, and gone back to his Somerville apartment. He taught classes Monday through Wednesday and usually held office hours on Thursday and Friday, even as he tried to finish the manuscript for *18th Century Boston,* the book he'd been researching and writing for nearly four years. But he and Kyrie were in the midst of making important decisions about their life together, and canceling his office hours for this week had allowed them to steal away on Wednesday afternoon and spend two nights and one lovely day in the White Mountains. He was sure that autumn in England held its own charms, but though he'd grown up in Florida, he'd grown to love the seasons of the American Northeast, and would miss them.

Oxford, he thought. An image of Maddie twirling in

delirious circles swam into his head and hesitation plagued him again. Not doubt, really, but worry.

Since arriving home, he'd walked to the market to pick up some essentials, done a load of laundry, and put away the clean dishes that had been in the dishwasher since he had left on Wednesday. He felt the pull of his desk from the second bedroom he used as an office. There were e-mails to answer and research materials to catalog, now that he was getting closer to finishing the book, but he had promised himself that he wouldn't work at all today. Tomorrow would be soon enough. Kyrie had work of her own to do and they'd agreed that Saturday would be a day apart, to focus.

He had just started to surrender to the inexorable pull of his desk when Wheeler finally phoned him back.

"Thanks for calling," Nick said as he answered.

"You left three messages. Didn't seem like you were giving up, though I don't know why. You made it pretty clear you didn't want me to call you."

"I never said that, Derek—"

"Are you calling me a liar, Mr. Devlin?"

Nick hesitated, disturbed by the real anger in the man's voice. He moved into his desk and slid into his chair. "Listen, I don't know what's going on here, but the last time you and I talked was Monday and at that point, we were very much on the same page."

The line went so quiet, Nick thought he had hung up.

"Derek?"

"You called me yesterday afternoon. Said some really unpleasant things about my business skills and about me, personally. Or don't you remember telling me you didn't think people would want to buy an apartment from a Realtor who looked like a troll?"

"Jesus," Nick whispered. "No, I don't remember that, because I never said it. I was up in New Hampshire with Kyrie. Whoever made that call, I swear it wasn't me. I hired you because I knew you would help me make the place presentable and get me a fair price for it. That hasn't changed."

Nick could practically hear him mulling it over.

"The guy said he was you. And he sure sounded like you," Wheeler said.

"I'm telling you—"

"You do realize how this sounds? I mean, who the hell does something like that?"

"I have no idea," Nick said, trying to make a mental list of people he and Kyrie had told about their plans. "A practical joker, I guess."

Wheeler sniffed. "I'm not laughing."

"No," Nick said. "Neither am I."

FOUR

In the gloom of his basement, Frank woke with a start. He whipped his head around, suddenly afraid that rats might get at him, there on the floor with his wrists cuffed behind the support column. Had he heard something in his sleep? Yes, there had been something—a skittering whisper that had chased him up out of his dreams and lingered in his thoughts now. His throat was dry and he wetted his parched lips with his tongue.

Rats. So stupid. He'd never seen rats in the basement. A couple of times he had needed to set traps for mice, but never rats.

Exhaling, he sagged against the post. His cheeks were stiff with dried tears and the memory of his breakdown this morning brought a fresh wave of humiliation crashing over him. The only saving grace was that nobody had been there to see it, not even the man who had his face. The impossible creature. The bastard.

The muscles in his shoulders burned, not just from his hands being cuffed behind him all the time but from the way his arms had been twisted into uncomfortable positions while he slept against the post. The blanket underneath him did not keep the cold of the concrete floor from seeping through and the stink of the waste bucket permeated the entire basement, making his stomach roil. The stench clung to the inside of his nostrils and mouth like the yellow coating of pollen that blanketed everything in springtime. He'd never be rid of it.

He'd die first.

The truth and the pain and humiliation made him tremble. His lips pressed into a thin line and he felt his eyes welling with fresh tears of exhaustion and fury.

Frank exhaled and then slipped back against the post so unexpectedly that his head struck the metal hard enough to clang. Pain echoed through his skull but suddenly he no longer had the energy to react to it. For several seconds he felt a *pull* inside him, an awful suction as if something had crept up into his chest cavity and begun to tug on his heart or draw the blood from it.

Like a leech, he thought. *Inside.*

His eyelids grew impossibly heavy, his limbs like lead. He almost surrendered to that dreadful, sudden weakness, almost lost consciousness entirely, but the sound of the basement door opening made him force himself to sit up. He blinked and shook his head, breathing deeply, and some of his meager strength returned.

The light clicked on and the man with his face came down the steps. He wore the tailored suit Frank had bought to wear at his mother's funeral and what looked like a brand-new tie, brighter and more stylish than anything Frank would ever have put around his neck.

Clean-shaven and with a neat haircut, eyes bright and smile wide, he approached to within a few feet and tossed the keys against Frank's chest. They fell onto his bare leg, then slid down to rest against his scrotum. The cold reminder of his vulnerability forced him to sit up straighter, but his flagging strength did not return.

"You don't look well, Frank," the man said with an air of false concern. "Very pale."

"Let me go."

The man cocked his head. "It's an odd combination of pitiful and adorable that you'd still be asking me that. I've told you, it's going to be awhile. When the time comes, you'll know."

Frank wanted to spit at him but couldn't muster the strength or the saliva.

"I'm going to be late with dinner for you," the man said, "but I figured you'd need to use the bucket, so I came down."

Mustering up what little energy he had, limbs heavy as lead, Frank drew his legs under him and began to slide around the pole until his cuffed hands could snag the keys that his captor had tossed his way. The bastard must have seen how much difficulty he was having and could have helped him, but no help was forthcoming.

When Frank had unlocked his cuffs and gone over to relieve himself in the bucket, the man turned his back. He'd been holding his piss for hours and the stream splashed loudly into the bucket. Frank had pissed and shit in the bucket with this bastard in the room many times by now, but the shame had not relented. He doubted that it ever would.

Just as he'd finished, the man spoke again.

"I also wanted to share the good news. I got the job. They loved my samples—"

"*My* samples," Frank said, his voice cracking as he turned, nakedness and humiliation forgotten. Anger made his heart race as he took a shaky step toward his captor. "You used my portfolio to get that job?"

The man with his face reached under his suit coat and drew the gun from his rear waistband, not even bothering to take aim. He could see Frank had grown too weak to be much of a threat to him.

"Every one of those articles was written by Frank Lindbergh," the man said, his smile returning. "And I'm Frank Lindbergh, now. That's my byline. My samples. My job."

Frank clenched his fists and howled. "It's my life!"

The new Frank pointed his gun at the original. "Not anymore. You had your chance and you blew it. Now put those cuffs back on so I can dump your shit bucket, and if I'm feeling generous later, I'll bring you something to eat."

Frank wanted to kill him. He wanted to cry. But he didn't have the strength for either. Drained and defeated, he turned and slunk back to the support column, sat on his smelly blanket, and put the handcuffs back on his own wrists. The son of a bitch had his face and now a job he'd dreamed of. Not the teaching post he'd dreaded, but the career rebirth he'd promised himself. Hell, the fucker had his name. Without those things, who was he?

Again he felt himself fading. Diminishing, as if his

very existence were a cup that had cracked, its contents bleeding off into nothing.

What use was a broken cup?

How long before the cup would just be empty? How long before it would be discarded?

FIVE

Tess stood beneath her black umbrella, rain pouring off the edges in drips and cascades that reminded her of a childhood spent on the corner of Little Tree Lane and Bosworth Road, waiting for the school bus. On rainy days the bus would always be late and the rain would crash down, and a fifth-grader whose name she could no longer remember would always be there without an umbrella, soaking wet. Tess sometimes invited her beneath the shelter of her own umbrella, but not always, and the *sometimes* of it had haunted her in her adult years. Why had she ever hesitated to offer the little girl shelter, waiting for someone else to do it? Had she worried that it would become her responsibility?

The way that childhood hesitation disturbed her had helped her become a better human, she thought. A better grown-up.

Or so she told herself. There had been times when she had seen homeless people in the area near her Boston office building and given away money, sweaters, and—yes, more than once—her umbrella. But not today. *Sometimes* had come back to haunt her, because today the rain poured down from the cold gray sky and her spine ached and she wanted to hold on to her umbrella. Today she wanted the man sitting beneath a makeshift poncho next to a shopping cart full of sodden belongings to be someone else's problem.

A finger tapped her shoulder and she let out an eep and spun around, heart pounding. Lili jumped back a step as they bumped umbrellas and they both laughed, there in the rainy gray Boston afternoon, with the after-work crowd rushing around them. Streams of people raced for cabs and parking garages and the T station, all clad in black and gray and brown. With the buildings of International Place looming nearby and the cars roaring through puddles, throwing sheets of rainwater onto the sidewalks, it seemed to Tess that Lili's red umbrella was the only patch of vivid color in the entire city.

Cold and damp, she lowered her umbrella and ducked beneath Lili's for a moment, embracing her friend, warmed by the connection.

"I'm so glad you're here," Tess said, rain trickling down the back of her neck, underneath her coat and her shirt. "Are we really doing this? It's supposed to be sunny on Monday."

Lili kissed her cheek and took her hand. Both of them had frozen fingers. "Do you really want to wait till Monday?"

Tess remembered the encounter at First Light Gallery last night and shook her head. "No. It's too weird. I won't be able to focus on anything else if we just go home, but what if he doesn't show?"

"Then we get coffee and warm up somewhere dry."

"Half an hour. That's it," Tess said. "Longer than that and we're going to feel pretty stupid instead of just freezing."

Lili agreed. They found a spot out of the way, near a granite circle that surrounded a small patch of grass and a single tree. The rain lightened a bit as they stood there, umbrella to umbrella, watching the sidewalk where Tess had seen Not-Nick the previous afternoon, but after ten minutes the wait became numbing.

"This is ridiculous," Lili said with a shiver. "It's not even October."

"Close enough, obviously."

They fell silent for a few seconds, listening to the rain around them. In the distance, thunder rumbled across the sky.

"Alonso called me today," Tess confessed.

Lili's eyes lit up with mischief and she grinned, about to speak before something caught her attention. She glanced at the river of umbrellas rushing past them and her expression flattened. Tess watched her mouth open into an astonished "O," and Lili's head turned to watch one of the black umbrellas float by.

Tess understood. "Is that him?"

Lili nodded. Her head slumped a bit and she stared at nothing, as if trying to make sense of what she'd seen. They had come back to the spot where she had first seen her ex-husband's doppelgänger, thinking they might encounter him again in the after-work pedestrian rush. And now here he was.

"Let's go," Tess said, taking her by the arm.

A sixtyish woman cussed them out as they cut her

off. Tess's foot splashed into a puddle, but they bulled their way into the sidewalk foot traffic and she tried to keep an eye on that particular umbrella. She saw the man beneath it, the set of his shoulders, the fingers wrapped around the umbrella handle, and she knew them. Even from behind, she knew her ex-husband.

"That's Nick," Lili rasped in her ear, leaning in and keeping her voice down, though in the rain and with cars roaring by, the man who was a half-dozen people ahead of them would not have heard.

"It's not," Tess said. Windswept rain had soaked through the right arm of her jacket and slicked her cold legs, but she felt flushed with the heat of the moment, with stealth and pursuit and the impossible mystery of it all. "It's not him, Lili. I know it looks like him—"

"*Just* like."

"Did you think the gallery owner last night was reacting to you just bearing a passing resemblance to this Devani Kanda woman?"

"I guess not. But still . . ."

"I know," Tess said.

They followed him south at first, heading along High Street and trying to keep track of him in the flow of people. Tess lost track of where they were until they turned west onto Boylston for a block or so, and then they were headed south again, into the theater district. Lili walked alongside her in a silence Tess found unsettling. With every step, Lili's reaction reinforced the uneasiness that Tess had been trying so hard to ignore. The resemblance this Theo guy had to Nick Devlin wasn't just startling, it was uncanny.

Coupled with their experience at the art gallery last

night, though, it became more than that. Tess felt her
skin crawl as she kept her eyes on Theo. Unless Nick
and Lili both had identical twins from whom they'd
been separated at birth, the existence of Theo and
Devani Kanda felt impossible.

Impossible means impossible, she told herself. So
obviously they weren't. But still this act of tailing him
had an air of unreality about it that made her feel a bit
queasy, and she was glad to have Lili with her.

The pedestrian traffic thinned out considerably
and they had to drop back, worried that the man might
notice them, but the rain fell harder and Tess realized
this was an empty concern. Under his umbrella, with
the gray sky and the hammering rain and the daylight
fading, he wasn't going to be paying any attention to
the city around him, only his destination.

Unless he's worried about being followed.

For half a minute she let this idea trouble her, but
she realized that he hadn't turned to glance back even
once during the long minutes they'd been trailing him.
He barely paid attention when crossing the street, as if
his thoughts were entirely elsewhere.

When Theo turned down Charles Street, they hung
back fifty yards. Two blocks farther, he stepped under
the awning of an elegant old brownstone and shook out
his umbrella. Lili tugged Tess to a halt and they stood
watching for a few breathless seconds, wondering if he
had figured them out. Then he walked up the four steps
at the front of the building and went through the revolving doors.

"Shit!" Tess hissed. "Hurry!"

Together they bolted along the sidewalk, dodging

around a pair of older, wool-coated men. Tess splashed through several more puddles until her feet squelched in her shoes and she knew they would be ruined. Their umbrellas bounced along above them, sparring together, until they ran under the brownstone's awning and came to a huffing stop. Heart pounding, Tess shook off her umbrella and closed it, wet and cold in spite of its protection. Six o'clock had come and gone, perhaps half an hour left before night fell, but with the storm raging it had grown dark already.

Warm lights glowed beyond the frosted glass doors and windows at the front of the building. Stenciled on the glass panels on either side of the revolving doors were the words:

NEPENTHE—A BOUTIQUE HOTEL

Tess glanced at Lili, hesitating, but when Lili nodded they went up the steps together. Theo had seen Tess before, so she nudged Lili ahead of her and they went through the revolving door, which spilled them into the warm golden glow of a lobby full of marble and brass and red velvet, a pristine elegance that belonged so completely to another era that it felt like stepping back in time.

The Nepenthe Hotel took Tess's breath away.

"Do you see him anywhere?" Lili asked.

Tess forced herself to ignore the Victorian elegance of the lobby. Professionals in business suits moved in clusters from the elevator foyer across the marble floor. An elderly couple in earth-tone wools sat in chairs and entertained a boy of nine or ten, their grandson no doubt. A pair of teenage girls made up to look older hurried ahead of several adults, maybe headed out for a night of theater, wanting to be noticed for themselves instead of as part of a family unit.

No sign at all of Not-Nick. *Theo,* she reminded herself.

"Check the bar," she told Lili, hurrying off toward the entrance to the elevator foyer. If Theo was staying in this hotel and hadn't gone into the bar, he would have headed for his room.

"Text me if you see him," Lili called back as she strode for the little pub restaurant just off the lobby.

Tess wore a small purse across her chest. She tapped it, feeling the comforting weight of her cell phone inside almost like a talisman, and then she picked up her pace. The elevator foyer was actually a short corridor that led to restrooms and an old-fashioned wooden phone booth. Two similar corridors opened off the foyer, both of them housing elevators. A handful of people waited in the first offshoot but Theo was not among them. Numbers on the wall indicated that these elevators allowed access to the fourth through fourteenth floors. Tess darted around to the second elevator bay, barely aware that she was holding her breath. Her heart crashed around inside her chest as if it were trying to escape. Three men in suits, waiting for an elevator. Two the right height. One could've been Nick, but then he glanced up at the glowing numbers above the elevator to his left and she saw his face.

"Shit."

The word came out before she could stop it. Two of the three men glanced at her curiously but otherwise they had no reaction to her presence. The numbers on the wall showed that these elevators went to the ballroom and mezzanine levels. Tess exhaled as an elevator opened and the three men stepped on. When the doors slid closed she was alone and she dug out her cell phone.

She texted Lili. *Any sign?*

Waiting for a reply, she wandered back into the lobby, scanning the front desk, the concierge station, and the entrance to the bar. She expected Lili to appear any moment and glanced down at her phone, but there had been no reply to her text.

She told herself it was stupid to be afraid. What could Not-Nick do to Lili in a pub full of people? Still, an icy prickle ran up the back of her neck. The wrongness of these impossible twins had been right there on the surface, but the world felt tangible and real and ordinary, and so it had seemed totally natural to poke their noses into this, to try to get answers. Now, though, in that moment when Lili was out of her sight, it occurred to her just how surreal and off-kilter the situation truly was. Her sense of reality felt unbalanced.

A little boy knocked into her and Tess jumped, a little gasp escaping her lips. Flush with embarrassment and fear, her heart galloping hard, she spun to stare at the boy. He held up some kind of spaceship toy and used his mouth to make a sound that must have been its engines firing but sounded more like a wet raspberry. The kid did not run onward, only stared at her as though daring her to issue a reprimand.

His mother rushed up, full of apologies for Tess and stern chidings for the boy in a foreign accent Tess could not place. As the mother led the boy away, Tess glanced past them, through the lobby, past the various enormous planters and the tables and chairs arranged for guests to linger. Past the darkened glass window and door of the gift shop, whose sign read CLOSED.

At the very back of the lobby was an entry to a wide hallway of the sort Tess associated with restrooms and staff-only areas, but something didn't jibe with that assumption. The left side of the entryway was blocked by the sort of podium typically manned by hosts and hostesses at restaurants worldwide. In front of that was a freestanding sign, though she couldn't make out the letters on it from this distance.

Another glance at her phone. Still no reply from Lili.

She set off toward the rear of the lobby, walking normally at first but picking up her pace until she knew she must have looked like she was in some sort of race. A group of older women sitting in plush chairs and sipping tea stared at her as she passed, but Tess did not slow down.

Movement in her peripheral vision drew her attention to the right and her step faltered. She halted and turned away, feigning interest in the offerings in the window of the darkened gift shop. Forcing herself to breathe, she counted to three and glanced over at the man now making his way toward the closed-down restaurant at the back of the lobby.

She knew him, but it wasn't Nick. Or Not-Nick.

Aaron Blaustein stood about five feet, nine inches tall. He was in his early fifties, slim, and athletic. He wore stylish glasses and his once-black hair and well-groomed beard were shot through with a great deal of silver. The last time Tess had seen Aaron, the man had been serving as the curator at the New England Historical Museum. He was a brilliant man with a winning smile who had proven himself prickly and easily agitated during their brief acquaintance. The kind of man you defended for a while until you realized at last that he really was as big an asshole as everyone else had been telling you all along. Right now, though, she welcomed the sight of a familiar face. Her thundering heartbeat calmed just a bit.

Tess forced herself not to call out as Aaron walked past the podium and into the shadowed restaurant. She exhaled, drew in another breath, and then set off after him. The sign in front of the podium read:

THE SIDEBOARD
BREAKFAST DAILY 7–10:30
LUNCH NOON TO 2

Why the hell would Aaron Blaustein be at the Nepenthe Hotel? More important, why would he be walking into a restaurant that wouldn't open for business for nearly twelve hours?

Heart fluttering, she glanced at her phone but still had no text from Lili. With a glance over her shoulder, she strode to the podium and peered along the short hall into the darkened restaurant. She moved along that short passage, past restroom doors and up to the entrance of an enormous, high-ceilinged dining area. There were small tables throughout, perfect for breakfast, and a long wood and glass buffet, all of its food stations empty and dark for the night.

Tess pressed herself against the passageway wall, peering around the corner into the larger room. Her breath hitched in her throat. Silently she stared, refusing to believe her own eyes.

Aaron Blaustein stood talking to Not-Nick. In the part of her brain that had been struggling to make sense of the existence of someone who could have been a clone of her ex-husband, the presence of Aaron—someone they both knew—slipping into the hotel's shadows . . . the coincidence was too much. *Of course* they would be together.

But it wasn't the sight of the two men together that had caused her to catch her breath. Nervously, she glanced at her phone, quickly texting *Where are you?* to Lili. Reality felt soft and spongy beneath her feet. Tilty and blurred. Her heart buzzed with something between wonder and terror.

No, Aaron talking to this Theo guy wasn't the thing that had made her heart skip and her breath freeze in her lungs . . . it was the thing in the far corner. The restaurant had been decorated in the same Victorian style as the rest of the hotel, the nineteenth-century aesthetic influencing everything from the carpet to the curtains and light fixtures. Anywhere else, the structure in that far corner would have been dramatically out of place, but here it was a mere curiosity.

Twelve feet wide, the strange gazebo-like structure had been erected as an artifact of days gone by. The thing had been painted and dark portraits hung on its outer walls, but inside she knew there would be no paint and no artwork—only mirrors. Mirrors were the entire point of a psychomanteum.

Even from her hiding place, Tess could see through the thing's open doorway. The hotel had put a table and chairs inside the psychomanteum so that patrons could enjoy their meals within it. She wondered if there might be a plaque nearby that explained to visitors the nature and history of the structure, that occultists and spiritualists had been using psychomanteums for centuries to attempt to contact the so-called other side. She could still recall the first time she had ever seen one. Nick had called it an apparition box and aside from the paint and artwork, it had been identical to this one.

Not identical. It was *this one,* she thought.

With Aaron and Nick there . . . Not-Nick . . . the idea that it could be some other psychomanteum seemed absurd. Of course it had to be the same one. Except it had been dismantled; Tess had watched it being done.

The cell phone in her hand buzzed and she jerked back, startled. *Shit,* she thought, pressing her back to the wall and not daring to look around the corner. A quick glance told her it had been Lili responding at last. *No sign of him,* she'd texted. *Where are you?*

Tess forced herself to be calm. Even if they'd heard her, there was no reason for her to be nervous. There were dozens of people in the lobby. A single scream would bring them running. She could retreat if she felt threatened.

The part she didn't understand was why she felt threatened in the first place. Not-Nick had no reason to hurt her, and Aaron would never think of harming her.

If that's Aaron.

Unable to rein in her fears, frustrated with herself, she steeled herself and looked around the corner.

Both men were staring right at her. The buzz of her phone, or her startled reaction, had halted their conversation. Anger simmered in their expressions and then Not-Nick tapped Aaron's arm and guided him toward the psychomanteum's open door. Aaron stepped inside the mirrored box and out of sight, but Not-Nick paused to glance back at Tess. His eyes gleamed in the darkened restaurant as if they were mirrors themselves.

"Go away, woman," Not-Nick warned. "This needn't concern you."

He followed Aaron into the psychomanteum. The fading gray light beyond the curtains provided enough illumination that she could see a little way inside the octagonal structure and she glimpsed shifting reflections in the mirrored panes.

The wrongness of the strange tableau remained, but as she stood staring, listening for any sign of movement within the psychomanteum, Tess grew irritated. *Go away, woman,* he'd said. Whatever might be transpiring here, whoever these people really were, Tess would not be dismissed. Her fear had gotten the better of her, but now anger and curiosity overcame it.

Her phone remained in her hand. She shot Lili a quick reply. *Empty restaurant in the back. U won't believe this.* Just communicating, thinking of Lili joining her, slowed her racing heart. The tinge of sarcasm in her text helped, too. It stiffened her spine, gave her a bit more strength, so that she managed to take a deep breath and approach the apparition box. Quietly, she moved within ten feet of the mirrored booth.

Her phone buzzed. *I'll find you,* Lili had texted.

Tess glanced up, uneasy with the silence emanating

from the psychomanteum. Frowning, she shifted her
position and craned her neck to get a better look through
the doorway. The mirrored interior walls of the booth
were silvery blue in the dim light, the color of the ocean
on a cloudy morning. But the only things she saw in
those reflections were the table and chairs the hotel had
put there.

What the hell?

Two steps forward and one to the right, still wary.
Not-Nick's words had angered her, but where was he
now? *Theo.* She remembered the way the name had
sounded when he'd spoken it, like he was trying it on
for size.

She moved up to the doorway of the mirrored room,
knowing even as she did that she ought to wait for Lili.
The lure of the impossible was too strong. She bent
and looked under the table, then stood gaping at the
otherwise empty booth, at the reflections, wondering
how the two men could have just vanished. Had the hotel tricked the thing out as some kind of magician's
apparatus? The mirrors might lend themselves to such
an effect, but why?

"Hello?" Tess said softly, stepping over the threshold into the psychomanteum.

Each of the walls had a half-dozen mirrored panes
and every one of them reflected her face back at her.
The cautious eyes, the knitted brow. Tess ran her fingers
over the mirrored surfaces, searching for some kind
of latch or gap, anything to explain how the men had
vanished. Her mind would not accept the reality of
what she had just witnessed—not at first. When it began

to sink in, she felt queasy, staring around at her many reflections.

Tess backed toward the door, staring at one mirrored pane. Her reflection looked back. The gray light had faded further, the mirror darkening, and she blinked as she studied her own face, noticing a dull spot on the glass, a ripple in the image that seemed to be spreading.

"What . . ." she began, cocking her head and leaning closer, thinking it must be just a trick of the light.

Human eyes watched her, the reflection of a man behind her, as if he'd been there all along. Tess whipped around, hands up to protect her, cell phone flying from her fingers. It struck the table and skidded off onto the floor as she stood wide-eyed, heart machine-gunning against her rib cage.

No one.

She stood alone in the psychomanteum.

The reflection had belonged to her ex-husband. Those eyes had gazed at her with such love over the years but not tonight.

Tess pressed her eyes shut. *How?*

Woman, she heard him say.

Not breathing, heart clenched, she turned slowly to glance over her shoulder and saw the reflection there, in one mirrored pane. The reflection, but no one to cast it.

"No," she whispered.

Keep away!

In that moment, she watched her husband die. One blink of her eyes and the shadowed reflection was that of Nick Devlin, and the next it turned to rotted muscle and skin stretched tight across an eyeless skull . . . jaws splitting open in a terrible, yearning maw that stretched toward her, darting outward as if the mirror were an open window.

Tess screamed as she jumped back, smashed into a chair and caught her leg. She fell, crying out again as she scrambled through the doorway and hurled herself out of the booth. Whispering prayers to a God she'd almost forgotten, she flipped over to face the psychomanteum, certain the dead thing must be right behind her, sure she could feel its breath on her neck. She scuttled a dozen feet back from the mirrored booth until she realized that nothing had pursued her out into the gloom of the empty restaurant.

Gaze locked on the psychomanteum, she began to rise, remembering its other name. *Apparition box.*

"No way," she whispered, feeling her heart pounding in her throat and temples.

"Tess?"

She twisted around, darting away from the voice, only to find Lili frowning at her from two tables away.

"Whoa," Lili said. "Relax, you spaz."

Tess raised a trembling hand to cover her mouth, afraid she might scream again.

Lili moved toward her, alarmed now by the depth of her fear. "Tessa?"

With a shake of her head, Tess turned to look at the psychomanteum again. Nothing moved inside that little room, an archaic curiosity meant to be nothing more than ornamentation. She wanted to tell herself that her imagination had gotten the better of her, but what of the two men who had vanished inside the booth? *A magician's trick,* she told herself again. *All of it.*

She didn't believe it, but the idea gave her the strength to speak again. In halting tones, her heart slowly returning to normal speed, she told her friend what she had seen. Lili chimed in with a litany of quiet profanities and wide eyes that kept glancing over at the damned box.

"You dropped your phone in there?" Lili said when she'd finished speaking.

"Fuck the phone," Tess whispered, moving toward the exit. "I'll ask someone from the hotel to get it."

Lili started toward the psychomanteum.

"What are you doing?" Tess asked.

"Getting your phone."

"You don't believe me."

Lili paused just outside the mirrored box. "I mostly do. But you're not alone, now. Something happens to me, you can get help."

Before Tess could protest, Lili stepped into the box. Tess could see her moving a chair aside and getting down on one knee to retrieve the cell phone. As she stood, Lili glanced around at the mirrored walls. In the fading gray light, she hesitated a moment and craned her neck as if she wasn't quite sure what she had seen in the mirror, but then she stepped out of the psychomanteum. Tess imagined the thing in the mirror coming after her, a hand reaching out from the gloom inside the apparition box.

"Shit," Lili said, tsking as she strode over to hand Tess her phone. "Screen's cracked."

Numb, Tess took the phone. Lili walked beside her and they left the restaurant. Only when they had strolled through the lobby and moved through the revolving door to stand beneath the hotel's awning, rain pounding down, did Lili speak again.

"You want me to come home with you?" she asked. "We can get some Chinese food, send the sitter home early."

Tess scoffed. "Hell, no. The gallery manager said Devani Kanda's going to be there tonight. We're going."

Lili offered a thin smile, hugging herself against the damp chill of the oncoming evening. "You really want to go over there after this?"

Tess fought the tremor in her hands as she opened her umbrella, forcing away the memory of the hideous death face she'd seen in the mirror.

"We have to go," she told Lili.

"Why?"

"This is still some kind of mystery to you, just a puzzle to solve," Tess said. "You're not afraid. But I have a feeling that when you see this woman, your double . . . maybe then it'll get under your skin."

She turned and marched off into the rain and Lili followed. As night fell, every window in the city seemed to hold the promise of dead faces and whispered warnings. Tess tried to breathe and told herself that the rules of the solid, tangible world she had always known still applied. But she knew a lie when she heard one, even one she very much wanted to believe.

SIX

Tom Belinski didn't mind the rain. A good thing, because his three-year-old German shepherd, Kirby, never stopped to consider the weather when it came time for his walk. They had an apartment on Boylston Street, but their walk always took them over to Beacon Hill, past the golden-domed State House and into the neighborhood of exclusive mansions at the top of the hill. Belinski had been a history professor for years but now, well into his fifties, he'd dropped the professor part of his job description to concentrate on being a pure historian. His work in progress was a book about the old Granary Burial Ground, just blocks from where he and Kirby now wandered. Each chapter offered a slice of Boston's early history by profiling the lives of some of the city's early denizens—every grave in that burial ground, from Benjamin Franklin's father, Josiah, to the victims of the Boston Massacre, had its own story. His publisher had flipped over the idea, but Belinski had missed his deadline by months and still had months to go, and they were profoundly displeased.

Kirby tugged at the leash, sniffing the leg of a mailbox where some other dog had no doubt left its mark. He loosed a short stream of urine not because he had to go but because he wanted to obliterate the other dog's claim of ownership over that spot. Over his life, Belinski had owned four dogs and he had learned that each had its own personality, but Kirby had proven to be the oddest, by far. Like graffiti artists, dogs marked their territory almost as a challenge to others to take it back. Normal behavior for canines. But Kirby took it one step further. When they went to the Common on their morning walk he would always antagonize other dogs by stealing their toys and balls, running off to drop them on the ground nearby, just to piss on them.

Belinski had been told that his dog was an asshole, and he never argued the point.

"Come on," he said, tugging the leash until Kirby fell into step beside him.

The shepherd stopped every dozen feet or so to sniff the sidewalk or the front of a building, undeterred by the puddles or the falling rain. It had eased up a little, but Belinski kept beneath his umbrella, making no attempt to shield the dog. He kept a towel by the front door to dry Kirby off so that they could both avoid provoking the ire of Belinski's wife, LeeAnne.

Kirby paused in front of the granite wall that hemmed in the yard of the second Otis Harrison House, the only freestanding mansion on Beacon Hill. The house had always been one of Belinski's favorites and he had written about it more than once. After the latest restoration a few years back, the brick building looked more magnificent than ever. He'd always found the use of Corinthian pilasters more than a bit odd, but who was he to question the great Thomas Bulfinch, who had designed the whole thing, right up to the octagonal cupola on the roof?

A low span of wrought iron separated the street from the tiny green yard. The leaves on the two oaks in front had turned a vivid red and orange, but in the rain and after dark they looked almost black.

He gave Kirby's leash a tug but the dog did not respond. Kirby had paused in his sniffing of the granite wall and as Belinski tried to pull him away, the dog began to growl. Belinski rolled his eyes—the dog had always indulged in this sort of drama—but he gave in when Kirby tried to drag him nearer to the house.

"What do you smell, boy?" he asked. "That little French bulldog?"

At the corner of the house, a curtain of rain spilling off the edge of the Federal's roof onto Belinski's umbrella, Kirby started barking. Just a few growling yaps at first, but they grew in ferocity. The dog backed up a step, hackles raised, barking wildly. Kirby had snapped at people before, but Belinski had never heard him like this.

"Hey, dummy, quit it!" he said, yanking on the leash.

Kirby stood his ground, straining against his collar. The dog howled, paws scratching the rain-spattered sidewalk as he threw his weight into an effort to pull away from his master. Belinski wondered if he'd caught some animal scent that had whipped him up into this frenzy, but couldn't imagine what it might have been.

With his merely human nose, he couldn't smell anything except the rain.

"Jesus, Kirby, come on!" Belinski said, holding firm. "What set you off?"

The dog began to whine between snarls, digging in harder. Belinski gave up being gentle and tried to drag Kirby away from the house. Snarling, the dog refused to turn away, forcing Belinski to haul him backward, nails scraping the sidewalk. The wind gusted fiercely and blew up under the umbrella, which bent sideways and popped inside out. The rain swept down on him and suddenly Belinski had lost all patience.

"That's enough," he said, pulling his way along the leash like they were playing tug-of-war.

He shouted the dog's name as he dropped to one knee on the rain-slicked sidewalk and grabbed hold of Kirby's collar, reaching around to force the German shepherd to look at him. Wild-eyed, slobber drooling over his black lips, the dog paused, huffing for breath. He whipped his head side to side to pull away from his master's grip, but Belinski held the collar tightly.

"Let's go, boy," he said. "There's nothing for you here."

The dog sniffed the air. His upper lip curled back in a silent snarl, and then he lunged. Belinski shouted in alarm and anger, grabbed Kirby's throat, and held him back for a few seconds until the dog twisted sideways and sank his teeth into his master's left wrist. Bone crunched and blood sprayed as the dog clamped his jaws down and shook his head back and forth, digging in.

Belinski screamed. His right hand slipped off the

dog's collar. Kirby felt it, released his wrist, and went for his face.

And then his throat.

And then the meat of his arms.

And then the soft things inside his belly.

SEVEN

The cab ride passed mostly in silence, save for the African music playing through the speakers. The driver kept a clean taxi and unlike many of those in his occupation, didn't try to engage his passengers in small talk. Occasionally, voices crackled over the radio as the dispatcher ordered other drivers to addresses where they would pick up their fares. The wipers sluiced rain off the windshield. The taxi shot through a vast puddle, tires throwing a tidal wave onto the sidewalk.

"You're mad at me," Lili said.

Tess kept her breathing steady, trying to ignore the throbbing in her spine. "I'm not."

"But—"

"Let's just get there, okay?"

Lili pressed her lips together and turned to stare out the window. After twenty seconds or so she spoke a single, quiet word. "Okay."

Minutes passed during which Tess reminded herself that they had been incredibly fortunate to get a cab. In retrospect they could have had the doorman at the

Nepenthe call one for them, but neither of them had been thinking clearly when they had emerged from the hotel. Tess had just wanted to get away from the place. Fortunately they had passed Octavian Steak House, which was high-end enough to have a doorman all its own, and he'd had them in a taxi ninety seconds after they'd asked.

The African music quieted and the driver gestured to the street corner ahead. "Any particular spot for you, ladies?"

Tess bent to peer through the window and saw the bright white of the First Light Gallery's shop window. She wanted to tell the driver to keep going, give him her address and tell him to take her home.

"Right here's fine," Lili replied.

"All right," he said, his accent thick. "But you'll want those umbrellas. It's nasty out there tonight."

The driver pulled up to the curb, creating a smaller, slow-motion tidal wave. Tess opened the door, not waiting while Lili paid. She popped open her umbrella and slid out, sheltered herself from the rain, and stared at the gleaming white light pouring out of the gallery. It seemed impossibly cheerful on such a dreary evening.

"Hey," Lili said.

Tess glanced at her, then blinked in surprise as she realized the cab had already pulled away—was halfway up the block—and she hadn't even noticed.

"You okay with this?" Lili asked.

Tess managed to nod and start walking. Lili caught up, hiding from the storm beneath her own umbrella. The wind whipped the rain sideways and Tess felt it slicking her legs, colder than before now that the temperature had dropped. Her back ached a little, but the tightness would work itself out as she moved. It always did.

They passed a gourmet cupcake shop, empty though its lights were still on. Nobody wanted a cupcake badly enough to deal with the rain. Not tonight.

Just beyond the shop was a narrow alley between buildings, rain pouring off the roofs. If it hadn't turned so cold—if it had been a different night—Tess might have found it almost beautiful. Instead she hurried on, wanting to get this over with, needing to know without question that Lili believed her. What had happened in that gloomy restaurant in the back of the Nepenthe— what she had seen in the apparition box—had been like stepping across the threshold from one world and into another. Like crashing her house down on a witch and opening the door into a world of bright and frightening colors she had never known existed. She couldn't stand the idea of being in that world alone.

Clutching the collar of her jacket closed, she approached the steps that led up to the gallery's entrance. A couple hurried along the sidewalk from the other direction, huddled under a single huge umbrella of the sort that infuriated people on a crowded sidewalk. Tess caught a glimpse of them as they turned to go up the steps, a leggy blonde in a scarlet dress and an artfully disheveled young guy in a 1980s-inspired suit.

Lili mounted the first step to follow them in, but Tess halted.

"What are you doing?" Lili asked.

A tight little ball of nausea burned in Tess's gut. The voice inside the psychomanteum echoed in her head, the warning still fresh as a slap in the face. Nick's voice. She remembered the words he had spoken prior to that as well, just before he had stepped into the mirrored room. *This needn't concern you.* Not the kind of phrasing her ex-husband would have chosen.

Lili took the edge of her umbrella and tipped it back so they could look eye to eye. "What are we doing, babe?"

Tess stepped up beside her, moving under Lili's umbrella as she closed her own. "Listen to me, Lil. I can only imagine what your brain is doing right now."

"I've kind of shut it off for the moment."

"Exactly. Trying not to analyze any of this, because it's crazy. I know all that. I want you to see your clone or whatever, but I think maybe it's not a great idea for her to see us."

Lili nodded slowly. "Let's just look inside."

Under that single umbrella, they went up the last couple of steps and peered through the glass panel in the door. Tess had only been to a couple of gallery shows in her life—both during her college years—but both of them had been thinly attended affairs, a handful of friends and curious art lovers, wine and cheese and pompous talk. It surprised her to see that First Light had drawn a crowd. People milled about in clusters, admiring the work hung on the walls and installations. A closer look revealed glasses of wine and small plates of cheese and grapes, so maybe First Light wasn't that much different from those art school shows after all.

Tess scanned the crowd. "I don't see her."

"I do."

Lili had leaned to the left, looking through the shop

window instead of the door. The artwork hanging there must have blocked most of the view—Tess certainly couldn't see more than the tops of a few heads and an arm or two—but Lili stood positioned to see between two of the displayed paintings. Her face had gone slack and she let out a loud breath that seemed to deflate her.

"Is this real?" she said quietly.

Tess held tightly to her arm, aches and pains forgotten. "It is."

"I don't . . . Oh, my God, Tessa. To be told is one thing, but to see . . . to see her . . ."

Lili pulled away from the window and reached for the door.

Heart lurching, Tess held her back. "No, no. Honey, I think that's a very bad idea."

Lili hung her head and breathed in and out, steadying herself, then looked up at Tess. "It's like *A Christmas Carol*. Like the Ghost of Christmas Past is showing me myself."

"But it's not you. Her name is Devani Kanda and she's an artist."

Lili leaned over to stare back through the window, peering between those two paintings behind the glass. "I saw the guy. Theo. I saw how much he looked like Nick, but this is different."

"We should go," Tess said.

Lili didn't argue. They turned together and descended the steps, staying under the one umbrella. Tess held on to her own umbrella as they reached the sidewalk, knowing that she and Lili needed to talk, to make sense of things that made absolutely zero sense, but she didn't have the words yet. Didn't know how to begin.

"Tessa," Lili said, yanking her to a stop.

Tess glanced up and saw the homeless man standing in the rain. She jerked back in surprise. The man turned toward them, perhaps as startled as they were, and she saw the dirty rag he had tied like a blindfold over his eyes. The white lights of the gallery cast him in a dim glow. His gray hair was slick with rain, beads of it running down his stubbled face. He wore a ratty, full-length, black coat over clothes that looked baggy and torn and stained with colors she did not want to think about.

The blind man stood too close.

"Excuse me, sir," Lili said, edging Tess sideways to go around him.

A dank, animal smell wafted off him, an unpleasant musk even the rain could not wash away. Tess held her breath as she moved past him, but then the man put his head back, lips curling, and his nostrils flared as he sniffed the air.

Lili muttered something and nudged Tess, who kept going but could not take her eyes off the blind man as he sniffed again, like a hunting dog trying to pick up a scent. His head swiveled, tracking them as if he could see perfectly well through that filthy blindfold, and then he smiled. The grin became more of a leer, showing broken, crooked teeth.

He shot out a hand and grabbed a fistful of Lili's hair. She swore, grabbing his wrist, and smashed the open umbrella against his head. Even over Lili's furious shouting and the rain and the noise of the umbrella, Tess could hear him sniffing again . . . breathing them in. The sound broke something inside her.

"Off me, you crazy fucker!" Lili screamed, then she cried out in pain as the blind man dragged her forward by the hair, batting the umbrella away and pulling her closer. His mouth opened as if he meant to bite or lick her.

Tess struck him in the temple with her closed umbrella. He reeled back, still holding on to Lili's hair. She swore again as she tried to force his fingers free. Tess went after him, hit him in the skull twice more, then turned the umbrella around so she could hit him with the handle, and smashed it across his throat.

He let go, wheezing as he grabbed his throat with both hands.

With a snarl, his smile returned. He lunged for Tess, arms waving, hands searching blindly. She swung the umbrella again but somehow he caught it and ripped it from her grip.

"Oh, darling girl," he said, and stalked toward her, hands raised, ready to lunge.

Tess saw the frown form on his face, saw his brows knit. He paused in confusion and sniffed the air again . . . and then again.

"No, no," he said, turning in a circle as if he had forgotten them entirely. "What happened? I had the scent. I know I did."

Muttering and cursing, he dropped his arms and slumped into a sulk. Sighing, he bent his head back and began to sniff at the air again, wandering along the sidewalk until, hands in front of him now and searching the rainy night, he turned into the narrow alley beside the cupcake shop and vanished into the shadows.

Lili stared after him. "Could you please tell me what the hell that was about?"

Tess could not erase the image of the filthy blindfold from her mind.

"I think I'm glad I don't know," she said. "I just want to go home, have a mug of tea, and climb into bed."

They were standing in the rain, Lili's umbrella ruined and Tess's still closed.

"Can I come?" Lili asked.

Tess did not need to answer. She put up her umbrella and they sought out the nearest hotel, knowing they would never find an empty taxi on such an ugly night. If Lili hadn't asked if she could come over, Tess would have invited her. Maddie was at home with the babysitter, so Tess wouldn't have been by herself, but she did not want Lili to have to go home alone.

Not on a night like this.

The thought brought a rueful chuckle to her lips. *A night like this.*

As if there had ever been a night like this.

EIGHT

Tess lived with six-year-old Maddie in a Victorian house in Cambridge, an easy trip on the red line from downtown. Mother and daughter shared the spacious first floor of the house, which consisted of a kitchen, a home office that had once been the front parlor, a gorgeous living room that had once been a dining room, and two small bedrooms. The hardwood gleamed and the high windows washed the apartment in sunlight when there was sunlight to be had.

It wasn't cheap. On her salary alone, Tess could never have made the rent every month, but Nick shared the cost with her. On her angry days, she told people that the divorce settlement required it, which was true. But she knew that he would have paid his share even if the court had told him he didn't need to kick in a dime. Despite how often he found himself in a bubble of self-interest, Nick loved his daughter and he wanted the best for her. And, after all, he hadn't been solely responsible for the dissolution of their marriage. Post-accident, Tess had needed attention and found herself married to a man uniquely unsuited to give it to her.

There had been some discussion of moving to the suburbs, raising Maddie in a town where she could have a house all her own and wouldn't have to live with the sound of neighbors walking over their heads. They would all have moved, Nick getting an apartment nearby so Maddie could still feel that he was close. But over the years they had become city people, and the suburbs seemed too much like a foreign country. Living on the first floor of the Victorian, Maddie had a backyard and access to Cambridge public schools, which were excellent, and her father was just a short drive away in Somerville.

"You like living here?" Lili asked as the two women approached the house by foot.

Tess took in the street ahead. There were trees growing from squares cut out of the sidewalk and streetlights made to resemble some nineteenth-century gaslight district. At the end of the block she could see the Victorian, its red paint almost black now that night had fallen.

"It's not the life I imagined for us," she said, shifting the brown paper bag in her arms, "but we're okay."

"Well, it's *mostly* the life you imagined," Lili chided her. "You have Maddie and a job that's ideal for you, living in a nice house in Cambridge with pretty much anything you could ask for either a short walk or a few subway stops away. It's a good life."

Tess smiled. Lili had conveniently left out her divorce and her chronic pain and the fact that this life was supposed to be the one she and Maddie shared with Nick. But she couldn't argue.

"Tell that to Maddie," she said.

Lili moved the plastic bag she carried from one hand to the other. "What's wrong with Maddie?"

"She's very unhappy with me right now," Tess said gravely. "She wants to live in the turret room. Reminds her of Rapunzel in *Tangled,* I think."

Lili laughed. "Hell, I'd like to live in the turret room."

"Shame we live on the first floor instead of the third."

"Maybe the third-floor tenant would let her move in."

Tess rolled her eyes. "There are days I might let her, but I don't think Mr. Mariano would go for it."

They stepped around the empty garbage barrels one of the neighbors hadn't taken in after trash pickup that morning and then started up the Victorian's front stairs. Tess inhaled the delicious, spicy aromas rising from the bag in her arms and then set it down to dig out her keys. As she unlocked the door and pushed it open, picking up the bag, she heard voices coming from inside.

"Hello?" the babysitter called.

Maddie piped up with an echo. "Hello?"

"It's Mom!" Tess called. "And I have two surprises!"

"Surprises!"

A thump came from the living room, followed by the sound of running feet. Maddie came bombing down the corridor dressed in flowery pajamas and a pair of dirty socks.

"Mommy!" she said happily. Then she turned her run into a slide, gliding along the hardwood floor in her dirty socks like she was on a surfboard, arms out to steady herself.

Tess caught her in a one-armed hug, joyful in a way that could always make her feel better. If her spine and shoulder cried out in protest, she pretended she couldn't hear them.

"Is Aunt Lili one of the surprises?" Maddie asked, still hugging Tess.

"I am," Lili admitted.

"The other is Chinese food!" Maddie said, poking the bag. "I can smell it."

The babysitter, Erika, appeared in the hallway. "Did you think I wouldn't feed her?"

"I knew you would," Tess said, mussing Maddie's hair. "But no matter how full my girl is, I knew that if I brought home Chinese food and didn't get her some fried dumplings, she'd be heartbroken."

"True! Very true!" Maddie said, trying to tug the bag from her mother's arms.

"You're home early," Erika said.

"Change of plans," Tess replied. "If you want to take off, you can. I'll still pay you for the night."

Erika shook her head. "I wouldn't take it, but I can't leave yet."

Before Tess could ask why, dramatic Maddie let go of the Chinese food bag to hold up both hands as if to block Erika's potential departure.

"You bet you can't, young lady!" Maddie piped. "We had a deal. I watched your movie, and now you've gotta watch *Frozen* with me again."

Erika crossed her arms. "I wouldn't miss it, madwoman. But you can't complain if I sing along."

"Fine," Maddie said, then turned and tried to pull the bag from her mother's arms again.

"I've got it," Tess said, thinking about the various sauces in the bag.

"Mom, I can do it," her daughter insisted with a darkly serious look. "I'm not little. I'm in the *first grade*."

Tess relented, letting her take the bag. "Straight to the kitchen table. We need plates."

"I *know*. I'm not *messy,* either."

Lili and Erika laughed. Sensing that she'd trumped her mother, Maddie marched victoriously down the hall past her babysitter with the Chinese food in her arms.

"Wait till she's twelve," Erika said, reaching up to pull her thick red hair into a ponytail. "My mom says that's when the sassiness hits critical mass."

"I can't wait," Tess replied, but the truth was that she loved her daughter's confidence and wanted to encourage it whenever possible. If that meant indulging a little sass, she thought they would both survive.

Erika greeted Lili, who saluted with her plastic bag.

"What've you got there?" the babysitter asked.

Lili grinned. "If I recall correctly, your favorite Ben and Jerry's flavor is still cheesecake brownie."

"Oh, my God!" Erika squeaked. "You didn't!"

"I did."

Seventeen-year-old Erika threw her arms around Lili almost as enthusiastically as Maddie had hugged her mother, snatched the bag away, and dashed down the hallway toward the kitchen making happy humming noises. Her skintight yoga pants and stylish green knit sweater might have made her look mature, but it seemed there was plenty of little girl left in her.

Tess smiled. "I guess we're all little girls at heart."

She and Lili were left alone in the foyer. They could hear the clatter from the kitchen as Erika and Maddie got out plates and utensils.

"You guys coming?" Maddie called.

Tess took a deep breath.

"Ice cream's gonna melt," Lili said.

"We need to talk about this," Tess replied.

Lili moved in front of her, close enough that Tess could feel the warmth of her friend's breath. Lili searched her eyes.

"We're going into the kitchen and we're gonna eat our dinner while it's hot," Lili said. "Then we're going to watch *Frozen* and sing along."

"We can't just pretend—"

Lili raised her eyebrows. "We can chill out with Maddie until she goes to bed and Erika goes home. It'll give us both time to breathe and sift through all this crap. And then you're gonna call Nick and I'm going to call Aaron Blaustein—"

"It'll be ten o'clock by then. If you're gonna call him, don't you think you should do it now?" Tess asked.

Maddie called from the kitchen again.

Lili smiled. "No. I do not. Aaron, if you recall, is a prick. I'm not worried about getting on his nerves. I didn't see what you did in the hotel, but with the psychomanteum there, and having seen the things I *have* seen . . . we have to tell them."

Tess exhaled, trying to rekindle the joy she had felt upon walking through the door. The rest—the impossible stuff—would keep for a couple of hours. It would have to.

"You know there's someone else we need to call," Tess said. "Unless we're both completely insane, there's something . . . unnatural . . . going on here. Which means we need to get in touch with—"

"Audrey Pang," Lili interrupted.

The name echoed off the walls and ceiling, and for a few seconds the women said nothing further. Then Maddie gave an exasperated, singsong shout of "Mo-om," and they turned together and hurried to the kitchen.

The four of them talked and laughed over Chinese food and then took their ice cream into the living room so the girls could resume their movie. Tess barely tasted any of it. Nothing seemed to have flavor. She smiled as they sang along and chuckled in all the right places during the film, but she knew she was only pretending. The shadow of the evening's experiences loomed over her, an invisible weight that she could never forget completely, even when Maddie curled up beside her on the sofa and began to drift off to sleep.

There were no ghosts in this house. She believed that with all her heart.

But still, she felt haunted.

NINE

Nick lay in bed, head propped on his pillow as he watched old sitcoms with the volume turned low. Kyrie had one leg thrown over him, her head on his chest. The strangeness of the day had unsettled them both, anxiety rippling inside them, and though they had talked more about their plans for England and their future together, that mutual anxiety had established an awkward distance between them. Only when they had agreed to slip into bed early, ostensibly to watch TV, had the tension begun to ease like the exhalation of a long-held breath. Kyrie had stroked his arm almost absently and Nick had turned to smile at her, reaching up to push a lock of her hair away from her eyes. She had kissed him and he'd run a hand along the curve of her hip, and then desire and momentum carried them along.

With her full cheeks and button nose, Kyrie looked lovely and peaceful in her sleep, but she also looked even younger than she was, emphasizing the age difference between them. She snored softly beside him and he stared at the TV, the volume low enough that he could barely hear the laugh track. Her naked body felt warm against his skin and he kissed her forehead, envious of her ability to sleep. The clock had not yet struck eleven and it was rare for him to drift off before midnight. Tonight he thought it would be especially difficult.

What have I done? he thought, hating the melodrama of it. *Fuck, what am I doing?*

Late-night doubts often plagued him and usually revolved around the same concerns. Tess had been the one to ask for a divorce, but Nick had not put up much of a fight. Even before her accident, before her scars, and before she'd kissed another man, she had often told him that his focus on his work would be detrimental to their relationship. Then came the crash. Tess had been out Christmas shopping, Nick home watching TV with two-year-old Maddie asleep on his chest. During a commercial break, he'd seen the brunette meteorologist in her strangely formal dress talking about the dangers of black ice and thought nothing of it. Tess had always been a careful driver.

But she hadn't come home.

At 9:30 he had sent the first text. Half an hour later, he'd left the first message on her cell phone. Shortly before eleven o'clock, he'd received a call from Lawrence Memorial Hospital in Medford and answered, heart pounding. Maddie had woken up, sensing his agitation, and he'd been trying to calm her for twenty minutes when the nurse rang to tell him Tess had been in an accident. At first, the woman had tried to put off giving him any substantial report on his wife's condition, suggesting he come down to the hospital and speak to the doctor. Nick had insisted, which was how he had discovered that she had lost control of her car on the ice, slid over an embankment and into a stand of trees, broken multiple bones and been impaled through her left shoulder by the limb of a tree.

Before the accident, he had often been distracted in the company of his wife and daughter. Tess had told him that she and Maddie needed to know that when he was with them he was *with them*. Nick had mostly pretended to listen and made some halfhearted attempts to assuage her concerns, not because he didn't love his family but because the things Tess said were true. His focus was elsewhere. When he came home late on a night they'd scheduled a dinner date, he apologized profusely and he meant every word.

After the accident, he had spent weeks hovering by her, wanting to help but unsure how to go about it. The doctors insisted that Tess would be fine, but as she healed, she often seemed lost in her own thoughts. She would mention her pain, but never in a manner that seemed like complaining. Awkward and unable to offer her any real comfort, Nick had returned his focus to teaching, secure in the knowledge that Tess would be all right. That she didn't need him.

It turned out she did.

One night, when he'd stayed particularly late at his office at the university, Nick had finally seen the anger on her face . . . and the hurt.

"Where is your daughter right now?" she'd asked.

Nick had frowned in confusion. He had worked late on plans for a symposium he wanted to pitch to the university—a project that had taken up a great deal of his time. When he had rolled in around eight-thirty, Tess had been reading a book in a chair in the living room, a basket of fresh, folded laundry beside her and an ice pack on the shoulder that still gave her trouble. The external wound had scarred over, but the internal damage was done.

"Maddie's sleeping," he said. "Of course she's sleeping."

"How would you know if she wasn't? Maybe she's at her first sleepover."

"She's too young for—"

"How would you know?" Tess had barked. He could still see the pain in her eyes, the moisture there as she fought against her tears. "You haven't read to her at bedtime in seven months! You and I haven't had a night out in six! And do you even remember the last time we had sex?"

Nick hadn't been able to remember. That was the night she had told him about letting another man kiss her. It was also the night she had asked for a divorce.

He'd been angry about the kiss, but inside he also felt relieved it had not been more than that. In the midst of his anger, though, he realized he was not terribly surprised. Not that he expected Tess to be unfaithful, but he had always been aware of the bubble he lived in, his too often distant manner. She had always loved him in spite of the difficulties he had in understanding others and making himself understood. But the tether that connected them had frayed over time, and he knew he was far more to blame than was Tess. He and black ice. He and pain.

"You can't say you didn't have fair warning," she'd

told him. "I talked to you about this over and over. I deserve to have someone in my life who wants to be with me, who can't *wait* to be with me! Maddie can't swap you for another father, but sometimes I really wish she could, because *she* deserves a dad who puts her first."

When he'd stopped fuming about that damn kiss, Nick had wanted to make it up to them. He had started to argue and faltered, shaken by the realization that everything she had said was the truth. That the door to that part of his life had closed.

Now he had a chance to really start over, to do it right, and guilt hung over him like the sword of Damocles. He and Tess had been getting along well enough, even if only for Maddie's sake, but the move to England would douse their détente in gasoline and set it ablaze. He knew it. She would be furious, and why not? He had promised over and over that Maddie would always be his number-one priority and now he was about to prove that to be a lie.

It's not a lie, he told himself. *They'll both understand. Maybe not right away, but in time.* Maddie would get to see England, maybe other parts of Europe as well. Nick might not get his weekly visit with her, but when he did see her he would be able to give her his full attention. They'd be longer, concentrated visits, and it was only for two years. Afterward, he and Kyrie would come back to Boston. There'd likely be a wedding. The visits would go back to their previous pattern but with a new dynamic, a new future for all of them. By then, he thought, Tess would surely have found someone new of her own.

All of this felt true to him. He could make it true. Yet the guilt still lingered.

Kyrie shifted against him, soft breast pressing against him. The smell of her hair filled his nostrils and she breathed warmly against his chest. He slid his hand along her skin and felt himself stirring with fresh arousal.

Nick laughed quietly at himself. "Idiot," he whispered.

No way he could shut his mind off just yet, not with all that was swirling around in there. Kyrie would not have protested if he woke her up for a second round, but he needed to wrestle his demons into submission, not fuck them away. Sexual oblivion worked nicely as a distraction, but he knew it would only be temporary.

He forced himself to focus on the sitcom, turning the volume up. When the ads came on, though, his mind wandered back to the day he'd had with Kyrie, to their conversations, and to the weirdness with the real estate agent.

Buzz.

Surprised, Nick glanced over at his nightstand. Kyrie's cell was in the kitchen, but his sat beside the lamp on the bedside table. Just about eleven o'clock. Before he had become a parent, late-night texts had been filled with the promise of mischief, but now they worried him.

He picked up the phone one-handed so as not to disturb Kyrie, and tapped it to view the text message. His pulse quickened with worry when he saw it was from Tess.

Hey. Can you meet Lili and me tomorrow? It's im-

*portant. Nothing to do with Mad. Some weird stuff go-
ing on and we need to put our heads together.*

Nick stared at the words, wondering what they
meant. With Kyrie's head nestled in the crook of his
armpit, he had to hold the phone right above her head
in order to text a reply. It felt wrong, somehow. Sneaky,
although Nick knew the idea was absurd.

Maddie's okay? he asked.

*Fine. Full of late-night Chinese food. This isn't
about her.*

Nick stared at those words long enough that the
cell phone screen went dim and he had to tap it to
wake it up again. What did he and Tess need to talk
about if not Maddie? And why was Lili involved? They
were professors in the same department at Boston University, but other than that, they had very little contact.
Nick had always heard that after a divorce, friends
were divided up just like the rest of the marriage's belongings, and Tess had certainly gotten Lili. That
was only right, given how long they'd been friends,
but . . .

"Shit," he whispered.

Kyrie murmured something in her sleep, but his focus remained on his phone. Had word somehow gotten
around the department that he had applied for a position at Oxford? If Lili had heard about it and told Tess
already, things would get very ugly.

You're not going to tell me what this is about? he
texted.

Work. In a way, she replied. And then, *Look, we just
need to see you. I told you it's important. Are you going to make time or not?*

A sour kernel of suspicion grew in the back of his mind. *You haven't talked to Derek, have you?*

Would Tess have done it to him, even out of anger? Would she have had someone call his real estate agent, pretending to be him, and fire the guy? He had trouble imagining her capable of it, and yet Tess had changed. They both had, since the split. Maybe the new Tess was capable of all kinds of things the old Tess would never have done.

Who's Derek?

Kyrie shifted in her sleep, relaxed, and began to snore lightly again. Nick wanted to put the phone away, wished he had never looked at the text. The laugh track on the TV seemed to be aimed at him, mocking him for how easily a simple text from his ex-wife could have him chasing his tail.

Tess never asked him for anything that didn't have to do with Maddie. She hadn't been that kind of ex. It made him both grateful and a little sad to know that their daughter was the only connection with him she wanted to preserve.

Where and when? he asked.

Eleven am at Diesel Cafe.

Nick hesitated, but only for a second. *See you there.*

He set the phone back on the nightstand and drew his arm from beneath Kyrie's head. Turning away from her, he stared at the wall. The TV would play old sitcoms all night. He often left it on while he slept, the flicker and the voices offering the comfort of familiarity as he traveled through dreams. Tonight he lay there, Kyrie drawing tight up behind him, cleaving to his warmth, and he listened to those voices. They gave him no comfort this time. He had never imagined being the kind of man who would neglect his family, never mind get divorced. He had grown up with an image of himself as a good man, a righteous man, his father would have said.

Now he wasn't sure.

Midnight came and went and Nick stared at the wall, wondering who he really was. Wondering if he would ever know.

TEN

Frank needed a drink. He'd fought the nausea and endured the chills and sweats that had come and gone. *Fucking alcoholic,* he scolded himself. How had it come to this? All those years promising himself he would never become his father, and here he was. Maybe not as far gone, but still, enough of an alcoholic that his body had decided to torture him until he gave it what it craved. The need had come on in fits and starts. He had been able to push it aside while dealing with the fear and fury of being imprisoned in his own cellar, and the impossible riddle of seeing this man who wore his face again and again. Now, though, the thirst had its hooks in him deep.

He sat slumped against the metal post, unable to sleep or even to pass out from exhaustion. His stomach knotted up with pain and his entire body ached. He would have screamed if he had any hope that someone besides his double might hear him. His mother always said that men were babies when they were sick and even her drunken asshole husband had never argued the point.

This is more than sick, Frank thought. *I don't have the flu. I'm a prisoner.*

For a while he had told himself that eventually someone would come. He would be discovered. The sick knot in his gut, the craving that clawed at his eyes and made his skin prickle with an unscratchable itch . . . maybe it gave him clarity, because he knew nobody would be coming. As far as the outside world knew, Frank Lindbergh had started to turn his life around, gotten a new and better job, better clothes, and a brighter attitude. Down there in the basement with the knot in his gut, he had neither the time nor the inclination to lie to himself, which meant he accepted the truth— people would like the new Frank better. How could they not?

Nobody's coming.

If he didn't do something, he would lose his mind. He would scream.

The night before, he'd had a stupid idea. An idiot's idea. But he'd still been fooling himself then, even had a little fantasy in which his double would build this beautiful new life for him and then let him go, stepping back to let Frank take over, like some kind of sadistic guardian angel. Why keep him alive, otherwise? If you wanted to replace someone, wouldn't you erase them first? Nothing else made sense.

Then he had remembered how weak he had been when new Frank had told him about the job, recalled the feeling of his vitality being leeched out of him and the way his thoughts had gone blank for a minute. To-night, after his last piss in the bucket, his last visit from new Frank, he realized that he couldn't remember his mother's first name. For a little while he had chalked it up to stress or the pressure of trying to remember, the way that some words seemed to become nonsense if you thought too long about the way the letters fit to-gether. But his mother's name had not come back to him, as if he had never known it, but that was impos-sible. He felt the hole in his memory where her name ought to have been and a kind of panic had set in.

New Frank had done something to him.

And Frank—*original recipe Frank,* he was starting to think of himself—couldn't let it happen again. He thought it would be very bad if he allowed new Frank to keep it up. Which meant he had to get the hell out of the basement. But nobody was coming for him, which meant his stupid idea, that idiot's idea, had started to seem more attractive.

Stupid or not, it was his *only* idea.

Taking a deep breath, fighting the nausea and the aching and the chill of the sweat trickling down his back, he pressed himself against the pole and slid up-ward. Rising to his feet, he moved around the pole so that now his back was to the stairs and he faced the op-posite direction. Hands still cuffed behind him, he settled to the concrete, his bare ass shrinking from the cold floor. The blanket remained on the other side, in his usual spot.

Frank twisted his wrists and pressed down, getting the handcuff chain flush with the concrete. He dragged it toward his back and felt the metal lip at the bottom of the post. Pulling, sawing the cuffs from side to side, he forced the chain beneath the metal lip. It didn't slide very far under the lip, but it didn't have to—not at first.

He exhaled, refusing to hope. *Stupid. It'll never work.*

But he had nothing better to do, and at least his stupid idea would take his mind off the booze. Maybe the effort would help him fight the pain in his gut and the craving.

Slowly and deliberately, Frank pulled the handcuff chain toward his back and began to grind it left and right. The day before, when new Frank had set him loose to do his business in the bucket, he had noticed that the metal post had not been sunk into the concrete. It was bolted to the support beam overhead and to the concrete floor below. One bolt on either side of the metal lip, and the ones on the floor were rusty from the times water had seeped into the cellar.

He couldn't let new Frank see, which meant he had to work from this side of the pole. That way, he could use the blanket to cover that metal lip—if he'd made any progress at all, which didn't seem likely.

Still, he sawed right and left, scraped the chain against the rusty bolt under that metal lip. Would one bolt do? If he could grind it down, break through, could he use his body and smash the post off its mooring? Maybe, or maybe he'd have to do both bolts.

He wondered if the cuffs would break before the bolt gave way. Or if his wrists would bleed so badly he would have to stop. He wondered if new Frank would catch on before he could find out just how stupid his idea really was.

But he kept sawing.

If he could free himself, a little voice in his head whispered, there was whiskey waiting for him right upstairs.

He worked the cuffs a little harder against the rusty bolt.

It was thirsty work.

SATURDAY

ONE

On Saturday morning, Audrey Pang woke an hour before dawn. Years of insomnia issues had taught her that it was a very bad idea to look at the clock. The numbers would stress her out—she would start calculating how many hours she had slept and how many she might be able to sleep if she could just manage to drift off again. It never went well. Her wife, Julia, had taken to turning the clock toward the wall every night before bed.

Audrey forced herself to take a deep breath, inhaling the comforting aromas of the little nest they made of their bed at night, pillows all around them. She reached out and took Julia's hand, watched the rise and fall of her chest and the way her lips pouted in her sleep. Pale and freckled and innocent, her face had a kind of sweet joy in repose that made Audrey jealous and filled her with love all at once. With a sigh, she ran her hand gently over the curve of Julia's belly, thinking of the baby growing within. Only three months along, but soon to change their lives forever. She closed her eyes, drawing a certain peace from her wife's presence and thoughts of their future, but her mind had started to buzz.

She glanced at the curtains and saw that the darkness outside had an indigo hue that signaled the approach of day. Even if she fell back to sleep, she would manage an hour and a half at best before she had to get up. Audrey turned her pillow over to the cool side and closed her eyes again. Breathing evenly, she tried to slow her thoughts. Four and a half hours. That was how long she reckoned she had been asleep. Audrey could make it through the day on that, but it wouldn't be fun.

Inhaling the warm scent of Julia's presence—her shampoo and her body lotion and the musky smell of her body—Audrey let herself slide into a meditative state. A song by Radiohead had been running through her mind the previous night and now it returned on a loop, even as snippets of her week's research floated through her mind like images in Dorothy Gale's tornado. A wizened old man named Paul Sorenson had set himself up in a little house in Quincy and word had spread that he was a genuine psychic medium.

Audrey had spent days gathering background on Sorenson, established that nearly everything he claimed about himself—his age, work history, supposed work with the police in his native Sweden—had been fabricated. Sorenson's latest mark was a woman named Farrah Myers, who firmly believed that the medium was allowing her to communicate with her son, who had taken his own life two years ago. Sorenson had been bleeding Farrah Myers dry, and the old woman's daughter, Elena, wanted to force her mother to see the truth. There would be people who insisted these lies did not negate his powers as a medium, so in the coming week, Audrey would attend a group session with Sorenson, set him up, and expose him.

She didn't mind the work—pulling back the curtain to reveal the truth about liars and thieves like Sorenson was its own reward—but she took the cases for other reasons as well. Museums, universities, authors, and police departments paid her good money as an expert in spiritualism and the occult, so it helped to maintain recent credentials.

Shifting in her bed, she finally admitted to herself that there would be no falling back to sleep if she did not empty her bladder. Reluctantly, she left the nest of her marital bed, pushing pillows out of the way. A glimpse at the window was enough to show her that the sky had become even lighter, though she still kept her gaze averted from the clock in case Julia had not turned it around.

When she hit the switch, the bathroom light flickered to life, accompanied by the buzz of the overhead fan. The white noise never disturbed Julia—Audrey had been awake often enough in the middle of the night to know—and somehow it soothed her nerves a bit. With a sigh, she relieved herself and then stood, dragging up her underpants. She turned on the tap, water hissing into the sink, and then a wave of nausea hit her. Her stomach cramped and she slumped against the wall, breathing in and out through her clenched teeth.

Gritted, not clenched. Audrey huffed loudly, gripped by a sudden animosity she could not explain. She looked at her reflection in the mirror, saw hatred in her own eyes, and wondered at its origin. Hunger began to claw at her, a deep yearning, an emptiness that made her want to scream every second she spent not filling it. Her entire body tensed, and then released.

She breathed as her eyes brimmed with tears.

"What the fuck was that?" she whispered, blinking as she wiped at her eyes, trying to puzzle out those crippling emotions.

Emotions that had not been her own.

Washing her hands, she stared again into her own eyes but then glanced away, afraid of what she might see. She turned off the tap and then the light, slipping out into the bedroom where she stood, and studied Julia's sleeping face. She loved the freckles across her wife's slightly pudgy cheeks and the bright orange hair that framed her features, loved the shape her voluptuous curves made beneath the covers . . . but the urge to strike out at Julia, to hurt her, throbbed inside Audrey like the ache of an old injury that never quite went away.

"Jesus," she whispered, feeling sick again.

Never, she thought. She'd never hurt her wife. Julia had been her life's greatest happiness, her greatest gift. Whatever had touched her with this malice, she needed to burn it out of her system.

Quietly, careful not to disturb Julia, she changed into her yoga pants and tugged a Tufts University sweatshirt over her head. She picked up her sneakers and padded downstairs to put them on. Her stomach still hurt and the memory of the hatred and the hunger she'd felt burned in her, made her feel flush as she went out the door, locked it behind her, and set off down the center of the pale, cracked pavement.

The faded 1960s split-level she and Julia called home had very little going for it. Their neighbors were mostly old folks and blue-collar families whose houses had been passed down for two or three generations. Backyard cookouts, street hockey, and police responses to domestic disturbances were part of most every weekend, which would be fine if the neighborhood had any idea how to engage with the lesbian couple in the pale blue house on the corner.

The neighbors were perfectly nice, always tried to include them. Julia had grown up in neighboring Chelsea and been tormented all through high school, so she had been stunned by how accepting they all were. But sometimes Audrey grew tired of the awkwardness of even the nicest gestures and wished she had persuaded her bride to settle in Northampton, where families like the one they hoped to build were practically the rule instead of the exception.

But Revere had the ocean, and Audrey could forgive a great deal to be this close to the water. It didn't hurt that they lived half a mile from Wonderland station, so a trip to Boston meant just a few minutes on the blue line. She ran to the end of the street, up a steep section of hill, and then turned toward the beach, a long drag of dingy hotels, condo complexes, restaurants, and houses.

She padded along the road, the soles of her sneakers skidding on sand blown inland with the last storm, and in no time she reached Revere Beach Boulevard. Though the western horizon remained dark, the eastern sky—out over the Atlantic—had begun to lighten, and she turned south to run, passing other early risers, mostly old Sicilian men walking their dogs and young women jogging. Nobody did early morning yoga on Revere Beach. Audrey sometimes had daydreams about California, but Revere wasn't that kind of place.

Now that she could see the waves, hear them crashing, and breathe the salt air, she opened up her stride, cleansing herself. Only then did she allow herself to remember that wash of terrible emotion, to let it back in.

Audrey had felt such things before and knew they were unnatural. Maybe worse than that—maybe evil, if such a thing as evil existed outside the human world. She spent a great deal of her time studying the occult in history books and archaeological files, not to mention debunking the claims of bullshit spiritualists. A childhood fascination with witchcraft had led her into a lifelong study of a wide spectrum of related topics. She had master's degrees in history and sociology, spoke French and German and could read Latin, though she often outsourced translation when delving into a forgotten cult or deciphering some medieval grimoire.

Over the years, she had concluded that magic was mostly gibberish, but that did not mean those who called themselves witches were not dangerous. There were arcane energies in the world, and people sometimes stumbled into the power lines and got themselves or someone else burned. Ghosts fell into another category entirely—Audrey had seen and experienced too much not to believe that spirits sometimes lingered on after death.

As for psychics and mediums . . . she had exposed dozens of charlatans who took advantage of people's grief and loneliness, but there had been a handful who weren't so easy to dismiss. On the rare occasions when she ran across anyone with a real connection to the dead, she left those individuals to their own devices. If she'd been hired to debunk their efforts, she returned her clients' money and kept quiet about her findings, made excuses that did not involve admitting she believed anyone might be a genuine medium. Any such declaration would be very bad for business, which was also the reason she kept quiet about her own psychic experiences.

They were small things. Over the years she had programmed herself to doubt, and that infected her thought process even when it came to her own experiences. Yes, she could always guess the sex of an unborn child, and her ability to find things others had lost was uncanny, but that didn't make her psychic.

Sometimes, though . . . sometimes she would get a feeling. She would enter a house or a room or pass over a patch of ground that filled her with joy or dread or confusion and she would *know*, down in her bones, that these emotions belonged to someone else. Whether these were echoes of past events or the powerful emotions of the lingering dead, she never tried to guess. At least half a dozen times she had been in the presence of a self-styled medium and known with utter certainty that there were indeed spiritual echoes in a place. But she had never felt anything like the wave of ugly emotions that had struck her this morning.

Troubled, she ran on, relishing the pumping of her blood and the sound of the crashing waves. The wind cut in across the water and swept over her, but she only picked up her pace, letting the effort warm her.

No way our house is haunted, she thought.

Trying not to think about it. Trying and failing.

No way. They had been living in the house more than three years. If some malignant spirit had been left behind by an earlier owner, she would have felt its presence sooner. Julia worked as a copywriter for a Boston ad agency, an ordinary-world job, but she believed in ghosts and she believed in Audrey. The two of them had insisted that the real estate agent search the history of the house to find out if anyone had ever died inside. There were no guarantees, of course. Babies died in their cribs and old folks passed in their sleep—not everything would be in the available records. Julia worried about what she called her wife's "sensitivity," but they had been satisfied that the house was clean.

Three years, and now this, Audrey thought, racing along the sidewalk. A pair of fiftyish women were walking a dog ahead and she stepped off the curb, running past them in the street. *It makes no sense.*

Without breaking stride, she returned to the sidewalk. The streetlamps began to flicker off, though the sun had yet to crest the horizon. Down on the beach, a tall guy in a knit cap tossed a Frisbee along the sand for his dog, who darted and barked like a happy maniac. The sight brought a smile to Audrey's lips and finally she felt as if the last of the morning's lingering emotions had bled out of her.

The cramps hit her again.

Hate and hunger like twin daggers in her gut.

She doubled over, moving too fast, and pitched to the sidewalk. Hands too slow to break her fall, she drew them toward her instead, twisted on her side to avoid breaking an arm. Her right knee hit the sidewalk just before her shoulder and then her skull. In the back of her mind, buried deep behind the violent animus that filled her, she realized she had made a mistake. If she'd sacrificed the skin of her palms, risked a broken forearm, her skull wouldn't have struck the sidewalk. Pain shot through her head and she blacked out, coming to a moment later in a fog of ill will. The desire to hurt someone had never been so strong. It seemed to her that only with her hands around a throat or gripping a knife with which she could draw blood—only then could she fill the void that carved itself into her core.

Lying on the sidewalk, she felt the tears burning her cheeks. The emotions frightened and humiliated her.

This is not me, she thought furiously. *I am not made like this.*

Audrey smelled blood and knew it must be her own. Spikes of pain jabbed her skull and she could feel cold air on her right knee where her yoga pants had torn. Hot blood steamed in the chilly morning air, soaking the fabric. She felt it trickling into her hair, sticky, and she wanted to reach up to touch the spot where she'd banged her head but she worried what she might find.

The hostility roiled in her, ebbing and flowing like the ocean.

"Stop," she said through gritted teeth, one hand on her belly. The nausea came in waves that matched the surging emotion and she fought them both.

This is not me, she thought.

Fighting the pain in her skull—real pain that belonged only to her—she used her left hand to push herself up until she could kneel. On hands and knees, body aching, right knee bleeding, she breathed deeply and tried to cycle that poisonous hatred out of her body again.

Glancing up, she saw him.

A homeless man in a long black coat that hung open and flapped in the wind, revealing torn rags for clothes and a lining that seemed woven of impossibly dark shadows. Across his eyes he had tied a filthy strip of a cloth like a battlefield dressing. A blindfold.

A blind man? she thought.

The blindfolded man—the rag man—cocked his head back and inhaled deeply, breathing in the ocean air. A fresh paroxysm of revulsion and hatred clutched at her. Pain spiked through her skull and her stomach convulsed. Audrey felt bile burning up the back of her throat and she twisted and vomited so hard that her entire body went rigid. Her vision swam with blackness and she nearly fell unconscious again. The smell of vomit forced her to shuffle on her knees, wincing in pain, away from the puddle she had made and she breathed tentatively, afraid she would throw up again.

Distant cries reached her and at first she thought they came from seagulls wheeling overhead. She frowned deeply as she realized the cries sounded muffled, and that they came from straight-ahead.

Again she lifted her gaze and stared at the rag man with his dirty blindfold. He had come no closer but she winced as she realized that she could smell him, and that the stink of him was worse than the smell of the puddle she'd left behind a moment ago. She groaned in disgust and stared at him, stared at the shifting black shadows inside his coat.

The hatred drained out of her and with it that hollowness. Fear slid into the vacancy they left behind and suddenly she wanted to run.

"Stay away," she said, the pain from smashing her head jabbing into her with every word.

An icy chill swept over her, gooseflesh prickling her skin, but it had not been the wind. This chill had come from inside her.

The sun crested the eastern horizon, out over the water, and she squinted and glanced away from its brightness.

When she glanced up again, the blindfolded man was gone.

TWO

As she parked her car around the corner from the Somerville Theater, Tess did her best to fight off the guilt of having left Maddie at home. It wasn't just that she had left her daughter with the babysitter again—though just for a couple of hours today. What troubled her was that she and Nick were going to be together and she had not brought Maddie along. It would have been impossible to have the conversation that needed to take place if her daughter had been there, but she knew she was sinning by omission, not telling Maddie about it.

Tess went to pay at the meter, irritated to find it was one of the old styles, requiring coins. She dug around in the various cup holders in her car until she had enough quarters to buy her an hour and fifteen minutes of parking, plunked the coins into the meter, and then hurried along the street. Her phone marked the time as 11:18 A.M., nearly twenty minutes after the others would have arrived. She wondered how much Lili would have told them—wondered if Nick and Aaron would even have stuck around after that.

It was Saturday morning in Davis Square. People stood on the sidewalk and read the marquee of the Somerville Theater, which showed movies but also still hosted the occasional concert. Tess and Nick had seen The National there back before Maddie had been born. The lyrics to one song had stuck in her brain. *It's a terrible love and I'm walking with spiders.* The song had resonated with her afterward as she tried to figure out how love could ever be terrible. Eventually she realized that a love full of doubts and reservations could never be anything *but* terrible. Full of spiders.

She waited for the light to cross the street. Hipsters played hacky sack. A little anti-oil demonstration had been set up on the island across from the T station. A white guy with thick dreadlocks played guitar and sang "Skinny Love" with the voice of an angel. Once, Davis Square had been run-down, just a spot students had to pass through on the way to Harvard Square, but now Harvard Square was full of chain stores and business lunches, and Davis had become the home of the authentic hipster. The hippie atmosphere had a vitality that made her glad to be there, no matter the circumstances that had brought her.

On that crisp morning, Davis Square felt solid and real. After the previous evening's events, she needed real.

A chilly breeze whistled along the sidewalk as she made her way toward Diesel Cafe. Tess shuddered and turned up the collar of her jacket, wishing she'd worn a scarf. As she passed a restaurant, she glanced at her reflection in the plate glass window, and it unsettled her to see that ghostly, transparent version of herself.

Others passed by in the reflection. She could see them in the glass, crossing the street. A little Volkswagen passed by, itself the ghost of a car.

She reached Diesel Cafe, smiling in spite of her troubles when she saw the rocket ship logo on the front door. She grabbed the door handle, glancing at her reflection in the glass door. Behind her, a woman stood on the sidewalk across the street—a woman her height, with the same curls and the same hue to her skin. A woman with her face.

Tess froze, staring at the reflection of that distant figure. Inside the café, a man tapped on the door and she jumped, startled by the sound.

"Sorry," he said as he exited the café. "You looked distracted and I didn't want to smack you with the door."

Tess smiled and brushed it off, barely aware of the words she was speaking. As he left, she held the open door and turned to look across the street just in time to see the woman entering a small stationery store. *Not my imagination,* she thought, but was this really her double, or just a woman with similar hair?

"Tess. You coming in or are you just gonna stand there?"

Blinking, Tess turned to see Lili standing in the open door of the Diesel Cafe. She glanced again at the stationery store, feeling the powerful urge to go over there, to see her double face-to-face, if that had indeed been her double. Her skin prickled with revulsion. If she went over there anything might happen, and she had a daughter to take care of. She told herself it wasn't just the fear that stopped her from investigating.

"What is it?" Lili asked, her expression darkening as she realized something was truly wrong.

Tess shook her head. "Nothing. Something for later, maybe. Sorry I'm late."

Lili stared across the street as Tess entered the café, but if she saw anything strange, she said nothing. Instead, she led Tess toward the back of the café to a four-top table where Nick waited with Aaron Blaustein. It gave Tess a shiver to see Aaron, after she thought she had seen him last night at the Nepenthe Hotel. She told herself that could not have been the same man as the one sitting in the corner at the back of the café, sipping tea and picking at a slice of peach coffee cake.

When he spotted Tess, Nick rose to greet her.

"How's Maddie?" he asked as he leaned in to kiss her cheek, one hand on her arm. No smile, and no recrimination for the strange phone call she'd made to him two days earlier.

"Home, coloring with Erika," she said.

Aaron kept his seat in the corner. They hadn't seen each other in more than a year, but he did not even glance up—just held his teacup and kept swirling the last of its contents in a circle as if the motion of the brown liquid mesmerized him.

"I guess Lili's already laid it out for you," Tess said, glancing from Aaron to Nick.

"You were late and they were impatient," Lili said.

Nick searched Tess's eyes. "I'm trying to tell myself this is some kind of gag, that you guys are playing a joke, and maybe if we were still married that would make some sense to me. But we don't have that kind of relationship anymore—"

"Why don't we sit down?"

He hesitated, looking at her almost angrily. Lili took a seat next to Aaron, so Tess slid out a chair and sat across from her. Nick stared at her.

"You two must be—" he started.

Aaron set his teacup down hard enough to get their attention. "Nick. Take a fucking seat."

After a moment, Nick complied. He glanced at Aaron but then turned a laser focus back on his ex-wife.

"Stop looking at her like that," Aaron said.

He used a fork to split off a piece of his coffee cake, breaking it up idly with no apparent intention to eat another bite. Then he dropped the fork as if he'd caught himself doing something that offended him and looked around the table.

"This isn't a delusion, because it wouldn't be affecting both of you," he said. Aaron Blaustein had always come off as something of an asshole, but he wasn't stupid.

"No. It's not a delusion," Tess confirmed.

"Okay," Aaron said. He took off his glasses and rubbed the bridge of his nose. "There are some things you apparently saw at the Nepenthe Hotel last night that Lili wasn't in the room to witness. We've heard her version. I'd like to hear yours."

Tess took a deep breath, unused to speaking of impossible things to anyone other than Lili, who had reason to believe her. Still, this had been the reason they had asked the guys to meet them, so she launched into the story and told it as swiftly and succinctly as possible. When she had finished, Nick stared at her again.

"This guy," Nick said. "How much does he look like me, really?"

Tess felt her skin flush. "I don't think there's anyone who's seen you as up close as I have for as long a period of time. Not yet, anyway. If this guy was sitting here at the table, I think I'd be able to tell the difference, but only based on mannerisms and the fact that he's in a little better shape than you. I doubt anyone else would be able to tell. Maybe not even Maddie."

"Maddie's my daughter."

"That's what I'm saying."

Nick swore, shaking his head.

The server came over and smiled politely as she took their coffee orders, perhaps sensing the tension around the table. Lili ordered a cinnamon twist but Tess could not imagine eating anything.

"Tess," Aaron said when the server had departed, arrogant as ever, trying to be in control of something uncontrollable. "You're sure the psychomanteum at the hotel is the one we found at the Otis Harrison House?"

"Not a hundred percent," she said. "How could I be? But it shouldn't be hard to find out."

"Come on," Lili said. "What are the odds of there even being another psychomanteum in Boston?"

Aaron blinked. "Admittedly not great."

A quiet came upon them. The sounds of the café continued unabated, voices and clinking spoons and Amos Lee playing softly from the speakers overhead. Tess figured they were all thinking about the project that had first brought them all together, the dig that had taken place in the cellar of the Otis Harrison House. A man named Silas Ford had bought the historic mansion and hired contractors to restore it to its original grandeur. In the process, Ford's contractor had discovered a stairwell hidden behind a false wall. Since the wall was not part of the architect's design, the contractor had removed it and then descended into a rear cellar that was not in any of the records Aubrey Ford had found referencing the house.

In that cellar, the contractor had found the psychomanteum, covered in dust but otherwise intact and in pristine condition. But it wasn't the apparition box that had brought about the intervention of the New England Historical Museum and the Bostonian Society, or drawn in an archaeological team from Boston University. In the center of the room, a section of the stone floor had fallen into what the worried contractor told a justifiably panicked Aubrey could only be a sinkhole underneath the house. The walls and floor around the sinkhole had been covered in occult symbols.

The contractor and the house's owner cared more about that sinkhole than they did about the five withered corpses they had found in a circle around it, or the one they had discovered inside the psychomanteum itself. Though Aubrey Ford admitted to the temptation to making the bodies vanish, knowing that such a find could seriously impede his restoration of the house, his fear that the contractor and his employees would be unable to keep the discovery secret forced him to involve city officials.

Ford's fears had been justified. The restoration had been put on hold while experts were consulted, and soon a small archaeological team was at work beneath Beacon Hill. Lili and Nick had been brought in to oversee and catalog the work and any discoveries, with Tess and Aaron as consultants for the Bostonian Society and the museum, respectively. Given the obvious occult elements of the site, Tess and Nick had asked around and eventually brought Audrey Pang in to advise the rest of the team on what, exactly, they might be dealing with.

It was Audrey who had identified the psychomanteum and who had explained what she believed the dead people in that cellar had been doing on the day they died.

Summoning a demon, she had said.

Tess remembered the conversation well, even though two years had passed.

You mean trying to summon a demon, Nick had replied.

Audrey had arched an eyebrow. *If you say so.*

Tess had not taken her very seriously after that. Audrey had a great deal of knowledge, but her beliefs were of the sort that the pragmatist in Tess had always scorned. Among the other items found with the corpses had been a journal in which their leader, Simon Danton, had identified them as a group of occultists who called themselves the Society of the Lesser Key, after a seventeenth-century magical grimoire entitled *The Lesser Key of Solomon*. In the journal, Danton had made it clear that they were conducting a séance, trying to replicate the work of someone they called "the master," and that they had built the psychomanteum as some sort of safeguard, to prevent them from sharing his fate . . . whatever that had been.

An autopsy had not offered any conclusion as to the

cause of death for the six corpses in that cellar, though a journalist who had taken an interest in the case would later suggest that the occultists could have taken poison. Tess had allowed herself to believe the explanation of poison because there was something tidy about it, and it allowed her not to wonder anymore.

Audrey had gone through Danton's journal and translated the bits that had not been written in English, but learned little more. Frustrated, she had pursued outside research that eventually led her to uncover the writings of an arcane scholar who had actually mentioned the 1897 disappearance of the Society of the Lesser Key in his memoir. According to Audrey, the society had been following in the footsteps of Cornell Berrige, a man of distinct wealth and occult beliefs of his own. Berrige had bought the Otis Harrison House in 1868 and vanished two years later without an heir.

When the archaeology team had excavated the sinkhole in the middle of that claustrophobic cellar, they found it to be thirteen feet deep. At the bottom of the hole they found another corpse—older than the six in the cellar—that Audrey persuaded them all must be the body of Cornell Berrige. His bones had been charred black, but they could find no sign of the presence of fire anywhere in the hole or the cellar. Audrey had an explanation for that which involved things none of them believed in. She had managed not to be insulted by their skepticism.

Or, at least, not to show that she had taken offense.

Aaron cleared his throat as the server returned with coffee for Tess and a refill for Lili, along with her cinnamon twist. Normally Tess loved the smell of cinnamon, but today it made her stomach clench and she had to edge away from Lili.

"You know we're going to need to talk to Audrey Pang," Tess said, shifting in her seat to alleviate the deep ache in her spine. "I'm not saying what's going on here is black magic or something. I don't know what I believe. But there's obviously a connection to the Harrison House project and we need to get a better handle on what exactly happened in that cellar."

Lili sipped her coffee. "I spoke to Audrey an hour ago. She agreed to meet with me tomorrow, so I can fill you all in after that. I'm not gonna lie, though. She seemed a little *off.*"

Aaron sniffed. "She's an occultist. Isn't that off to begin with?"

"Occult expert. Not that same thing," Tess said curtly. "The woman was incredibly knowledgeable and her research was top-notch. Don't dismiss her just because she believes in things you don't."

A chilly silence went around the table. Tess felt as if she could hear the ticking of an invisible clock.

"You haven't seen what we've seen," Lili said quietly.

"What Tess has seen, you mean?" Aaron replied.

"I saw a woman who looked so much like me that it felt like I'd woken up in the *Twilight Zone,*" Lili told him. "So maybe keep an open mind, Aaron. Don't be so sure Tess is having a breakdown or whatever."

Tess froze, staring at Aaron. "Is that what you think?"

"Take a step back to Thursday morning, before this all started for you, and ask yourself what you would have thought if I'd come to you with the same story," Aaron said. "Come on, Tess. We're friends."

Tess took a long sip of her coffee, glancing toward the plate glass windows at the front of the café. "I *thought* we were."

Nick rapped his knuckles gently on the table. "This doesn't help anyone. Aaron, it's obvious Tess and Lili aren't just messing with us. Let's ask the obvious questions and worry about the answers when we get them."

Blinking, Aaron nodded. "Sorry, Tess. It's just . . ."

"We know," Lili said, ripping off a piece of her cinnamon twist and popping it into her mouth. "Crazy."

"Whatever's at the bottom of this," Tess said, "we've all agreed it's connected to the Otis Harrison House. We need to contact everyone who worked on that project and see if anything similar has happened to them."

"If they've run into their doppelgängers on the streets of Boston?" Aaron asked.

The rest of them ignored him.

"Nick," Tess said, "you still have the files, right? When you moved out—"

"I have them," he agreed. "The number's fairly small, really. The four of us, Audrey Pang, Bob Costello and his partner, the three students—"

"Jalen, Marissa, and the girl from Sicily," Lili said. "What was her name?"

"Hilaria," Nick replied.

Tess drank her coffee. "You'll call them?" she asked.

"Of course."

"Don't forget the writer," Lili said. "What the hell was his name?"

Nick froze, then glanced stiffly at Tess. "Lindbergh," he said, signaling the server that she should bring the check. "Frank Lindbergh. I've got his number some-where, too."

Tess tore off a piece of Lili's cinnamon twist with-out asking and put it in her mouth. Her shoulder throbbed and she wished she had taken a Vicodin this morning. But it wasn't really her chronic pain that had tensed her up. It was the mention of Frank Lindbergh's name.

"Glad you're feeling better," Lili said, amused that Tess had helped herself.

Tess smiled. Lili was her best friend, but there were things she didn't know. Tess had told her about kissing another man at a party and the way that moment had lit the fuse that detonated her marriage . . . but she had never told Lili that the man had been Frank Lindbergh. They'd all met Frank at the same time, during the Harrison House project. Handsome and smart, the jour-nalist had been of immediate interest to Lili, but Tess had lobbied against her getting involved with him be-cause he talked too fast and drank too much and seemed not quite certain where his career was headed. Tess had talked Lili out of pursuing Frank, and then gotten drunk and made out with him at a party. At the time, the news would not have gone over well with Lili. Now enough time had passed that it wouldn't be the act that would piss her best friend off, but the fact that Tess had kept it from her.

So she shot Nick a dark look and said nothing.

The server gave him the check and he handed her his American Express card.

"You don't have to—" Lili began.

"It's just coffee," Nick said, turning to look at Tess.

She saw worry in his eyes. Worry for her, but maybe something else as well.

"Something else on your mind?" she asked.

He frowned. "Nothing that won't wait till Tuesday."

Tess hesitated.

"Really," he said.

She nodded, sliding her chair back as she finished her coffee. "Okay. Thanks, then. For the coffee, and for keeping an open mind."

They all rose except for Aaron. He sat alone, clearly troubled.

"You coming?" Lili asked.

Aaron tried on a smile that didn't fit his face, picking up his fork again and cutting into the peach coffee cake. "I think I'm going to finish this and get another cup of tea. I'm not in any hurry."

One of them could have stayed with him, kept him company, but Tess didn't like him enough to spend time with him, and anyway she had the feeling that Aaron didn't want their company. He took a forkful of his coffee cake and put it in his mouth, then waved good-bye with the fork. The server noticed that he had remained and started over toward him.

Tess, Nick, and Lili left him there. Outside, they all set off in their own directions. It was a Saturday, and they all had other obligations.

They all had their own lives to lead.

THREE

Tim felt his heart thrumming in his chest and the flush of blood rushing through him as he cycled up Pinckney Street. The tires hummed against the pavement as his legs pumped, breath steady and deep. The smell of the city could be toxic at times, but not here at the top of Beacon Hill. Every time he rode his racing bike through the rows of wealthy antique homes, he felt like some kind of time traveler, slicing through dimensions.

Or maybe you've just watched too much Doctor Who, he thought, grinning as he cycled. Legs pumping. Wheels spinning.

It had started fifteen months earlier on a summer vacation with friends. Tim and his wife Kathleen had rented a cottage on the Bass River down on Cape Cod and invited the O'Briens to join them for a week. Kathleen had been wary at first. They'd never vacationed with anyone but her sisters before, and she didn't know Ben and Sydney O'Brien well, never mind that they had two kids who were a little younger than Tim and Kathleen's girls. But the trip had turned out beautifully, the families very simpatico. There had been turns taken at the stove and loads of wine. The cottage had a little dock that stuck out into the river, and late at night the adults had brought plastic cups down to the water and polished off two bottles of Sicilian red while gazing up at the stars. The wives had sworn they had seen a falling star and Tim had backed them up, though he had missed it.

A perfect week . . . until Tim saw the pictures. Saw his belly, and how out of shape he'd gotten.

Monday night after they'd returned home, he'd started on his research. By that Friday he had bought his first racing bike and registered for his first triathlon. Now, forty pounds and a dozen races later, he felt more alive than he ever had in his life. Kathleen and the girls had become healthier themselves, just by dint of their living with him. They ate better, they exercised more, and he and Kathleen had a hell of a lot more sex than they had when he had been out of shape. He liked to think it was because his good health gave him a higher sex drive and not that she had been put off by his earlier weight gain, but either way it was the end result that counted.

He slowed a bit and cleaved nearer the curb as a sparkling new Lexus slid by him on Pinckney. Glancing over his shoulder, he turned into Louisburg Square. A crew was repainting the short black wrought iron fence that ringed the park in the middle of the square, and he had to slow down a bit to glide between a white box truck and the sidewalk, but then he picked up speed again. Tim had a habit of infuriating the neighbors in Louisburg Square, cycling too fast past people walking their angry little dogs and making uptight neighbors dressed for the symphony jam on their brakes as he whipped past their gleaming cars, but he loved it there. Red brick and white trim on the beautiful row houses made him wish he could see inside, but he knew he never would. He and Kathleen did very well for themselves, him in advertising and she as a cellist for the BSO, but they would never be wealthy.

He flew through Louisburg Square like a ghost, knowing he did not belong.

Which was okay, actually. Tim liked his life. On a cloudy Saturday afternoon, his girls had gone to Copley Place to go shopping and see a movie with some of their friends. Kathleen, who had met her mother for lunch, would surely be home within an hour or so. They would go to the market and decide what to make for dinner—on the weekends they always cooked together—and they would make love before the girls came home.

He turned left on Mount Vernon Street, taking the corner wide so he could keep his speed. Far ahead he could see a yellow taxi moving his way, but otherwise the street was devoid of moving vehicles. He sped past parked cars, irritated by the enormous brown UPS truck that took up much of the street. Even a typical compact would have trouble getting past the truck. The driver had left it double-parked in front of a house on the left-hand side of the street, hazard lights blinking.

Something moved in his peripheral vision, just off to his right, and Tim glanced up to see a pigeon diving toward his head. He ducked and it glanced off his helmet, striking hard enough to make him twist to one side. Too late, he realized his mistake. In the last sliver of a second, he tried to compensate, but the front wheel whipped horizontal and he sailed over the handlebars, one foot still in the pedal strap. It came loose, but not before it tugged the bike along behind him, so when he smashed down onto the street the bike came down on top of him.

Tim bounced, cracked his helmet and his left forearm, and skidded along the road with the bike in his wake. Pain exploded in his arm and his back and then he rolled several times and lost consciousness, darkness swallowing him.

He came awake with a groan. The sound alone hurt him. Something in his chest had cracked and just drawing breath spread such pain through his body that tears came to his eyes. He blinked against the gloomy daylight and listened to the familiar sound of a bicycle tire spinning.

Shit. My bike, he thought, feeling a different sort of pain. The crash would have wrecked it. Tim's head rang with what must have been a concussion, but he only vaguely recognized that the ruin of his bicycle was not the worst of his troubles.

He thought of Kathleen, and immediately felt the reassuring presence of his cell phone zipped into the little pack at the small of his back. If he could only reach it, he could call her. He tried to turn on his side and pain screamed inside him, so vivid that he went rigid and began to fall unconscious again. Breathing carefully, wincing, he tried to clear his head.

Fucking pigeon, he thought, remembering.

Wondering what had happened to the taxi and when

some other car might come by and stop to help—not the same thing, he thought, knowing that many people would just keep driving—he let his head loll gently to one side. A crunching in his neck filled him with a dread he had never felt before.

He had rolled up beside the UPS truck, legs tucked beneath it, up against the right rear tire. It had been double-parked, blocking in a silver Audi, but the car's owner had not appeared. Beyond the Audi, he could see a short wall and some trees, and then a Federal mansion that he knew was some kind of landmark. *Famous architect,* he thought. Maybe famous owner. He couldn't remember.

Tim frowned. He couldn't remember much.

The pigeon lay dead on the sidewalk.

Someone coughed nearby. Tim blinked, heart racing. How hurt was he? He smelled blood but could not be sure if it was his or the pigeon's. But someone was coming. Someone was here.

"Hello?" he wheezed, lips trembling from the pain in his chest, the grinding in his rib cage. "Are you . . . are you there? Can you help me?"

A shuffling step came from around the side of the UPS truck, between its bulk and the silver Audi. A thump made him jerk and the pain caused him to cry out, then hiss through his teeth.

"Please?" he ventured.

Another thump, and then another. Someone banging on the metal wall of the truck. For a few seconds he considered the possibility that it had come from inside, that somehow the driver had gotten locked back there and couldn't get out.

Then the shuffle step came again and he could see under the truck, could see the bottom cuffs of the brown uniform pants and the driver's boots. The sound of an engine approaching gave him a flicker of hope, but now that the driver had come back to the truck, he could call an ambulance. *And Kathleen,* Tim thought, feeling so sorry for his wife, knowing how she would worry for him now. The girls, too.

Thump, thump.

The driver came around the back of the truck. A big man with thick brown hair. The driver kept his head down, hanging, as if he'd done something of which he was terribly ashamed.

"Please . . ." Tim gasped.

Without lifting his head, the driver smashed his fist against the side of the truck. *Thump.* Only then did Tim see the blood on the man's knuckles.

The driver took another step forward, head still hung, and then froze on the street, staring down at the dead pigeon. The big man began to tremble and for a second, Tim thought he might cry. A mute protest raged inside him. *Come on, asshole! I'm right here, and I'm hurt. Seriously hurt. It's just a damn pigeon!*

The driver reached down, picked up the dead pigeon, and began to eat it.

Tim stared, unable to breathe. His tears dried and his pain ceased, frozen with the rest of him.

At last the driver looked over at him. Tim wished he hadn't. Bloody feathers stuck to his lips. His eyes were dull, his gaze empty. Then he blinked several times as if waking from a trance and seemed to really *see* Tim for the first time.

The driver looked at the dead pigeon in his hand and winced in disgust. He dropped it, wiping its blood onto his brown uniform. Tim allowed himself to breathe.

"Help?" he wheezed.

The driver wiped his hand again, stared at it in revulsion, and then looked at Tim with the same disgust on his face, as if somehow the dead pigeon and the broken bicyclist were one and the same.

A light seemed to go on inside the driver's eyes.

A glint of malice.

Trembling, the driver wiped his hand again. Then he cocked his leg back and kicked Tim in the side with one steel-toed boot. A scream of agony ripped from Tim's throat. A car engine grew louder, someone stopping to investigate, but something inside the delivery driver had been unleashed. He grunted with effort as he kicked Tim in the ribs again and again. Bones cracked and agony arced through his body.

The driver lifted his foot and drove that boot down on Tim's head.

The man from the newly arrived car screamed for the delivery driver to stop.

The driver brought his boot down again. Tim saw gum on the worn sole of the boot.

He heard a crack as his skull caved in.

FOUR

Nick glanced at the clock over the stove. The minutes were ticking toward seven P.M. and Kyrie had yet to arrive. She had texted to say she was running a little late, but that had been nearly an hour ago and he had begun to worry. While he waited, he sliced the chicken breasts into thin cutlets. Pounding them down seemed to be the more popular method, but his mother had always believed it damaged the flavor of the meat, and Nick agreed. While he dredged the cutlets in milk and coated them with shaved Parmesan, he kept an eye on the pot of water boiling on the stove.

The doorbell rang and he frowned. Kyrie had her own key.

Uneasy, he washed his hands and hurried from the kitchen. The image of police officers on his front steps, there with dreadful news, swam up into his head and he pushed it away. Tess and Lili had filled his head with ghost stories at coffee earlier and he scowled at his own foolishness. Inside, though, he knew the scowl was a mask to cover his disquiet.

His door was solid, but through the frosted glass of the sidelight he saw a single figure, and exhaled a breath of relief to which he would never have admitted. Had Kyrie forgotten her key?

He unlocked the door and drew it open, and then he understood. Beaming at him with her adorable grin, Kyrie had a bottle of Italian white in one hand and her other arm clutched a brown paper bag to her chest.

"Well, hello," he said. "What've we got here?"

Her eyes sparkled. "Mad Maggie's closes for the season in three weeks. With us headed to England, who knows how long it'll be before I can have their double brownie fudge again?"

Nick stood back while Kyrie slipped inside.

"I take it we're making brownie sundaes tonight."

She grinned. "I got hot fudge and everything."

"In that case, you're forgiven for not telling me just how late you'd be," he said, closing and locking the door behind her. "Perfect timing, actually. Dinner should be ready in a half hour."

Kyrie stood on her tiptoes, smiling with spritely mischief, and kissed him. "In that case, my dear," she said with mock formality, "I shall pour the wine!"

They went into the kitchen. The water had started to boil and the cast-iron frying pan had heated up nicely. He dumped the uncooked risotto into the pot and poured a bit of oil into the pan. It hissed and crackled and he felt a familiar satisfaction as he laid the first of the Parmesan-coated cutlets onto the cast-iron.

Kyrie fetched a pair of long-stemmed crystal glasses from the cabinet and uncorked the dry, white Italian.

"We didn't have much chance to talk today," she said, pouring the wine. "How was coffee?"

"Odd," he said without thinking.

Kyrie arched an eyebrow as she handed him his wineglass. "Meaning?"

"Tess and Lili ran into someone we all worked with at the Otis Harrison House project and he acted kind of freaky, I guess. They have another project that he might be involved in and they wanted to get feedback from me and Aaron Blaustein from the museum before they agreed to work with him."

Nick lied without even looking up. He wasn't sure why.

"Okay. Kind of weird that she couldn't just call you, but at least it gave you an opportunity to tell her about England without Maddie around."

He turned the cutlets in the frying pan. Stirred the risotto. Checked to make sure the peas and mushrooms and grated Parmesan were ready to go into the pot once the water had boiled off.

Really, he knew why he had lied. If he told Kyrie the truth about the bizarre story Tess and Lili had told that morning, he would end up defending his ex-wife to his girlfriend, and that was not a position he cared to put himself in. Tess and Lili might have been behaving strangely, but it was clear they had experienced something bizarre. He had seen the uncharacteristic fear in the eyes of these two usually sensible women, and though he had been trying to tell himself there must be a rational explanation behind these doppelgängers—if that was indeed what they were—he could not deny that he had been unsettled by their certainty.

"Nick?"

The first batch of cutlets sizzled in the pan, edges beginning to brown. He swore to himself and plucked one out with a fork, some of the Parmesan sticking to the pan. Earlier he had put some paper towel on top of a clean plate and now he laid the first cutlet down so the paper would soak up the oil.

"Babe?" Kyrie said.

He forked the other cutlet out of the oil and glanced at her. "Yeah?"

"Did you tell Tess about England or not?" Her eyes burned with sparks of irritation. She already knew the answer.

Nick started to put the next batch of cutlets into the oil. "There was just no good opportunity. Lili and Aaron were there the whole time. It would've been awkward."

He had his back to her as he stirred the pot and watched the frying cutlets. His stomach growled at the aromas coming from the stove, but he could not focus on the task in front of him. He felt Kyrie's gaze on his back, felt the climate of the room change like an atmospheric pressure shift that preceded a storm. There would be no storm here—Kyrie wasn't the kind of woman to shout or throw things—but the silence that came from her had a polar chill.

When she appeared at his elbow, he only glanced at her.

She sipped her wine, studying him closely. "You didn't want to call her because you wanted to tell her in person. Now you've seen her, but you didn't tell her."

"I told you—"

"It's not okay, Nick. I know it's not an easy thing, telling Tess. I know it's complicated with Maddie. But if you're committed to us doing this together—"

"I am."

"I love you," she said, taking another sip of wine. "But this is not okay."

Nick turned the second batch of cutlets, then took her wineglass. He kissed the back of her hand, then her forehead, and then her mouth.

"Other than the birth of my daughter, there isn't anything I've ever looked forward to more than the adventure we've got coming. There was no opportunity to talk to Tess today, but I'll see her Tuesday when I drop Maddie off. I will have the conversation with her then."

Kyrie pursed her lips, trying not to smile, but it wasn't in her nature to stay mad very long. She stole back her wineglass.

"You'd better."

The topic did not come up again that night. The Parmesan-crusted chicken wasn't perfect, but it tasted delicious in spite of that, and the risotto more than made up for any imperfections. Kyrie had specifically requested it and Nick was happy to oblige. The hint of garlic was the key to balancing the flavors.

"I'll mix the brownie batter," she said when the last bite had been eaten. "And I'll clean up while they're baking. You said you had some calls to make tonight?"

Nick glanced at the clock and saw that it was closing in on eight o'clock. "If you don't mind."

He retreated to his office, closed the French doors, and fished through his files for the Otis Harrison House project. The need to do this had been weighing on him ever since he had returned from Davis Square earlier in the day, but he had been putting it off. The last thing he wanted to do was call Frank Lindbergh. But really, he didn't want to call any of the people who had worked on the project if it meant one of them might say, *Yes, Nick, so strange that you'd ask that question, I did see someone who looked exactly like someone from that project but turned out not to be.*

Once the file lay open on his desk, he hesitated.

The psychomanteum convinced him. As persuasive as Tess and Lili's demeanor had been, it troubled him that the Nepenthe Hotel had acquired and reconstructed the apparition box. At least one person had died inside it and half a dozen others nearby. If the psychomanteum was going to be rebuilt and displayed, it ought to have been at a museum and not as some Victorian-era curiosity for hotel guests to gawk at over brunch.

His first call was to Bob Costello. He and his partner, Carlos Soares, had been indispensible when it came to the painstaking work of examining and photographing every inch of the cellar at the Harrison House, but more important they had been the ones to shore up the pit in the center of the floor and set up the lighting. Carlos and one of their grad students, Hilaria Guarino, had been the ones to plumb the depth of the pit and lower ladders. Hilaria had found the body of Cornell Berrige, but Nick remembered holding his breath the entire time, afraid that the floor they'd hit was only a blockage and that the pit really was a sinkhole that would cave in beneath them.

Bob and Carlos were happy to hear from him, though he could hear the puzzlement in Bob's voice. After more than a decade together as partners in business and life, the couple was finally getting married in the spring. Bob told Nick to expect a save-the-date card in the mail, and Nick was touched. He had worked with them on several projects but would not have expected an invitation to their wedding.

"So, to what do we owe the pleasure?" Bob asked.

Nick hesitated, momentarily stumped. He had planned to spin a line of vague bullshit, but now that he had Bob on the phone he felt he owed the man something more.

"This is a weird question," he said, glancing at the French doors, craning his neck to make sure Kyrie remained in the kitchen.

"My favorite kind," Bob said.

"My ex, Tess—"

"I know who Tess is, Nick."

He gave a polite chuckle. "I know. Anyway, Tess and Lili Pillai have run into some really odd things the past couple of days, including a guy who could basically be my twin. Also, there's a hotel in town whose designer apparently bought and reassembled the psychomanteum from the Harrison House for decorative display."

"That's messed up."

"Agreed, though they may not have any idea of its background," Nick said. "Anyway, I just wanted to know if you or Carlos had encountered anything strange yourselves lately."

"Huh," Bob grunted.

Nick's pulse quickened. "Is that a 'yes'?"

"No, that's a 'you're right, Nick, that's a weird fucking question.' I haven't seen Tess or Lili in probably a year. Why would anything they've run across have anything to do with us?"

Nick felt his cheeks flush. He muttered something about them wondering if the weirdness might be connected to the Otis Harrison House, but when he wouldn't elaborate further, the tone of Bob's voice went from amused to dubious and then to maybe-you-won't-get-a-save-the-date-card-after-all. By the time Nick managed to extricate himself from the phone call, he never wanted to make another one.

Then he remembered the look in Tess's eyes at the Diesel Cafe and he picked up the phone again. Neither Hilaria nor Jalen answered their phones. When he got Marissa on the line, he kept it as vague as possible, mentioning the psychomanteum to see if that triggered a response and asking if anything peculiar had happened to her lately. Marissa became wary, asking if she ought to be worried that something peculiar *would* happen. He assured her that he had no reason to think so, and then undermined that assurance by asking her to call him if anything strange did transpire.

The last call he made before rejoining Kyrie in the kitchen was to Frank Lindbergh. With the smell of baking brownies filling his apartment, he listened to the ringing on the other end of the line. He had never confronted Frank after Tess's admission. The Harrison House project had been completed by then and Nick had figured the problems he had with Tess had very little to do with that kiss. But in the back of his mind, he had wondered what he would do if he ever ran into the guy again. They'd never heard anything more about Frank's plans to write a book about Cornell Berrige and his posthumous acolytes, the Society of the Lesser Key, and Nick assumed he had abandoned the idea.

"Hello?"

Nick had been expecting an answering machine. "You're home."

"Who's this?"

"It's Nick Devlin. From the Otis Harrison House project?"

The line went so silent that Nick thought he had lost the connection.

"Frank?"

"What can I do for you, Nick?"

The question came out less than friendly, but that was no surprise. Nick would have been wary himself if he received a phone call from a man whose wife he had tried to seduce. He had no interest in small talk, so he forged ahead, being just as vague as he'd been with Marissa.

"What do you mean 'strange'?" Frank asked, laughing quietly. "That's a pretty nonspecific word. I got a new job. My mother died. Also, I saw a dog jumping in the air today, trying to eat bubbles from a little kid's bubble wand. When the bubbles stopped, the dog kept snapping at nothing. That was pretty weird."

Nick sighed. Had Frank always had such a dry sense of humor?

Reluctantly, the memory of Bob Costello's reaction fresh in his mind, he mentioned that Tess had twice run into a man who she and Lili said could be his identical twin. He expected Frank to ask what that had to do with him or with the psychomanteum, how the things could possibly be connected.

Instead, the line went silent again. Nick wondered how Tess and Lili had convinced him that making these calls would be anything but an embarrassing waste of time.

"Wow," Frank said, "that *is* strange."

Nick frowned. "Are you making fun—"

"No, man. No," Frank said. "I mean it's really weird, because the last couple of weeks I've seen this guy—I don't know, twice at the T station and once on the street—and I swear to God he looks just like me. He wears a hat, a black ski hat thing, and usually has his collar up. Twice he had sunglasses on, but he looks so much like me that I thought it was some kind of prank."

Nick could barely summon words. Part of him wanted to laugh, but the icy dread spreading across the back of his neck and his shoulders wasn't at all amusing. What was this all about?

"Did you approach him?"

"The first two times I saw him when I was getting on a train and he was on the platform. The other time he was across the street and then he got on a bus. Listen, Nick, what's this about? How does this connect? I mean, it's got to, right?"

"I think it must, yeah, but I don't have a clue how."

"Oh, shit, I didn't realize the time," Frank said. "I'm sorry, man, but I've got to head out. I have a date for drinks and I don't know what tomorrow looks like. Maybe we should get together? You, me, and Tess. Monday after work, maybe?"

Which was how Nick made plans to have dinner with the man wearing Frank Lindbergh's face.

SUNDAY

ONE

Sunday morning brought blue skies and seventy degrees. The forecast called for a radical temperature shift overnight, with a twenty-degree drop between today and tomorrow, but as Lili Pillai drove through Revere with the windows down and '90s pop music on the radio, she felt clarity spreading like daybreak through her mind. Saturday had passed without any further weirdness, and now the conversation she'd had with Tess, Aaron, and Nick at coffee yesterday seemed awkward, embarrassing, and a little crazy. The memory of seeing Devani Kanda—the artist who was virtually her twin—through the window of the First Light Gallery still gave her a chill, as did Tess's story about what she'd seen in that room with the psychomanteum. But today it seemed much more plausible to think there must be a rational explanation for all of it.

The breeze through the open windows brought the scent of the ocean and Lili smiled broadly, tapping the steering wheel along to the music. She felt a bit guilty to be enjoying herself, but she forced that aside, shoving off the heavy shroud of fear and dread. There were things that required explanation and maybe the fear that had been suffocating her was entirely reasonable, but just for these moments she refused to let the unknown destroy the beauty of the day.

The GPS guided her to Audrey Pang's driveway and she turned in, surveying the location. The blue-collar North Shore neighborhood was not at all where she would have expected to find an adorable lesbian couple, but the country had been changing, and maybe this neighborhood was no more or less welcoming to them than many others would have been. During the Otis Harrison House project, Lili and Audrey had gotten to know each other enough to share personal details of their lives, and Lili had been envious of the love Audrey had for her wife, Julia. When the starry-eyed belief in a lover's perfection passed and the ravenous lust of a relationship's early days began to abate, it was adoration that people really wanted. When just being together was enough to make two people happy, that was the real deal.

Lili shut off her Prius and climbed out of the car, eyes slitted against the sun's glare. She chuckled quietly at her musing. *These are the places your brain goes when you're single,* she thought.

As she strode up the flagstone path, the front door opened. In black yoga pants and an Arsenal soccer sweatshirt, Audrey leaned against the doorjamb and sipped from a mug of coffee.

"Good morning, Lili. I'm glad you found us all right."

Lili smiled as she approached the door. "Last time we saw each other you had scarlet hair."

"I'm going for a more professional look these days," Audrey said. "Listen, a day like this . . . what do you say we go for a walk on the beach while we talk?"

Lili saw her gaze flicker toward the inside of the house for a fraction of a second and wondered if Julia had objected to this Sunday-morning visit.

"I hope I'm not intruding," she said.

Audrey smiled. "You're fine. The house is a disaster and Julia wanted to pick up before you came, but we overslept."

"A walk would be perfect," Lili agreed. "We're not going to have many more days like this before winter. I don't want to squander it."

"There's a place with wicked good coffee a couple of doors down from Kelly's now," Audrey said. "Let me just put this down."

She left the door halfway open as she retreated into the shadows of her home. Lili imagined her giving Julia a farewell kiss-and-nuzzle and felt another twinge of envy. Then Audrey returned, now empty-handed, and pulled the door closed behind her as they started down the driveway.

"It's a hard life," Lili said, "living two blocks from the beach."

They kept the conversation light all the way to the ocean. On a summer weekend, Revere Beach would have been packed, and even today the sun had brought out many of the locals. People biked along the road that ran parallel to the sand. Old men sunned themselves as if they'd never heard of skin cancer, their hides brown and rough as leather. Sixtysomething women in tracksuits walked in clutches of three or four, pumping their elbows enthusiastically as they engaged in savage gossip. Lili preferred her beaches a little more picturesque, but Revere Beach had a sense of preserved history whose appeal she could not deny. Once upon a time there had been a roller coaster here. As they crossed the street and started north along the sand, she fancied that the joyful cries of the coaster's passengers could still be heard on the occasional gust of wind.

Here you go with ghosts again, she thought. And that put a stop to the small talk. She couldn't pretend that she had only come here to chat with an old friend.

"There's something freaky going on," she said.

Audrey smiled as they moved across soft sand to the darker hardpack near the surf. "So you implied. And as much as I like you, Lili, we're not the kind of friends who go for Sunday morning walks on the beach for no reason. People who call me usually have something freaky to talk about."

"You don't believe in any of this stuff, though."

Audrey hesitated. Lili glanced at her and saw a kind of skittishness in her expression, in her eyes, as if she wanted the conversation to be over already, even though it had really just begun.

"That's not really true," Audrey said after a moment. "I believe most of what people claim to be supernatural experiences is misinterpretation, hallucination, or invention. Most, not all. I've seen things I can't explain. I've had some experiences myself. . . . I don't want to go into it, really."

"But at the Harrison House—"

"The Otis Harrison House creeped me the hell out because when they went down into that cellar it was full of dead people who had been trying to summon a demon to do their bidding, or whatever. But I found no evidence that . . ."

She faltered.

Lili came to a stop on the sand, watching her, and Audrey stopped as well.

"What?" Lili prodded.

Audrey turned to stare out at the waves. The wind kicked up and even with the sun out, the air grew colder.

"There's no evidence that the Society of the Lesser Key succeeded," Audrey said, watching the surf roll in. "But I didn't like the psychomanteum. So much malignant energy coming off it. And that pit in the cellar—"

"Wait, you felt that stuff?" Lili asked quietly, going back over their time at the Harrison House, seeing it all again for the first time. "You never said a word."

"You hired me as an occult expert," Audrey said, turning toward her again. "You didn't want a medium. I was there to explain what you had found—who you had found—and help you determine its historical value. That's all. Not to mention that, honestly, none of you should have needed me to tell you there was something *wrong* down there. You all felt it. You especially, Lili. Don't you remember how sick you got while the pit was being excavated and all of the writing on the walls was being transcribed? There were a few days there when you couldn't keep a bagel down, never mind a whole meal."

"I had a stomach bug."

"Yeah," Audrey said. "There was a lot of that going around."

Now that she'd brought it up, Lili remembered how bad it was—how nearly every member of the team had been sick at some point.

"Hilaria," she said.

Audrey nodded. "The Italian girl—"

"Sicilian."

"—somebody took her over to the hospital and they had to give her drugs to stop her from throwing up. She was out for days. By the time she came back your team had dismantled the psychomanteum and filled that pit with dirt and rocks and mortar. For me, that was the end of it. Whatever unpleasant echoes were left over from the things those creepy fuckers did . . . they didn't matter anymore."

Lili threw her hands up. "Except the psychomanteum's out of storage. It's been dusted off and put on display as a curiosity."

Audrey frowned. "The curator? Blaustein? Was this him?"

"Nothing that simple," Lili replied. She shook her head and gestured for Audrey to walk with her again, and they set off along the sand.

Lili told her everything, beginning with Tess on the sidewalk with the man who looked like Nick and ending with the events of Friday night, outside First Light Gallery, and the blindfolded man sniffing the air and then staggering off into the shadows.

"*The raggedy man,* I call him. In my head, anyway," Lili said.

Then she saw the way Audrey's eyes had widened, the thin line of her lips where they pressed so tightly together.

A knot of ice tightened in Lili's stomach. She felt nauseous, as if Audrey's reminder of her earlier sickness had summoned it up again.

"What?" she said quietly, reaching out as Audrey stopped short on the sand.

Audrey started back the way they'd come.

"Hey!" Lili said. "Come on, you can't just give me that look and then take off."

"We're going back," Audrey said.

"What did I say?" Lili asked, hurrying to catch up. "Was it the raggedy man? I saw your eyes, Audrey. Have you seen him, too? If you know who he is, you need to—"

She caught up and clutched Audrey's arm.

"I don't know!" Audrey snapped, yanking her arm away. Her gaze went faraway a moment and then she turned to stare across the beach—across the street— back toward her home. "I have no idea who he is. I wasn't even sure I'd really seen him. I get these . . . spells, I guess you'd say. I passed out a second, maybe, and I thought I saw this man and then he was gone. But it happens sometimes. I've seen things that are like waking dreams and . . ."

Audrey stared. Put up a hand, though it wasn't clear if the gesture was meant to halt her words and train of thought or to warn Lili to keep back.

"I don't want this," she said quietly. "I don't owe you guys anything. I like you, Lili. But I want to stick to research and helping people who are being taken advantage of by assholes pretending to talk to the dead. There's a dark streak through all of this, something that goes back to that cellar. I felt it then and I don't want anything to do with it now. I owe it to Julia to—"

"I didn't bring this to you," Lili said.

Audrey started for the road again, picking up her pace. "You called me, remember?"

Lili chased after her. When Audrey crossed the road too fast, forcing a growling Ford Mustang to jerk to a halt on the pavement, Lili caught up. The driver laid on the horn and swore at them out the window, but both women ignored him. On the other side of the road, they hurried away from the water toward Audrey's street.

"I called you, yeah," Lili said. "But if you saw the raggedy man, you were involved with this before I picked up the phone."

Audrey sagged as she walked, slowing enough that Lili didn't have to hurry to keep up with her. Eyes closed, Audrey hung her head.

"Fuck."

"You're in it, Audrey," Lili said gently. "And you're the only person we know who has any hope of figuring out what the hell is going on."

"What do you expect me to do?" Audrey asked as they turned the corner onto her street.

"Come to the hotel with us. Figure out who these doubles are. Maybe they're another group like the Lesser Key assholes and this is some kind of glamour or whatever. See if you see or feel anything weird. I don't know, Aud. This is your area."

Audrey gazed sadly at her house. "I don't want it to be my area anymore."

"You know, on my way here I had half convinced myself it was nothing. Just coincidence, or someone screwing with us somehow. Then you started talking about what you sensed at the Harrison House and it felt like I couldn't breathe. None of us wants anything to do with this. You're not alone in that, and you're not alone, period."

They reached the driveway. At Lili's car, Audrey stopped and looked at her. When she spoke, it was with her voice low, just in case Julia might be within earshot of a window.

"I'm on another case," she said, "so I can't do it tomorrow. I'll meet you Tuesday. Just tell me when."

"Six o'clock," Lili replied. "If you want to go earlier, we can manage, but we have jobs we're supposed to be going to."

"Fine."

The ocean breeze kicked up, but instead of the clean salt air that Lili had smelled before, this time the wind brought that other ocean smell. Low tide and dead things.

"One other thing," Audrey said, pale with worry. "I'll go with you to the hotel, but not over to the Harrison House. I don't care how many raggedy men we see. I won't go back to that place again.

"Not ever."

MONDAY

ONE

Tess came awake in the middle of the night, body heavy with sleep and head full of muzzy cotton. Her eyes itched, and she blinked a few times while her head made sense of the clock she kept on top of the tall jewelry cabinet between her bedroom windows. The little red dot indicated that her alarm remained set, but it was the time that confounded her. It felt as if she'd been sleeping most of the night, but the numbers told a different story: 2:37. She'd been asleep less than three hours.

She tugged the covers up to her neck, nestling further into the bed, expecting to drift back to sleep. A tightness formed across her forehead and she felt herself tense. Insomnia had not plagued her in some time, but she was familiar with its army of small anxieties. *Not tonight,* she thought, shifting to make herself more comfortable. Suddenly nothing felt right to her. The pillow felt too warm, so she flipped it to the cool side. Her neck ached, and the cable box beneath the TV on her bureau buzzed too loudly.

She sighed in frustration.

Behind her, someone else sighed.

Tess froze, breath trapped in her lungs. Fear crawled over every inch of her skin on tiny insect legs. Her back felt soft and yielding, the perfect home for the sharp plunge of a knife. Her itchy eyes burned with tears and her lungs with that held breath, her unvoiced scream. Seconds of paralysis ticked by without another sound and she tried to convince herself that she hadn't heard it, but really there was only one way to do that. Only one way to *know.*

How many times had she woken up in the night to a creak or a knock, or blinked and seen a jacket hanging from the closet door that for just a moment seemed an ominous shape? Only one way to ever really know for sure.

She drew a breath, steeling herself.

Behind her, someone else drew a breath. Followed by short exhalation, just a little thing. A quiet laugh.

She pressed her eyes together, then opened them and stared again at the gleaming red numbers on her alarm clock.

"Please," she rasped. *Please don't hurt me. Please don't kill me. Please just go.*

A floorboard creaked, and a rush of very different emotion swept over her. If it meant a knife in her back or strangling hands around her throat, none of that mattered. Her visitor could not leave the room.

Because Maddie slept right across the hall.

This fear had a different hue, a cold and violent red, and she whipped back her covers and hurled herself off the other side of the bed. Her right hand found the nearest thing, the alarm clock, and she ripped it off the table, tugging the plug from the wall as she spun to face the sighing, laughing intruder.

The alarm clock hung by its cord in her hand.

Of course, Tess thought.

The clothes were unfamiliar. Dark turtleneck sweater and yoga pants. The earrings that glittered in the dark had to be real and expensive. Otherwise, the woman was Tess. Her mirror.

Seeing Nick on that street corner and understanding that it wasn't really him had been one thing, but this was something different. Lili had seen the artist through the window at First Light Gallery and had paled, unraveled by it. Tess felt herself unraveling now, faced with the impossible, the simply-cannot-be. In her mind she could almost hear the tearing of fabric, as if all her life she had been wandering through a grand performance and never understood that other truths existed beyond the curtains.

"You can't be here," she said.

The double opened her hands, palms up, and gave a small shrug. "And yet I am."

My hands, Tess thought. *My shrug.*

And in the next room, her daughter.

"I'm not kidding," she said, her voice lowering as she made her way around the end of the bed, heart thundering, still holding the clock by its cord. "I don't know what you people are or what you want with us, but you can't be *here*. You want to meet, tell me where and when and I'll sit down with—"

The woman sneered. It made her ugly.

She took a step forward. Tess took a step back.

That was all it took—that step back.

The double came at her in terrible silence. Tess tried to lift the alarm clock, to swing it at the woman's face, but the step back had set her off balance. As she whipped the clock around, the double lunged inside the arc of the swing. One hand on Tess's throat, she thrust backward and the two of them careened into the wall just inches from a window frame.

"Don't you fucking—"

"Don't I what?" the woman whispered, tightening her grip on Tess's throat. "Don't I *dare*?"

With her free hand, she smashed Tess in the face once, twice, a third time. Blood filled Tess's mouth and she struggled to get an arm up, blocking the next blow. One foot against the wall, she pistoned forward and hurled the woman across the room. The double smashed into the bureau, shattering the mirror attached to its back. She cried out in pain and Tess *relished* the sound, wanted to make her do it again.

My daughter, my baby, is in the other room. You think you can come in here . . .

Her thoughts trailed off. The double stood there, sneering again, and Tess saw that somehow she'd snagged the cord of the alarm clock. Tess looked down at her own hand, opened and closed it, finding it empty. For half a second, she wondered if it was possible that she was the double and the other woman was Tess. What could she truly say was impossible?

But no. Tess wore a faded Tufts University T-shirt. The bitch wore black.

"Mumma?" Maddie called from her room, woken

by the shattering mirror, voice plaintive and afraid.
"Mummy?"

The bedroom door stood open. The night-light in the
hall cast a dim golden glow. Tess looked through that
door and prayed that Maddie would not appear, that she
would not see this. She glanced back at her double and
froze, paralyzed by the sight of the woman's face . . .
by the desiccated skin and the wisps of hair and the
gaping pit where one eye had been. Tight gray skin like
dry parchment stretched tautly across the skull and
the lips had receded to reveal yellow, too-sharp teeth.
Something moved and buzzed beneath the dry skin of
the woman's throat and Tess blinked and took a step
back when she *saw*. When she understood. A wasp
crawled out of a split in that withered flesh—they had
built a nest in there.

Shaking, Tess barely realized she had screamed.

Then Maddie called for her again.

"Stay there, baby," the double called, the skin at the
edges of her mouth ripping as she grinned. "Everything's all right. Mumma's coming."

Tess could not breathe. But she could not let that happen. "Not a chance—"

Her double whipped the clock up and around on its
cord. Tess dodged too late. The woman put ferocious
strength into her swing and the clock struck Tess in the
skull, shattering plastic and drawing blood. She went
down hard on the floor, cut her hands on broken shards
of mirror, and felt the hot trickle in her hair and on her
scalp, blood spilling down her cheek. The world went
sideways and blurred around her, flickering like some

nightmare zoetrope vision of her bedroom, her safest place, her home.

The woman stepped in and kicked her in the gut and Tess twisted sideways and threw up on the carpet. Saw stylish boots, zipped on the side. One boot kicked her again, this time in the side, and she couldn't breathe or think.

Maddie cried out again, much more afraid.

"Mumma!"

Once again the image of Tess, as if that death face had never existed, turned toward the corridor with a thin smile on her lips. "Coming."

She kicked Tess again.

Turned and left the room.

Tess closed her eyes on darkness. Opened them on darkness, save for the golden light from the hall. Smelled her own blood but didn't try to staunch it. Stood uneasily and propped herself with a hand against the wall, driving a shard of mirror glass deeper into her palm. Bright pain snapped her alert. The world blurred again as she stepped back but she shook her head, snarling in pain as she tugged the glass from her palm, then whipped her head around again, thinking of the hallway. The night-light.

Her daughter.

"No." The word came out a whisper that did not reflect the roar building inside of her.

Breath coming hard, she stumbled for the door and into the hall. Into that golden night-light glow where dreams and nightmares had always seemed possible to her. Tess braced herself on the wall, streaked her bloody palm along the paint, but froze just outside Maddie's room. From within came a soft maternal shushing.

"It's all right, baby. I just made a mess," the double said softly. "Sorry if I scared you. Just go back to sleep and everything will be all right in the morning."

Tess leaned on the doorframe and turned to look inside the room. The other one—her other self—sat on the edge of the bed, hugging Maddie to her. The two of them, not-mother and daughter, had their faces buried in each other's hair the way Tess and Maddie always did when they hugged good-night.

"I was scared," Maddie said quietly, the hitching remnants of a sob still in her voice. "It was *loud*."

"It was," the other mother agreed.

No. The other me, *but Maddie only has one mother.*

It tore her heart out just to look at them. Not-Tess had perfect hair, even in the middle of the night. In the starlight streaming through the windows, her skin seemed impossibly smooth and pale and perfect. Fit and stylish and in control, all things that Tess wanted to be but never quite achieved.

"Mumma," Maddie said quietly, content and snuggling against a stranger. "You smell really good."

The double glanced up at the doorway, at Tess. Her smile had sharp edges.

Something fled her then. Not just strength—what remained of it—but spirit. Tess staggered backward, clutching at her nightshirt and staring down at her chest as some invisible hand sank into the core of her and pulled, ripping loose a fragment of her everything. Love, passion, fear, self-image, motherhood. It all leeched from her and made her less, drained far more from her than blood loss ever could, and she felt it go.

Whimpering, she collapsed to the floor, wanting nothing more than to lie there. To recover some of what she had lost. But in the bedroom Maddie was still cuddling with something wrong, something that shouldn't exist. Her daughter couldn't see that it wasn't her mother who comforted her. If the woman who was not Tess wanted to lift her up and carry her away, Maddie would not balk. She wouldn't know any better.

Hate fueled Tess now as she turned and dragged herself along the hardwood, slipping once on her bloody palm but then plodding ahead, more determined. At her bedroom door, she managed to prop herself up into a crawl. Always wary of power outages, she maintained one phone in the apartment that plugged into the wall instead of being portable and battery-powered. The ugly yellow phone sat on her nightstand, and it was this that kept her moving.

She dialed 911, telling herself that this was the only way—that going into the room and confronting the woman who had beaten her heightened the risk that her double would harm Maddie. She told herself Maddie would be all right, that she could keep the trauma of this night to a minimum, even as she tried to imagine explaining any of it to her daughter.

"My name is Tess Devlin," she said into the phone. "There's an intruder in my apartment. She attacked me and I'm afraid she'll hurt my daughter. . . ."

Tess answered questions, but vaguely. Her mind could summon little else, and she knew that was good—that details would hurt her later. How could she accurately describe the woman in Maddie's room without them thinking she must be some kind of lunatic? If they thought she'd done this all herself, they might think her a danger to Maddie, and she couldn't live with that.

"Please, ma'am, just wait there until you hear the police arrive. They're on the way," the 911 dispatcher said.

Tess scowled, face numb and heart hollow. "I can't do that. My daughter—"

"Ma'am, please."

She dropped the phone, leaving it off the hook in case they still needed to trace the call or something. *No, she said the police are on the way*. But the phone stayed off the hook, and that was okay. It didn't matter. She had made the call and now she had to get back, to distract the woman somehow, to make sure Maddie was safe.

Her head swam with black motes as she forced herself to stand, clutching the bedpost. Taking deep breaths, she felt slivers of herself returning, just enough to reel out of the room, somehow avoiding the shards of broken mirror on the floor. Still cloaked in the smell of her own blood, she sailed down the hall in a lurch and turned into Maddie's room.

Her daughter lay alone in the starlight, buried under her covers, only her head poking out, a fan of hair on her pillow. Tess whipped around, breath coming too fast, staring along the hallway toward the steps. Only then did she feel the cold wind sweeping through the apartment. Taking deep breaths, she mustered her strength and went back into the hall. In the foyer at the front of the house, the door stood open to the autumn night, leaves blowing in over the threshold. In the distance, she could hear sirens.

"Mumma?" Maddie called to her.

Relief washed over her as she understood—the woman had gone and her daughter was still here. Safe in bed. Emotion welled up and overflowed, tears sliding down her cheeks as she made her way back along the hall.

"I'm here, baby," she said, and a ripple of nausea went through her as she realized how much she sounded like the other woman. The other Tess.

"Who were you talking to in the other room?" Maddie asked.

Tess hesitated. The sirens were growing louder. The police would want to talk to Maddie, too, and the girl would see her mother's blood and bruises and the broken mirror and she would never understand. An intruder, that was all she had to know. It didn't need to make sense to her and the police would not expect it to. She was only six years old, after all. Only one thing mattered.

"You're safe, my love," Tess said, standing in the golden glow of the night-light, that place where—in the small hours—all of the best and worst imaginings had always seemed possible. "You're safe."

But she knew that she couldn't *keep* Maddie safe.

And that was going to have to change.

TWO

Frank jerked awake. His shoulders hurt the worst, an ache that went to the bone. His lower back muscles were knotted so badly that the nerves around them were like tiny bombs, ready to go off if he shifted his weight or tried to rise. The groan that slipped from deep within him seemed too loud in the dark and he moved almost without thinking, exhaustion and malnutrition clouding his mind.

And something else, he thought. *Something else.*

His consciousness ebbed and flowed, but he knew there was more to the tide that shifted inside him than just the lack of proper rest and food. More than just the oppression of being a captive. Something else had been drained from him, and the hollow it left behind kept getting deeper. *I'm fading,* he thought, and far from the first time. *Fading fast.* He felt like a shadow of himself. For now the shadow seemed dark enough to have some texture, some substance, but as the hours crawled by he held a picture in his mind of the sun rising higher in the sky and the shadows growing thinner, until eventually the sun would be right overhead and the shadows would vanish altogether.

But he could feel his shadow burning away.

Frank could smell the stink of his own body, rank after so much time down here with the concrete and the damp, and he feared that soon that stink would be all that remained of him. With a deeper groan, he shifted himself against the post and all the little bombs in his lower back and shoulders exploded with bright, lancing pain. Muscles and nerves. The movement made his eyes brim with moisture but he cherished every little agony. Better that than the numbness spreading inside him, the chasm of nothing within.

Grunting, he dragged the chain of his handcuffs under the metal lip between the bottom of the post and the concrete. By now he could force the metal snug against the first of the bolts that anchored the post. One more breath, shoulders on fire, and then he started to saw back and forth again.

Fucker, he thought, imagining his own face. He wanted to smash it in.

You're gonna die.

Frank couldn't quite be sure which of him he was talking to. The one he wanted to save or the one he wanted to kill.

THREE

The dashboard clock in Nick's car read 8:03 when he rolled up to the curb in front of Tess's place. In his mind he could still see the tightness around Kyrie's mouth when she had told him to go. *Just go. Your daughter needs you.* But in those same words—beneath them—had been others. *Your ex-wife doesn't, and don't forget it.*

The dynamic would not go away. For a while he had imagined that his new relationship could exist in harmony with the complications of the old one, that the two women occupied separate space in his life. He'd been an idiot. Whatever equation he had thought he could fit them into, whatever Venn diagram he'd hoped for, it had been a fantasy. Maddie threw off all calculations, because when he took her into consideration, nothing else mattered.

If Kyrie had difficulty separating the idea of him rushing to comfort his daughter from the image of him doing the same for Tess, there was nothing Nick could do about it. He would navigate those waters later. Right now, the only thing that mattered was being Daddy.

He turned off the engine and climbed out of the car, reaching back in for the hot cup of Dunkin' Donuts coffee he'd picked up along the way. As he slammed the door and clicked the locking mechanism on his key fob, he realized with a pang of regret that he ought to have brought hot chocolate for Maddie. Even coffee for Tess. He'd never been good about such things, spent too much time inside his own head, but he had been teaching himself to pay more attention to the needs of those around them. It wasn't always easy for him to read people, but he'd been making an effort.

His ex wouldn't expect him to have thought of her—might even be shocked if he had—but Maddie might be hurt. The thought was nearly enough to make him leave his own coffee on the roof of the car, but he shook his head and kept walking. If Maddie asked for hot chocolate, he'd take her out to get some.

Nick turned up his collar as he walked to the Victorian's front door. The second- and third-floor neighbors had their own entrance around the side of the building. Morning had come but the night's chill remained, as if winter hastened to claim its turn. He knocked, and saw his fist tremble. The coffee cup shook in his other hand and he bent forward, a momentary fog passing through his thoughts.

Frowning, he shook his head. With a deep breath, the sudden wavering passed.

"What the hell was that?" he whispered to himself.

Then the door opened and he saw what the intruder had done to Tess the night before. He screwed up his

face in concern as he reached for her. She flinched
backward as his fingers nearly grazed her cheek. For a
second he thought she was afraid to be touched—afraid
it would hurt—and he felt bad. Then he saw the confusion and distaste on her features and realized Tess
had jerked away because she didn't want to be touched
by him.

"Sorry," he said, glancing at his hand, which hung
uselessly in the air for a moment before he dropped it
to his side, almost embarrassed to own such things as
hands.

Tess gingerly traced the swollen, raging-red bruise
that the left side of her face had become. "It's all right.
I've seen me in the mirror. I know it's a shock."

Nick studied her eyes. Bloody red lines shot through
the left one. "You okay?"

She laughed softly, wincing from the pain it caused
her. "Seriously?"

"You know what I mean."

She exhaled, letting him off the hook. "I do. Okay
as I can be, I guess."

The past hung between them, an unwelcome companion whose presence would not allow them to speak
freely. Nick still felt love for Tess, and believed the same
must be true in reverse, but he couldn't take her in his
arms and give her the kind of comfort a husband ought
to. Nor would Tess welcome the attempt.

"I'm sorry," Nick said, frown deepening. "This—"

Maddie appeared behind Tess in the doorway.
"Daddy?" She had dressed for school and wore a bright
pink backpack with cartoon monkeys all over it.

Nick grinned, but it felt like a lie. Tess stepped back

to allow him inside, reminding him that she had kept him until then on the threshold. He knelt in front of his daughter and took her in his arms.

"Good morning, my love," he said, voice muffled in the little girl's hair.

"What are you doing here?"

Nick pulled back and studied her querulous expression. "Mommy told me what happened last night, so I decided to come and check on you guys."

Maddie glanced around, suspicious of the shadowed corners of the room. "The bad lady's gone, though. Mom said—"

"Of course she's gone," Nick said quickly. "And she won't be back. Nothing to be afraid of, now. But it's like when you wake up from a nightmare and you want to be hugged for a little while. The bad dream's over but you still feel a little scared, right? You're safe, bug. I just thought I'd hug you for a little while before you left for school."

Her smile bloomed slowly, but when it came it lit up the room. "I could use some hugs."

Nick laughed and swept her into his embrace again. He saw Tess smile and the sick feeling that had been roiling in the pit of his stomach returned. The bruises would fade. The cuts would heal. But how could they ever recover from the unwelcome knowledge that had been inflicted upon them?

"Maddie, honey, give me and Daddy a minute to talk, okay?" Tess said.

"We're already late," the girl said.

"I called the school. You won't be in trouble," Tess

promised, caressing Maddie's hair. "Go on in and watch TV for a minute."

Nick kissed his daughter's head and she poked him in the nose before running down the hall and into the living room, ponytail bouncing behind her. Rising to his feet, Nick turned to Tess.

"You need help cleaning up?"

Tess shook her head. "Already took care of the broken mirror and I've got a locksmith coming at one o'clock. I'll give you a copy of the new key."

"You don't have to do that. It's your house—"

"She's your daughter," Tess interrupted. "Like it or not, part of your life is here."

Nick winced.

She waved the moment away. "I'm sorry. That's not fair. I know how much she means to you. I'm just . . . you haven't seen your double yet. It's the strangest thing, like someone's tearing down the walls around you and showing you what's really been there all along."

"Not to mention what she did to you."

Tess visibly shuddered. "I don't care what she did to me," she whispered. "She had Maddie in her arms, Nick. And Maddie . . . she didn't know it wasn't me."

Nick covered his mouth, trying to hear these words in his head and make them sound like something other than batshit crazy. He ran his palm over the stubble on his face, wishing very hard that he could make himself not believe in any of this. If Tess had lost her mind, that would create a hundred difficult complications, but it would be easier to process than any of this.

"Shit," he rasped, shaking his head.

"I know how it sounds."

Nick nodded. "Yeah. But I'm here. I'm on your side, Tessa. We're meeting up with the others tonight. Audrey will be there. So will Frank."

They both took a minute to let that sink in, giving each other a few seconds to bring up the elephant in the room. When Tess said nothing about seeing Frank again, Nick realized he had no interest in bringing it up either. That battle had already been fought, and as far as he was concerned all three members of what had once been the Devlin family had lost.

"We're going to figure out who these people are, how the hell they're pulling this off, and then we're going to the police," he went on. "The woman who did this to you? She's got to be in cuffs after this."

Tess smiled thinly. Painfully.

"What?" Nick demanded.

"Nothing. Go visit with Maddie. How much time do you have?"

"I'm going into the office later, but I have as much time as you need."

"How does Kyrie feel about that?"

A barb hidden inside a seemingly innocent question. The past would never really be past. The blades might grow dull, but they'd still be stabbing each other with them for as long as they lived. Nick forced himself not to bring up a defensive shield, not to jab back.

"She's fine."

Tess hesitated, perhaps deciding whether to stab at him again. "I need a shower and a few minutes to breathe and deal with this. Do you think you could run her to school for me?"

"Of course," Nick said, turning toward the living room.

"First, though, maybe you can tell me what you're hiding."

Nick glanced at her, saw the glint of half knowledge and full-on suspicion in her eyes, and guilt flooded through him. Frustrated, he pushed it away. Now was not the time to have this conversation—not even close to the right moment—but the part of him that still loved Tess looked at her bruised face and knew that she'd been beaten up body and soul in the past couple of days. He couldn't lie to her now.

So he told her about the plans he and Kyrie had for London.

The revelation was not well received.

FOUR

Tess let the water run so hot that it seared away much of her hurt and anger. As she soaped and shampooed, wincing at the pain in her face and ribs, she fantasized about ways she might kill her ex-husband and get away with it. Running him down in her car gave her a certain grim satisfaction. Then she reminded herself that Maddie would have to suffer through the tragic murder of her father and it seemed less palatable.

Stop, she told herself. *You love him.*

And she did, even still. Not that she yearned for him—that ship had sailed—but she did care deeply for her former mister. Enough to forgive him, even though she wanted to strangle him. Enough to recognize that, no matter how inconvenient his plans to move to London for a couple of years with his too-smart and too-adorable girlfriend might be, he had a right to his own life. To his pursuit of happiness.

Truth was, if Tess could get out of the way and help her daughter over the feelings of abandonment that would certainly arise from Nick's decision, Maddie would get to see London and beyond, to really experience another part of the world. It might be good for her, in the end.

She let out a feral roar in the shower and felt much better.

Turning off the shower, she squeezed excess water from her hair and slid open the door. With Maddie off to school, she had left the bathroom door open, and now the chilly air made her shiver as she reached for her towel. The beating she had taken had distracted her body from the daily pains left over from her car accident, but whenever she dried herself off after a shower, her shoulder and spine reminded her.

She glanced into the half-steamed mirror and saw that the near-scalding water had turned her brown skin into a pinkish copper, which had already begun to fade. Hot and cold both felt good, balancing out the deep ache in the places where her double had punched or kicked her, but she felt another ache that persisted. Ever since she had seen her double in Maddie's bedroom, she had felt an awful absence at her core. A loss not unlike grief. But now, at last, she sensed herself recovering. The pit remained in the center of her, but it didn't seem so deep now.

As she did after any shower, she studied the vivid pink scar tissue that stretched across the top of her left breast and curved up toward her shoulder. The tree limb that had impaled her had done a savage job of it. She knew that plastic surgeons could do wonders for her— not make the scar vanish entirely but near enough—yet somehow she wasn't ready yet. The scar felt like an out-ward expression of inner pain, like evidence, and she wasn't ready to erase it.

Tess lifted her eyes to confront herself in the mirror, and recoiled at the sight of her dead face. She cried out, jerked back, and whipped her head around, heart thumping hard, primal fear crashing through her.

No, no, no. This can't be.

She forced herself to look back. In her mind, she saw the death's head again. The wisps of hair and parchment skin. The empty eye socket and too-sharp, heinous yellow teeth. But now she blinked and realized the image lingered only in her mind. Steadying her breath, trying to calm her heart, she put her hands on the sink and leaned over, doing her best not to throw up. She ran cold water and splashed her face.

"Jesus," she whispered, thinking about how deeply the fear had been planted in her mind last night. *That's all it was,* she thought. But it felt like a lie.

Tess dressed quickly, pulling on dark green pants and her favorite old sweater, a cable-knit burgundy turtleneck that had seen better days. The clothes made her feel better, and she dried and brushed her hair out into a mass of curls while she forced her thoughts away from the death mask she'd seen on her double, and thought she'd seen in the mirror. Instead, she turned her ruminations back to her ex-husband. Her marriage had died a long time ago. So why was she mourning it now?

Barefoot, feet chilly on the hardwood, she moved carefully across her bedroom, wary of mirror shards that her broom and vacuum job might have missed. *Shoes would be nice,* she chided herself, but by then she had reached her bed and she lay down and stared at the ceiling. Her ribs throbbed, but the EMT who had prodded her side during the night had not thought anything was broken, so she endured it.

Tess breathed, listening to the autumn wind outside and the rattle of the windows in their frames. She and the rest of the crew from the Otis Harrison House weren't gathering until six o'clock, which meant she had all day to do nothing but fume or be afraid or both. If she'd gone into the office, her bruised and swollen face would have elicited more questions than she felt like answering, but the others were working.

Read a book, she thought. She did her stretching routine, relieving some of the pain in her joints but doing nothing for the bruises she'd incurred last night. It occurred to her that she should get out of the house, maybe go to the gym, but on the heels of the realization came a second one—she'd already put on very comfortable clothes. Her subconscious had no intention of going to the gym.

Instead, still trying to flush the nightmare imagery from her mind, she took her phone from the nightstand and slid under her covers. Head on her pillow, she texted Lili with the same intensity her fifteen-year-old self had used to write emo poetry in her journal back in high school.

Dickhead moving to London with spunky GF, she tapped. *Oh and btw, intruder in the house last night. Beat the shit out of me.* Tess considered elaborating, but didn't want to put the truth in a text, didn't want to talk about doppelgängers or mention that the intruder had her face in a communication that the police might read someday. Lili would call her as soon as she saw the text and then Tess could elaborate.

But the phone remained still and silent in her hand. Minutes passed before Tess realized that Lili must have been teaching a class. Her head throbbed, pain wrapped in cotton, and she clicked on the television to distract herself. A blond bobblehead and a friendly giant co-hosted a morning chat show and Tess left the channel on, thoughts drifting, half her mind still focused on the phone that lay beside her on the bed.

When the nine o'clock chat show had given way to a ten o'clock version with a different host, she called Lili and listened to the ringing on the other end of the line. The call switched to voice mail and Tess left a message. "Call me." Nothing more.

Insidious worries gnawed at her.

Her double had come for her in the night—or come for Maddie, or both. The woman had slipped away when she'd heard the police sirens, but Tess knew that she and her daughter might both have been killed. So where was Lili? Had she received a visitor in the night as well?

She texted again. *Not kidding. Call me asap.*

The television audience laughed. To her ears, it sounded like they were mocking her, so she clicked it off. Turning on her side, she held the phone in her hands like some kind of talisman. The flannel pillowcase felt soft against the unbruised side of her face and she breathed in, exhaling in a shudder of exhaustion and uncertainty.

Her head and her side throbbed with pain, but a

shroud of weariness enveloped her and in moments her eyes drifted shut.

Tess jerked awake at the buzz of the phone in her hand.

Lili, she thought, and she blinked as she held up the phone to stare at the screen. For a few seconds the words made zero sense. *Not Lili. Alonso.* Who was Alonso? Still half lost in dreams, it took her a moment to remember the bartender.

We still on for tomorrow night?

The screen dimmed and she had to tap it to wake it up again. What could she say?

The week hasn't started off great.

Tess watched the ellipses that signified Alonso was typing a reply. The pain in her face and side had been magnified by rest instead of healed by it. A giant bottle of Advil and a whiskey would have helped but she had neither of them at her bedside.

Is this your segue into canceling? I had this fantasy about a romantic dinner and dancing under the stars. Or pizza and beer. I can go either way.

She smiled until she remembered her double. Felt the kicks in her side all over again. In her mind, she saw the woman holding Maddie, whispering comforts to her.

I'm not really in any shape to go out. Had a break-in last night. Woman assaulted me.

The ellipses blinked.

Holy shit. Do you need anything? Are you okay?

Tess began to tap a reply but paused. Of course she was not okay. She'd had some truly surreal and frightening encounters in the past couple of days. But the team from the Harrison House project was gathering in seven hours or so. She had allies and friends. Their presence would not erase her fear, but just being with people would make her feel better. Maybe the psycho-manteum was just as much magician's trick as it was a mirror box. Maybe she had been too quick to believe in the impossible.

Definitely not okay, but I will be, she texted.

Sounds like you really need a night out, but I understand if you don't feel up to it.

Tess stared at the message from Alonso and found herself exhaling. Some of the tension eased from her shoulders. The pain had not ebbed, but some of the cobwebs that had cluttered her mind this morning were swept away. For a few seconds, she considered actually keeping the date, but then she pictured herself trying to flirt with Alonso while in a constant state of anxiety and creeping unease. Never mind that she looked like she'd gone a few rounds in a boxing ring.

I swear this isn't a blow-off but I need a few days to deal with last night. Can we talk at the end of the week?

Not that she had any confidence that things would be resolved by Friday. It just seemed nicer than telling him she'd call him when she could make the time.

However you want to play it.☺ Rain check.

Absolutely.

The conversation with Alonso over, Tess glanced back at the bathroom door, tempted to go and look in the mirror to see which face would be looking back. Instead, she stayed in bed, thinking about the mirrored walls inside the psychomanteum and what she had seen there. *Mirrors,* she thought. It was all connected, of course. The apparition box and the woman who had attacked her last night.

They're apparitions. Ghosts.

But the bitch who had her face hit pretty damn hard for a ghost.

Tess stared at her phone, willing Lili to call her back.

FIVE

The first thing Lili felt was the dryness of her throat. Awareness crept in like dusk gathering outside the windows of her mind, somehow slow and deliberate, and yet sudden at the very same time. She took a shuddering breath and her eyes fluttered open. Her stomach ached badly and her eyes burned. She rolled onto her side and curled into a fetal ball, hoping to alleviate the clenching pain in her belly, and only then did she feel the carpet against her cheek.

Groaning, she forced her head up and looked around her living room. Her eyes took a moment to focus but she managed to read the clock on her DVR: 10:37. Judging by the light outside, it was 10:37 A.M., but her thoughts were in such disarray that she had needed the sunlight to be sure.

Her skin crawled with dread. How had she ended up here? Blackout?

There had been a time when drinking enough to black out was common enough for her that she would not have woken up in confusion. She'd go on a date—

not a first date, she was expert at those, but a third or fourth—and the guy would be sweet and want to take things further and instead of curling up into a fetal ball the way she often wanted to, she would undress him. Then herself, but always with the lights on. She told herself it was safer with the lights on, that she'd be fine if she looked at his face the whole time and focused on how she felt and how she was making him feel. Sometimes the sex would be mediocre or even unpleasant and other times it would be sweet or even, occasionally, mind-blowingly excellent. Sometimes she managed to prevent her subconscious from firing up the home movie projector of her mind and showing bits and pieces of the night she'd been raped at a frat house on Professor's Row. But many times she waited until the guy had left and then drank herself into oblivion.

The trauma had receded over time. She'd been in love more than once, had sex many times without getting shitfaced afterward. Sometimes she went days without thinking about it, and other times she studied other women and wondered what they had endured. Tess had been through her share of ugliness, but not like this, and Lili envied her that. There were days she just wanted someone to take the memories away or wanted to be someone else.

She sat up fully and the floor tilted under her. Her stomach rebelled against the sudden movement and she had to prop herself up on both hands and take long, slow breaths to avoid puking her guts up. Was that where the pain in her stomach came from? Had she thrown up during the night? There was no sign of it, but the whole evening stretched behind her into vague shadows.

"Shit," she whispered, an ugly certainty forming in her mind. That night at the frat party she had drunk a cup of punch a guy had poured for her and had woken up seven hours later in the basement laundry room. The whole punch bowl had been roofied. Lili knew from whispers that she hadn't been the only one raped, but as far as she knew none of the others had come forward.

She had worked hard to put the pieces of herself back together and she felt strong now. Stronger than ever before.

Lili knew she was strong, because she suspected she'd been drugged last night and instead of panic she felt anger. She ran her hands over her body, finding all of her clothing still in place. Her thoughts were fuzzy and her stomach a bit queasy, but if someone had drugged her, it didn't seem like they had done anything worse. Relief drained all of the air out of her for a few seconds, then she forced herself up and sat on the edge of the coffee table. The sofa seemed too far away.

The ache in her stomach began to abate, but her thoughts still felt muddy and her mouth and throat seemed even more parched. She'd had her share of hangovers, but the only empty cup in the room was a mug she presumed she had used to make tea. Presumed, because she could not recall. There were no open bottles around, nothing to suggest she had gotten herself drunk or taken any pills. Whiskey would not have surprised her—even beer—but Lili had never been a fan of drugs, so what the hell was this?

Rubbing her hands over her face, she tried to remember the night before. Images flashed in her mind, entirely mundane flickers of the past twenty-four hours.

She had watched television, maybe old episodes of something on Netflix, and had eaten leftover sesame chicken, but even those details she saw in momentary fragments.

On the glass table beneath the television set, her cell phone vibrated. It created an echo in her head—had it been vibrating before she came around? Lili felt pretty sure it had. Moaning quietly, she forced herself to stand and walk over to her phone as it buzzed a second time. Plucking it from the table, she blinked in surprise as she saw that she had three missed calls from Tess and a litany of texts from her as well.

"What the hell?" she whispered.

Her doorbell rang and she flinched. Figuring it must be a package delivery, something she ordered from Amazon, she tapped the phone to open her texts, but then whoever had come to her door began to knock heavily. Four times in rapid succession—*thumpthump-thumpthump.*

Lili caught her breath. Phone forgotten, though still clutched in her hand, she stared toward the arched doorway that led into the foyer. She took two steps in that direction, feeling strangely vulnerable, exposed in her own home. Her baby blue pajama pants and long-sleeved white T-shirt seemed thinner, and she put an arm across her breasts, wishing she had passed out wearing a bra. The absurdity of the idea struck her— what possible shield could a bra provide?—but somehow she felt more in danger without one.

The doorbell rang again. She reached the archway and froze.

"Who is it?" she called.

Three knocks now, firm and quick. Then a voice. "Police, ma'am. Open up!"

The pain in her gut gave a fresh twist. What the hell was this? Lili went to the door and pulled back the sheer curtain tightly drawn across the sidelight. She saw a badge and a uniform. Irritation battled with lingering fear inside her. What was so urgent?

She opened the door and stared into the face of the palest man she'd ever seen. The sun made her squint her eyes and raise a hand to block the glare, even as the fall chill swept in around her, red and brown leaves eddying in around her feet. The cop smiled at her, goofily handsome.

"Long night?" he asked.

"I'm sorry?" Lili said, hackles rising, arm still across her breasts. "You scared the crap out of me with that banging. What is it?"

He winced and she saw a flash of hurt in his eyes. "Huh. Not what I expected. After last night I figured we were good. My shift starts in an hour and I know you don't teach until after lunch on Mondays, so I figured I'd . . . I mean, I wanted to see you. Thank you, 'cause I thought you'd forgiven me."

Lili felt something stirring in the back of her head, unfurling like a cat rising from sleep.

The cop shrugged. "I guess not."

He started to turn away and she darted over the threshold to stop him.

"Steven," she said, blinking as he turned to face her. Horror spread through her as his features painted themselves into her mind. A thousand images filtered in, more than a year of shared history. "Oh, my God."

The hurt in his eyes vanished, replaced by concern. "Hey . . . What's going on with you? Are you okay? Last night you seemed—"

Lili hurled herself at him, wrapping her arms around his waist and burying her face against the stiff blue fabric of his uniform. Her heart beat so fast it felt like a swarm of furious bees inside her chest.

"Steven," she said again, anchoring the smell of him in her mind along with the image of his face. Somehow she had lost him for a minute, forgotten him entirely. It couldn't be, and yet it was.

"Something's wrong with me," she said.

Steven took her by the arms and held her away from him, studying her eyes. "You look terrified. Talk to me, Lili. You left my place eight hours ago and you were fine. Happy. What happened?"

Lili shook her head, feeling as pale as Steven looked. Another breeze rustled the leaves that had already whispered through her open door.

"That's just it," she said. "I don't think I did."

Her memories were a strange archaeology all their own, fragments of artifacts left behind, but what little she could reconstruct told her she had not left her apartment at all. Pajamas, leftover sesame chicken, and something on Netflix. *Gilmore Girls,* she thought. *The one when Rory's grandfather rigs her Yale interview.*

"I don't think I saw you at all."

Steven stiffened. Something in her manner had triggered him, altered the gravity of his thoughts, and she saw him shift from ex-boyfriend to police officer in the space of a single moment.

"That doesn't sound like you're talking metaphorically," he said. "Maybe you'd better tell me what you mean."

Lili thought about it. Last she knew—last her sudden resurgent memories told her—she had been furious at Steven for cheating on her, but not really surprised. Things had been tenuous between them for a while and she had started to freeze him out, afraid of how serious things had become. How adult. That didn't mean she forgave him for cheating, but she had engaged in her share of infidelities with past boyfriends and knew that behaving like an asshole for a little while didn't make him a monster.

Whatever his flaws, he was a good man and a good cop, so far as she knew. If he thought her mind had begun to unravel, he would be honest about it.

"Come inside," she said. "It's a long story."

At her kitchen table, over cups of coffee, she told Steven everything. It was clear that he did not believe her, but he didn't laugh at her either.

Steven sipped his coffee and watched her warily over the rim of his mug.

"Tell me again," he said, as if her story were some scientific theory and he was her competition, wanting to find fault in her research.

Drained, she told it again in a near monotone. When she was done, she held up a finger for him to be patient while she called her TA and told him he would have to take her afternoon classes. The grad student inquired after her health and Lili told him she'd been feeling poorly all morning, which was true enough. He wished her a speedy recovery and she almost laughed.

Steven had gotten up while she was on the phone and gone to look out the window over her kitchen sink. The autumn light limned his pale face in a shade of gold, as if he existed in a world slightly out of step with Lili's own. Perhaps that was true.

"So?" she asked as she ended the call. "You ready to lock me up?"

He turned around, but stared at the floor, and Lili hugged herself, feeling alone.

"This would be a pretty elaborate story to make up if you just wanted to pretend it wasn't you in my bed last night," he said.

"You think I'm making it up?"

Steven gazed at her, brow knitted, wrestling with a question he did not like at all.

"You're meeting Tess and the others at six?" he asked.

Lili nodded.

Steven rested his right hand on the butt of his service weapon. "I go on duty at noon. You should sit tight here or go and hang with Tess until tonight. I'm not *telling* you, by the way. I know how you feel about being told to do anything. I'm just suggesting. I'm off at ten o'clock. If you're okay with it, I'll swing by my place and get a change of clothes and then come and stay here tonight."

"What about what's her name?"

Regret shaded his features. "That was . . . self-medicating, I guess. I've already forgotten her. If I could make you forget her, I would. For now, I just want to make sure you're not in any danger. I'll sleep on the couch if you want. I'm off rotation for the next three days, but tomorrow I want to go over and have a look at the hotel, and the Harrison Otis place—"

"Otis Harrison House," she corrected.

Steven gave her a lopsided smile. "Yeah. I'm on duty, or I'd go over today."

"No," she said, breathing a little more evenly. "I appreciate it."

"Look," he said, "I know you've got your friends in this thing with you, and I know you don't need me sticking my nose in—"

"No, I do."

He cocked an eyebrow at her.

Lili fixed him with a withering glance. "Not because you're a big, strong man, jackass. Because you're a cop and you carry a gun, and that feels like tangible reality, which I could really use a little bit of right now."

"I'm glad you made that clear," he said, crossing the kitchen to hug her good-bye. Steven kissed her on the top of the head and she let him. "When I see you again, make sure to call me *jackass* so I know it's really you."

She walked him back out to the foyer, glancing into the living room and shuddering as she remembered waking up on the carpet.

"About tonight," she said as he opened the door, letting the cold breeze back in. "I'd welcome the company."

He grinned, a mischievous sparkle in his eyes.

"You're sleeping on the couch," she added.

Steven held up his hands like she had him at gunpoint. "Whatever you say."

They both knew where he'd be sleeping.

"Keep your eyes open," he told her.

Lili promised she would, but as she watched him

walk back to his patrol car, she thought about her blurry memory and the fact that she hadn't recognized him—this man she had been afraid to really love—when she opened the door.

Would keeping her eyes open really make a difference? If her double came for her, would she even remember it afterward?

In the pocket of her pajamas, her cell phone buzzed again. She shut the front door and tugged out the phone, reading the messages from Tess again, including the latest one, which consisted of four words: *Please don't be dead*.

Lili shuddered and locked her front door, then leaned against it as she held down the control button on her phone. "Call Tess," she said once it had beeped.

"*Calling Tess,*" the phone replied.

It seemed they both had stories to tell.

But as she listened to it ring, she thought about the visitor Steven had received the night before, and for the first time she wondered if it would really be Tess who answered the phone.

SIX

Audrey stepped off the train at Porter Square T station and felt the warm rush of subway tunnel air envelop her. Her nose wrinkled with distaste. Down in the subway, she always felt far too cut off from the world, the air clammy and insinuating. Slipping off her small backpack, she unzipped it and stuffed her copy of the latest Carlos Ruiz Zafon novel inside. She hated the laziness of an escalator but Porter was one of the deepest stations she'd ever seen, so she rode up instead of using the stairs. Moving past a throng of commuters, she emerged into Porter Square and took a moment to orient herself before crossing the street and then turning left, toward Harvard.

Tess lived a mile or so from the station, a brisk fifteen-minute walk. It would have been faster for her to drive over from Revere—she'd taken the blue line into Boston and then switched for the red line out to Cambridge—but this time of day she would have been stuck in stop-and-go traffic on Route 16, breathing exhaust fumes, and this way she had been able to relax and read her book.

Well, maybe not *relax*. Julia had tried to hide her irritation, but it had been clear she would have preferred that her wife stay home tonight. Audrey would have preferred it that way, too, but she felt an urgency inside her that even the things Lili had told her could not quite explain. Julia had noticed that she had been feeling lethargic and out of sorts, and Audrey had said she just hadn't been sleeping well enough. Which was mostly true.

But there was more to it than that. When she'd stumbled on her morning run and gotten sick, and seen that blind man, something had happened to her. Then Lili had come to her with her story about doppelgängers and genuine fear in her eyes, and Audrey had sensed the connection. This morning she had wrapped up the case she had been working on, and all afternoon she had been thinking about the Otis Harrison House.

When Lili had called to plead with her to come and meet with her and Tess and the others tonight, Audrey had wanted to refuse. Tomorrow she had plans to go and investigate the presence of the psychomanteum at the fancy Boston hotel where it had unexpectedly turned up. If she could be any help to these people, it would be tomorrow. Yet here she was, disappointing her wife and ignoring her own anxiety for a subway ride and a chilly evening walk to Tess's house to spend a couple of hours with people who weren't her friends. Sure, she liked them, but not enough for this.

So why are you here? she asked herself as she walked

away from Massachusetts Avenue and past a small bar with live music thumping from inside its windows.

Audrey knew the answer. Something had gone wrong. Most strange happenings had ordinary explanations, but not this. This was real. Fear had spread through her like a low-grade fever, lingering, threatening to settle in more deeply, and she didn't like being afraid. So she had ridden the subway and now she walked past a convenience store and an Italian bakery and then turned left at a stoplight, moving into a gentrified Cambridge neighborhood. Fewer cars passed by, and three blocks along she came to an intersection, this one with a darkened gas station on one corner and a Tex-Mex takeout place on the other. The smell of the food made her stomach growl.

Tugging out her phone, she checked her position against Tess's address in her GPS, then turned right past the Tex-Mex place. Another hundred yards brought her within view of the Victorian she remembered envying the only other time she'd been here—for a celebratory dinner after the Otis Harrison job had ended. In the early evening, the house was lit up with a warm golden glow, as if every light inside had been turned on the moment night had fallen.

Audrey shifted her backpack straps as the wind picked up. Walking had seemed like a good idea until now, but the house was so close, just across the street and fifty yards ahead. There were several cars in the driveway and another pulled up to the curb even now. She watched its headlights wink out and the driver's door opened. In the white glow of the Dodge's dome light, she could make out a familiar face. That reporter . . . what was his name? Like the famous kidnapping case.

Lindbergh, she thought. *Fred or Frank.*

Then someone climbed out of one of the cars in the driveway and she saw that it was Lili Pillai. The wind gusted again and she bent against it, noticing something blowing along the sidewalk toward her. Black cloth, perhaps a scarf or rag. In the wind, it seemed almost serpentine, twisting along the concrete before it caught on her leg. Idly, she tried to shake it off, and somehow the rag *unfurled.* It flapped upward, wind blowing it open, so that suddenly instead of a scrap of cloth it seemed an entire bolt of flowing fabric, still wrapped around her leg at the bottom as though her presence there was its anchor.

Audrey felt its presence. How could she have missed it?

Then the stink hit her and her throat closed up with fear.

"No," she rasped as spindly gray fingers thrust from within the flapping fabric and grabbed hold of her throat.

The wind whipped the rag to one side and the face of the blind man loomed before her as if he had always been there, grim and solid, with his hideous teeth and soiled blindfold. He cocked his head back and sniffed the air. Inhaled her scent.

And he grinned.

Audrey screamed and tore from his grasp, struck him in the face with a dry crack of flesh on cold flesh. Then she was past him and running, and she had taken a dozen steps before she realized her mistake. She was running away from Tess's house, away from the people she knew, and the blind man was giving chase.

She heard him breathing hard, right at her back . . . heard the slap of his shoes on the sidewalk. He grunted and she thought she heard his voice, a muffled word or two that she couldn't make out. Farther back she heard Lili and Frank shouting and someone hammering on the door to Tess's apartment.

Stupid, Audrey thought. *He's blind and old. Stop running.*

Jaw clenched, backpack bouncing on her shoulders, she dodged to the right and started to turn back the way she'd come. The blind man whipped around, sniffing the air and then baring his teeth in anger. He lunged after her, somehow sensing the curb, and for the first time she wondered if he could see after all, even through the blindfold. She darted past him, picking up speed, and then his fingers snagged her hair. His fist tightened and he hauled her back. Audrey let out a scream as the blind man twisted her around and hurled her to the cracked pavement.

He loomed over her, steaming fetid breath in her face, and she saw the blood and dirt that stained his blindfold, saw the yellow and brown dental wreckage in his mouth, and tried to scramble backward on the street. The blind man grabbed the front of her jacket and yanked her upward, inhaling her scent again. A wave of cold spread inside her, like an ice storm had begun to churn in her chest.

"Get the hell away from her," a voice snapped.

The old man snapped his head up just as Lili Pillai barreled into him, both hands straight out in front of her. She shoved him backward with enough force that he ought to have been knocked off his feet. Instead he seemed to flow backward, his long coat flapping in the breeze as part of the fabric wrapped around Lili's wrist, dragging the two of them closer. On her ass on the street, Audrey stared in breathless horror. Whatever this was, it was real. For just a moment the jacket gaped open and she saw a swirl of motion in the shadows within . . . heard a whisper of voices.

Lili threw a solid punch—feet set, shoulders square, snapping her hips around to put her strength behind it— and Audrey heard the old man's jaw crack as the blow connected. He snarled again, baring those hideous teeth, and grabbed Lili by the throat.

"No," Audrey said, rising to one knee, reaching for the blind man's coat.

Blindfold obscuring his eyes, somehow he studied Lili. Inhaled deeply, head cocked, taking in her scent. Then he let her go. Staggered back a step, forehead creased and lips curled back in confusion. Blindfold a blank slate, he turned at the sound of the others running toward them. Audrey spared only a glance for the sight of Tess and Nick rushing toward them, with Frank hanging back on the opposite sidewalk, face slack with fear.

"*Where?*" the blind man seemed to say. "*Where are you?*"

But Audrey could not tell if the words came from his lips or from the shadows inside that coat.

He turned away from them. The long coat flapped around him, collar flipping up to block his profile, and in a gust of icy wind the fabric folded in upon itself. It fell to the street, seeming to shrink until all that remained was that one black rag, no larger than a scarf. It blew along the road for a dozen feet and then circled in the wind, carried up off the ground until it sailed into the air, eddying and rippling in the night sky until it vanished over the roof of a house.

"Oh, my God," Audrey said as she stood and reached for Lili. "Thank you."

But when she took Lili's hand, the other woman's skin felt ice cold. Lili looked up at her as though waking abruptly from a dream and reached up to touch her own throat, where the blind man had gripped her.

"What just happened?" she asked.

For a moment all the color had drained from her face, so pale that it almost seemed that the moonlight passed through her skin. Then Nick and Tess were there, talking to both of them, and Audrey had to turn her attention to them.

"Tell me I didn't just see that," Nick said. "That's gotta be some kind of illusion, right? That guy didn't just fucking vanish."

The women ignored his efforts to make it all less surreal. Less impossible. Tess took Lili in her arms and Audrey felt relieved. The cold she had felt when the blind man had touched her seeped deeper, aching in her bones, and she had enough terrors of her own without trying to comfort Lili.

Audrey glanced up and saw Frank walking toward them. He attempted to collect himself, but fear still radiated from him.

"Can we go inside?" he asked Tess. "I don't think we should be out here."

They all looked up into the night sky, at the place above the house where the shred of black fabric had disappeared into the dark. Audrey started to move first, and then they were all walking toward Tess's apartment in a tight cluster. Frank fell into step beside Audrey and he no longer seemed so afraid. She understood. The cold had taken deep root inside her, but she felt safer with the others around her.

Safety in numbers, she thought as they reached Tess's front door. Frank seemed to intuit her feelings. He smiled thinly and put a hand on her shoulder in solidarity as they waited for Tess to unlock the door.

At his touch, Audrey shuddered. She turned to study him, searching his eyes, startled by an aura of malice that seemed to surround him. He drew back his hand and gave her a darkly curious look, but then Tess opened the door and they were all filing inside, and there were other things to discuss. If Frank bore her some animosity, Audrey would deal with it later or not at all. After all, what was he to her? Just a man she'd met once on a job. Compared to the malign entity that had come for them tonight, Frank's hidden feelings mattered not at all.

Tess closed the door behind them and Audrey exhaled, feeling safer.

But she kept glancing at dark corners and the shadows beneath chairs and tables, wondering if a locked door could do anything to keep them safe.

SEVEN

Tess felt numb. She asked Lili to make sure everyone had something hot to drink, but it was Nick who filled the teapot. While Lili fetched mugs, Tess checked on Maddie, whom she had left watching a movie, nestled in her own bed. She pushed open her bedroom door and saw Maddie propped on a pile of her mother's pillows, entranced by *The Princess Bride*. Though the little girl had no interest in most films of a similar age, Maddie had latched on to the story of Buttercup and Westley and their friends.

"Hey, punkin," Tess said, hating the quaver in her voice. She exhaled, steadying herself. "You okay?"

"I'd be more okay if I had cookies!" Maddie said brightly.

Tess smiled, some of her tension and fear burning off in the light of her daughter's presence. "Coming right up. Okay if I send Daddy in with them?"

Maddie rolled her eyes as if to say *of course* it was okay.

Back in the kitchen, she sent Nick down the hall with a cookie delivery and checked to make sure that everyone had what they needed. The teapot hissed as it heated the water inside, and Tess was grateful to see that Lili already had put a tea bag in a mug for her and left it in front of her usual seat at the table.

"Audrey. Frank," she said as she slid into her chair. "Thank you both for coming."

Frank nodded, still pale. If he felt at all awkward about having made out with her at a party when she was still married to Nick, he didn't show it. Instead, he glanced at the window over the kitchen sink. "You want to tell me what we saw just now, out there?"

"We're not sure," Tess replied.

"But it's related to the Otis Harrison House somehow," Lili added.

"It was a revenant," Audrey said, slowly rotating her coffee cup in a circle on the table. "A dead person, but with a spirit still inside. Maybe the spirit of the dead man himself or maybe someone else's."

Frank stared at her. "Isn't your job to say things like that don't exist?"

"I have several jobs, Mr. Lindbergh. One of them is to evaluate situations in which someone has claimed the presence of something supernatural. Most of the time, those claims turn out to be either superstition or fraud or wishful thinking, because some people *want* to find ghosts in their houses. But I've never said things like that don't exist. I know that they do."

She'd been firm in her reply, even harsh, but now she faltered. Dropped her gaze.

"Never seen a revenant before. I've read about manifestations like that, but wasn't sure they were really possible."

"Audrey," Tess said, "there's something you should know."

Nick had come back in and now they were all staring at her.

"The blindfolded man," Tess said. "We've seen him before. Lili calls him the raggedy—"

"The raggedy man. I know." Audrey shook her head. "Lili told me yesterday. Thing is, I've seen him before as well. Sunday morning, early. I was out for a run and I felt really terrible all of a sudden. Nauseous, like my stomach had just dropped into a pit. I threw up, actually. I saw him then, just for a second. When I looked back, he was gone. I thought . . . shit, I hoped I'd imagined him. Didn't feel like myself for the rest of the day."

Nick retrieved the steaming teapot and carried it to the table. "So what does this . . . dead thing . . . have to do with the doubles Lili and Tess have been seeing?"

Frank huffed and held up his hands. "Can we just . . . can you all start over? I just saw something my brain is telling me I could not possibly have seen."

Audrey sipped her coffee. "You're hiding something."

As Nick poured her tea, Tess stared at her. "What?"

"Frank's scared. We all are. But there's something he's not telling us. Not all of this is a shock to him," Audrey said.

All eyes turned toward Frank.

He pointed at Audrey. "You're some kind of occult

expert. When Nick called, he told me this all had to do with the mirror thing, the ghost box, whatever it is, and that you were going to be here. I figured there was something bizarre going on—I did a ton of research on that house and the bodies you found there, remember? Cornell Berrige and the Society of the Lesser Key. I wrote half the book already. The manuscript is printed and in the top drawer of my desk. . . ."

"And?" Tess prompted when his words trailed off.

Frank looked at her, an edge of hostility in his eyes. "And I never thought any of this was true until I saw your raggedy man out there vanish in the middle of the street. So maybe start at the beginning, okay? Get me caught up? Because I've got to reset every thought I've ever had about this sort of thing."

Tess glanced at Audrey, who still looked at Frank as if she wanted more. But if they were going to figure any of this out, they needed everyone on the same page.

"What about Aaron?" she said, turning to Nick. "He's late."

"Lucky him," Lili muttered.

Tess began. She had spoken to Lili earlier in the day and they had exchanged their own stories, Lili telling her about her certainty that her double had visited Steven during the night. Now they shared their experiences with Frank and caught Audrey up on things she had missed.

"There's something else," Nick said.

Tess narrowed her eyes. "You saw something?"

"Not exactly," he said, keeping his focus on Frank and Audrey. "This morning I told Tess that my girlfriend and I are likely to be moving to London. The other day, someone who sounded very much like me called my Realtor and fired him."

"Your double," Audrey said.

"I don't understand," Lili said. "Why would they care if you went away? Wouldn't they have been less likely to be discovered if they tried to build lives far away from us? It'd be better if you were gone."

Frank ran his thumb over the handle of his coffee mug. "Unless they need you."

They all looked at him.

"If they need us," Tess said, "why are they trying to kill us?"

"I haven't heard anything that indicates they've tried to kill you," Audrey said. "At first, they were keeping clear of you entirely. If you hadn't run into Nick's double on the street, we might never have known that these people exist. Now they're showing up in your lives and intruding. Tess, your double wanted to be close to Maddie. Lili's double did the same with her ex."

"It did something to me," Lili said.

"And to Tess," Nick added. "Mentally and physically."

"I still haven't recovered," Tess admitted. "It's like a part of me's been . . ."

She searched for the right word. It was Audrey who supplied it.

"Siphoned," the medium said.

Tess tapped on the table. "You know what this is. What they are."

"Suspicions only."

"What about the raggedy man?" Lili asked. "The others may not be trying to kill us, but he attacked me and Audrey just now, and I'm pretty sure he had murder on his mind. That didn't feel like he just wanted to be buddies."

They were all silent a few moments. Tess hadn't experienced the raggedy man's touch, but she could see it haunted Audrey and Lili.

"I wonder if he's got eyes under that blindfold," Audrey said.

Tess saw Frank stiffen, as if he'd understood something in the comment that the rest of them hadn't.

"What difference would that make?" Nick asked.

Audrey sat back in her chair. "As part of the original ritual down in the basement of the Harrison House, our friend Berrige ripped his own eyes out."

Lili gave a hollow laugh. "You think the raggedy man is Berrige? They found his bones down in that pit in the cellar of the Harrison House."

Audrey fixed her with a grim stare. "I did mention that revenants are dead."

"That still wouldn't explain why he's coming after us," Nick said, looking pale and haunted himself. "They buried his bones. He should thank us, not try to kill us."

"I can't even believe we're talking about this," Frank said. "Dead people do not wander around and—"

"You saw him out there just now," Lili scolded him. "Your eyes don't lie. That was no magician's trick. I agree with Nick, though. Why is he coming for us?"

Tess hugged herself tightly, tea forgotten. She stared at the center of the table, but her thoughts were on Maddie. Whatever happened to the rest of them, herself included, she would not allow any harm to come to her little girl.

"It's possible he's not coming for us at all," she said. "The way he sniffs the air . . . outside the gallery where Lili and I first saw him, he very clearly said something like 'I had the scent.' He thought whatever scent he was tracking had led him to us. But maybe the scent he was following belonged to Lili's double, and her pretending to be Lili confused him."

Everyone looked to Audrey, then. None of them dared comment on the lunatic impossibilities of Tess's theory without her chiming in first. She had her head down, fingers to her lips as though preventing herself from speaking until she could be sure of her words. When she glanced up at Tess, she nodded.

"There's logic in that. Whatever these doubles are," Audrey said, "whether they're revenants or living people who've used magic to hide themselves behind your faces—"

"Our," Nick said.

Audrey frowned. "Sorry?"

Nick shrugged. "*Our* faces. If your raggedy man is Berrige or if he isn't, either way, you saw him before any of us brought you into this thing. If he's hunting our doubles and getting confused by their scents mingling with ours—and his hunt led him to you—that means there's a double of you out there somewhere, too."

Audrey looked like she might throw up. She sagged in her chair. "Fuuuuuck."

Tess snapped her fingers impatiently. "C'mon, Audrey. Freak out later. You were talking about the doubles."

"All I'm saying is, whatever they are, they started out

just using your . . . our faces. Like a reflection," Audrey said. "But it's more than just faces now. More than an image. They've started leeching something from us. Do they need it to survive, to sustain their appearance—"

"Or is it just to confuse the raggedy man?" Tess interrupted.

Audrey stared thoughtfully at her. "They need us for something, that's for sure. Nick wants to move far away and they don't want that to happen. And if we're some kind of danger to them, my guess is if they didn't need us they would just kill us."

A knock came at the front door and they all jumped in their chairs. Tess's breath caught in her throat and she turned to stare at Lili.

Nick was the first one to rise. "I'll get it."

"No," she said. "It's my place."

But he followed her to the door. Nick tensed, ready to fight, but when she opened the door it was only Aaron Blaustein, wearing an apologetic look.

"Sorry I'm late," he said. "What'd I miss?"

Beside her, Nick exhaled.

"Come in, Aaron," Tess said. "I'll get you a coffee and we can start at the beginning."

EIGHT

The noise of a door opening made Frank shift in his sleep, muttering to himself. Then came the creak of footfalls on the stairs. He frowned, resisting the urge to wake for several seconds, but then consciousness seeped in and he felt the weariness of his bones and the throbbing soreness of his muscles. His shoulders were the worst of all, alight with blazing pain from using the chain of his handcuffs to saw at the rusty bolts holding the support post in place behind him.

His eyes popped open. *The post.* He'd passed out in the middle of his work and as he jerked the cuffs to one side he found the chain still caught beneath the metal lip at the base of the post. With a waking groan for cover, he sawed the cuffs back and forth, but this time he pushed back, yanking them out from beneath the lip. The dust of rust and concrete would still be there. He had no time to clean up after himself.

The basement light was on. The power flickered as if a storm roared outside, but he wondered if it might not be something else—some energy that had nothing to do with electricity. Now that his momentary panic subsided, he remembered passing out . . . remembered the sudden irresistible fatigue that had swept over him. In the midst of working the cuffs against those rusty bolts, he had begun to tremble and then felt his muscles slump as if something had just given way inside him, his last vestiges of strength flowing out of him.

Waking to the sound of those footsteps had given him a small burst of adrenaline, but now it subsided and he bent his head, taking small sips of breath. His thoughts felt thin, his heartbeat shallow. Though he felt no hunger, the emptiness within him had gotten worse, as if there was little left of him now but a shell. In his mind, he pictured one of those Russian nesting dolls, their layers thin and fragile, and imagined himself one of them—with all of the smaller dolls removed, only the largest one, hollow and empty, left behind.

"Not feeling quite yourself tonight, are you?" a voice asked.

He blinked, jerking his feet as he glanced up. Frank Lindbergh looked down at him. The face was so familiar. He knew Frank well, but couldn't focus on how they knew each other or the nature of their acquaintance. Too tired. The pain made it hard for him to concentrate.

"Frank," he rasped.

The visitor laughed softly. He wore a gray suit with a thin black wool scarf, very stylish. His shoes were charcoal black, barely scuffed, and he had trimmed his facial stubble so that he had a silhouette of a beard rather than an actual one. Frank looked good. Maybe better than ever. The best possible version of Frank Lindbergh.

The prisoner shifted. Smelled the stink of his own body and of his blood, felt the sting of the wounds at his wrists where the handcuffs had chafed and cut him.

The cuffs, he thought. His brow creased as he remembered sawing the chain against the rusty bolt under the post at his back. The explanation for that memory seemed out of reach for a moment, but then he managed to reach into the fog of his thoughts and grab hold of it, drawing it close.

He lifted his eyes and stared at the stylish man. Was it cologne he smelled over the stink of his own blood and piss? He thought it was.

"I'm Frank Lindbergh," he whispered, all that he could manage.

The other Frank crouched in front of him, black scarf dangling. The scent of his cologne grew stronger.

"You're a shadow," he said. "Pretty soon, you'll barely be that."

Frank focused on his breathing. In and out. He stared at the other Frank.

"Fuck you," he grunted.

The visitor laughed softly. "I have to say, I admire the way you've held on. You didn't have much of a life to begin with, so building a better one was easy enough. Tonight really ought to have taken most of what you had left of yourself. I mean, I sat down with people who are your friends. They're scared but they're smart enough that they've started to figure out what's been happening to them, but even so, they looked at me and saw you. To them, I *am* you, and belief is a powerful thing.

On top of how well things are going for me at work, I expected that to finish you. So well done. Truly. You've got my admiration."

The man who wasn't Frank rocked back a bit on his heels, still in a crouch. He laughed, rolling his eyes.

"Hell, could that be it? What an irony if my admiration of you is keeping your self intact."

Frank grunted. He ran his tongue around the inside of his mouth, thirsty and repulsed by how long it had been since he had brushed his teeth, never mind bathed. He shifted, twisted his wrists inside his cuffs just a little—not enough for his visitor to pay attention to the cuffs or to come around and look at the concrete and rust that had been disturbed there, but enough to wake Frank up. Bring him back to himself.

For long moments he had let his mind slip away. It felt like he was holding on to his identity by mere threads and at any moment it might be torn from him, dragged off into an abyss. But it wasn't his doppelgänger's admiration helping him hold on. Frank felt sure of that.

It was the pain in his wrists and shoulders. The scent of his own blood. The way he gritted his teeth when he worked the handcuff chain against that rusty bolt under the post. He might be a shadow of himself, withering to nothing, but he *wasn't* nothing yet. Instead, he felt alive with the knowledge that a moment before he had forgotten that the man in front of him was *not* Frank Lindbergh. Still brittle and gutted, but maybe not completely hollow. Not yet.

Not when he knew he had made progress with that rusty bolt.

His self would continue to fade, leeched away by the bastard in front of him. Frank knew that his time was running out. But he wasn't a ghost yet.

"What are you doing to me?" he asked.

The man wearing his face smiled as if this were the most precious, most adorable question he had ever heard. He stood up from his crouch and slipped his hands into his pockets. Slowly, his smile diminished.

"All right," he said. "I suppose you deserve to at least understand what's happening to you while there's still a 'you' in there. Considering what you're giving up for me, I owe you that much. For you, this began the first time you stepped into the psychomanteum."

"You mean the . . . the spirit box?" Frank rasped.

"The apparition box," the man with his face replied. "Yes, the very one. You and your friends just stood there, looking into the mirrors . . .

"While *we* were looking out."

TUESDAY

ONE

Steven Parmenter took the steps up from Park Street station two at a time. By the time he stepped out into the cold gray morning light, his heart was pounding in his chest and he had to draw long breaths to calm it down. He was a young man, but his gym schedule had been falling apart over the past few months and he had hurried up the steps to get in a little of the cardio he had been missing. Today was Tuesday. Captain Monahan had told him that he would know by Friday whether or not he would be promoted to detective. For the past six months he had been working his ass off, ignoring nearly everything else in his life in favor of the job. If Saturday morning came and he was still Officer Parmenter instead of Detective Parmenter, he wondered if he would feel it had all been for nothing. He hoped he would not have to find out.

With a glance up at the golden dome of the State House, he threaded his way along the path that ran parallel to Park Street, up the concrete stairs to Beacon Street, and took a right. It was worth going half a block out of his way to get a coffee from Dunkin' Donuts. Maybe on a detective's salary he would be able to afford to drink Starbucks all the time, but even then he knew he would stick to Dunkin'. Really, there was no contest.

Hot coffee in hand, he retraced his steps through the shadow of the State House, took a right up Walnut toward Mount Vernon Street. He wore jeans and a green cable-knit sweater, a black leather jacket and gloves, and a thick New England Patriots hat with a red, white, and blue pom-pom on top. He spent so much of his time immersed in serious, sometimes grim work, and the pom-pom made him feel silly. It reminded him that not every situation was life or death.

What this thing with Lili was, he had no idea. It sounded insane, but city cops encountered more than their share of crazy people, and he had never gotten that vibe off her. Which meant that something was going on, that someone had been messing with Lili and Tess, and Steven could not just let that go. He had spent the past twenty-four hours trying not to think about some of the things she had told him. Last night he had started on the sofa and ended up in her bed, but there had been no sex. Instead, he had just held her in his arms while she fell asleep and eventually drifted off himself.

As afraid as she was, the only way for him to take some of what she'd told him seriously was to assume that she and Tess had been victims of a prank or some Hollywood-level makeup FX. If he found out later that it had all been a gag—that Tess's ex-husband had done it all as some kind of joke—he would make sure Nick regretted it.

For now, though, he had decided to poke around on his own. His first stop this morning had been the Nepenthe Hotel. He'd gone into the restaurant at the back and looked at the mirrored box. It was odd, but its antiquity did make it a good fit for the room, and he could see how some of the hotel's guests might find it intriguing to have breakfast or brunch inside the whatever-it-was-called. Steven had examined it closely and found nothing but mirrors, wooden walls, bolts, and a kind of musty odor.

No ghosts, no strange faces, nothing unusual about it at all.

He stuffed his hands into his pockets as he walked through Beacon Hill. The wind whipped around him and he shivered. His coat had a collar he could have turned up, but his mind was wandering, focused on other things. The morning he had met Lilandra Pillai, he had just come off duty and had stopped into a café near Boston University for a coffee before heading home. She had turned from the counter, focused on the cup in her hand, trying to get the lid fastened properly, and she had collided with him. Hot coffee had spilled down the front of his uniform and they had both backed away from the fresh puddle of coffee on the linoleum, raising their arms like startled birds ruffling their wings.

She'd looked up at his uniform, rolling her eyes with an expression of disgust, and said the words every guy wanted to hear from the lips of a beautiful woman: "Oh, you have got to be fucking kidding."

Steven knew what she saw—a big ginger guy in a police uniform, with a coffee-stained badge and a gun at his hip. What he had seen that morning had been something entirely different, a formidable, no-bullshit woman of stunning beauty.

He wiped droplets of coffee off the front of his uniform and arched a single eyebrow. "So, is this what they mean by 'meet cute' in all those romantic comedies?"

The question shocked her out of her momentary paralysis and then she was grabbing a handful of napkins, trying to dab at his uniform while a sighing employee came out from behind the counter with a mop. Steven had promised her it was not a big deal, that he was on his way home. She insisted on buying his coffee and they had sat in the front booth in the sunshine coming through the plate glass, talking for an hour, until she had to run or risk being late to teach a class for which she was now woefully unprepared.

That had been the beginning of the best thing that had ever happened to him. Somehow, he had managed to screw it up. Now there seemed like the possibility of rapprochement, a new start.

If he could just prove to himself that this woman he thought he might love was not completely out of her fucking mind.

The sidewalk lit up with sunlight and Steven glanced toward the sky to see a break in the clouds. The horizon remained a thick blanket of gray, but this one patch of blue had opened just ahead. The light warmed even the façades of the buildings on both sides of the street. The fall leaves burned with color, and the patch of grass on the small, raised front yard of the Otis Harrison House looked rich and green. In moments it would pass, but it was a blessing in the moment to be reminded of the vivid colors of the world.

Up ahead, a fiftyish couple moved along the sidewalk opposite the Harrison House. A taxi had pulled to the curb and an elderly woman stepped out as Steven approached. A bicyclist came around the corner, and Steven watched with a deepening frown as the rider shifted across the street—toward the taxi—buzzed within inches of the yellow cab's door, then passed Steven himself before shifting back to the other side of the street. It was as if he had gone out of his way to avoid riding directly in front of the Harrison House.

Steven paused on the sidewalk. A seagull flew overhead and he glanced up to track its passage across the sky. It sailed to the left, arcing toward the top of a row house and alighting there, lining up with several other gulls. There were other birds around, including a crow on the crest of a dormer window and a host of sparrows on a telephone cable of the sort you hardly ever saw anymore. On the branches of trees in front of the Otis Harrison House, not a single bird roosted.

Odd, certainly, but what did it mean? Nothing. Not a single thing. But the small hairs stood up at the base of Steven's neck and he felt gooseflesh rise on his forearms. There'd been a dog attack here a few days ago, not to mention the violence that had erupted with the UPS driver. How many had been killed? It shamed him that he couldn't remember. When Lili had told him about her history with the house and the connection she believed existed between the old place and the bizarre things that had been happening in her life, he had bitten his tongue to avoid mentioning the recent violence up here. He had been unwilling to add to the fear and anxiety already driving her.

Now that he had arrived, however, he had to tell himself it was all just coincidence. Had to tell himself, because he felt a frisson of something in the air, some static that made his skin crawl.

The old woman who had exited the cab slammed the door and the host of sparrows burst into the air in a cloud of flapping chaos. The birds flowed upward in the elegant stroke of a paintbrush, first one direction and then the other, moving with a single mind, in that impossible way he had always found so beautiful. The swirl of sparrows arced toward the roof of the Otis Harrison House, but just before they reached it the flock turned away. Not as one. Not in any natural way of birds. Instead, they scattered in all directions, peeling away from their previous course in what seemed a dreadful panic. One sparrow caught itself in the branches of a tree and flapped madly. Steven thought it must have injured itself, because after a moment it just stopped fighting and hung there, dead or in despair.

Despair, he thought. *Birds don't feel despair.*

But as the taxi pulled away, driving too fast down the narrow street, the old woman stood and stared at the birds as well. The fiftyish couple had vanished, presumably into their own home, but the elderly lady stood in her wool coat and colorful scarf and gazed sadly at the bird dangling from the autumn-bare tree. The rest of the birds began to regroup, alighting back on the roof where they had begun, but Steven watched one of them begin to chase another away. He'd seen gulls and pigeons do that, fighting over scraps on the street or the beach, but this looked different.

The larger bird attacked the smaller in midair and then both were falling. They recovered in time. The smaller bird landed on the fence in front of the Harrison House and then the larger one sailed right into it, the collision knocking both sparrows off the fence and onto the grass of that elevated yard. From the sidewalk across the street, which was lower than the little yard, Steven couldn't see the birds anymore. He heard a flutter of wings, and then nothing.

The old woman crossed herself and then turned her back to him, heading up the street in the other direction. Away from the Otis Harrison House, and very purposefully on the opposite side of the street.

Steven forced a laugh. "Okay, enough. Shake it off."

What had he really seen? Nothing. An old woman spooked by a couple of violent events happening on the same block in a span of days. Why wouldn't she be spooked? *The birds,* he thought. But what did he know about the flight patterns of sparrows? Hell, he wasn't even a hundred percent certain they were sparrows. They could have been swallows or starlings, for all the time he had spent studying the difference.

These were the things he needed to tell himself to get his feet to move off the sidewalk and cross the street to the corner in front of the Otis Harrison House. He walked up the side street until he reached the corner of the house, which had been built up high enough that it was impossible to see through the windows from here. A ripple of nausea began in his gut, just a queasy tickle, the first suggestion that he had eaten something that had not agreed with him.

Thinking of Lili—of the fear in her normally fearless eyes, and of the velvet smoothness of her cool brown skin beneath his hands—he went up the steps at the side of the house and right up to the front door of the Otis Harrison House. The property was for sale and a small sign jutted from the ground beside the path. Steven pulled out his cell phone, closing one eye and wincing as his head began to throb. He felt ill. And irritated. He wanted to shed his skin or flee this place, or both.

Instead he dialed the real estate office. The phone rang half a dozen times before clicking over to voice mail, but since he was not a part of any official investigation regarding the house, Steven hung up.

He left the front door and went to the nearest window. Hands on the brick sill, he leaned forward, pressing his forehead to the glass, trying to peer inside. The little ball of nausea in his gut blossomed into a churning wave and he slumped away from the window, whipped around, and put his hand on the lowest branch of a tree, sucking air through his nostrils and trying to keep the bile from erupting. His head pounded, the headache full blown now, and he took a few steps back along the path, needing to get away.

It's not the house, he told himself. *Don't be a tool.*

But such thoughts would not go away. He reached the few steps down to the sidewalk and paused to sit on the top one, bent over and breathing deeply. Already he felt a bit better. As he sat, a few drops of cold rain

pelted him and he looked up to see that a light drizzle
had begun.

A dry flutter came from above and Steven glanced
up to see the dying sparrow trapped in the branches
overhead. A single red leaf, shaken free, floated toward
the ground, danced on a breeze, and then slid across
the grass and the path until it caught on one of the
wrought-iron railings of the low fence at the edge of the
yard.

An engine rumbled. Steven looked up and saw a
white van moving along the side street toward the corner. It slid to a stop right beside the Otis Harrison
House. The words THIBODEAU HOME HEATING &
REPAIR were stenciled on the side. As he idled at the
corner, the driver, a gray-bearded man with thick
glasses, glanced over at Steven and scowled with startling disdain. Then he turned right, passing through the
shadow of the Harrison House and its retaining wall.

The sparrows came down then.

The crow had departed at some point, but the gulls
roosting on top of the row house remained, and they
watched with baleful eyes as the sparrows rose and
spread into a wave of silent flight, beautiful and dark
beneath the gray sky. Then the wave crashed down,
sweeping toward the white work van with precision, but
without mercy or hesitation. They struck the walls and
windows of the van with such force that each thump
sounded more like a gunshot than the breaking of hollow bones. There were at least a hundred of them, and
Steven ran along the sidewalk, the Harrison House's retaining wall rising up on his right, until he reached the

corner. There, he could only stand and watch as the sparrows killed themselves to shatter the windshield and side windows.

The van swerved right and then left, crossed the road and slammed into the front steps of the brownstone where the gulls presided over the proceedings, standing stern sentry. The van's horn began to blare and did not let up, something wrong under the hood or the driver jammed against the steering wheel instead of any effort on the man's part. *Mr. Thibodeau,* Steven presumed, who looked like an angry Santa.

The whole thing had taken perhaps twenty seconds. The street was littered with broken, bloody sparrows. Feathers skittered along the pavement like autumn leaves. The white van had been stained and streaked with their blood.

But not all of the birds were dead. Several began to emerge from inside the van, flying or hopping up onto the roof and hood and on the jagged sills of the windows.

Steven pulled out his phone, ready to call it in, when the first of the birds looked at him.

Looked *right* at him.

The sensation of its being aware of him was so strong that he took a step back, and when it took to the air and the other surviving sparrows followed, he backed up to the corner again, hiding in the lee of the retaining wall. He dialed 911, but before he could hit send, he noticed motion in the ceiling of his peripheral vision and looked up to see the six seagulls taking flight. Circling. And the sparrows joined them.

That doesn't happen, he thought. *Not ever.*

Phone clutched in his fist, mind awhirl, he turned and bolted back up the sidewalk to the side door of the Harrison House. Its dark windows loomed behind him as he watched the birds. The flock drew backward a moment and then wheeled toward the house, hurtling toward him with such a sense of malign intent that he drew his gun, knowing as he did how ridiculous it was to think that he could protect himself from dozens of birds with a handful of bullets. Suddenly their wings were no longer silent, their cluster no longer elegant. The beating wings became a roar and he staggered backward along the sidewalk, finger on the trigger.

Again they scattered as if driven away, the flight pattern disrupted.

Most of them scattered, anyway.

The one stuck in the tree branches fell to the stone path, dead.

A pair of gulls alighted on either side of it, cocked their heads and watched Steven out of the corners of their eyes. He backed up again and bumped hard against the street level door, looked up and saw the flock massing and turning and flowing again, preparing for another attempt at him.

"Fuck this," he muttered, and he reached back and grabbed hold of the doorknob.

It turned, and the door swung inward so quickly that he nearly tumbled over the threshold onto his ass. He grabbed hold of the doorjamb and managed not to fall, but momentum had carried him inside. A brief thought about the Realtor and the unlocked door tried to form, but the relief that flooded him left little room for other rational thought.

He closed the door and put his back against it. A hoarse laugh escaped his throat and he holstered his gun, lifted his phone, and hit the Send button to call 911, thinking of dead Mr. Thibodeau out in that blood-smeared van. By now people would be coming into the street to investigate. Someone else would have called the police already. Probably more than one person.

Which was good, because he had zero signal at all inside the house.

Call Failed, the screen of his phone announced.

"Of fucking course," he growled, and shoved the phone back into his pocket.

Steven peered through the sidelight and saw that the gulls were still on the walk, and more had arrived. The wind gusted and the old boards of the Harrison House moaned and whispered. And yet Steven frowned, because in amid the old-age complaints of the centuries-old structure was a whisper that sounded nothing at all like the house, and very much like words.

He took a step deeper into the house, trying to make them out. Words, yes. Somewhere inside the sprawling home. They were not words in any language he knew, and yet he could hear the mocking tone in them. The disdain and malice.

Steven drew his gun again. He had no idea how all of this fit together—the violence of the past few days, the behavior of the birds, the story Lili had told him—but he knew one thing for certain.

He was not alone.

TWO

Audrey stood on the sidewalk in front of the Nepenthe Hotel and felt nothing. The chill in the afternoon air made her turn up the collar of her jacket while, behind her, Lili paid the cabdriver. It seemed strange to take a taxi in a city with such an excellent public transportation system, but Lili had offered and Audrey had readily agreed.

"Okay," Lili said as the cab pulled away. "You all set?"

"I wouldn't have run off, you know," Audrey said, still staring at the elegant, restored façade of the hotel. The wind gusted and she trembled, though perhaps the shudder in her bones had nothing to do with the cold.

"What do you mean?" Lili asked.

"I mean you didn't have to pay for a cab to keep me from escaping," Audrey replied. "I told you I'd come over here, and I keep my word."

Lili glanced at the hotel. "I don't doubt you. But after the conversation we all had, and the raggedy man . . . hell, anyone would have second thoughts about

coming over here. You're the only one of us who believed in anything remotely supernatural before this.
You'd have more reason to have wanted to just go
home."

Audrey smiled. "Oh, I want to go home, believe me.
But I said I'd have a look at the psychomanteum."

"All right. Let's get it over with."

Audrey followed Lili through the revolving door and
into the lobby, gazing around at the premature holiday
decorations and the faux-period décor and costuming
of the employees. It was meant to be elegant, but she
found the effect cloying. Lili moved around a bellman
with a cart loaded with luggage and through a gaggle
of tween girls who seemed to be in Boston for some
kind of dance studio championship, if such things
existed. Audrey thought that if she and Julia had a
daughter, it would be fascinating to see what sorts of
extracurriculars she gravitated toward. Dance studio
championships seemed unlikely, but that was the beauty
of tomorrow. You never knew what it would bring.

With a smile on her face, Audrey trailed Lili past the
pub and the front desk and the main staircase to a podium at the back of the hotel where a smiling young
man in a tight suit and narrow tie greeted them with
an expression of barely summoned regret.

"Oh, ladies, I'm sorry," he said, "but the Sideboard
stops seating for lunch at two P.M. I'm afraid you've just
missed us, but the pub is still open."

Audrey hesitated, readying a long explanation for
why they needed to examine the psychomanteum. Lili
just raised a hand, grinned, and breezed past the young
host.

"No worries," Lili said. "We're just meeting a friend. We won't eat so much as a single French fry."

The host seemed about to argue, but by then Lili had already vanished into the restaurant, carrying Audrey in her wake. They wove a path among mostly empty tables while the staff cleared glasses and dishes. A mother vigorously wiped smeared ketchup from her toddler's cheeks. A husband sipped coffee while his wife checked her text messages.

Audrey felt her steps slow, though she had made no conscious decision to halt. Lili kept walking, but Audrey came to a stop between two tables that had already been cleared and reset for the next morning. In the far corner, beneath a ceiling of white Christmas lights that had been strung like stars overhead, a trio of middle school dance studio girls sat with two bleached-blond stage mothers at a table inside the psychomanteum.

Staring, Audrey felt her whole body go slack. Her palms felt strangely moist, and she reached up to wipe her sleeve across her forehead. A feeling overwhelmed her, the certainty that she was no longer clean, as if the whole of her skin had been coated in a film of grease.

The little dancers were poking each other and laughing while their moms finished their coffee or tea. One of the girls dipped a finger into some ketchup left over from her onion rings. Audrey wasn't sure how she knew about the onion rings—it was the sort of thing that just occurred to her, and always turned out to be true. They seemed so happy, as if they could not feel the aura of sickness that flowed from the apparition box. As if their skin was not covered in that oily coating.

Audrey forced herself to take a step. In her peripheral

vision, she noticed a waitress who had stopped rolling utensils inside cloth napkins to stare at her, troubled by her manner. Audrey swallowed hard, tasting something vile.

Lili paused beside the psychomanteum, clearly intending to loiter until the little dancers and their mothers vacated the apparition box. Audrey understood this, but once she had begun moving toward the psychomanteum she could not stop. Instead, she approached the mirrored chamber and stepped inside, crowding those already within. The dancers and their moms looked up in surprise, and already the waitress had abandoned her work. Audrey sensed the woman behind her, heard her calling out.

"Excuse me, ma'am? Can I help you?" the waitress asked, an edge of alarm in her voice.

And there should be, Audrey thought. *She should be more than alarmed. She should be fucking fleeing this place.* But of course the waitress was not unsettled by the presence of the psychomanteum. It had been the look on Audrey's face, or some slight buzz of her own sixth sense, that had set her off.

"She's okay," Lili said, unconvincing. "Just give her a second. She's not hurting anyone."

"Mom?" one of the little dancers asked with just the tiniest shade of fear.

Lili ducked her head in, right beside Audrey, exuding warmth and friendliness. "Sorry. Rude, I know. She can't help herself. She's just fascinated by this thing. Mirrors and antiques are, like, her two favorite things, so this just blows her mind."

The dance moms huffed.

"She could wait until we're done," one of them said.

"I know, right?" Lili agreed. "But since you're just sitting here and pretty much *are* done, you won't mind if she just takes a quick look."

Audrey heard all of this, sensed the irritation from the mothers and the anxiety from the little dancers. The waitress kept saying *Ma'am,* as if that would get her out of the psychomanteum. It wouldn't.

"I don't want to have to get a manager," the waitress said.

"Oh, come on," Lili started.

The two mothers huffed. One of them swore, causing the little dancers to giggle, hiding their smiles behind their hands, but then they were all getting up from their chairs and nudging past Audrey and Lili in a hasty, grumbling exit.

"Look at it this way," Lili said, "you'll have such a story about your trip to Boston."

"That's enough," the waitress said. She turned and strode off to fetch someone of greater authority.

Audrey felt Lili's hand on her elbow.

"Better make it quick."

Inhaling deeply, wiping her sleeve across her forehead and cheeks, Audrey stepped nearer to the mirrored panes of one wall of the psychomanteum. She stared into the mirror, studied many facets of her own features, refracted in a hundred panes from every angle, splintered into infinite variations that retreated into the sinking distance only opposing mirrors can create. An eternity of tiny realities.

She saw no faces other than her own and Lili's. Nothing at all out of the ordinary.

But she felt it. *Holy shit,* did she ever.

A malice as pure, a wrongness as deep, as any she had ever felt before.

Lili nudged her. "Hey. We have to go."

Audrey blinked, wondering how long she had been standing there, staring into the mirrored forever of the psychomanteum. Her mind had taken a sideways step somewhere, and now she looked around and saw the waitress returning with an older woman in a skirt and a coat with an important-looking name plaque pinned to her breast. The officious, skinny little guy from the host station followed up the rear as if he thought he might be called upon to physically remove the troublesome visitors. All but two tables were clear of customers now. The patient husband had finished his coffee and was slipping on his jacket, but his wife was still texting.

"We're going," Lili promised the parade as she took Audrey by the arm and escorted her back through the restaurant.

"Break it apart," Audrey said, feeling hollow. Transparent. It seemed as if she herself were a ghost, drifting through the room, trying to make the living see and hear her. "You can't keep it in here. It's too dangerous. Don't you feel it? You've got to dismantle it again."

"Antique dealer," Lili said. "She's just jealous. Wants it for herself."

"I don't want to call the police," the manager said, winking white lights overhead glittering off her name plaque.

"We're already gone. Trouble over," Lili promised.

Audrey felt Lili take her hand and she allowed herself to be tugged through the lobby and into the revolving door, which deposited the two of them one at a time on the sidewalk in front of the Nepenthe Hotel.

The cold wind whipped around her, scouring the oily film from her skin.

She gasped, inhaling deeply, and blinked as she looked around.

It felt exactly like waking from a dream, but she knew she had been awake the entire time. That bit of truth was the part that made it a nightmare. The way she had felt inside that room, near the psychomanteum . . . it had passed, but she knew that if she went back inside, that aura of malice would envelop her again. You couldn't wake up from reality.

The cold bit deep into her face and hands. Audrey wrapped her jacket more tightly around her as Lili stepped into the street and flagged a cab. The vehicle's brakes squealed as it pulled to the curb, and then Lili grabbed her arm and escorted her to the cab.

"Not the house," Audrey managed to say.

"Audrey—"

"I told you before, I'm not going."

Lili stared at her, perhaps fully understanding the depth of her fear for the first time. "We'll go to Tess's house."

"Good," Audrey said. "She needs us."

"What do you—"

The cabdriver honked, gesturing at them from behind the glass. Lili opened the door and Audrey slid into the backseat. When Lili followed her, Audrey nestled close against her simply because she was another human. A tangible, ordinary person, warm and alive.

As the taxi rolled out of the city, Audrey began to feel like herself again.

But there was still no way she was going to that house.

THREE

All the time he'd been using the chain on his handcuffs to saw away at the bolts connecting the post at his back to the concrete floor, Frank had poured all of his focus into that single, repetitive act. It ought to have been maddening, but he thought that somehow it had kept him sane, down there in the stinking, musty basement. His stomach growled as he paused for a breath, shoulders sinking. His muscles burned and his wrists skidded against the metal cuffs, slick with blood from where the constant friction and strain had bruised and chafed the skin.

Fury fueled this single-mindedness. He wanted to find the other Frank—*Not-Frank, he's not Frank*—and smash his skull against the concrete floor. He wanted to chain the son of a bitch down here and make him piss and shit in a bucket, make him eat a few feet away from that bucket, turn his life into the three-foot circumference around that metal post bolted to the basement floor.

He scraped metal against metal. Skinned his

knuckles on the concrete. Listened to the rasp of the handcuff chain against the rusty bolt. Could smell the rust as it flaked away, the metal as he ground it down. For long periods, he thought of nothing but the rusty bolt and that sound, and in those times he forgot that such a person as Frank Lindbergh existed. The longer he worked, the more progress he felt he must be making, the emptier he felt. Memory seemed like another country, the nation where he'd been born but which he had long ago left behind. He felt bloodless and hollow, not a husk so much as a balloon that had never been fully inflated. Nausea simmered in his belly, never quite enough to boil over, and it occurred to him that he had no feeling or emotion powerful enough to boil over except for his anger at his captor and the desire to cut through that goddamned rusty bolt.

When it gave way, his hands jerked forward and down and his scabby knuckles dragged along the cement. He whimpered and pulled his hands up—or tried. The handcuff chain caught hard, jarring his swollen, contorted shoulders and sending a fresh wave of pain crashing through him.

He took a deep, ragged breath, and then his eyes went wide as understanding dawned. Tugging against the cuffs, sliding the chain back and forth, he realized that he'd sawn through the first bolt. Giddy laughter bubbled up from his chest. He hung his head and began to giggle and sigh, then banged his back against the post several times, overcome with manic glee.

When his laughter began to subside, he steadied his breathing, still trembling with happiness and exhaustion. Steeling himself, he hauled the handcuffs forward, tugging the chain farther under the post toward the single remaining bolt, the one nearer to him. The chain caught between post and concrete and he froze with a terror that screamed through the hollow place inside him without a single echo.

"No," he whispered. Or thought he did.

He yanked against the cuffs, tried to saw them from side to side. The chafed, raw flesh at his wrists began to bleed even worse, but the cuffs did not move. The bottom of the post was closer to the concrete on this side, against his back. With a groan, he pulled forward and slammed himself against the post. His skull banged off the metal and for several long seconds his vision went gray and black. When he blinked back into consciousness, he did it again, careful for his head. Six times. Nine times. A dozen times he smashed his back into the post. If he couldn't saw away at the second rusty bolt, he would use his weight to snap it.

Shaking with dreadful weakness, he slumped, without enough energy to hurl himself backward again. After a minute's rest, he found that the handcuff chain was no longer clamped between post and floor, and began to drag it back and forth again. The metal would scour at the concrete, but he did not know how far he had to go to reach the second bolt, or how narrow the space between post and floor might be. It would take days, he was certain.

He didn't have days.

A whimper came from his throat and he hung his head. Tears filled his eyes. When the first one fell, it ran cold down his cheek, no warmth in it or in his flesh. With a halfhearted roar, he slammed himself back against the post again, twice, and then a third time. He banged his skull backward on purpose, listened to the ring of bone on metal.

He frowned, thinking it seemed muffled, and then he just lay back against the post. A lightness filled him. He inhaled but could no longer smell the stink of his own waste or the filthy odor of his unwashed body. Staring at the bottom of the steps, he knew he would never use them, never escape this basement.

My basement? he wondered, unable to remember where he was.

Who he was.

A name danced along the rim of his thoughts but he could not quite grasp it.

Again he felt like a balloon, but now it was as if the air had begun to slowly leak out. He would die here, nothing and no one. His throat twitched, stomach convulsing, but there was nothing for him to throw up. Just emptiness.

He looked down at his stomach and froze. In the gray nothing light, for a moment it appeared as if his shirt had faded into transparency. Not just his shirt, either, but his body. For a sliver of a second, he thought he could see all the way through his abdomen to the concrete floor. Unable to breathe or to blink, he stared at his legs, which seemed mostly solid . . . but only mostly. If he tilted his head slightly, he thought they faded in the gray light, both there and not there.

Turning his head, he looked at his right shoulder, which was solid as ever.

Hallucinating. My mind is slipping. I'm dying.

But whe he glanced at his left shoulder, it looked

ghostly. It jolted him so hard that he slid to the right, trying to get away from the transparent part of him. He heard a clink of metal and frowned, unsure of its source. Then he felt his shoulders relax, felt them hunch forward to relieve the ache in his muscles.

"How?" he whispered in that gray basement.

He brought his left hand around and stared at it, trying not to scream at the sight of his transparent fingers. His chafed wrist had stopped bleeding. Then he pulled his right hand around and saw the handcuff tight around that wrist, the other cuff dangling from the chain, still tightly cinched.

The laughter returned, madder than ever. He doubled over, shaking as it bubbled out of him, uncontrollable. Tears ran freely and dripped to fall upon his bare legs, and this time he could feel their warmth. That brought him up short, choking his tears and his laughter.

Weak, unsteady, he leaned on the post and struggled to his feet. Taking a deep breath, he turned and started for the steps, pausing twice when his thoughts fuzzed and he worried he might pass out. When he made it to the stairs he turned around and stared at the post and at the bucket and he promised himself that he would never come down here again. Then he went upstairs, hoping to kill Frank.

No, he thought. *That's not his name.*

Confusion swirled inside him as he reached the door. It had a lock, but somehow he remembered that there was not much to it. Drained as he was, he only had to throw himself at the door four times before the wood around the lock splintered and the door swung into a gloomily lit hallway.

For the count of ten he waited, expecting shouts or pounding feet, but the house just breathed and creaked and then he knew he was alone. Jaw set with determination, he ignored the hungry roar of his stomach and made his way up to the second floor to the master bedroom. When he saw himself in the mirror, fresh tears sprang to his eyes. His skinny legs and dirty underpants were bad enough, but the scruff of his beard and dark circles under his eyes made him look like a savage.

He glanced around the room and a kind of weight settled on his shoulders. A good weight. Solidity. The framed photos on top of the tall bureau stirred a bitterness in him that he did not yet understand, but he knew those faces.

Go, he thought. *Run.*

He glanced at the clock and saw that it was just after two in the afternoon. Since he could not remember what day it might be, he could not be sure when his captor would return, but he could not leave the house half-naked and without shoes. He needed clothes . . . and not just clothes.

Staggering into the bathroom, he got a closer look at himself in the mirror. He turned the faucet and fresh water spilled out, turned quickly hot, and began to steam. With his hands under the hot, clear flow, he let emotion overwhelm him again. Staring into his own eyes, he turned off the sink, reached out to open the medicine cabinet, and took out shaving cream and a razor. The razor felt comfortable in his hand, but he put it down.

A shave would come after a shower.

He opened the shower door and turned the water on.

Stripping off his filthy T-shirt and underpants, he gagged from his own stink. He waited for the steam to rise before stepping beneath the spray. Only then did he look closely at his left hand, turning it over and pressing it against the shower tiles. He bent to investigate his legs, thin but solid.

As he soaped his body under the hot spray, the scent of Irish Spring triggered a memory of his father. Suddenly he knew his own name, and that he had been on the verge of vanishing from the world. Of forgetting himself forever.

It all came back to him, then, and he knew he wasn't the only one in danger. Once he had climbed from the shower and dried off, he went to the closet in his parents' old bedroom, hoping but doubtful that his double had continued to store his father's SIG Sauer in the same place. To put it back in the same shoe box every morning when he left the house. But when he pulled the box down from its shelf, he felt its familiar weight and he smiled.

After that, he hurried. For the first time in a very long time, there were people who were depending on him.

They just didn't know it yet.

FOUR

Driving to pick Maddie up from school, Tess felt her strength ebb. At first she thought it was just the stress and exhaustion of recent days catching up with her. Her eyelids fluttered and she sat up straighter, clutched the streering wheel a bit tighter, and opened the window to let the chilly air flow in. When she felt a twinge of emptiness in her gut, she tried to remember what she'd eaten that day. But as she turned into the street that ran alongside the schoolyard, she slumped forward against the wheel like someone had just hit a cosmic switch and powered her body down.

The car horn blared. She couldn't lift her head from the wheel, her cheek pressed against its ridges. From the corner of her eye she saw the chain-link fence surrounding the playground and the after-school children chasing one another across the grass. The teacher tasked with overseeing them began to turn in response to the sound of the horn. The front-end alignment had been slightly off for a while—she'd been meaning to take it into the shop—and the car drifted to the right, toward the fence. All the strength gone from her, Tess had let her foot slip off the accelerator, but even as the car slowed it had enough momentum to take a section of fence down. The bodies of small children would fare no better than the chain-link.

One breath. Teeth gritted, she slid her foot back onto the brake. The teacher minding the kids in the playground shouted something, but the kids hadn't had time to really understand, or to scream. Tess mustered up all that remained of herself and pushed down on the brake. The car slowed, but only when she put her hands back on the wheel and pushed herself back against the seat was she able to overcome her weakness. The car rolled to a stop inches from the fence.

She breathed. Put it into park. Lay her head back against the seat and let the chilly breeze blow through the windows. Her shoulder and spine throbbed with the old pain, strangely distant now. The teacher shouted at her, striding angrily toward the fence as autumn leaves skittered around her ankles and children gawked at the car that had just come to a stop kitty-corner with the fence.

"What do you think you're doing?" the teacher barked at her. Then she must have gotten a clear look at Tess through the windshield, because her anger turned to worry. "Oh, my God, are you all right?"

Thinks I had a seizure or something, Tess thought. And then, *well, didn't you?*

Her injuries throbbed, but that was good in a way, because it meant she could feel again. She wasn't herself, but she could move. The empty hollow in her chest and her gut seemed to shrink, but as she put the car in gear and drove slowly around to the front of the school, carefully joining the pickup line, fear screamed into a crescendo within her. What had her doppelgänger done now? How she felt reminded her of the night she had seen the woman holding Maddie. It had drained away some of what made her who she was, and this felt the same way, as if her essence had grown somehow thinner, the way the air thinned at high elevation. There just wasn't as much of her to breathe.

Paranoia crackled inside her, kept her moving. She needed to call Lili, not to mention Nick. The certainty that they ought to stay together had just become concrete in her mind. None of them was safe until this was over.

The car engine idled as she waited in the line, moving up one vehicle at a time as parents picked up their kids. Three cars back from the pickup point, she could see the vice principal and two teachers who were herding the kids, ducking their heads to greet the parents through car windows. When the Ford in front of her pulled away and Tess hit the gas, advancing to the designated point at the curb, she rolled down the passenger window. Mrs. Kenner, who taught third grade, knitted her brows in confusion as Tess drew to a stop.

Tess didn't see Maddie in the string of children waiting to be retrieved.

"I'm sorry, Mrs. Devlin," Mrs. Kenner said, bending to peer through the open passenger window. "Maybe you and Mr. Devlin got your wires crossed today?"

Perhaps sixty, Mrs. Kenner had been negotiating the politics of broken families for decades. Tess could hear the kindness in the phrasing and the way the woman turned the words into a question. But panic would not allow her to be diplomatic.

"Where's my daughter?" she demanded.

The kindness vanished from Mrs. Kenner's face. Icy and stern, she leaned a bit nearer and put her hand on the door.

"Your husband was in school earlier. I saw him in the corridor. I assume that Maddie left with him. She's not my student, of course, but if there's a problem—"

The vice principal, Leonard Moss, appeared over Mrs. Kenner's shoulder. "Please pull ahead a bit, Mrs. Devlin," Moss said. "So Mrs. Kenner can continue with pickup."

"But Maddie—"

"I'll explain as soon as you pull ahead," Mr. Moss said.

Numb and hollow, Tess drove another twenty feet, keeping her car by the curb. Mr. Moss walked alongside and then took up a position at the passenger window, leaning on the car the way Mrs. Kenner had.

"Mr. Moss—"

"It had slipped my mind," the man interrupted, "but your husband—"

"Ex-husband."

"Mr. Devlin said he couldn't reach you and that you might have forgotten that Maddie had a doctor's appointment today. He thought you must be busy, but he asked that if you had forgotten, and came to collect her, that I tell you he would wait with Maddie at your house until you came home."

The arrogant little man gave her a condescending smile, peering through the open window. "I find in talking to them that most of our parents check their cell phones often, just in case of emergency."

Tess trembled with fear and rage. Moss's tone only stoked that blaze higher.

"Go fuck yourself," she muttered.

She hit the gas, skidding in a patch of sand. When Mr. Moss shouted, she remembered that the vice principal had been leaning against the window, but she didn't slow down. The world blurred around her and she felt as if she floated outside of herself. The other cars on the road were just moving colors. Only out of habit did she manage to stop at traffic signals and stop signs. More than ever, her body felt like a husk, and she saw herself as a ghost holding on to herself by some invisible tether. Only love and fear gave her strength to drive, to turn the corner at the DiMarino's Ristorante and drive past the little Catholic middle school whose patron saint she could never remember.

Just a hair shy of four miles later, she sped around a corner and turned into her street, struggling to hold on to the wheel. The engine roared as she accelerated. A skinny, elderly man raking leaves shouted at her to slow down as she drove by. The front windows on both sides of the car were still open—she had not even noticed. As she blew through the stop sign at an intersection, a dervish of multicolored leaves spinning up in her wake, she gripped the wheel—felt it anchor her a little—and slipped back into her body. The scar on her chest and left shoulder felt stretched too thin.

A gleaming Lexus sat at the curb in front of her house. In the driveway, a red Mercedes waited as if it belonged there. Either car might have belonged to guests of her upstairs neighbors, but she knew that wasn't true. It was the middle of a workday afternoon. Nobody would be home in the second- or third-floor apartments in the old Victorian.

Bile rose in the back of her throat as she hit the brakes and pulled up across the street. She only barely remembered to put the car into park before she popped the door, leaving it open and the engine running as she stumbled out. Her thoughts felt as if they were floating again, but her body—what little remained of her physical shell—seemed weighed down. She staggered across the street.

The front door opened the moment she reached the front lawn and she saw herself emerge. Her eyes burned with tears she could not shed. Numbness reached all the way to her bones and she could only stare as the new Tess gazed at her with horrifying pity and came down the steps and across the grass toward her.

The new Tess. That's what she was.

Her replacement wore jeans and cuffed boots and a belted leather jacket with a teal blue scarf, a casual ensemble that somehow looked elegant on her. Everything about the new Tess seemed to gleam in the fading afternoon light, her skin clearer and her eyes brighter and her spine straighter as she approached.

The original Tess fell to her knees on the lawn, hooks anchored deep inside her, dragging more of the essence from her. She barely had the strength to lift her head and stare at her doppelgänger. The new Tess knelt by her, put a hand on her shoulder.

"Don't fight it," New Tess said. "Really, it's only going to make you fade faster."

The original glanced at the doorway, wanting to scream for Maddie but lacking the strength. Even her love for her daughter felt thinner somehow. She lifted a hand and reached toward the door, but her arm dropped when she spotted Nick standing in the doorway with Maddie in his arms. He looked so handsome, so thin and young with his hair freshly cut, wearing a beautifully tailored suit and a red tie. This Nick and Tess looked as if they had just stepped off a movie screen.

In New Nick's arms, Maddie cried out for her mother.

New Tess turned toward the house. "I'll be right in, darling."

"N-no . . ." Tess managed to mutter, but her breath would barely come. She felt thin. Faded. Not unraveling so much as drifting, like fog burning off at sunrise.

"But who is that?" Maddie asked, frightened and pleading for understanding. "Who *is* that?"

New Tess bent to whisper to the original, hand still firmly on her shoulder. Her eyes glinted with ice, sharp enough to cut. "You're nothing now, understand? You're not welcome here. We . . . my *husband* and I . . . we're moving in. Maddie will have both parents again, the family together. You can't give her that, but we can. She'll be happier if you just stop resisting and let go. Run away, now, nothingness. Stay away. *Fade* away."

Maddie had begun to cry, but the sound became muffled and the original Tess glanced up to see that Nick had taken her back inside. The door still hung wide open.

"Go," New Tess whispered.

"Nnnhh," was the closest she could come to *No.*

The grass felt strange to her touch. She'd gone down on all fours and her palms itched where the grass touched it, passed through it. So little remained of her now that she imagined herself made of glass, just a thin pane of transparency, awareness slipping away. The poisonous fury faded in her and she looked up at the beautiful face of a woman she might once have been, pleading with her eyes.

New Tess might have smiled kindly, seen her off gently. Instead, she sneered. "There wasn't much to you to begin with, was there?"

She felt her eyelids flutter. Darkness swept in around her, long before evening would have brought it on, and she felt a sorrow unlike any she had ever known. She had very little feeling left, but the weight of New Tess's hand remained on her shoulder. This woman had no scars, no old pains, none of the heartache of the original. Surely that made her more worthy of the name and the life? She was *pure* Tess, a new beginning. Would it be so bad to fade out, to make way for an unbroken version of herself?

A car horn blared, three long, rattling sounds, as if an alarm had gone off. She blinked and glanced up at New Tess, saw the irritation on her face . . . and then saw worry there. The original blinked, a frisson of awareness passing through her, and she managed to pick her head up at the same time that two car doors slammed, one after the other.

"Tess, get up!" a voice shouted. "Come over here!"

For a few seconds, she thought the voice had spoken to New Tess. Then she mustered the strength to sit back on her haunches and turn toward that voice. For a few seconds, she did not know the two women running up the driveway toward them.

"Tess!" one of them called again. To her. The woman had spoken to her.

"Lili," she rasped. And then she recognized the other woman, too. Audrey Pang.

"Get the hell out of here!" Lili said. "Right now, or I swear to God I'll cave in your fucking skull."

The original Tess blinked. For the first time, she saw the crowbar in Lili's hand—the kind that nearly every car had in the trunk with the spare tire.

"But we live here," New Tess said, so reasonable. Even polite. "I think you two ought to go before my husband and I call the police."

Nick came out the front door. Maddie, screaming in fear and confusion for her mother, tried to follow him out but he pushed her back inside and yanked the door shut. Just before it closed, the original Tess met her daughter's gaze, and suddenly she didn't feel like the original anymore. She felt like the *only*.

"Go on and call them," Audrey said. "I'd love to have a conversation with them about who you are and who that woman on the lawn behind you might be. Especially once we get the real Nick Devlin down here."

Not-Nick strode angrily up beside the imposter. "You're making a mistake. This doesn't have to be painful for any of you."

Not-Tess snickered. "Oh, I disagree."

Tess took a hitching breath and forced herself to stand. Wavering on her feet, she nearly puked. Instead, she spat on the grass between herself and the doppelgängers.

"I still have the bruises to remind me how much you disagree about hurting us," Tess said, then glanced at Lili. "Knock her goddamn head off."

Lili started forward, crowbar cocked back, but Audrey grabbed her arm to stop her. Audrey took her free hand from behind her back and revealed her cell phone.

"I've already called 911," she told the imposters. "You want to be here when they arrive?"

The false ones exchanged a glance. Not-Tess twisted her mouth into an ugly sneer, turned, and grabbed Tess by the hair. Audrey shouted and Lili swore, rushing at them with the crowbar. The man who wasn't Nick caught her wrist and she punched him in the throat with her free hand. He grunted and took a step back, still holding her. Twisting hard enough that she screamed as she brought the crowbar down on his arm.

Not-Tess yanked Tess toward her, put her lips to Tess's ear.

Her breath felt like winter on Tess's skin.

"You will wish you had vanished," the double hissed. "I promise."

She hurled Tess to the grass and stormed toward her red Mercedes. Lili swung the crowbar again, hitting Nick's double in the side, but he only winced and shoved her away. He pointed a finger at Audrey and for just a moment, in the waning afternoon light, his features shifted to the rotting death mask Tess had seen in the mirrors of the psychomanteum.

Audrey screamed, raising her hands and wheeling backward in fear.

"Just stay right there," Not-Nick warned, flesh shifting again.

Audrey lifted her chin defiantly, visibly fighting her terror. "As long as you're leaving."

He ran to his Lexus, climbing behind the wheel even as Not-Tess hit the gas and her Mercedes rocketed backward out of the driveway. The car tore away, and an instant later, the Lexus roared after it, leaving Lili, Audrey, and Tess standing on the grass exchanging looks of relief and disbelief.

Audrey reached Tess first, grabbed her by both shoulders and studied her closely. "You're all there."

Tess frowned.

"When we drove up," Lili said, "it was like you weren't all there. Like part of you was invisible."

Tess still felt a million miles away, as if she had retreated deep inside herself now and could see these events unfolding from far off. She took several deep breaths and squeezed her eyes shut and the feeling abated, but she knew it would come again.

"We have to stay together from now on, no matter what," she said without opening her eyes. Her knees began to buckle, but Lili and Audrey caught her and held her up.

Lili and Audrey, she thought. But could she be sure?

She opened her eyes and studied first one, then the other. How would she know, really, if one of them had already been replaced, the way her double had tried to take over her life? Her double, and Nick's.

"For safety," she said.

"And so we know who's who," Lili replied.

Audrey nodded in agreement, but Tess could see in her eyes that her thoughts had already gone to that same, dark place. It was too late to be sure who was who. They would have to pay very close attention to the words and actions of those around them, just in case. Beyond that, they would have to proceed on faith, which was in very short supply.

The front door opened and Maddie rushed out, leaped from the top of the steps and nearly fell on the front walk before careening toward her mother.

Me, Tess thought as the little girl rocketed into her arms. *I'm her mother.*

"I love you so much," Tess said, as Maddie cried, babbling out a dozen frantic questions.

Tess put a hand behind her head and gazed down into her daughter's red, teary eyes. "I don't really know who they were," she said, and it was neither the truth nor a lie. "But I'll tell you what I can once we get everyone inside."

Lili came over and took one of Maddie's hands while Tess held the other, and then headed back toward the house.

"First, though," Tess said, "we have to call your dad."

"That man wasn't Dad," Maddie said. "At first I thought he was, but then he was so mean, and Daddy would never . . ."

Tess squeezed her daughter's hand. She had so many misgivings about who Nick had turned out to be, but she never wanted to shatter Maddie's faith in the man. That might happen soon, when Nick told her that he and Kyrie were moving to London, but Tess wanted no part of it.

"That's right, sweetie," she said. "Daddy would never.

Let's get him on the phone and you can hear his voice. You'll know right away that you're right—that mean guy is nothing like your dad."

But Tess stumbled going up the front steps, still weak and hollow and barely tethered to her body. Though all the old pains were surging back, the feeling of fading remained, and she wondered about Nick. Had they already gotten to him? What if he had already been taken, vanished completely? What if the man who had slammed the door in Maddie's face was all that remained of her ex-husband?

"The phone," she said to Lili as they walked into the apartment. "Hurry and get the phone."

FIVE

Nick sat on a bench just inside the Voodoo Lounge on St. Paul Street, just down the block from the office of WBUR, the university's radio station. St. Paul Street was narrow and intimate in comparison to Commonwealth Avenue, one of Boston's main arteries. Boston University sprawled for miles along Comm Ave and there were dozens of chains, pizza joints, and cafés lining that stretch, but Nick had always preferred the spots that were sort of tucked away—the places you had to search for. Voodoo Lounge had several locations in the Northeast, but he didn't think it would be fair to call it a chain. In his mind, it would have been impossible for a chain to serve food this good. He'd always liked Cajun and Creole food, and that was the specialty of the Voodoo Lounge—that and about ninety-nine kinds of beer.

Sitting on that bench, he gazed out at St. Paul Street and watched the sidewalks, waiting for Aaron to appear. They were all supposed to gather again tomorrow, but Aaron had called a little after noon and asked if Nick could meet for a beer or a coffee in the afternoon. Nick figured it was as good a reason as any to walk the four blocks from his office at BU's archaeology department to the Voodoo Lounge. They served the best gumbo he'd ever had outside of New Orleans, and on a chilly, gray day, a cup of steaming gumbo would be just the thing to warm his insides. He felt poorly—numb and lost in a fog, as if he were coming down with the flu.

Not all there, he thought, scanning the sidewalk across the street.

He had chalked it up to distraction and worry. No matter how good the gumbo might be, it couldn't cure him of those things—but as he sat there waiting for Aaron, he could smell the spicy aromas in the air and he knew that the gumbo would help, at least for a little while. He wouldn't feel quite so cold or so empty.

His stomach growled at the thought. The clock on the wall behind the hostess stand put the time at just about three o'clock, much too early for dinner, but a cup of gumbo was just a snack. An early appetizer. Tonight he needed to sit Kyrie down and try to explain the madness that had entered his life, so a little sustenance in advance of that conversation would not go amiss.

He spotted a familiar figure bobbing along the sidewalk across the street, beneath a tree whose leaves had begun to turn a fiery red. Aaron glanced in both directions before stepping off the curb and sailing toward the front door of the Voodoo Lounge. His eyes darted around, and Nick knew he wasn't scanning for oncoming cars. Aaron looked skittish, and when he came through the restaurant's door and saw Nick waiting for him, he exhaled with relief.

"You look like you're about to jump out of your skin," Nick said.

Aaron nodded, glanced right and left. "Not in here."

Nick's stomach growled, yearning for gumbo. "What are you talking about?"

"Walk with me," Aaron said, gesturing back through the door with a tilt of his head.

"You think something's going to happen in here?" Nick asked, trying not to let himself say the word *paranoid* out loud. Yes, they had things to fear, but not inside the walls of the Voodoo Lounge. Not now, in the middle of the afternoon.

"I just want to keep moving," Aaron said, his features pale. He stared into Nick's eyes. "We all need to keep moving now. I'm out of this, my friend. Earlier today I packed up my car and tonight I'm driving out of here."

Nick frowned. "Where are you going?"

Aaron rolled his eyes in frustration and pushed open the Voodoo Lounge's door, holding it for Nick. Mentally bidding farewell to the gumbo he'd so desired, Nick walked outside. St. Paul Street had fallen mostly into shadow as the sun crawled down toward the horizon. They had hours until sunset, but already the daylight had turned even grayer. The trees along the street and the closeness of the buildings gave the road a twilight gloom.

"It doesn't matter where I'm going," Aaron said, starting south along the sidewalk. "That's the thing that troubles me the most. I can't even be sure that you're you. So I'm leaving, and I'm not coming back for a few weeks, and you don't need to know where I'm going because by the time I come back, all of this will be resolved one way or the other."

Nick shoved his hands into his pockets, his skin crawling in the presence of the crazy emanating from Aaron. He took half a dozen steps as he tried to understand what had happened to set the man off like this.

"Your double is out there," Nick said quietly as leaves skittered around his feet.

"Why do you think I'm leaving?"

"But if we can't stop these people . . . if they kill us—if that's what they're trying to do—then your double will be waiting for you when you come back. And how the hell are you explaining all of this to your wife?"

Aaron grew more agitated. He glanced around again, anger flashing in his eyes.

Nick stopped walking. "Enough of this shit, Aaron. You tell me what happened to set you off like this. If there's more trouble, the rest of us need to know. What've you seen, man?"

His cell phone buzzed in his pocket but he ignored it, staring at Aaron to press him for an answer. The anger in the other man's eyes flared more brightly.

"We need to go, Nick. My car is just up around the corner. I want you to come with me."

"Out of town? I've got a daughter here, remember? And what about the others? Hell, my double tried to mess up my relationship with my Realtor to interfere with me trying to move out of the area. What makes you think they'll *let* you go anywhere?"

Aaron grabbed him by the arm and tried to propel him along. "Walk, damn it. I'll explain it all to you when—"

Nick tore his arm away, face flushing as he rounded on the smaller man. "Fuck off, man. Seriously."

"I'm not asking you to leave Boston," Aaron said, jaw tight as he tried to contain his temper. "But we need to go."

The phone began to buzz in Nick's pocket again and a tremor of worry went through his heart, defusing his anger. Aaron was pissing him off, but two calls that close together felt like trouble to him. It had to be Tess or Kyrie. His breath quickened. If something had happened to Maddie—

Aaron grabbed his wrist.

"Jesus!" Nick snapped. "I said 'fuck off!' " He dug into his pocket for his phone and turned away. "If you want to tell me what your problem is without this paranoid bullshit, I'm here to listen, but I've got to worry about the people I love, and I'm not going to let you take me away from . . ."

His words trailed off. He'd turned around, his back to Aaron, but now he saw Aaron again, up ahead of him, standing in front of the Voodoo Lounge. This Aaron seemed just as harried, but pale and insubstantial, almost ghostly. As Nick stared at him, this other Aaron shifted position, staring back, and nearly vanished in the deepening afternoon shadows.

The double, he thought, a sinking feeling in his gut.

"Shit," he said, turning back toward his friend. "Do you see—"

"Nick!" the ghostly Aaron shouted. "Stay away from him! The son of a bitch is *not* me!"

Frozen, Nick stared at the solid Aaron, the one who had come rushing into the Voodoo Lounge and hurried him away. The one who had seemed so paranoid, so skittish about who might be coming after him. Of course he couldn't be sure—the faded one had shouted that the other Aaron was not him, but the double could easily have said the same thing.

Yet he knew. He saw the duplicity in the double's eyes now.

Revenant, he thought. *Dead man.* The world seemed too solid and ordinary for that to be true, but his skin crawled with the idea of it. *Inhuman.*

"Nick," said the anxious one, the one who'd been so keen to lead him away.

"Fuck you," Nick said again, practically whispering it this time. Driven by terror, he grabbed the skinny, balding man by the front of his coat and slammed him against the stone façade of an office building. The doubles were strong, so Nick knew he had to be fast. He smashed the bastard's skull off the wall three times in rapid succession. "What do you want, asshole? What do you *all* want?"

The double inhaled, stood taller somehow, and pushed away from the wall. He swung a punch that Nick barely saw coming. The blow crashed into his cheek with a crack he hoped wasn't bone and for an eyeblink he just reeled backward, forgetting where he was. Aaron's double followed and hit him again. Nick threw an arm up to block and nearly managed to dodge his head out of the way. The double's fist clipped him on the temple and he staggered off the sidewalk and into the street. A car horn blared and he saw a red compact swerve to avoid hitting him.

The double hit him again, and this time he went down, lip split, mouth bleeding. He sat in the middle of the street and stared up at this man who looked so much like Aaron that Nick could feel his understanding of the world collapsing beneath him. A dead man he might be, but the double had substance. Flesh and bone.

The double crouched by him, head cocked, studying him. "We want what you want, Mr. Devlin. What anyone wants. We want to live."

The man with Aaron's face stood. In a hundred little ways he no longer looked like Aaron at all. He was too confident, too strong, and too cruel.

"I want to thank you," the double said. "I heard your friend planning to meet you here right before I got my hands on him. When he got away from me, I thought I'd come in his place, get you out of the way, and then finish him off when he came seeking help, as I knew he would."

He smiled and turned toward the shadows in the lee of the building, where the daylight had already abdicated its hold.

"And here he is."

In the shadows, the fading Aaron took a step forward. Nick saw the terror on his face, but also a determination he would never have expected.

"Run!" Nick snapped at him.

The double marched toward the fading Aaron.

Nick shook his head to clear his thoughts and forced himself to stand and go after him. "Damn it, Aaron, take off! Get the hell out of here!"

His voice seemed to snap Aaron out of whatever ridiculous bravado had come over him. He stared at his double and took a step back, then two. Nick picked up his pace, knowing Aaron would not be able to run far or fast enough now, not as weak—as insubstantial—as he had become.

When the double came to a startled halt, just at the edge of the sidewalk, Nick nearly collided with him. He grabbed the back of the man's jacket, wondering what had stopped him, but then he saw the shadows deepening behind the faded Aaron. The darkness swirled and took shape, building itself into a figure, and Nick swore under his breath as his grip on the double gave way.

The raggedy man stood just behind the real Aaron, wearing the same tattered clothes and the same filthy blindfold.

"Aaron . . . come this way!" Nick said. "Now!"

But Aaron only frowned in confusion, staring at his double as he shook his head and took a step backward . . . toward the raggedy man.

The double turned and fled on foot, running swiftly across the street and toward a narrow fire lane between buildings. Nick watched him go, just a glance, and he shouted for Aaron again.

The raggedy man sniffed the air, moving his head back and forth. Then he smiled.

"No!" Nick shouted, but he took only one step. Just

one step, and he wondered if Aaron might have always been the braver of the two of them.

The raggedy man grabbed the fading Aaron with one hand and opened his coat with the other. Aaron shouted, beating insubstantial hands against the raggedy man's arms and chest, but the blind man thrust him into the darkness inside his coat. A susurrus of voices, a cascade of satisfied groans, rose from inside that coat, and then Aaron screamed as he was dragged further inside, as if something had been waiting for him in the tattered folds of that black coat. A dry tearing noise followed, and Aaron vanished inside the raggedy man's coat with no shape or bulge that would indicate anything at all had changed. He was simply gone.

Numbed, Nick stared at the raggedy man in disbelief, until the coat twitched and billowed and went still, and then the raggedy man put his head back and sniffed the air again. He frowned as if unsure whether or not he had found a new scent, and Nick knew he couldn't worry about Aaron anymore. He had a daughter, and that meant he had to worry about himself. The raggedy man cocked his head, sniffing and considering, and Nick turned and darted across the street. A truck rolled by, then a taxi, and several cars. He ran toward Commonwealth Avenue, glancing back at the gray shadows in the lee of those buildings and beneath the autumn-leaved trees. Every turn, he caught a glimpse of the raggedy man sniffing curiously at the air, until at last he reached the corner at the end of the block and turned, and there were only shadows again.

No raggedy man. No Aaron.

But though he was sure Aaron was gone, he had no doubt he would see the raggedy man again.

In his pocket, his cell phone began to vibrate. Heart thundering, he answered it.

SIX

Tess sat on the edge of her daughter's bed, one hand on Maddie's back. The room was silent except for the ticking clock on the nightstand and the creaking of the house as the wind blew outside. Simply being in her daughter's presence, comforting her little girl, had restored much of her strength, making her feel more solid and real and alive, but she was more worried about her daughter than she was about herself.

"I just don't understand," Maddie said. She glanced up at her mother, lower lip trembling. Her eyes were red from crying but her tears had dried. "I mean . . . they looked exactly like you guys. Are they related to us?"

"No," Tess said quickly. "They're con artists or something, trying to rip us off."

"Criminals," Nick said from the doorway. He had his hands stuffed in his pockets, as if he was afraid to come farther into the room. A dark bruise had swollen his mouth and another had turned a deep purple on his temple. "But we're going to get the police involved, honey. You'll be safe. I swear."

Maddie took a deep breath and sat up straighter, gazing defiantly at her father. "I don't want just me to be safe. I want you guys to be safe, too."

"We will be," Tess said. She hated to lie to her daughter, but the truth would terrify the girl even more than this lie. "We'll take care of this, honey. Your dad and I may not be married anymore, but we're still on the same team. We'll back each other up, just like we'll back you up, always."

Nick came into the room, taking his hands from his pockets. He went down on one knee in front of Maddie.

"Sweetie, Mom and I need to talk to Aunt Lili and our friend Audrey in the kitchen—"

"About the weirdos?"

"Yes, about the weirdos," Nick agreed. "Are you going to be okay here in your room for a little while? Can you read or watch some TV for a bit, or are you scared to be by yourself?"

Maddie exhaled. "I'll be okay," she said bravely. "You guys aren't leaving, right?"

"Not without you," Tess promised. "We just need to handle this situation as quickly as possible, and it's—"

"Grown-up stuff," Maddie said. "Probably with swearing."

Nick laughed. Tess felt a twinge in her heart. He wasn't her husband anymore, but she would always love the way he laughed when the wonder of having a daughter caught him by surprise.

"Lots of swearing," Nick admitted.

"Can I just ask one question?" Maddie turned to her

mother. "How did they do it? Make themselves look so much like you? They talked like you and . . . Mom, the lady even kind of smelled like you. Like your body lotion, I mean."

Tess felt a twist of nausea in her gut. Fear skittered along her flesh like a hundred crawling spiders. Keeping that fear from showing on her face might have been the hardest thing she'd ever done, but for Maddie, she had to be brave. Whatever might happen to her, she had to protect this little girl, who was the greatest gift that either she or Nick had ever received.

She grabbed Maddie and hugged her tightly. "This is me, kid. Right here. If you ever have a question about that someday in the future, we need a password. Something only you and I and your dad will ever know. We tell nobody."

Tess held Maddie away from her. "What do you say? Pick a word."

The little girl knitted her brow, thinking hard, and then she giggled a little.

"You have a word, Mad-girl?" Nick asked.

"Linguini." Maddie smiled softly and gave another quiet giggle. "It's such a funny word."

"Linguini it is," Tess said, kissing her forehead.

Nick stood and did the same. "Okay, honey. Give us half an hour or so."

A moment of worry creased Maddie's forehead, but then she nodded. "No problem."

Tess clicked the TV on for her and handed her daughter the remote control, kissed her one more time, and then followed Nick out of Maddie's bedroom. She shut the door behind her, wanting to be sure the girl could not overhear the conversation the adults would be having.

As she walked into the kitchen, Lili was just finishing a phone call. Nick had gone immediately to the counter to pour himself a fresh cup of coffee and Tess found that she did not mind him helping himself. This wasn't his house, but they were in this together, whatever came next. She would not begrudge him making himself at home.

If it was really Nick.

He could've had the other Tess punch him a few times to make them believe his story. Anything was possible. People said that all the time, but now Tess understood what it really meant. *Anything* was possible. So she liked having Nick around right now, needed him there, but she had to remember that Maddie was the only thing that mattered.

"Audrey," she said, "do you want another cup of tea?"

Hollow-eyed, Audrey shook her head and turned to Lili. "Well?"

Lili stuffed her phone into her pocket. She had been pacing while finishing up the call and had ended up in front of the refrigerator. Now she leaned one hand on it, as if for support.

"I reached Frank Lindbergh," Lili said. "I only gave him a snapshot of today's insanity, but he's on his way over. Half an hour or so, he said."

"I thought he had a new job," Tess said, sitting at the kitchen table beside Audrey. "He can just leave like that?"

Nick brought his coffee over and sat down. "How much did you tell him, Lili?"

Lili shrugged. "That you got your ass kicked. That Aaron might be dead. That your doubles basically abducted Maddie but we got her back. That Audrey got a reading at the hotel that made her want to run screaming from the fucking building. How much more do you think I'd have to say for him to be willing to help? He's part of this too, remember? He said he saw his double."

"I wonder if that's all of us," Tess said, glancing around the kitchen. "I mean, we don't really know, right? Nick contacted most of the others involved with the Harrison House project, but if we see any of them at this point—"

"We keep our distance," Lili agreed.

"Whatever happens, we stay together until this is over," Nick said.

Audrey shifted uneasily. "Look, I get it. I'm . . . not okay. Just being in the same room with the psychomanteum today messed me up pretty badly. But I have a pregnant wife at home. I can't just abandon her for however long it takes to—"

Tess stared at her. "What you *can't* do is put her in danger if you can avoid it. You want to bring her into this?"

Seconds passed as little waves of frustration and anger swept over Audrey's features. Then she shook her head and stared in disgust at the floor.

"Shit."

"Yeah," Lili said. "That's one word for how I'm

feeling. There are others, though. Terrified. Confused. Fucking furious."

Tess felt her heart racing. She stared at Lili, surprised that there wasn't one more word in that string of emotions, because she herself had a terrible feeling growing inside her that she felt sure the others must have shared. *Suspicious.* She wished that she had a password with each of them like the one she and Nick had just set up with Maddie.

"Audrey," Nick said, "please tell me you have some idea of what we should do next, because if we just sit around here and wait for these things—these people— to decide to just kill us and be done with whatever game they've been playing, I'll lose my mind."

Tess was about to reply when she hesitated. "Did you all hear that?"

Nick frowned, but Audrey had pricked up her ears, too.

"Is it Maddie?" Lili asked.

Tess shook her head, slid back her chair, and started out of the kitchen. "No. I think someone's at the door."

"Hang on," Lili said quickly. "Don't go alone."

Tess waited for Lili to catch up, and a moment later all four of them made their way to the door. Nick went to look out the window to try to get a glimpse of the front steps, but Tess did not wait for him. If the doubles had returned, she intended to fight them. It would be four to two, now, and she thought that might make the difference.

Unless they've brought reinforcements, she thought, too late, as she opened the door.

The sight of the figure on her threshold made her

breath hitch in her throat and she backed away from the door, startled. Lili let out a cry of fear and Tess felt ice trickle down her spine. In the fading afternoon light, skies gray and nightfall only an hour or so away, the man on her doorstep looked only halfway real. Parts of him seemed solid, but the left half of his face, the right side of his torso, and his left hand all seemed almost to have been erased from the world. As he shifted toward her, gazing at her with pitiful, pleading eyes, she realized that she could see those portions of him, but that they were transparent, as if the man was half a ghost.

"Frank," Nick said. "Jesus—"

He started to reach for the man but Lili grabbed fistfuls of his shirt to stop him. Nick started to shrug her off.

"Wait," Tess said, staring at the emaciated thing at her door that might once have been Frank Lindbergh. "How did you get here so fast?"

Frank could barely lift his head to look her in the eye. "What?"

"I just talked to you five minutes ago," Lili snapped. "You said half an hour!"

"No," Frank said weakly. "You didn't talk to *me*."

SEVEN

Frank sat at Tess Devlin's kitchen table wondering if he might be asleep and dreaming. He blinked to clear his blurry vision and took a deep breath, feeling the solidity of the wooden chair beneath him. Tucked into the rear waistband of his jeans, the gun pressed against the small of his back. His stomach felt a bit queasy, but when it growled he realized what he felt was not nausea but hunger. Nick was in the middle of asking him a question—there had been a lot of questions—but Frank found it hard to focus.

"Am I dreaming?" he asked.

"What?" Nick asked.

Audrey Pang—whom Frank had nearly forgotten before discovering her here in the kitchen with the others—leaned over and pinched his arm. Pinched hard, with a twist.

"Jesus!" Frank inhaled sharply, rubbing at the place she'd pinched, and realized that the flesh felt solid. His thoughts were clear.

"Does that feel like a dream?" Audrey asked. It was a smart-ass thing to say, but there was no smirk on her face when she said it. Frank looked into her eyes and realized that she genuinely wanted to help.

"What the hell was that?" Nick said, staring at the woman.

Audrey shrugged. "We don't have time to be gentle. If this is the real Frank, that means the other one's still on the way."

"Frank," Lili Pillai said, warming her hands around a fresh mug of coffee. "You think you can string a few sentences together now? You look like hell, and I'm inclined to believe you're the real thing. From what we've seen, our doppelgängers are always slick and healthy . . . like the best versions of us."

Frank heard Tess mutter something he couldn't make out, saw the others shift uncomfortably. He laughed softly, vision blurring a bit again.

"Always liked you, Lili," he said, blinking his eyes. "Your subtle way of saying I look like shit."

"You showed up at the door with parts of you fucking transparent. Literally transparent," Nick said. "Flesh and bone can't do that. So if we have a hard time believing you're you—"

"That's no indicator," Audrey interrupted. "Tess looked the same when Lili and I arrived in the middle of the chaos with your doubles."

They all hesitated, then, staring at Frank as they tried to digest the idea that human beings could just fade into intangibility, like living ghosts.

"Can I get something to eat?" Frank asked. "I've

been in my basement for who knows how many days, eating whatever the guy wearing my face felt like bringing me."

"So we believe him now?" Nick asked sharply.

Frank winced at his tone and glared at him.

"Nick, don't," Audrey said softly, gazing at each of them in turn, a calming presence. "We're all scared. We'd be stupid to be anything but terrified, but we need to remember that the only help we can expect is from the other people around this table. Now, Nick, what's your issue? Why don't you trust him?"

Nick studied him intently. "Why are you here?"

"I told you why," Frank said. "The guy—my *double*, to use your word—he didn't tell me everything but he told me he'd met with you all, that you believing he was me was one of the things letting him suck the . . . the *me* out of me."

"No," Nick said. "Why are you *here*? At Tess's house? How did you know we would be here? How did you even know where she lives?"

Frank sighed. "I've been here before."

Nick glanced at Tess for confirmation.

She nodded.

"We stayed in touch after the Harrison House project," Frank said, glancing awkwardly at Audrey and Lili, wondering if they knew about the night at the party when he and Tess had gotten cozy. From her expression, it was clear Lili did.

"Things have not been good for me since most of you have seen me. I've lost both of my parents. After my mother died, I needed someone to talk to, and Tess

and I met for coffee. I dropped her off here afterward."
Frank looked at Nick. "That's all."

Nick raised his hands. "None of my business anymore."

"Even so," Frank said. Then he turned to Tess. "My
double talked about you. I came to you because we're
all in danger. Can I get something to eat now?"

Tess smiled wanly as she rose and turned toward the
refrigerator.

"What else can you tell us?" Audrey asked. "Tell me
everything you remember your double saying about us,
or about what was happening to you."

"I don't—" Frank began.

A knock at the door interrupted him. They all froze,
staring at one another. After a second or two, Nick got
up and padded quickly toward the front of the house,
taking pains to be as quiet as he could. Frank stood, but
had to steady himself by leaning on the table a moment,
stronger but still too weak to rush anywhere. He took a
breath and then followed Nick into the hallway, past
bedrooms and a bathroom. Nick had slipped into
the living room just to the left of the foyer and Frank
watched him draw back the curtains for a quick look
out the window at the visitor on the front steps.

"Who is it?" Frank whispered.

Nick let the curtain fall back into place. He'd gone
pale as he glanced back over his shoulder.

"It's you, Frank."

EIGHT

On the first floor of the Otis Harrison House, Officer Steven Parmenter leaned against an interior wall and caught his breath. The birds had stopped slamming against the door, but how long ago had that happened? He narrowed his eyes and shifted his feet, staring at the nearby window. Had the slant of afternoon light been altered? Moments ago, it had seemed the sun was higher in the sky, but now the angle of the shaft of daylight coming through the window had moved. A blizzard of dust motes floated across that span of sunshine.

Steven glanced away, listening to the muttering voices deeper inside the house, and when he looked back the light had shifted again. His legs felt stiff, as if he had been standing in that one position much longer than he imagined.

The muttering inside the house, that whispering that seemed to come from other rooms and yet from just beside his ear simultaneously . . . stopped. He cocked his head and listened, holding his breath, and just when he thought it had ceased completely, he heard the voice again. It spoke a language he did not understand, but that pause and the words that now flowed made him feel as if his presence had been noted. As if someone inside the Harrison House had said, *You. I can see you. Come closer.*

"Fuck you," he murmured. The whisperer in the dark heart of that old home might not know English, but he was sure it would understand his tone.

He blinked and the daylight dimmed just slightly.

"Fuck you," he said again, and forced his legs to move.

He had to drag himself forward as if he were wading up to his chest in the ocean, slogging toward the door he had used to enter. Focused on the knob, jaw clenched tight from the effort, Steven grabbed hold of it and turned. The knob rotated perhaps an eighth of an inch and then clicked. Steven rattled it back and forth. The door had been unlocked when he had needed to enter to escape the birds, but that had changed. He twisted again, heard the click, felt the resistance.

Locked.

The voice again, a variation on the same words as last time. Still unintelligible, but something inside his chest translated them as a summons. A beckoning, like a hook planted in his heart and dragging him forward. Steven turned from the door and went deeper into the dark, letting his fingers trail along a wall. The gloom in the room had grown ever dimmer, but he did not allow himself to glance at the window again, not wanting to see how swiftly the day bled out.

He wore a thin flashlight on his belt and now he unsnapped it and clicked it on, shining the tight beam into the corridor. Visitors to the Otis Harrison House could have argued over which was truly the first floor. He had come in from the side entrance, which was on street level, but the front door of the house was elevated, the tiny front yard with its path and trees higher up than the road. The front door opened into what was technically the second floor. Steven shone his flashlight down the corridor, attentive for the whisper or creak that might reveal the location of whoever spoke to him now in that dreadful old parchment voice in that ugly, guttural language more foreign than any he had ever heard. He heard no sound, not even the natural shifting, the breathing that came with a house as old as this one.

The voice had gone silent.

As if he'd been released from the drag of the amniotic sac that had seemed to engulf him, his arms and legs were his own. He took a breath and hurried across the darkened hall. His penlight picked out the bottom treads of a stairwell going upward, and he took the steps two at a time. The hair stood up on the back of his neck and he shivered. Only as he reached the top step did he feel the bounce of his service pistol against his hip and he froze, reaching for the gun.

Why hadn't it occurred to him to draw his weapon? He felt sure it had, but somehow he had not done so. Steven did it now, drawing the gun as he turned into the second-floor hallway. The stairwell had been almost pitch-black, but here the rooms and hall were lit by the late-afternoon light that came through the windows. Time had passed—far more than the few minutes he thought he'd spent inside the house—but it hadn't been skimming by at the speed he had feared.

Unless it's no longer Tuesday, he thought.

"Stop," he whispered, angry with himself for imagining such things.

The voice returned, so cold and close and intimate that he spun around, sure whoever had uttered those words must be standing just over his shoulder. He stared back along the corridor, the dry, papery voice prickling his skin with gooseflesh, and he retreated toward the front door. Gun in one hand, he had to make a choice about what he would put down and the penlight made far more sense, so he clicked it off and snapped it to his belt. Reaching backward, he kept watch over the corridor, heart thumping so hard in his chest that every beat pained him. His fingers found the cold metal knob and he gave it a twist, not at all surprised that it did not budge. A quick glimpse showed him the dead bolt and he managed to twist it, unlocking the door.

It wouldn't open. Steven turned to seek another lock but saw none. He twisted the knob harder and shook the door in its frame, but it was wedged firmly in place. Cursing under his breath, he moved into the front parlor. Cobwebs hung in the corners of the ceilings and small tumbleweeds of dust eddied about in the currents of air his entrance had disturbed. He looked out the window at the front steps and the small green patch of yard. There were dead birds on the grass and half a dozen of them on the steps. His pulse quickened when he saw the blue lights flashing and zeroed in on a pair of police cars that were parked half a block away, down at street level. Reporters were out there as well. He saw a camera truck from Channel 5 and one from the local Fox affiliate.

The voice of Harrison House whispered in his ear, and Steven batted at its insinuating tone as if it might be swatted away like a fly. The voice was more than a nuisance, but he couldn't listen. Couldn't think about it.

"Hey!" he shouted, slapping the glass. "Up here!"

He turned the lock on the window and tried to force it up so he could call to the officers or the press down below. The lock moved, but the window would not. As if it had swollen in its tracks, the wood refused to budge.

"That's enough," he said.

Stepping back to avoid flying glass, he smashed the barrel of his gun against the window, which showed no scratch or crack. Holding his breath, he tried harder, striking the glass again. The whisper came in his ear, but it seemed much louder now. Much closer. As if the thing speaking to him were inside his own skull.

Baring his teeth, Steven struck the window a third and a fourth time, then backed away from it. His hands were shaking as he wiped sweat from his brow. How could he be sweating when it was so cold in here? He left the parlor, returning to the front door, and saw his breath fogging the air. With his heart thrashing inside his chest, he did not even attempt to open the door again. Instead, he took aim and fired three times, tearing up the wood around the knob and smashing the mechanism so that it hung loosely from the hole. He fired again, shooting at the part of the doorframe where the latch protruded into the metal strike plate. With a single pull, he yanked the wreckage of the knob out of the door and it clattered to the floor. Thrusting his fingers in through the hole, he tried to pull the door toward him but it didn't budge.

Hollowed by despair, he slumped against the door and it gave way, swinging outward. With nothing to grab hold of, he pitched onto the steps and fell, end over end, in a darkness that was impossible. The gun flew from his hand and preceded him, thumping down the stairs. He struck his right knee and the back of his head and racked his spine on the steps—too many steps— until he landed in a sprawl on cold, uneven stones, in a dank, moldy darkness that was not the late-afternoon sunlight of the front yard of the Otis Harrison House.

Frantic, reeling at the impossibility of it, he reached for his penlight and was surprised to find it still there. With a click, he shined the narrow beam into the darkness of what could only be the cellar. His gun lay on the stones just a few feet away and he scrambled over to pick it up. Blood dripped down the back of his neck, and his knee and back throbbed as he rose shakily to his feet.

The urgent whisper came to him again, beckoning him forward. Shaking his head in mute refusal, he backed toward the stairs. Three steps, then three more, and another two before he realized the staircase could not be so far away. Steven turned to find that he'd advanced deeper into the cellar . . . deep enough that he now stood only half a dozen steps from a pit in the center of the room, a place where the stones had collapsed down into a yawning hole. His breath fogged the air, so cold and yet thick and humid, a greasy film coating his skin and clothes.

Despair bubbled within him and he nearly burst into tears. Penlight in one hand and pistol in the other, he took aim at that sighing, breathing pit, waiting for the moment when he would pull the trigger, when he would have something at which he could shoot.

But the voice . . .

The voice spoke to him so intimately, cajoling and commanding all at once. Imperious and knowing. Yes, it knew him.

The words were gibberish, the language made of words he did not imagine a human mouth could form. He could not understand those words, but he felt their meaning. The need.

The thing in the pit had a purpose for Steven. It required him. There was a task he would have to perform. He felt reborn. Baptized. Thought, this could be the start of something beautiful.

Gun in hand, he stood in the cellar of the Otis Harrison House.

And waited.

NINE

Tess opened the door for Frank's double as if nothing at all was amiss. She stepped back, smiling in welcome, and held the door open for him. Not-Frank walked in, worried and apologizing for the delay. As he started to ask how Maddie was handling the whole thing as if he gave a damn about the girl, Nick stepped out from behind Tess with an aluminum baseball bat.

"Don't even say her name," Nick sneered, and swung the bat.

Not-Frank got one arm up in time, and the first crack of the bat broke his forearm. The second swing struck him in the side and then he turned as Nick rained blows down on his back. Tess wanted the thing dead, but not yet. Not now. As Nick cocked back the bat, gaze locked on Not-Frank's skull, she knew that her ex-husband had no such hesitation, and she grabbed the bat. Held it tightly.

"We need answers," she said.

Nick looked at her. Instead of rage, his eyes were full of fear, though she knew it wasn't for himself. These people—if they had ever been people—had tried to take their daughter earlier, and the knowledge of that made the temptation to destroy them almost impossible to resist. The only way to be sure they would never succeed in taking Maddie was to make sure they never had the chance. But the only way they could truly hope to achieve that end was to find out who or what the doubles really were. They needed to know how to stop them.

Hissing, jaw set in rage, Not-Frank began to rise as if he might want to make a fight of it. Nick swung the bat hard at his broken forearm and the double cried out and went back to his knees. His eyes rolled back and he collapsed to the floor, blacked out from the pain.

Tess kicked him in the legs and back, trying to wake him, until Lili arrived with a glass of water and dumped it on his head. The man sputtered awake, glaring hatred at them.

"What the hell do you think you're—" he began.

Then he saw the real Frank, pale and thin and shaking, standing farther back along the hall, and it all became clear to him. The real Frank reached behind his back and his hand reappeared holding a gun.

"Jesus, Frank!" Tess cried, jerking backward at the sight of the weapon, though it wasn't pointed at her.

Not-Frank ignored the gun. He launched himself at Tess, one good hand hooked into a claw, and Nick smashed the bat across his head. The sound reminded Tess of a hammer striking the last blow on a nail, driving it at last into the wood.

With Lili and Audrey to help and the real Frank standing by and spitting on his double, weapon still aimed at him, Tess managed to drag the impostor into the kitchen. They put him in a chair and bound him with an entire roll of duct tape. Tess left his mouth uncovered—the whole point of holding him was so that they could hear what he had to say.

"Mom?" Maddie called from the hall. "Who's at the door? What was all that?"

"Go back into your room, honey!" Tess shouted, trying not to snap. She glanced up at Lili, who nodded and rushed down the corridor to make sure that Maddie did not try to come into the kitchen. In the girl's room, Tess knew Lili would turn the TV volume up.

"Frank," Nick said coldly, "put that away. My daughter's in this house."

The real Frank nodded, clicked on the thumb safety, and slipped the gun back into the rear waistband of his pants.

Turning to stare at the unconscious man taped to the chair, Tess marveled at how much he looked like Frank. How much better a version of Frank he was. More handsome, more confident, better dressed, better haircut, better complexion.

She slapped him hard to wake him up. When that didn't work, she poured a mug of hot tea on his head and he sputtered and shook and opened his eyes to swear at her.

"You bitch," he growled, "you have no idea the mistakes you've made."

Tess sat on the chair beside his and leaned forward. "Tell me all about them."

The double's expression softened. "Why, Tess? Why are you helping the ghost?"

For half a second, the tone of his voice cut into her—betrayal, disappointment, and sorrow implying that he was the real Frank Lindbergh and the withered thing whose hand she had held at her kitchen table was the *other*. The double. But then the last word resonated in her mind and she studied him carefully.

"Is that what you all are, then? Ghosts?"

Audrey returned to the kitchen—Tess had barely noticed her absence—carrying a pair of mirrors. "Of course they're ghosts."

Nick whacked the double in the back of the head with an open hand, came away with blood on his palm. "Pretty solid for a ghost. And he bleeds."

"I imagine it's complicated," Audrey said. "Now we're going to find out just how complicated. Give me a hand with these mirrors."

"What are you doing?" Tess asked.

But Audrey had a purpose now, and she was no longer listening. The real Frank had been standing in the corner of the kitchen as if the idea of getting too close to his doppelgänger made him want to run screaming. Tess understood the urge, but now Audrey instructed him to take a seat. She handed the mirror she had taken off the wall in the living room to Nick.

"Hold that up next to his head," Audrey said.

Nick positioned himself on Frank's left and Audrey hoisted the mirror she had taken from Tess's bedroom, holding it in place on Frank's right. They angled the mirrors so that Frank could see almost nothing but his own reflection.

"We know these . . . manifestations . . . have been siphoning your strength by imitating you," she went on.

"The more they become you and inhabit bits of your life, the more other people perceive them as you, and the more you become the ghost and they the reality."

Audrey glanced at Nick. "Who is the man in the chair in front of you?"

Nick seemed about to argue, maybe mock Audrey's methods, but Tess saw the flicker of resignation in his eyes. They had seen too much for him to doubt anything else that might occur.

"It's Frank Lindbergh," Nick replied.

"Tell *him*."

"You're Frank Lindbergh. Always have been. When you're feeling better, I might just break your fucking nose for making a move on my wife when we were still married, but you're Frank fucking Lindbergh."

Lili did a double take. "Wait, what?"

Audrey ignored her. "Tess?"

Tess couldn't see more than a sliver of Frank's features through the gap between the mirrors. She turned to look at the false Frank, the double, who seemed fascinated in spite of himself. She should have been afraid of him. If he was a ghost or revenant or whatever Audrey wanted to call him, he was dead. He ought to terrify her, but her fury had surged to the fore, tamping down the fear. They'd put their hands on Maddie, tried to take her little girl away. The fear still shivered in her heart, along with disbelief, but she would face anyone or anything that dared to threaten her little girl. She stared at the thing that was not Frank Lindbergh. As strong as the doubles were, the bastard wasn't going to be able to tear through the thick strips of duct tape they'd used to strap him to the chair.

She moved around the table and crouched beside the real Frank's chair, nudging Nick over. She took Frank's hand in both of hers and held it tenderly.

"You're Frank Lindbergh. We've both had a rough time of it the last couple of years, but I believe my best days are still ahead, and so are yours."

He made a small noise and Tess thought he might be crying, just a little.

"Frank," Audrey said quietly. "This may be painful, but I want you to talk now about the ugly things in your life. These manifestations have crafted perfect versions of you . . . of us. The idealized versions. Tell me the things the perfection can't embrace, the things you never want to say out loud."

Tess saw him shudder, but then Frank exhaled and sat up straighter in his chair.

"You're a fool, little witch," the doppelgänger said, but he thrashed in his seat, testing the strength of the duct tape.

"I'm no witch," Audrey said. "I just have a sense of things. I may not really understand what you are, but I know the things you aren't."

"Think you're so fucking—" the false thing began.

"I'm a drunk," Frank interrupted. He exhaled. "All my life I swore I wouldn't be anything like my father. He didn't have the balls to make a better future for himself. When I was a kid I thought it was because he was a drunk. By the time I hit twenty, I realized that was just what he wanted everyone to think, but the reality was that the booze was a handy excuse. He wanted people to think he could've been something better, something more, if not for the booze."

Tess clutched his hand and he held on tightly. She heard a moan behind her and glanced across the table at the impostor. The sight made the breath catch in her throat. Instead of the face of Frank Lindbergh, its features had become a death mask. She'd seen glimpses on her own double, the hellish, rotting faces of the malignant spirits masquerading as human beings. Tess flinched back a little, though the dead thing had stopped struggling and only sat bound to its chair, staring at the backs of the mirrors that shielded Frank's face from view.

"Keep going," Audrey said quietly.

Frank hesitated. "I . . . I get it now. My dad taught me well. Anytime someone went for their dream and got even a fraction of it, I resented the hell out of them. Still do. I bitch about the universe being against me, but I know . . ."

He drew a shuddery breath and let the words trail off.

"How do you feel?" Audrey asked.

"Better. Stronger," Frank replied softly. "Ashamed of myself, but not enough to try to pretend any of what I just said is something other than the truth."

"Good," Audrey said, and lowered the mirror.

Nick put down the other mirror, turned to lean it against the kitchen wall. Tess studied Frank and realized that he didn't look much different than before. Healthier, maybe, but not markedly so. Still pale and too thin and unshaven. The vital thing was that he looked solid and alert, like he was *all there* for the first time since he had shown up on her doorstep.

Tess glanced at his double again, only to find that he no longer looked like a living corpse nor did he still look anything like Frank Lindbergh. Taller and thinner, with high cheekbones and a sharply pointed mustache above a thin strip of beard on his chin, he looked like a man transported from another era.

He is, she thought. *Of course he is.*

"Let's start again," she said, moving back around the table toward him. "What's your name?"

The ghost—or incarnation, or whatever he was— lifted his chin in arrogant defiance.

Lili spoke and Tess glanced up, surprised to see that she'd returned to the kitchen.

"You seem calm," she said, "but if you could look in one of those mirrors you'd see that the right side of your head is a bit see-through. Left shoulder, too."

Fearful, the double glanced down at his left shoulder and saw that Lili was right. Not only had he lost the Frank masquerade, but he'd faded a little. She wondered if the duct tape could hold him now or if it would just pass right through. If he kept fading, she was pretty sure they were going to find out.

Lili walked calmly toward him, wound up, and slapped him hard across the face. Blood flew from his mouth. *Not ghosts,* Tess thought. *Not really.* Ghosts couldn't bleed. Audrey had called them manifestations and Tess had thought of this thing as an incarnation, which made more sense to her. Incarnate. In the flesh. However they had done it, they were real and solid, at least for now.

"What is your name?" Lili demanded.

Nick grabbed the baseball bat from where it leaned against the wall. He didn't swing it—didn't even raise it—but the promise was there in his eyes.

"You don't need his name," Audrey said. "I've seen his portrait. Meet Simon Danton, the second-class magician who founded the Lesser Key."

Tess whipped around to stare at her. "The occultists—"

"Who tried to finish the summoning Berrige started in the cellar of the Harrison House," Audrey finished. "Danton was the ringleader of that band of—"

"Mind your tongue," Danton snapped, then turned a sneer of hatred into a grin. "You have no idea what real magic is. We came back from death. We gave ourselves new flesh!"

Audrey dragged her chair over so that she could sit right in front of Simon Danton. Tess saw fear glittering in the woman's eyes, beads of sweat on her forehead, and she hoped that Danton could not see how afraid Audrey was of him.

"I know that the only magic that matters is the magic that works," Audrey said. "If you botch the spell, that doesn't make you a magician, it makes you a fuckup."

Danton made a noise in his throat as if he might spit at Audrey and Lili slapped him again. Tess stood back to make room for the blow, an observer now. She glanced over at Nick, who had put the baseball bat over his shoulder as if he was waiting for his turn at the plate. Casual, aware that these women did not need him to step in for them.

"Let me see if I've got you figured out," Audrey went on. "You built the psychomanteum because you thought you could trap the demon inside it, but you screwed up and ended up trapping yourselves instead. Maybe you were already planning how you could get out when they dismantled the thing and put it into storage. That gave you time to plan but you were stuck there until the hotel management bought the psychomanteum and reassembled it. You'd all latched on to the reflections of people who'd looked into those mirrors before it was dismantled."

Frank—the real Frank, more himself now—coughed quietly.

Lili took the moment to jump in. "I don't understand. You could make these bodies for yourselves. Black magic whatever, okay fine, but when the others slipped out they tried to build lives for themselves, separate from us. Why didn't you?"

The thing that had once been Simon Danton looked to Audrey, arrogant and expectant. He cocked an eyebrow.

"No? You don't want to offer your theories on my motivations?" Danton asked.

Audrey glanced at Lili. "It's the raggedy man. We suspected it was Berrige and we were right."

Tess shivered. She crossed her arms, hugging herself, and stared at their captive as she tried to reconcile how he could be both a dead man and a living thing, a creature who could bleed. Images of the raggedy man swam through her mind, the memory of the first time she and Lili had seen him outside the gallery, sniffing the air like a dog searching for a scent. *I had the scent. I know I did.*

He'd shown up around them more than once, confusing her and her friends for the doppelgängers who were engaged in this masquerade. And then Aaron . . . the way Nick had described his death at the hands of the raggedy man. Tess had never liked the man, but nobody should have to die like that.

With the way Audrey had put things together, it was as if she had laid out a puzzle with missing pieces, gaps that they were waiting for others to fill. Tess stared at Lili for a moment, thinking about the life that her double, Devani Kanda, had made. These ghosts had created bodies and identities, used magic to influence the world around them. Why would the Lesser Key work so hard to build lives for themselves and then throw it all away by coming after the people whose faces they had all stolen?

"You knew," she said to Danton.

The man smiled thinly.

"Knew what?" Frank asked.

Nick glanced at her. "What are you—"

"Audrey already told us they were following in Berrige's footsteps, trying to replicate the . . . summoning spell or whatever that killed him," Tess said, skin prickling with a rush of heat as little epiphanies clicked in to complete the puzzle in her head. "When we figured out the raggedy man might be Berrige, I thought they were all working together. Berrige and the doubles."

"They've all been haunting us," Lili said. "Tormenting us."

"No," Tess said, shaking her head. "That's just it. The Lesser Key wanted nothing to do with us until I saw the one with Nick's face and we started poking around, trying to make sense of it. When we saw the raggedy man outside the gallery he wasn't looking for us. He was hunting your double, Lili, just like I said."

Nick had one hand on the back of a kitchen chair,

hanging his head as he listened. Now he pushed away from the chair, snapping his head up.

"What about Aaron? Berrige just . . . tore him apart. I saw it happen. Whatever Aaron had been reduced to, the old man ripped him to shreds and stuffed him inside his coat. I'll never . . ." His voice broke, and Tess's heart broke for him. Part of her would always love him and she hated to see him in pain. "I'll never be able to scrub that image out of my head, or the way Aaron screamed."

Tess slid into a chair beside the thing that had once been Simon Danton and stared at it. "Berrige had no idea that was Aaron, did he?" she asked softly. "He thought it was one of your people. That's what they've been doing to us, what you were doing to Frank . . . feeding on whatever makes us who we are, so that when Berrige came hunting he would get confused and think we were the ghosts."

"Of course," Audrey said. "That's exactly what they've been doing."

"Holy shit," Lili whispered.

Tess turned to Frank—the real Frank. "But Danton knew. The rest of the Lesser Key had no idea, or maybe he warned them and they didn't listen. He figured Berrige would be out there hunting for him and the only chance he had of surviving was to become you, Frank. To replace you, so when Berrige came looking, all that would be left was something so faded and dim that the sorcerer would assume you were the ghost."

"Just like he did with Aaron," Nick said.

They all stood around the table now, staring at the fleshly manifestation of the ghost of Simon Danton.

Tess caught her breath. The daylight coming through the kitchen windows had dimmed, the afternoon shadows growing long, and in the gray light she could see his true face—the withered features of the corpse—superimposed upon the false flesh like the golden aura that limned the outer edges of the moon on a foggy night.

Tess slid to the edge of her chair, so close to the dead thing that the little hairs stood up on her arms and the back of her neck. Her nose detected an odor she had not noticed before, the rancid stink of death, and she wondered if it was the smell of his breath. The thought smashed through her, an overpowering reminder of just what this creature was. Not just a dead thing. Not just a ghost. Danton had been an occultist in his lifetime, a would-be sorcerer who wanted nothing more than to summon a demon from whatever Hell might truly exist. This wasn't just death sitting before her . . . it was evil.

In her house. At her kitchen table. With her daughter down the hall.

"I want to tell you something," she said, so softly that the others had to lean in to hear.

Danton arched an eybrow. The afternoon light grew dimmer and his death face began to supersede that of the man he'd once been.

"Go on," he urged, his voice like the rustle of dry leaves. From one angle, she could still see his eyes, but from another they were only dark hollows with the glint of sickly yellow light within.

"I didn't believe in ghosts or magic before all of this," she said, even more quietly. "I live in almost constant pain and I never pray, because I know my prayers will not be answered. Yet now, here you are—"

"You think I'm God?" Danton laughed.

"I think you may be proof there is something out there for me to pray to," Tess said quietly. Behind her, Lili put a hand on her shoulder and Tess went on. "You terrify me, but not the way you'd like to, because the thing we really need to be afraid of is Cornell Berrige, and he's the one hunting the members of your cult."

"Tess," Nick said, the warning of his tone very clear.

Danton cocked his head in fascination. "I'm listening."

"You wanted to live again," Tess said. "I understand that. And except for what you did to Frank out of your own fear, your people left us alone until Lili and I started interfering. So what if you tell us what you know about why Berrige is doing what he's doing and we figure out a way to stop him? You and your friends can keep our faces. Build your own lives. We'll promise not to go so far away that it will undermine whatever spells you've cast that have allowed you to escape the psychomanteum. We work together, destroy Berrige, and call it a day. Truce. Détente."

"No," Nick snapped.

Tess whipped around to glare at him.

Audrey shifted closer to Lili and Tess. "Hear her out, Nick."

Across the table from Danton, Frank Lindbergh rose shakily to his feet. "Tess, do you have any idea what this fucker did to me? I've been pissing in a bucket for—"

"Sit down, Frank," Tess said.

"I will not—"

"Sit down, Frank," Lili barked. Then she softened and turned to him. "This is not about revenge. It's about survival."

"After what they did to you?" Nick asked, staring at his ex-wife. "After they came here and tried to take Maddie, to push you out of your own house? Your life?"

Tess reached for his hand. Nick flinched and tried to pull away but she grabbed his hand and held on tightly. "It's Maddie I'm thinking of."

Nick looked about to continue debating the point, but then he just clammed up and shook his head.

"Why don't you go look in on her?" Tess suggested. "Make sure she's not eavesdropping."

After a moment's hesitation, Nick glared at Danton, then turned and left the room.

Tess turned back to face the dead man strapped to the chair beside her. "Well?"

In the fading light, the death face grinned. "If you destroy Berrige, I'm sure my friends and I will have no problem letting you live."

Audrey dragged out a chair, its feet squealing on the kitchen floor. She sat down and stared at Danton. Tess wondered if she could see the pits of his eyes, the dead skin tight against his skull.

"Berrige tried to summon a demon. Carved out his own eyes as part of the ritual," she began.

"Clawed them out, not carved," Danton corrected.

"Jesus," Lili whispered.

The name only made the death grin widen.

"We thought Berrige had failed," Danton went on. "When we built the psychomanteum and tried to replicate the ritual in a safer environment, to infuse the magic of the ritual into our reflections, trap that power in the mirrors of the box—"

"What do you mean you 'thought' he'd failed?" Frank asked. But unlike the others, he made no effort to move closer to the creature who had kept him captive and stolen his identity.

Danton shifted, straining against the duct tape. Tess thought he might ask her to free him, but he did not. They had a fragile peace at the moment, but he knew that did not make them allies.

"The ritual failed," Danton went on. "But not completely. The demon rose but the summoning was flawed. It emerged only halfway into our world and became stuck there. When Berrige tried to end the ritual, it killed him and trapped his soul. It's held him there ever since, gnawing on his soul like a dog with a strip of rawhide. When we used the psychomanteum, it tried to take us, too. We were trapped, but we fled into the mirrors. The damned box saved us."

The cadaver looked at Audrey. "The rest you know. We spent years knitting these magicks together, stealing your reflections and building substance."

"But how can you just *make*—" Lili began.

"They're not natural flesh and blood," he said. "They require ritual and focus to keep up the heft and weight of human bodies, to keep us tangible. But the illusion of life is better than none at all. We have to return to the psychomanteum for at least a short while each night, or we'll begin to fade out of existence."

"Just fade?" Tess asked.

"As if we've been erased," Danton said.

"And if you'd succeeded in diminishing me so much that you'd completely become me?" Frank asked. "You said I would have faded."

Danton hesitated, but only for a second. "That's correct. Unless you made your way back to the psychomanteum. But that would be its own hell. You'd have been trapped there forever."

Frank looked as if he might be sick. "You see what you're dealing with here, Tess? Those are the options he had in mind for me. Either one of them would have been worse than dying."

Tess flushed, hating every moment, every word that came from her own lips. But she ignored him, keeping her focus on Danton.

"You said the demon had Berrige trapped. So how can he be the raggedy man? How can he be wandering around looking for you?"

Danton lowered his head. The wan, dying light of the afternoon silhouetted him, showing the wisps of hair on a corpse's head, though his living face was still visible as well, as if she might close one eye and see one visage or the other.

"I glimpsed him once," Danton said, and she could hear the fear in his voice. Fear of the abyss of nothingness that awaited his soul if Berrige caught up to him. "Hunting me. I barely got away. It's why I went to Frank's house that night, how I knew that it was all beginning to unravel before the others did. I thought I could hide until Berrige had caught the others, thought I could feed Frank to him in my place.

"He's still in the demon's power, you see. It's the only thing that makes any sense. If Berrige is wandering free, it can only be because we've freed ourselves. He is doing the demon's bidding, like a dog hunting for his master, but he remains on a leash. Its influence will be bleeding from the house now, seeping out like an infection, but it can't get out. Somehow, though, it has managed to let Berrige out.

"I can only imagine that when we emerged from the psychomanteum, it sensed us, and now it wants us back. Perhaps Berrige has struck a deal—the six of us for his own freedom—but I can't be sure of that. Regardless, the other members of the Key know that Berrige is after them now, which is why they have been trying to . . . well, to diminish you, to use Frank's word. They want Berrige to take you in their places the way they did your friend Aaron, and now they know that time is fleeting."

Nick came back into the kitchen and they all paused to look at him.

"Maddie?" Tess asked.

"Napping," he said.

She smiled, but Nick had no smile for her in return. She could see in the set of his mouth and the stony glint of his eyes that he disagreed entirely with the way she had handled Danton.

"Now then," the death face said, "tell me, how do you plan to destroy the ghost of the most powerful magician of the nineteenth century?"

Somewhere not far off, a dog began to bark. They heard the squeal of brakes from some kind of truck, perhaps the very thing that had set off the dog. The sun had nearly set and only the last glow of the autumn afternoon remained in the kitchen, but nobody moved to turn on a light.

Frank shifted in his seat, puzzled by her hesitation. Audrey, Lili, and Nick all began to stare at her and frown. Lili opened her mouth to ask the question they were all on the verge of asking, virtually the same question that the dead man had just asked.

"How do I plan to destroy Berrige?" Tess echoed, sliding her chair back half a foot or so, moving away from Danton. "Thing is, I don't. Berrige doesn't want us, unless your fucking cult can confuse him into thinking we're you people. As far as I'm concerned, Berrige is your problem."

"You said—"

Tess sneered. "Your followers tried to take my place. Tried to take over my life and take my child from me. You really think I'm going to let you all just go about your business wearing our faces after that? You must have been dead a long time to have forgotten how mothers can get when you put their kids in danger."

Audrey leaned back in her chair. "What are you planning, Tess?"

Tess glanced around at her friends, ending on Lili. "I vote we go back to the Nepenthe Hotel with some baseball bats and shatter every bit of mirror glass in the apparition box. Mr. Danton and his friends might get lucky and fade out forever before Berrige drags their black fucking souls back to the demon at the Harrison House."

Frank slapped the table, a vicious smile on his face. "Seconded."

Danton's human face had vanished almost completely, and now only the sneering corpse face gaped at her, sickly yellow light burning in the hollow pits where its eyes ought to have been. It slammed against the duct tape binding it, rocked the chair and nearly tipped over. It opened its mouth and roared so loud that the windows rattled in their frames.

The screaming was sure to wake Maddie, but that was all right.

They would all be leaving soon enough.

TEN

Kyrie sat on the sofa in the living room of Nick's apartment, trying to decide whether she ought to be worried or pissed off. Upon her arrival nearly half an hour ago, she'd clicked on the television but had barely been aware of the sounds and images coming from the screen. Now she forced herself to focus and realized it was the Food Network—some cooking competition. In the front of her mind, she allowed herself to become caught up in the challenge faced by the chefs. In the back of her mind, though, a little voice she thought of as the Logical One was asking what the hell she thought she was doing.

The Logical One had been mostly quiet for the past couple of months as she allowed herself the fantasy of having this handsome, intelligent, quirky guy fall so in love with her that he was willing to uproot his whole life and move across the Atlantic Ocean just so he wouldn't be parted from her. When she and Nick had first slept together and then begun a relationship, the little voice had been screaming loud and clear, telling her she was an idiot to get involved with an older man, a professor, and worse, a man who'd recently split from his wife. There had been so many red flags that Kyrie had managed to ignore, and in time she had become convinced that she'd made the right decision.

Now she sat on Nick's sofa and waited for him—and his ex-wife—to bring their adorable daughter over for her to babysit. Kyrie had been at her apartment in Allston, preparing dinner with her roommates, when Nick had called. He'd provided no details, only told her that it was urgent—that he needed her—and that he'd explain it all eventually.

Define eventually, she should've said. But she hadn't thought of it then.

The skinny little Latino chef won ten thousand dollars because he hadn't screwed up the dessert course as badly as the woman he'd been up against. Kyrie clicked off the TV and got up from the sofa, glancing around the apartment. Sometimes Nick's OCD and the cocktail of other little spectrum issues he had could drive her crazy, but she appreciated the fact that they made him compulsively neat. She walked across the room and looked out the window at the parking lot, wondering how much longer they would be.

The building had once been a factory, but it had been converted to upscale apartments within the past six or seven years, all exposed brick and wooden beams and high windows. Nick lived on the fifth floor in a two bedroom with a gourmet kitchen he never used to its potential. *And now we'll be leaving,* she thought.

Down below, in the dim glow of the streetlights, she saw Nick's car pull into the lot followed by a red Toy-

ota she didn't recognize. Nick drove up the front entrance of the building and parked at the curb, turning
on his hazard lights. He popped open the driver's door
and climbed out from behind the wheel, but by then Kyrie was barely looking at him. The passenger door had
opened as well, and she held her breath as she watched
Tess get out.

Tess *Devlin*.

Kyrie loved Nick, and she thought he loved her in
return, but if Tess decided that she wanted her ex-
husband back and was willing to fight for him, the out-
come was far from certain. Tess had been with him so
much longer, knew him so much better, had shared so
much with him. Beautiful and intelligent . . . Kyrie flat-
tered herself that she could compete in those arenas,
but Tess had given birth to Nick's daughter. Unless and
until Kyrie and Nick had a child of their own together,
she couldn't compete with that.

Unless he really loves you, the Logical One whispered in the back of her mind, for once saying something helpful instead of hurtful.

She watched Tess help Maddie out of the backseat,
a happy flutter in her chest at the sight of the little girl.
Maddie's imagination sparkled so brightly that she
always made Kyrie smile.

In the light from the lampposts in front of the building, it was hard to make out how many people might
be in the red Toyota, but a woman got out of the passenger's seat and joined Nick, Tess, and Maddie on the walk
up to the lobby door. Kyrie glanced around the apartment for a second, then hurried to the kitchen and poured
herself a glass of raspberry seltzer before returning to

the living room sofa and clicking the TV back on. She wanted Tess to see her looking comfortable and at home here, not like she'd been anxiously awaiting their arrival.

When she heard the key in the door she nearly spilled her drink. She forced herself to wait until Nick had opened the door before she looked away from the TV. With a smile, she put her glass down on the coffee table, expecting some forced niceties with her boyfriend's ex-wife.

Instead, Tess made a beeline to her as soon as she came through the door. Worry etched on her badly bruised face, she swept across the room and pulled Kyrie into a hug.

"Thank you for doing this," she said. "You have no idea what it means to me."

Tess stepped back, still holding her by the arms. Kyrie tried to hide the awkwardness she felt behind a half smile. Nick had told her about the intruder who'd broken into Tess's place, but now that she saw the bruises and sensed the tremor of fear in the other woman, she realized she had badly underestimated how serious the attack had been.

"It's nothing," Kyrie said, hoping her smile looked more genuine than it felt.

Maddie walked over wearing her favorite backpack and waved a shy greeting. "Hi, Kyrie."

"That's all I get? Your mom gives me a hug but I just get a wave from you?" Kyrie said, dropping to her knees. Maddie smiled tiredly and walked over to embrace her. "I'm so glad to see you, munchkin. We're gonna have a fun night. Have you eaten, or do you want me to make some mac and cheese?"

That was the trigger she'd needed. Maddie smiled brilliantly and pumped her fist. "Mac. And. Cheese!"

They high-fived and Kyrie sent her over to the TV to pick a movie, then turned to face Tess again.

"I know you must have questions—" Tess began.

"About a thousand," Kyrie replied, studying the pain and fear in the other woman's eyes. Nick had walked up behind Tess by then, and Kyrie turned her attention to him. "I don't need the answers right this second. Especially not with the munchkin around. But I *am* going to want them. I hope that doesn't come off as bitchy, but—"

Tess touched her arm. "No. You deserve the answers."

She looked at Nick, and a little knife of jealousy thrust deep into Kyrie's heart. With all of the other things the two of them shared, it hurt her that now here was this new thing, this secret they were going to keep from her, at least for a little while.

For the first time, Kyrie glanced past them and smiled at the other person who had arrived with them. The woman stood just inside the door looking profoundly uncomfortable.

"Hi," Kyrie said. "You okay? Want a drink or something?"

The woman sighed deeply. "I'd kill for a shot of tequila, but even if you had it, we don't have the time."

Kyrie looked at Nick and Tess, hoping for some explanation, but she could see by their anxious expressions that she wasn't going to get even a hint of one. Troubled, she turned to the woman at the door.

"What's your name?"

"Audrey Pang," she said, crossing to the same window from which Kyrie had watched them arrive. She looked down at the parking lot, practically vibrating with the same urgent energy that coursed through Nick and Tess.

"I'm Kyrie," she said.

Audrey did not turn toward her. "Nice to meet you."

A tight ball of fear formed in Kyrie's gut as she studied the tension visible in the woman's stance. She turned to Nick.

"I'm trying not to ask questions. I know you need to go. I can see you're ready to bolt out of here," Kyrie said. "But the way you're all acting, and after what happened to Tess the other night . . ." She looked over her shoulder at Maddie, who had the remote control and was surfing through the on-demand offerings on the TV set. Kyrie turned back to look Nick in the eye. "Are you in danger? Are *we* in danger?"

Nick stepped up and kissed her as if his ex wasn't standing three feet away. Kyrie knew he was trying to alleviate her fear and hated that it was so easy for him to do. She kissed him back fiercely and then let him go.

"That's not an answer," she said firmly, holding his hands so he could not avoid her question.

"It's the only one we have right now," Nick said carefully. "Ask me again when I come home."

His tone held something uncertain, but she refused to pursue it further. Was it that he could not be sure he *would* be coming home? It couldn't be. Something that serious . . . he'd tell her. He'd explain.

Wouldn't he?

"You've just got to trust me," Nick said.

Kyrie studied his face, on the verge of changing her mind and demanding they explain what the hell had them so spooked. Then Maddie cried out in victory.

"Look! Kyrie, look!" the little girl said. "Daddy's got *Finding Dory* on demand! We can watch it, right?"

"Of course we can, honey," Kyrie said. "Just give me a minute and I'll get things cooking for your mac and cheese, and then we can start the movie. Give your mom and dad some love before they go."

Maddie dutifully raced over and hugged her parents in turn, then grabbed Kyrie's hand and tried to drag her to the sofa. Nick gave Kyrie another quick kiss and a look she could have interpreted as apologetic but chose to see as grateful. Then he called Audrey away from the window and they moved for the door.

Tess knelt by Maddie and took her hand so that she would let go of Kyrie.

"Settle down, punkin. Kyrie's going to make your dinner and then you can watch your movie. Go on and find something on Disney Channel till she's ready."

Maddie smiled, but her gaze rested on her mother's bruised face and she gave Tess another hug before returning to the sofa.

"Thank you again," Tess whispered to Kyrie. "Truly."

"Of course," Kyrie said.

Tess moved in closer to her, one hand on her arm, and whispered again, so quietly that nobody else could hear.

"I know this must be strange for you. I know it's hard," Tess said. "But after tonight, you can have the future you're hoping for. I believe we all can."

With a final, searching glance, Tess turned and strode out the door. Audrey was already gone. Nick smiled softly and pulled the door shut with a solid click that echoed in the apartment, even over the cheerful voices on the television.

Kyrie hurried to the door and locked it, the image of Tess's bruises still fresh in her mind. She ought to have felt safe, but she did not. Not at all.

She walked back to the window and waited until she saw Nick, Tess, and Audrey leave the building. Without Maddie there to connect them, Tess got into the passenger seat of the Toyota while Audrey climbed in to ride with Nick. The jealous part of her, perhaps the sister of the Logical One, felt better, but Kyrie found it cold comfort in light of the fear and anxiety stirred up by their visit.

As the cars left the parking lot, the Toyota in the lead, she began to turn from the window but paused when she saw the dark figure of a man step out from the shadows between two cars on the far side of the lot. He was little more than a black shape in the night, but she shuddered. Something about the way he stood and watched the two cars depart troubled her.

"Kyrie, come on," Maddie pleaded. "I wanna watch the movie. You *said*."

She turned and gave the little girl a half smile. "I did say. You're right. Mac and cheese coming right up, and then we go find Dory."

Kyrie glanced back out the window and gave a little

start. She stepped closer to the glass, craning her neck to search the parking lot for any glimpse of that dark figure, but whoever it had been had vanished.

Something caught her eye, up in the air, almost level with Nick's fifth-floor apartment. A swath of black fabric flapped and danced in the night wind, blowing across the sky roughly in the same direction the cars had gone.

Kyrie watched it float and roll on a hard gust of air, and then she turned away, happy that she and Maddie were safe inside, out of the wind and the dark and away from whatever so terrified the little girl's parents.

ELEVEN

With Maddie safe, Tess switched cars, letting Audrey ride alone with Nick. Leaving their daughter behind troubled her enough without also having to share another drive with her ex-husband during which Maddie was sure to be the topic of conversation. Maddie or Kyrie, and right now Tess could not manage to talk about either. Instead, she rode shotgun in Lili's Toyota.

In the backseat, Frank Lindbergh pointed a gun at the creature who had once been Simon Danton. The ghost who had once worn Frank's own face. The doubles were strong, so they had been careful when cutting away the duct tape that bound Danton to Tess's kitchen chair. They'd waited until Maddie was safely out in Nick's car and the real Frank had kept the gun aimed at Danton the whole time.

She glanced over the seat at Danton as they pulled out of the parking lot at Nick's building. He cradled the arm Nick had broken with the bat, but it seemed to have begun to heal itself.

"So, what will happen, really, if Frank puts a bullet through your skull?"

Danton relaxed against the seat, seat belt tugging against his left shoulder and passing through a part of it that had faded, less solid than the rest of him.

"I honestly don't know," Danton replied. "But I'm not eager to find out."

"Audrey said it might kill him," Frank added. "Destroy the construct, unmoor the spirit. But she also said that at the very least it would be inconvenient, and it would hurt." He glared at Danton with seething hatred. "That's okay by me."

Tess watched the streetlights flicker off the dark hood of the Toyota as Lili picked up speed. Soon they were wending their way through Harvard Square and then over the Charles River into Boston. As they crossed the bridge, Lili glanced at her.

"Do you think her life is better?" Lili asked, her voice low.

In the green glow of the dashboard lights, she looked more haunted than ever.

"Your double, you mean?" Tess said quietly.

Lili bit her lip, her fingers flexing before she gripped the steering wheel again. She kept her eyes on the road. "I know they've used . . . influence, somehow. They've only been around for a few months and Devani Kanda's got her art in a gallery on Newbury Street. They have driver's licenses and other identification, presumably. They've got to be nudging people, pulling strings, so nobody questions them too closely. I can't believe I'm talking about magic, but that's magic right there, isn't it?"

"Something like that," Tess replied, knowing that the dead thing that had once been Simon Danton must be listening, that he could answer Lili's question easily enough. That he must be laughing inside at their fear and self-doubt.

"It got me thinking," Lili went on. "I started wondering if maybe she deserved it more than I did."

"Deserved what?"

Lili slowed, the engine idling as they waited for a red light to turn. She exhaled, wearing an apologetic smile.

"Life," she said.

Tess turned in her seat. "Don't be—"

"I know," Lili said, waving her to silence as the light turned green and they slid through Boston traffic. "Trust me, I've been through it all in my head. I'm saying I spent some time thinking about the idea that the ability for them to have a better life—happier and more successful and without so much pain and worry—made them more deserving. I mean, I'd have liked an easier path in my own life."

"We all would."

"But the more I thought about it, the more I realized I've earned this life. Yeah, I've lived through some ugly times, but I'm more than the things I've survived . . . I'm the life I've built on top of those things. Y'know, there was a time I wanted to be you."

The road seemed very loud beneath the car's tires.

"Why would you want to be me?" Tess asked. "You're so much stronger than I am. Ever since my accident I've been in pain, but when it gets really bad I tell myself that pain won't break me. That you never let it break you, and if I gave into the despair that comes with it, then I wouldn't have learned anything from being your friend. And I have."

Lili reached for her hand. They drove that way for a little while, taking strength and courage from each other. Tess could feel the weight of the gaze of the men in the backseat—one living and one dead. Frank had faced his own struggles, his own darkness, and found himself not as strong as he would have hoped. But tonight he was taking that part of himself back, the part that he'd surrendered.

Danton, though . . . he was another story. Just being in his presence made her skin crawl. The doubles were the spirits of men and women who had opened their hearts to real evil, the kind of darkness that Tess had always convinced herself must be just a myth. But evil was no myth—it was real, and vibrant with such power that it flexed and trembled and breathed all around them, a live wire waiting for someone foolish enough to grab hold of it.

She'd been so afraid, but her future depended on whether or not she would stand and fight. Her life with Maddie—and maybe Maddie's life itself—hung in the balance. Fear burned away to nothing in the light of that knowledge.

Tess turned in her seat and glared back at Danton. "You're awfully quiet. I'd have expected mockery from you."

All of his arrogance had fled. The dead man only sat calmly, his cadaverous face looming in the flickering city lights as Lili drove through Boston.

"You want to live, just as we do," he said at last. "I cannot mock that desire."

Tess stared at him a moment longer, aware that he was just biding his time, waiting for an opportunity. In his place, she would have done no different. Danton was right, they both wanted the same thing—to live.

When they drove past the Nepenthe Hotel, the dashboard clock showed the time as 7:32 P.M. Tess directed Lili down a side street a block from the hotel. Boston was a bustling city most nights of the week, but they managed to find a parking spot. Tess saw Nick's car drive past them, Audrey waving to indicate that she'd noted their location.

Lili killed the engine, glancing at Tess as if to say *what now*? Somewhere along the line, Tess had taken the reins, but that was all right with her. She would hold them tightly.

"Frank," Tess said, glancing into the backseat. "We can't let him get very far from us, but I don't want to take Danton inside."

The dead man sneered.

"I'd like to take a hammer to the psychomanteum," Frank replied, so different from the withered thing that had come through her front door only hours ago.

"I know and I'm sorry," Tess said. "But I don't know what he might do to interfere. To stop us. I need you to stay here with him, keep that gun on him, and if he tries to get out of the car or makes any move to hurt you, put every bullet you have in his head."

Frank took a deep breath as if he might be frightened, but Tess remembered the things he'd said about being held prisoner in his cellar and knew he wouldn't hesitate.

"We'll wait right here," Frank promised.

Danton leaned forward slightly. Frank pressed the barrel of the gun into his side but the dead man only glared at Tess.

"What do you suppose will happen if you manage to do this?" Danton hissed between his teeth. "The demon will still be there. Still hungry."

"Trapped there, yeah," Tess replied. "File that under, not my fucking problem."

She popped open the door and stepped out, buzzing with the anger and determination that protecting her daughter had given her. The cold autumn wind whipped around her and leaves skittered by on the sidewalk. The night made her more alert, attuned to a purpose that the people driving by her could never have understood. She slammed the door as Lili climbed out of the driver's seat. As they crossed the side street and headed back toward the hotel, Lili clicked the automatic car lock and its familiar tweet seemed to originate in another world.

On the other side of the street, Tess and Lili waited while Nick and Audrey parked. Tess saw Nick go to his trunk and retrieve a duffel bag. He glanced around guiltily as he closed the trunk, as if afraid the police might suddenly arrive to prevent the crime about to be committed.

"Don't look so twitchy," she said as Nick and Audrey approached. "You've got guilt radiating out of you so bright you could glow in the dark."

"You ready?" Nick asked, ignoring her jibe.

"Not even close. But we're doing this anyway," Tess said. She took Lili's hand, gave it a squeeze, and then dropped it. "You'll see the windows for the restaurant. It shouldn't be hard to figure out which is the right door."

"Tess," Audrey said quietly.

They all looked at her. Of the four of them, she was the outsider. The other three were so intimately connected, but Audrey was a colleague more than a friend. At least until tonight that had been the case, but Tess thought that was about to change. Audrey might have been the smallest of them, but her presence loomed the largest. She sensed and understood things that Tess did not envy.

"I know," Tess said. "Be careful."

"If you could feel how wrong that room is, the sheer malevolent weight of the psychomanteum, I doubt any of you would even go in," Audrey said, glancing around. "I'm only here myself because I don't see any other choice. We're only going to get one chance with this so if anyone tries to stop you—alive or otherwise—you can't let them."

Nick seemed about to speak. Instead, duffel hanging heavily in one hand, he drew Tess into a one-armed embrace. No matter what else they had been through or what the future held, they shared a bond that would never fade. Tess hugged him back, but only for a moment before she released him.

"Go on," she said. "I'll see you all in a minute or two."

He nodded and started around the side of the hotel
with Lili and Audrey, leaving Tess alone on the sidewalk. She steeled herself, turned into the wind, and
marched toward the awning at the hotel's front entrance. The doormen paid no attention to her as she
entered. Loud voices and the sound of clinking plates
and glasses came from the pub, but there were very
few people in the lobby and she knew that one of the
staffers behind the desk was sure to notice her if she
headed directly toward the other restaurant. Instead
she smiled at the concierge as if she belonged and
went to the central staircase, padding up the Victorian
carpet runner as if she were a guest.

Quiet reigned on the second floor. The carpet whispered under her feet as she hurried down the corridor
past the elevator bay and the doors to more than two
dozen rooms. At a turn in the hallway, she found the
entrance to another stairway. There was a service elevator there, but Tess feared that might draw more attention, so she slipped through the door marked STAFF
ONLY and started down.

Back on the first floor, Tess opened the door quietly
and slipped out, walked past the restrooms, and glanced
into the lobby. Several people were checking in and others were passing through, either leaving the hotel or
heading into the pub. No one had noticed her.

She slipped along the wall and moved past the hostess station. Heavy curtains had been drawn across the
narrow hall that led into the Sideboard restaurant at the
back of the hotel. She pushed through the curtain and
found herself alone in the room. Alone in the dark. The

only illumination came from outside, the light from streetlamps and passing cars and the neon sign from a pub across the street.

The psychomanteum remained where it had been the last time Tess had been in the Sideboard. But now, in the quiet and the dark, it seemed to pulse with malignant awareness. Nothing moved around or within it, though she could see the mirrored panes inside glinting with light from the nighttime city beyond the windows. Yet she could not escape the feeling that somehow, in the invisible heart of the thing, it buzzed with malevolent power, an enormous wasp nest of ominous potential.

Tess did not hesitate. She moved through the darkened restaurant without searching for a light switch. If she allowed herself to be daunted by the abhorrent aura emanating from the apparition box, the others would be waiting outside forever.

"What the hell are you doing here?"

She jumped, startled by the voice, which she recognized even before she spun around to see Aaron Blaustein standing just inside the curtains she had parted moments before. But it wasn't Aaron, of course, and from the naked hostility of his expression she could see that he knew his masquerade had ended.

Tess took a step backward, toward the psychomanteum. "You'd better call your friends. If you have a plan B, the time has come."

The dead thing wearing Aaron's face smiled at her. "You honestly think I need help to hurt you? To hold you here until Marketa comes to steal what's left of your *self*?"

Marketa, Tess thought. The name of the occultist

who had stolen her face. This dead man had no reason to lie to her when he thought she had no hope remaining.

"And I thought your friend Danton was an arrogant prick," she said.

The thing that wasn't Aaron flinched. "What are you—"

"You were all so full of yourselves, weren't you?" she said. "Cornell Berrige was the most accomplished magician of the nineteenth century and even he couldn't safely summon real evil into the world, but you amateurs thought you'd dabbled enough that calling yourselves the Society of the Lesser Key would lend you a sophistication and a level of skill none of you really had."

As she spoke, Tess kept backing toward the psychomanteum, knowing with every step that the other doubles might be inside, living within the mirrored panes of its interior. At any moment they might step out, might reach for her—the one called Marketa would try to leech more of her soul away, trap her inside the mirrors.

"Your tongue is going to get you killed, woman," Not-Aaron said as he began to approach her. In the soft shadows of the room he seemed to have three faces, one Aaron Blaustein, one she imagined he'd had in life, and the third his true face. Withered and dead, half his lower jaw rotted away.

Tess shuddered. She'd allowed fear and adrenaline to push away the knowledge of what these things really were and what it might mean to be drained completely, reduced to nothing but a husk of humanity, a forgotten shadow.

"I never liked Aaron Blaustein," she said. "But he had a wife and kids who loved him and now he's dead because you and your friends were so full of ambition that you were willing to sell your souls, but too cowardly to pay the price when it came."

"Hush, now, and die," the dead man said. His upper lip curled in disdain as he strode toward her, snatching a knife from a table that had been prepared for the morning's breakfast seating.

"You want to be careful telling a woman to watch her tongue," Tess said. "It never goes well."

She bolted for the emergency exit, smashed the safety bar on the door and it swung wide, blasted by the autumn wind. She turned back to look at the occultist, at the only thing left of Aaron. He picked up his pace, perhaps thinking she meant to run.

Lili was first through the door, this little Indian woman wearing leather gloves and carrying the poker from Tess's fireplace. Aaron's double slowed a moment, then gripped the knife tighter and lunged toward them.

Nick stepped through the door, aluminum bat held down by his side.

The dead thing hesitated.

Lili smashed him across the skull with the fireplace poker, gashing his skin. Blood spattered as he staggered into a table and then fell over a chair, his knife skittering across the carpet.

"Stay down," Nick said, pointing at him with the bat, even as Audrey came through the door with the duffel bag.

"Do it," Tess said, nodding at Lili.

Audrey pulled a pair of golf clubs from the bag and

dropped it onto the floor. She handed one to Tess, glancing around.

"No alarm?" Audrey asked.

"Maybe silent," Nick said. "Clock's ticking either way."

Tess gripped the golf club in both hands and followed Lili up to the psychomanteum. "Careful for the glass."

"Stop!" the dead thing said, its false face wavering. Not-Aaron scrambled to his feet, touching his bleeding head. "You don't understand."

Nick swung the baseball bat, breaking the dead thing's right arm. It cried out in pain.

"Thing is," Nick said, "we do."

Tess stepped into the psychomanteum, where Lili shoved aside the table the hotel managers had put there. She cocked her arms back, ready to swing the golf club at dozens of reflections of her own face.

Audrey began to scream. A wail tore from her throat, followed by desperate words.

"How . . . oh, God, how can you not feel that?" she cried as she fell to her knees.

As if the words had opened some window of perception in her, Tess did feel it. She doubled over, a pressure on her skull unlike anything she'd ever felt. Sweat beaded on her skin and she wanted to run, to get to fresh air, to water, to anything that might help clean the filth from her flesh. The ghosts of the Lesser Key had flesh and bone, they were solid, and somehow Tess and the others had persuaded themselves to look past what else they were. Dead things, yes, but black magicians.

Evil.

Three feet ahead of her, Lili leaned against the mirrored interior of the apparition box, tears streaming down her face as she used her free hand to swipe at imaginary things in her hair.

How foolish they had been to let themselves be brave. Tess wanted to tear her own skin off. Instead, she swung the golf club as hard as she could. Two mirrored panes shattered inside the octagonal booth, shards flying. One cut her face but she ignored the sting and swung again, smashing a third pane.

The thing that was not Aaron screamed and rushed toward the box. Nick struck him again with the baseball bat, shouting for them to keep going. Audrey struggled to her feet and staggered toward the psychomanteum, blood streaming from both of her nostrils from some kind of psychic overload.

Tess grimaced, lifting the golf club again. "Nice try," she managed to say, tears slipping down her face from pure revulsion and fear. "But mothers don't run."

Hundreds of Tess faces looked back at her from the mirrored walls. Hundreds of reflections of her, along with hundreds of Lilis.

"No," Lili rasped.

Tess glanced over at her. *Beyond* her. One of her reflections grew larger, looming. It wore the same clothes as Lili did and its hair looked the same, but it did not move when Lili moved. It had adapted to her reflection, but it lived, and its eyes gleamed with fury.

"No!" Lili cried, and swung the fireplace poker at the glass.

Too late.

The thing that called itself Devani Kanda lunged from within the mirrors, emerging as if thrust from darkness into light. The double wrapped her hands around Lili's throat, momentum hurling them both out of the psychomanteum.

Lili's double strangled her, screaming in hatred all the while.

The dead thing wearing Aaron Blaustein's face only laughed.

TWELVE

Frank sat in the backseat of the Toyota with his back against the door, as far from the revenant corpse of Simon Danton as he could get without fleeing the car. He wished he had thought to ask Lili to crack the windows because it was getting warm and close back there, despite the chilly night. Frank told himself they wouldn't be long. The plan had been for Tess to sneak in, open the emergency door to the outside and let the others in, smash all hell out of the mirrors inside the psychomanteum and then run out the same door before they could be detained and arrested.

Simple.

Batshit crazy, but simple.

He held his gun in both hands, rested on his thigh. For the first few minutes he had kept it aimed at Danton's skull but his arms were getting tired, and if he waited until they were too weary to hold the gun up, Danton might easily get the jump on him. This way the gun still pointed in the dead man's general direction and he could still get a shot off if Danton made a move.

Or even if he didn't.

Ghost or not, dead thing or living abomination, Simon Danton had masqueraded as him, chained him in his own basement, made him shit and piss in a bucket, mocked and laughed at him. Frank wanted very much to shoot him in the face. The strange part of that, however, was that he wasn't motivated by any of the things that Danton had done to him directly, or by horror at the hideous nature of what this inhuman thing was. He wanted to take aim and pull the trigger again and again for only one reason—because Danton had been better at being Frank Lindbergh than Frank himself had ever been.

"I'm going to miss it," Danton surprised him by saying.

Frank kept his arms rigid, ready to fire. "Miss what?"

The dead thing smiled. Frank wasn't sure what the rest of them saw when they looked at Danton, but to him the thing looked like what it was. A haunt. A withered human scarecrow, dried and desiccated. Dead except for the little points of ugly yellow light in the pits of its eyes.

"Miss being you," it said, as if it could read his mind. And maybe it could, after all the bits of him it had leeched away.

"You were never me," Frank said. "You were wearing a costume. Hiding and praying Berrige wouldn't come and make you pay for the evil you'd done."

"Is it so hard to imagine that we wanted a second chance at life?" the dead thing said, its voice the sound of autumn leaves crunching underfoot. "We weren't hiding, we were living."

Frank sniffed, almost a laugh, and saw Danton go rigid.

The dead thing swiveled its head to glare at him with those sickly, gleaming eyes. "What are you—"

"If you weren't hiding, you could have used your own faces."

The dead man glared at him, withered lips parted as if he might speak in his dusty, leathery voice, but he had nothing to say. The point had been made.

Something slapped the window just behind Danton and they both jumped. Frank lifted the gun, afraid the man who'd stolen his face—this man who'd once persuaded a group of others to dabble in black magic—would attack him. In a split second, he realized the sound was not Danton's doing. He'd seen that the dead man was startled but it took his conscious mind a moment to catch up with his instincts, for logic to catch up with fear.

Outside the car, a scrap of filthy black cloth billowed against the glass and Frank's heart beat wildly in his chest.

He knew, then. Even before Danton turned to look out the window, already more faded and diminished than an hour before. Even before the glass shattered and long arms reached into the backseat, spindly fingers like spider's legs closing around the dried flesh of Danton's throat and puncturing it like it was made of papier-mâché.

Even before he saw the grinning, thin-lipped mouth and its rows of black shark's teeth, or the filthy blindfold that covered the raggedy man's eyes.

Danton screamed as the blind man dragged him

from the car, half-vanished dead flesh ripping like parchment paper on the jagged shards remaining in the window frame. The raggedy man stuffed the fading remains of the ghost inside his coat, where the darkness roiled and breathed. Frank saw another screaming face in the shadows inside that coat, a damned soul trapped in a shifting indigo Hell, and beneath the screaming and the sounds of the city there came another voice, speaking a guttural, ancient language so laden with malice that Frank Lindbergh could do nothing but turn away, pressed against the opposite car door, weeping and waiting for the demon inside the raggedy man's coat to drag him into darkness.

When he glanced up, the raggedy man had gone and Simon Danton was no more.

"Oh," Frank whispered to himself. "Oh, no."

Then his hands were scrabbling for the door latch and the lock and he popped open the back door, stumbling into the street. A car horn blared and he turned into the bright headlights of a taxi, which swerved to avoid running him down. The driver shouted profanity out the window, but Frank barely heard. Numb, he turned to look at the side of the Nepenthe Hotel. Dead leaves skittered along the sidewalk and the road, fallen from the handful of trees that lined either side of the street.

He shut the car door softly, calmly. Pushed it to make sure it had clicked into place. For a moment he hung his head, heart thundering and face flushed, wondering if he could live with himself if he ran away now. Maybe if he hadn't already given up on himself so many times in this life that he'd grown sick of it. Maybe if the dead thing Simon Danton—whose screams still echoed in his mind—hadn't reduced him to a human husk before he'd reclaimed his name and his face. Maybe if he hadn't kissed Tess Devlin that night at the party, or if he couldn't remember how soft her lips had been and how kind her eyes on that night.

"Oh, shit," he said, wiping tears from his eyes.

Frank lifted his head, stared at the hotel, and then started to run.

Toward it.

THIRTEEN

In the darkness of the cellar of the Otis Harrison House, Steven found that he could still see. It made no sense, really. When he had come downstairs he had been carrying a flashlight, but now the flashlight was no longer in his hands. He vaguely recalled a cracking sound, though he admitted to himself that it might have been his skull when he had tripped over uneven stones in the floor and fallen.

Don't be stupid, he thought, flexing his fingers on the grip of his service weapon. His palm was dry against the surface of the gun. *If you'd cracked your skull, you wouldn't be standing here.*

Of course he wasn't standing, was he?

No. He was sitting, cradling the gun, letting its weight lie gently in his grasp like the hand of a lover.

The crack had been the flashlight. Almost certainly it had. Though he thought he smelled blood and it might have been his. He had to acknowledge the possibility. After all, he was a police officer, which meant he had to be an objective observer of the evidence. The flashlight, though . . . it was gone, and he remembered the cracking sound and now the cellar cloaked him in darkness.

But he could still see.

His friend whispered to him in words he had never heard before, but just as he could still see in the dark, he understood that rasping language and the things being said to him by that voice drifting up from the pit in the middle of the cellar.

Steven blinked his eyes, so different now. Vision so clear, so detailed there in the darkness. He sat just at the edge of the pit, dangerously close, and felt the cold draft that whispered past him as if the pit itself were breathing.

He cradled his gun and he nodded slowly, understanding the words and the dark, matching his breaths to the breathing of the pit.

FOURTEEN

Belly contentedly full of mac and cheese, Kyrie sat on the sofa at Nick's apartment with a cup of tea balanced on one leg. Maddie had been restless through the first half of *Finding Dory,* but at last she had rested herself against Kyrie, laid her head down on Kyrie's lap and promptly fell asleep. After the intruder the other night and whatever bizarreness had taken place today—hinted at in the girl's intriguing babble of an explanation— the poor thing was totally wrung out. Maddie would think it a betrayal if Kyrie watched without her. They would finish in the morning.

With the credits rolling, Kyrie only just managed to reach the remote control without waking the girl. She exited the on-demand menu and started surfing channels.

The knock at the door made her jump, a bit of tea sloshing out to dampen the leg of her pants. She swore quietly and glanced over her shoulder toward the front door. The knock came again and she grimaced as she slipped Maddie's head off her lap and set the mug down on the coffee table.

She took the chain off the door and was about to unlock it when an icy little tremor went through her. Nick and Tess had been angry and afraid. Ugly things had happened and she would be a fool not to be wary.

Kyrie looked out through the peephole in the door and exhaled, that momentary tension evaporating. Unlocking the door, she cast a quick glance over at a still-sleeping Maddie and then pulled it open, smiling at the woman who stood outside in the hall.

"What's up?" Kyrie asked. "Everything all right? I didn't expect anyone back this soon."

The woman smiled. "Can I come in?"

Kyrie shrugged and stepped back to let her pass. "Sorry, what was your name again?"

The woman stood watching Maddie sleep for a few seconds before she turned around. "Audrey."

"Right," Kyrie said, closing the door. "Sorry."

There came a rustling from the sofa. "Kyrie?"

Both women turned to see Maddie sitting up, sleepily rubbing her eyes.

"Hey, sweetie," Audrey said, moving toward the sofa. "Your parents sent me to pick you up."

"Whoa," Kyrie said, digging into her pocket and tugging out her cell phone. "I'd think I would have gotten a call or a text, at least."

Audrey shot her a hard look, edged with irritation. "Call Nick if you want."

Maddie sat on one of the big cushions on the sofa, frowning at Audrey and scratching the back of her head. Kyrie hesitated. Nick and Tess—together—had asked her to watch Maddie tonight, and that alone had been strange and awkward, though Kyrie had been touched by the way Tess had spoken to her, the acceptance she had felt just before they had left. It had been a stressful couple of days, so it wasn't impossible that their plans tonight had changed, but if that was the case—

"Why send you?" she asked. "If they want her, why didn't they just come get her?"

Audrey sighed and cocked her head, staring at Kyrie. "I'm tired. Truly. Could you just call him if you're concerned?" She glanced at the little girl. "Maddie, get your things."

Kyrie bristled at the woman's bitchy attitude. She enjoyed seeing Maddie but she had given up her night for this, dropped everything to come over and help out. Her hackles raised, she starting texting Nick.

"What's the password?" Maddie asked.

Kyrie looked up sharply, saw the confusion on Audrey's face.

"Sorry?" Audrey asked.

The little girl crawled forward to the arm of the sofa and knelt there, studying Audrey's face. "Mommy said not to go anywhere with anyone unless they knew the password."

Audrey stiffened and the corner of her mouth twitched into something close to a scowl. Kyrie's throat went dry. What the hell was going on? She stopped in mid-text and hit Nick's name on her contacts list instead, moving around Audrey to stand behind the sofa. Holding the phone to her ear, she listened to it ring, waiting for Nick to answer and explain it all to her.

Kyrie reached over the back of the sofa and put a hand on Maddie's shoulder.

"He's not answering," she said, turning to glance at the girl.

In her peripheral vision, Audrey looked dead. Rotting.

Kyrie let out a startled cry and whipped her head back around just as the dead thing leaped at her, wrapped both hands around her throat, and drove her to the carpet. Eyes wide with terror, Maddie began to scream. Kyrie beat at Audrey's hands and face but the woman's grip on her throat was impossibly strong. Black stars exploded across her vision as Kyrie tried to drag in even a single breath and found she could not.

If she could not get Audrey off her, there would be no screaming for her.

No scream. No breath.

No life.

FIFTEEN

As Tess screamed her name, she saw Lili's double drive her to the floor just outside the psychomanteum, and then they were rolling away. Two Lilis crashed into the legs of a table. One smashed the other's head against the carpeted floor. Tess ran toward her—toward them—and then she froze.

The clothes were nearly the same. The hair was identical now.

"Lili?" she said. "Lili, which is you?"

Shame filled her—how could she not know her dearest friend? One of them glanced at her, eyes desperate, and Tess cocked back her arms to bring her golf club down on the other one . . . when that other turned and said her name, pleading and full of emotion. Of *knowing*.

Tess lowered her arms, frozen with indecision.

"Just get them apart!" Nick said, racing past her and grabbing hold of Lili—one of them anyway.

Golf club in one hand, Tess dropped to one knee

behind the two Lilis and wrapped her free arm around the nearest one while Nick grabbed the other.

"What are you doing, Tessa?" demanded the one she'd grabbed.

"Just let go!" Tess snapped. "We can't—"

Then Tess felt a tug at her hair, hard at first, and then so much worse. She cried out in pain and raged as she was yanked backward. Twisting on the floor, she got her feet under her, going along with the momentum of her attacker to relieve the pain. She drove her head upward and smashed her skull into the bastard's jaw, and only then—as his grip loosened and the veil of her own hair fell away—did she see the rotting corpse face of the dead thing who masqueraded as Aaron Blaustein.

The Aaron thing grabbed her throat, cutting off her air. Her eyes went wide and she felt the desperate need immediately, the screaming lack of oxygen. The dead were stronger than the living, but Tess did not want to be one of them. Holding the golf club ahead of her, one hand on either end, she drove Aaron backward into a table, smashed her knee into his crotch and then smashed the club upward three times before she broke his grip. His hands flashed out, so fast, and tangled in her hair again. She rammed the golf club crosswise into his throat, but he had her now.

He slammed her face onto the table and pain exploded as her nose buckled. Blood poured onto her lips and down the back of her throat as she tried to get away from him. She looked up just in time to hear the whistle of the aluminum bat as it whickered through the air. Nick stepped into his swing and the bat caromed off dead Aaron's skull with a satisfying crack.

The blow staggered the dead thing and it took two steps backward. Tess crushed its windpipe with a swing of her golf club, then Nick struck it again, and then they were beating it, shattering bones and driving it to the ground. Tess saw the fear in its eyes that it was about to die again, for the last time, but she tasted her own blood in her mouth and remembered the way her double had comforted Maddie that night and she kept swinging. The old pain sang in her shoulder and spine, but it had become just another part of a symphony.

"Audrey!" Tess called. "Help Lili!"

But as she and Nick kept beating the thing that had stolen Aaron's life, she got no reply. With a final swing that caved in part of the corpse's face, she stepped back, heart pounding and breath coming in short gasps, and turned to see Audrey trying to force the two Lilis apart.

Nick grabbed her arm, tried to twist her around. "Tess!"

As she shook him off she saw motion in the corner of her eye and turned to see herself approaching. Herself and Nick. Their doubles had just come into the restaurant, pushing aside the curtain that led out into the hotel, and Tess could hear ordinary voices out there as well. An employee in Victorian garb came rushing in after them and Not-Nick turned, grabbed the employee's skull in both hands, and rammed his head against the wall. The employee went down hard, moaning as he rolled onto his side.

"Audrey!" the real Nick shouted. "The mirrors!"

Tess faced her double as the woman stepped toward her. In the shadows she could see the woman's death face and wondered if this was what she herself would look like after she had spent time in the grave.

From behind her came the sound of shattering glass and she saw her double's gaze shift. Not-Tess gave Nick's double a shove, sending him rushing across the restaurant to reach the psychomanteum. Nick stepped in his way. Tess swung her golf club at her double, putting all of a mother's rage behind the assault. The woman sidestepped, reached in and grabbed her wrist and hurled her to one side with such force that Tess landed on a table, sliding off the other side in a clatter of silverware and side plates and a tangle of tablecloth.

No, she thought, seized with panic. She couldn't let it be so easy. Fighting the dead would get them nowhere. They might have killed the Aaron thing but they were human and fragile and the odds were against them.

Stick to the plan.

Tearing loose of the tablecloth, Tess rocketed to her feet, already in motion. Her double came for her, confident and calm, and Tess dodged past her. She heard Nick grunt in pain as his double began to beat him, but she could not stop. She ran for the psychomanteum, where Audrey swung again, shattering more of the mirrored interior.

Two figures staggered across Tess's path. Both had Lili's face. With an anguished cry, one Lili drove the other backward into the psychomanteum, where they fell over the threshold and then scrambled to remain upright. Hands pressed into shards of mirror glass as they fell and rose and fought.

Audrey ignored them, shattered another mirrored pane.

Tess called her friend's name . . . and then froze, watching in horror as one Lili forced the other against the last mostly intact wall inside the psychomanteum. *Not against,* Tess saw, *but through.* The two Lilis swore and clawed at each other, but the one with the leverage kept pushing and Tess could only stare, open-mouthed, as the other slipped into the mirrored wall as if she were being lowered into a silver pool of water.

Lili whipped around. "Audrey! Give me that!" She snatched the golf club from Audrey's grasp and began to shatter that last full wall of mirrors. Her own reflection—doubled—screamed back at her from the other side.

Tess lowered her golf club. "Lili?"

Then she felt a cold draft whip around her, almost caressing, and she heard a scream that sounded hauntingly like her own. Tess spun and saw the predatory silhouette of the raggedy man crouched over the ruin of Aaron's double. She thought they had killed it, but the dead thing still lived, and now it screamed as the raggedy man dragged long, filthy fingers through its fading substance. The blindfolded thing that had been Cornell Berrige picked up the ghost and thrust it bodily into the shadows inside his jacket. The heavy coat hung open wide, a hungry maw of darkness, and when Tess got her first real glimpse inside that coat, her veins turned to ice. Sorrow like nothing she'd ever known came crashing down on her and tears spilled from her eyes, burning trails along her cheeks.

Inside the raggedy man's coat there were shapes, just hints of shadows, the faces of other ghosts. One of them might have been Berrige's own, and another was the real Aaron Blaustein. She saw his torment and heard his muffled cries and regretted every time she had ever thought ill of him.

"What have you done?" someone screamed. Her own voice.

The raggedy man flew across the darkened restaurant and landed upon Nick's double. The dead Nick cried out and tried to defend himself, but Berrige had the strength of cruelty in him and he began to feed the double into the suffering hell of darkness inside his coat.

A hand grasped Tess's arm and spun her around and she stared into eyes wide with unthinkable despair.

Her own eyes.

"What have you done?" her double asked again, crying the tears of the dead.

Two more employees came rushing into the restaurant, one in Victorian clothes but the other a security guard. They started shouting, but Tess saw their faces go slack with confusion at the chaos unfurling before them. Someone ran past Tess, then, and it took her a moment to realize it was Frank Lindbergh. She glanced over her shoulder at the door to the sidewalk and saw it slowly closing, a cold wind swirling into the room from outside. Frank ran toward the employees, gun aimed at them, snapping commands at them to silence them and make sure they did not try to interfere.

In the psychomanteum, Audrey and Lili kept swinging away, shattering pane after pane of mirrored glass. In her double's eyes, Tess saw defeat. The dead thing knew that the raggedy man had come for her and she had nowhere left to hide.

SIXTEEN

As the pressure built in her head, blood rushing to her face, Kyrie tried to find the strength to smash at Audrey's arms again. She twisted her shoulders, a primal effort to force away the hands that were strangling her to death. No air came in. Black pools formed at the edges of her vision as if her eyes were welling with shadows instead of tears. Her eyelids fluttered and she knew it was over for her. She flicked her gaze right and left, not wanting the last thing she saw to be the face of her murderer.

"Sorry, lovely," the killer said. "You're just in the way."

Kyrie's thoughts were leaves spinning in a dust devil. She tried to hold on to the few that remained. Her body went still but her eyes kept shifting, searching. Something moved to her right, blurry features that quickly resolved into those of a little girl. Maddie held a small lamp with a blue, stained-glass shade.

No, Kyrie managed to think. *Run.*

But then her eyelids drooped and she knew she was about to die.

Blue glass shards showered down onto her face and neck and into her hair. For half a second she didn't realize the hands were off her throat because she had given up trying to breathe. Then she inhaled sharply, air rushing into her burning legs. Her throat felt ragged, airways compacted but still open enough to drag oxygen painfully into her chest. The rusty wheezing of her own desperate breathing frightened her as she rolled onto her side and saw the terrified eyes of the little girl who'd been left in her charge.

Maddie dropped the ruin of the shattered lamp. Kyrie had not even heard the sound of it crashing against Audrey's skull. *You were dead there for a moment,* she thought to herself.

"Little bitch," Audrey sneered, wiping blood from her face. A blue shard jutted from her scalp, just behind her left ear.

"Please," Maddie whispered, lip quivering as she backed away.

Kyrie dragged in another lungful of air, her brain trying to force her body to obey. She pushed herself weakly up onto one elbow, panic surging through her as Audrey started after Maddie. The little girl ran around the front of the sofa to hide.

"Don't . . ." Kyrie managed.

Audrey strode over, murderous intent in her eyes . . . and then faltered. Her eyes lit up with alarm and she glanced down at her hands, then along the length of her body. Kyrie blinked hard, trying to clear her head, thinking oxygen deprivation had done something to her, or that she had begun to black out again and her perceptions could not be trusted.

Her attacker's hands were transparent. Audrey's whole body had begun to fade.

"No!" Audrey said, but even her voice seemed diminished, as if nothing more than a quiet echo in another room.

Voices droned away on the television, strangely loud now.

Kyrie propped herself up, hands on her aching throat as she stared at the woman who had attacked her. Fading, her face changed. For a moment she seemed taller, her hair blond. With mournful blue eyes, the woman turned to stare at Maddie and then her eyes sank back into her head and her face began to rot.

Maddie began to sob as they watched the ghostly woman turn into a corpse before their eyes.

Then the intruder vanished, leaving only an afterimage hanging in the air for a few seconds until even that was gone.

Maddie rushed to Kyrie's side. She gathered the little girl into her arms and they sank back onto the carpet in tears. Together.

Just a few seconds, Kyrie told herself. Then she would get herself together, get up, and call the police.

And Nick. She would call Nick.

Her tears dried in an instant. She clutched the weeping girl to her and stared up at the ceiling. Audrey had been with Nick before she had come here and tried to take Maddie.

No, she thought, shuddering. Nick had to be okay. He had to.

SEVENTEEN

Tess wiped blood from her mouth, glaring at her double. "It's time."

But amid the fear in her double's eyes, she saw a glimmer of desperate hope. She raised the golf club, but not quickly enough. The woman with her face rushed at her, ripped the club from her hands and flung it across the room. She grabbed Tess and hurled her to the carpet near where the raggedy man rose to his feet, forcing the grasping hands of Nick's double into the hungry shadows inside his coat.

A few feet away, the real Nick stood frozen with uncertainty.

"Her!" Tess's double shouted. "It's her you want! My name is Tess Devlin. I have a daughter named Maddie who is six years old. I have a life and friends and I live every day in pain. I've had my heart broken and I deserve to live, deserve a chance to keep looking for happiness."

"She lies!" Tess snapped, shaking her head as she backed away from the raggedy man. But as she held up her hands to fend the blindfolded man off, she realized they were partially faded. She staggered at the sudden pain in her gut as the double began to leech at her again.

"Your master wants the Society of the Lesser Key!" the double said. "He wants the ones who tried to control him!"

The raggedy man slid toward them, almost gliding. Behind the filthy cloth across his face, the pits of his eyes were sunken shadows. He put his head back and sniffed at the air, then cocked his head and turned toward Tess.

"If you could see," she said softly, "I would show you my scars." Her shoulder and spines throbbed with vivid pain. "These ghosts—these *fuckers*—ordinary life isn't enough for them. They wanted perfection. If you could look at my body you would see I'm far from perfect. No matter what she's stolen from me, you must be able to sense that. I'm broken, inside and out, but I'm still living. I don't know who the hell this is, but my name is Tessa Anne Boudreau Devlin. It's my name. They're my scars. Maddie's *my* daughter."

"Tess," Nick said, the echoes of their old love in his voice. Afraid for her.

The raggedy man whipped toward him, leaned forward and inhaled deeply. His brow furrowed above that filthy blindfold and his expression hardened, as though in some dark epiphany. Slowly he turned toward Tess's double and then took a step in that direction, hands rising and reaching, the souls inside his coat crying out. Yet with those voices was another, a deep and rumbling voice that spoke in a guttural tongue unlike anything she had ever heard.

"No!" Tess's double said, backing toward the shattered apparition box. "It's not me you want. It's not . . . please."

But the raggedy man had sensed the truth when Nick had called Tess's name, and even the demon he served could feel it now. Not-Tess begged, backing up farther. Behind her, Audrey and Lili stepped out of the ruin of the psychomanteum. Audrey had gone pale and her eyes were full of dread, and then Tess saw why. She lifted her right hand and a long jagged shard of mirror glinted in the light from outside. The scarf she'd been wearing was wrapped around one end to protect her from its sharp edges.

"Audrey?" Tess said.

In her terror of the raggedy man, Not-Tess did not spare her a glance. Nick saw them, though . . . saw Audrey and Lili as they lunged at the double from behind, both of them with daggers of broken mirror, and began to stab. Tess expected blood and screams. She expected them to pull back the blades and stab again, but instead Lili and Audrey thrust harder, plunging the mirrored glass of the psychomanteum as deep into the double's flesh as they could.

Not-Tess gasped and sagged on her feet, eyes rolling backward as she began to fade. In the gloom of the room she passed into a kind of twilight of substance. In the space of what seemed only two or three seconds she slipped from solidity into nothing more than a momentary afterimage. When Tess blinked her eyes, even that had vanished.

The room seemed to flex and breathe, a wave of malice erupting from the raggedy man and then flowing outward with such force that it staggered Tess. Curtains blew and tables shifted. Chairs overturned. Nick cried out in something like a prayer and clapped a hand over his chest, rocked by it. Lili had to catch Audrey to keep her from falling backward as the last of the mirrored panes of the psychomanteum shattered, showering onto the floor inside the apparition box.

The raggedy man hissed through his teeth, cracked lips peeling back in a seething fury. His coat undulated with a life of its own as he sniffed the air, caught the scent of the women in front of him and then ran at them with his hands outstretched.

Nick shouted in alarm and tried to grab hold of Berrige's coat as the raggedy man ran by. He cried out in pain and yanked his hands back as if he'd burnt them, but Tess saw ice on his fingers and knew hell did not have to be a place of fire.

"He's blind!" Tess snapped, running toward Nick, turning him and propelling him along with her. "Don't let him touch you!"

The employees by the door had begun shouting again. Frank aimed the gun at the security guard's head while the woman who'd come in with him knelt by the employee on the ground—the one the doppelgänger Nick had slammed into the wall.

Audrey dropped low as Lili skirted to her left. The raggedy man sensed them, but not clearly enough. He lunged, scrabbling for them, trying to get a fistful of their clothes or hair or the substance of them, a handful of the ghost-stuff inside everyone. Soul or spirit or humanity.

Lili stabbed him in the throat.

"No!" Tess said. "The jacket!"

Audrey's eyes gleamed with understanding and she slashed at the long coat, tore a rent in the fabric. Tess heard screams but they did not issue from the raggedy man's throat. The room vibrated with the bass thunder of the demon's displeasure. Tess hurled herself at the raggedy man's back and slammed into him, sent him crashing forward through the open door of the psycho-manteum. He sprawled on the floor, crashed into the table and chairs the hotel managers had put inside, stabbed by a thousand broken shards of the cursed mirrors that had hung there.

Tess followed him in. She stepped over him and ripped the thick white cloth from the table, then snatched up a long, wickedly sharp slice of broken mirror. The raggedy man tried to surge to his feet, reached up to stop her arm from descending, but scent and sense alone could not guide him. Tess batted his arm away and sank the mirror shard into the fabric of his coat, grabbed the cloth-wrapped haft with both hands and ripped downward. A gust of putrid wind enveloped her and she felt the touch of a malignance so vile that her stomach churned and she nearly collapsed beside him. Then she heard the rumble of the demon's voice and she looked into the tear in the jacket.

A single, terrified eye stared back at her, diaphanous and pale.

Tess screamed and took a step backward and that was all the raggedy man needed. He grabbed her by the throat, homing in on her scream, and lifted her off the floor. She slashed at the arms of his coat, hacked at the blindfold across his eyes, cutting his cheek and the bridge of his nose.

Then her friends were there, pushing inside the psychomanteum, each with a mirror shard in hand. Lili and Tess and Nick brought those gleaming glass daggers down in slashing arcs, tearing through the back of the raggedy man's coat, and he threw back his head just as her double had, mouth open in a silent scream.

He began to fade, and hope sparked a fire in her heart.

But when she tore her blade through that black fabric again, it fluttered in an unseen wind and seemed to expand, unfurling and billowing as it rose to hide his face. It enveloped him like a death shroud and then diminished, tightening and twisting down upon itself until it simply vanished.

Tess heard a heart pounding and knew it was her own. The four of them stood in a small circle inside the ruin of the psychomanteum, breathing hard and flush with the grim joy of survival. They stared at one another.

"Is he . . . ?" Nick began.

"He didn't fade out," Audrey replied.

"No," Tess agreed. "He ran."

"Only one place he'd run to," Lili said.

She nodded. She knew where Cornell Berrige would run. They all knew.

"Tess!" someone shouted.

They whipped around and saw Frank holding his gun at the three hotel employees who were still just inside the room. Tess could see in their eyes that they had seen quite a bit of what had just unfolded inside the psychomanteum, and it terrified them.

"Go!" Frank barked, covering the security guard and the other two. "I've got this. Just get out of here!"

"No!" the guard said. "Don't . . . don't move!"

Nick grabbed Tess by the arm. "Go!"

Then they were running, all four of them. The employees shouted as they bolted for the street door through which they'd entered. Audrey slammed it open and then they were in the street, racing for the cars. Frank did not allow the security guard to follow.

Tess still dragged the white tablecloth beside her, right hand clutching it around her shard of the psychomanteum. Somehow she had been unable to leave it behind, which was for the best.

She felt sure she would need it.

EIGHTEEN

Steven crouched in a corner of the cellar of the Otis Harrison House, cloaked in shadows deeper than the darkness around him. The stone floor vibrated with the power of the voice that came from that round pit in the middle of the room, insinuating words spoken in a language he had never learned but whose meaning he understood. He felt the words in his heart. Sensed the weight and shape of them.

The words made him feel strong and full of purpose.

Something shifted in the cellar and he twitched and whipped his head around to peer into the darkness. He bared his teeth, some small part of him reeling in horror at the savagery of the response, but the rest of him rejoicing in it. He sniffed the air, caught a strange scent—like the smoke from burning leaves—and then saw dust begin to swirl and eddy across the cellar. With a ripple of shadow, a scrap of dark fabric appeared amid that swirling dust devil. It billowed and grew, and Steven watched it sculpt itself into a man.

Berrige, he thought, but he knew the thought was not

his own. Even the voice inside his head was not his own voice. The name of this filthy, grizzled, blind-folded man had come from the pit.

Steven felt the voice's recognition. *Berrige is the servant,* he thought. *The previous servant.*

"You have failed," Steven felt himself saying, his throat barely able to contain the deep rumble of that voice.

The blind man glided through the shadows toward him . . . toward the pit. His long black coat had been torn to ribbons and long strips of the fabric fluttered around him, reaching out and floating in the dark like the tendrils of some terrible sea creature.

"It's not too late," Berrige said, pausing near the edge of the pit. He cocked his head back, sniffing the air, and then snapped his head around to stare blindly at the corner where Steven crouched. "There are others who will come. Tainted others. They will serve well enough."

Caressed by darkness, breathing it into himself, Steven felt what the voice felt. A bargain had been struck. There was to be a ritual. After ages trapped halfway through a doorway at the bottom of the pit, the voice might be freed at last if only Berrige would fulfill his promise. The yearning, the hunger, the hatred that seethed from the voice in the pit raged in Steven's own veins. He shook with it, dug his fingernails into his palms until blood dripped to the stone floor.

"It is not for you to decide what will serve," the voice of the pit whispered through him.

Berrige ignored him now, approaching the pit.

"You will have what you desire," Berrige said, hanging his head in obeisance. "We will both be free."

Steven's soul had shimmered with malice only a moment before, intent upon punishment. Now he felt the thing in the pit hesitate, and in that moment of uncertainty he blinked and found himself alone in the darkness. Panic seized him. He felt the wall at his back, heard the scritch of small stones under the soles of his shoes, but he could see nothing and could hear only the soft breath of the other man in the room and the hollow emptiness of the pit. He gave a quiet gasp as his mind replayed the past few hours, free from the horrid intelligence that had subsumed him.

Bile burned up the back of his throat and he clapped a hand over his mouth to keep from throwing up. To keep from screaming. With his other hand he sought his gun. He searched his memory in hopes that he could remember where he had dropped his flashlight.

His fingers bumped the gun, searched its contours, and then his training kicked in and he brought the weapon up and aimed it into the darkness where he had been able to see Berrige only seconds before. He opened his eyes wide but there was no light at all, nothing to give away the location of the pit or the blindfolded man except his memory.

He felt sick. Coated in a film of shit. Disgusted with himself in a way that made him want to scream and tear off his own skin to be clean, but even then he would have to thrust his fingers down his throat and vomit up the taint of the thing that had snuck inside him. The urge to spit hatred at Berrige, to speak his anguish, nearly overwhelmed him but he bit down on the words. These were not human things and he was only a man.

Gun hand steady, he slid two steps sideways. If he could find the wall he could make his way to the stairs.

Stop.

The voice in the pit would not allow him to go.

Feel it. Feel them, the voice said, and just like that it was inside him again. With a flicker his vision returned, a palette of grays. The words from the pit were no longer just guttural rumblings now. He understood, but in that instant when the demon wound its influence around him again, he knew that it was not that the voice had learned his language. It had infected him deeply enough that its words had become his words.

They're here, it said inside him, and in a rumble from the pit.

Steven did not have to interpret the words. He felt them arriving outside the house, felt them climbing out of the two cars they had driven here. He felt them because the demon felt them. Across the cellar, Berrige turned toward the outside wall and cocked his head back, inhaling deeply. Below the stained and tattered blindfold, he smiled a rot-toothed grin and uttered a sigh of cruel satisfaction.

"No," Steven whispered, or thought he had. His lips had not moved. The demon felt his reluctance and then burned it from his heart.

The gun grew lighter in his hand and he grinned a grin that mirrored Berrige's.

Lili, no, a tiny piece of him thought. *Run.*

But he began to creep toward the stairs, grin widening, grip tightening on the gun. The voice in the pit required that the ritual be finished. It had been interrupted so long ago, but tonight it would at last be completed.

That malice in him felt so good that he laughed.

"No," Berrige growled. "I will make the offerings. I will be free."

The dead magician swept across the cellar, savagely baring his teeth. Steven snapped around, took aim, and shot him twice in the chest. Berrige grunted, staggered backward a single step, and then the shadows of his coat stitched up the holes the bullets had left behind.

Berrige lunged and grabbed hold of him. Steven struggled but the dead man had momentum. Strips of torn fabric from Berrige's coat wrapped around Steven's forearms as the magician drove him backward, then twisted and hurled him along the cellar floor. The gun fell from Steven's hand as he struck the stones and rolled right over the edge of the pit. The gun clattered along the stones. It was the last thing Steven saw as his fingers grasped for purchase and found none.

He fell into a cloud of the demon's frigid breath.

Cold as ice.

As death.

NINETEEN

Tess stood in front of the Otis Harrison House for the first time since the day their team had completed work in the cellar—the day the psychomanteum had been dismantled and packed away. On that warm and rainy afternoon she had thought it just another job, fascinating but fleeting. One to remember, but nothing that would have any lasting impact on her life. Now she stared at the dead birds that littered the street and the sidewalk around the property.

"Over here!" Nick called.

She flinched, stared a moment longer at the face of the house, and then pulled her attention away. Nick and Audrey had gone to the corner of the house and tried the street door. Tess looked over to see it already yawning open.

"How did they manage that?" Lili asked.

Tess glanced at her, saw the blood-soaked scarf wrapped around her hand, and shuddered. "Let's go."

Lili nodded but made no move toward the open door.

Tess saw the terror in her eyes and went to her, put her left hand on Lili's arm, and waited until their eyes met.

"I'm with you, no matter what happens in there. We walk in together, and we walk out together."

The smile Lili managed then was spectacularly unconvincing, but Tess gave her points for trying.

A car went past on the street behind them, windows partway down despite the chilly fall evening. Music drifted into the night, receding as the car continued on its way as if nothing at all strange could possibly be unfolding there in that old house on Beacon Hill. Tess blinked and stared at Lili and then at Nick and Audrey, who waited a dozen feet ahead. She glanced at the steps that led up to the small front yard and the main door of the Harrison House, then turned and scanned the other buildings. Across the street, a slender man in an expensive suit hunched against the night wind and hurried by, briefcase in hand. Lawyer or politican, she guessed, and wondered if he was in a rush to get home or just to pass by this house as quickly as possible.

The real world—the ordinary world—might not want to see or acknowledge the malignant presence within the house, but they felt it. Tess knew they did. The house radiated such malevolent hostility that Tess felt as if she were pushing through some putrid, bilious membrane just walking toward that door.

The people who lived in the buildings around the Harrison House would go on pretending nothing was amiss because the evil inside its walls had not touched them. Had not caused the dead to try to steal their faces, to break into their homes and cradle their children. Tess knew the Society of the Lesser Key had acted out of fear and desperation, but she had no more sympathy for them than she did for Cornell Berrige. They had indulged in forbidden rituals and wielded black magic with the same breathless curiosity and trembling lust for power as small children starting fires just to watch things burn. The ghosts of the Lesser Key had been laid to rest or trapped forever in a prison of glass—she didn't care which. But the night wasn't over.

"Audrey," she said quietly as she and Lili reached the door. "What now?"

Nick frowned, glancing quickly around to make sure no one was watching them breaking and entering. "What do you mean, what now? We find Berrige and finish this."

"And after Berrige?" Tess asked.

Lili hung back, staring into the gray gloom beyond the street door. Somewhere not far off, a woman began to shout and then a man barked back as an argument ensued. Incongruous, but perhaps not entirely.

"I have a theory," Audrey said. "A hope, really. But let's save it for later. We know why we're here."

Tess exhaled loudly. They did indeed.

Audrey led the way, slipping into the gloomy interior of the Harrison House. Nick stepped aside, still watching the street. The voices of the arguing couple continued to rise, a hurricane of domestic frustration, but when Tess walked through that door it felt as if she had left all of Beacon Hill behind. The door remained open but silence claimed her, a deathly quiet that reminded her of winter nights from her childhood, snowbound with the power off and everyone else asleep.

Lili followed her in, and then Nick closed the door behind them.

The silence felt complete then.

"God, it's so cold," Nick said, and Tess could see his breath.

Her own breath, too. She shivered, wondering how she hadn't noticed. Chilly as the night had turned outside, in here every breath fogged the air. Crystals had formed on the walls and there were patches of ice on the windows.

"How . . . ?" Tess began.

Audrey glanced at her and she realized that it didn't matter how. Occult rituals had been performed in this place, more than once. Cornell Berrige had tried to draw a demon into the world, to part the curtains separating the ordinary world from whatever actual hell might exist beyond it. A crack had formed, as though Berrige had begun to open a window and it had gotten jammed. Invited or not, the malicious presence Berrige had summoned became stuck and after all of these years, it wanted out.

In the car, Tess had torn the tablecloth from the Nepenthe Hotel into strips. She carried the shard of mirror from the psychomanteum in her right hand, wrapped several times around the broken glass. It felt like a paltry weapon—she'd rather have had a shotgun or a crate full of grenades—but she didn't need Audrey's experience to know that they could not destroy evil with a bullet.

"Hey," Nick said, looming in front of her as if he'd appeared from nowhere.

"Yeah?"

He touched her face. Tenderly, the way he had in better days. "You're drifting."

Tess flinched away from him. "Don't touch me."

Nick stiffened, brow knitting. He held a shard of broken mirror as well, so he reached up with his left hand. "We're going downstairs, Tess. If you want to stay up here—"

A rush of alarm went through her and she glanced around to find that Lili and Audrey were gone. Farther ahead, she saw the door open—the door that had been uncovered in the renovation of the house, the discovery of which had led to them all coming here in the first place.

She'd lost time. "I . . ." she began.

The cold came rushing in. She shuddered and hunched forward a little, breath pluming in front of her. A little moan escaped her throat as she felt the pain in her shoulder and hip—the old pain, made worse by the icy chill in the house and by the exertions of the day. Adrenaline had pushed it away, overridden it with fear, and she'd been moving around quite a bit. Now the frigid air made the muscles contract and she felt grinding aches and the pull of scarred flesh.

The pain woke her. Reminded her of who she was. Not the perfect version of Tess, but the human one. A broken girl. The woman who endured.

"Something—" she began.

Audrey called quietly to them from the cellar door. She held a heavy-duty flashlight in her hand—the one that had been in the trunk of Lili's car.

"Stay here," Nick said, practically blocking her way.

"Better yet, go. I don't know what we were thinking. Maddie needs you."

Tess breathed in air so cold it hurt her lungs. "We hurt Berrige. You really think he's going to be forgiving? If we don't finish him, he'll come for us. What Maddie needs is for this to be over."

"Hey," Lili whispered. "Quiet."

"Can't you feel that?" Audrey said, hugging herself against the cold, face etched with fear. She clicked on the flashlight. "It already knows we're here."

Tess stopped breathing for a moment. The house seemed to do the same. She looked at the frost on the walls and floor, at the ice on the knob of the cellar door, and then she tightened her grip on the mirror shard and felt its edge dig into her palm, even through the strip of tablecloth she'd wrapped around it.

"Screw it, then," she said. "What are we whispering for?"

She pushed past Nick and joined Audrey and Lili by the door. Audrey started down and Tess went after her, not bothering to soften her footfalls. Nick and Lili followed, all of them careful on the icy steps. Tess let her left hand trail along the wall, the cold sinking invisible blades into her back and shoulder. There were stretches she could do . . . exercises . . . but not here, and not now. The pain didn't matter, really. If anything, it only cleared her mind.

Tess felt a comforting weight in the pocket of her jacket, but knew the time hadn't come just yet.

Her heart thrummed in her chest as they moved down the stairs. The cold and the dark enveloped them and she thought if it wasn't for the light of Audrey's flashlight, the ice might have swept in with the darkness and frozen them all there forever. She heard Nick breathing at her back, heard the creak of Lili's footfalls on the steps, kept her eyes locked on the beam of yellow light that cut the darkness below, and then they were at the bottom of the steps.

Something scritched against the stone floor.

Audrey swung the flashlight and the beam swept left to right. Tess frowned when she saw the pit—

"No," Nick whispered behind her. "They filled it. The contractors . . ."

—and the gun, just a foot from the lip of the pit. Where had it—

—and the black silhouette of the raggedy man.

Berrige stood off to their right, ten feet from the pit. Frost coated his jacket and his filthy blindfold. His head lay back and he inhaled their presence, then grunted out that air with a low snarl. Audrey's light locked on him, chasing away the darkness around him, but a simple flashlight could not push back the shadows inside the raggedy man.

"Kill him," Lili said. "Audrey, move. We've got to—"

Berrige rushed the stairs as if blown on an icy gale, coat flapping around him. Tess shouted Audrey's name, clutched the mirror shard in her hand and tried to move, but the dead man was too fast. By scent, Berrige found Audrey. With the flashlight beam whipping around, strafing the ceiling, he lifted her by the throat and hurled her across the cellar. As she tumbled on the stone floor and cried out, the flashlight bounced once, struck the stones a second time, and then winked out.

Between the first and second bounce, Tess lashed out with the mirror shard and snagged Berrige's coat. In the first moment of darkness, her urge was to rip, but destroying the coat was no longer the goal. The souls he'd trapped inside that jacket, in the shadowy interior of the fabric, had already been drawn out—stolen from the raggedy man and his master. So she fought her instinct and instead of tearing, she stabbed. The shard sank easily into the dead man's flesh, as if he was made of little more than skin and shadows, and Berrige hissed in pain and reeled away.

"Look out, Tess!" Nick snapped.

She darted left and heard a loud scrape, and then their end of the cellar blossomed into a waterfall of bright crimson light. Nick tossed the road flare to the floor where Berrige had been a second ago. Tess dropped to one knee, put down her mirror shard as she pulled two flares from her jacket pocket, ripped the caps off, and dragged them against the stone floor. They ignited in a rush of heat and light and she hurled them one at a time into the far corners of the cellar. The whole room was rimed with frost and the cold seared their flesh, but in the flickering crimson brilliance, the cellar looked like a proper hell indeed.

"Tess!" Lili screamed.

A shadow fell over her, blocking out the light, and Tess whirled to see Berrige looming above her.

"You hurt me," he snarled, his voice like bones grinding together.

Tess reached for her shard, hand closing on the loosened cloth, but too slow.

Lili raced past her in silence, one arm up to defend

herself as she plunged her own shard into Berrige's chest. The raggedy man grunted, then let out a groan so full of despair that Tess could almost have felt sorry for him. Lili stabbed him again and Berrige grabbed a fistful of her hair . . . and Tess hacked at his arm, slashing with her shard. He cried out and released his grip and then they were side by side, plunging the mirror shards into him. The cloth had slipped a bit on Tess's shard and the glass sliced into her palm. Warm blood trickled along her palm and down her forearm but she ignored it.

Nick grabbed Berrige around the throat and ripped him to the ground, dropped down on top of him, and used both hands to spear the raggedy man through the chest. He pulled the glass knife out and prepared to stab again.

Then Audrey was there, on one knee. "Don't just stab him! Drive it deep! Let it do its work!"

Tess and Lili did as she asked, drove their shards into Berrige's flesh and pushed, forcing the sharp glass as deep as it would go. Nick stabbed his heart again. Berrige's mouth hung wide open in a gasp of shock and pain and, Tess thought, a refusal to believe that he might be destroyed. The jacket fluttered and the raggedy man bucked against them. As Tess stared down at his withered chest, at the place where deadly edged mirror sliced deep into him, his clothes and flesh seemed to coalesce into shadows.

"No!" she screamed. "He's going to get away!"

Audrey smashed her mirror shard down through Berrige's left eye socket, slicing through the blindfold there. He twisted his head once, snapping the mirror shard, leaving most of it imbedded inside his skull. The blindfold fell away and they could all see the shadows spilling out of the empty sockets there. In the glittering red light of the road flares, she did not realize the shadows were an icy mist, but then she felt the cold seeping out of those dark sockets and saw the ice form on the scar tissue there.

Berrige began to sink in on himself.

"It's not working!" Nick shouted. "He's getting away!"

"No," Lili said. "Look at the shards."

Tess glanced down at the mirrored shard in her hands and saw that it reflected a shifting blackness, saw the flap of fabric and the button of a coat in the glass surface—but it wasn't a reflection.

Berrige's flesh collapsed abruptly, misting into a cloud of shadow. With the resistance of his body removed, her hand plunged downward and the mirrored shard snapped as it hit the floor, cutting a much deeper gash into her palm. Tess cried out and rocked backward, landed on her butt with searing pain raging in her hand. As the blood seeped out she took the strip of tablecloth and wrapped it tightly around her hand, holding it against her chest.

Berrige's empty coat and blindfold were all that remained of him. Nick picked it up, searching to make sure nothing of the raggedy man remained . . . except the rags.

"He's gone!" Lili said, a smile lighting up her face.

"This is wrong," Audrey said, rising slowly. She turned in a circle, staring around the hellishly lit cellar. She hugged herself against the cold, her breath pluming, ice crystals glittering in her hair. "Nothing's changed. Can't you feel it? I thought if we destroyed everyone involved in the summoning, the window they opened would be closed. The demon would be gone! But it's still here!"

She whipped around, shivering as she stared at them with pleading, hopeless eyes. "Why is it still here?"

Nick dropped his shard, which clinked as it broke apart on the stone floor.

"Oh, shit," he said softly. "What's this now?"

He and Lili were staring toward the pit, and Tess realized that was where they should all have been looking once they'd gotten rid of Berrige. If the evil remained, it could only come from there.

Tess clutched her bandaged hand to her chest and turned toward the pit. She heard Audrey mutter something too low to hear. A sound came from the pit, a kind of scratching and a low, almost human groan.

A hand reached out of the pit, scrabbled for purchase on the stone floor, and then the other hand stretched out and grabbed hold. Tess took a step away, back toward the stairs, but couldn't avert her gaze. Nick swore.

"Oh, shit," Audrey said quietly. "The gun."

Tess had forgotten the gun but she saw it now, flickering darkly in the spitting red illumination of the road flares.

"No," she said, or thought she said.

She bolted toward the pit, the stones uneven beneath her feet. The figure hauled itself from that hole in the middle of the cellar, hunched as it dragged its body up over the edge and onto the floor. One knee came up beneath it and it saw the gun, reached a long, powerful arm toward it.

Tess cried out as she kicked the gun away. It clunked across the floor and caromed across the wall. The figure from the pit grabbed her ankle and she went down hard, tried to break her fall with both hands and screamed as her slashed palm hit the floor. Powerful hands grabbed her and she turned over, kicked out at her attacker—at the thing, the demon—and only as it reared back did she see its face in that hellish strobing glow.

"Steven?" she said.

The thing from the pit was Lili's ex. He'd been beaten badly, or banged and scraped up, but she recognized his face.

But his face meant nothing. Not here.

The eyes were not Steven's eyes at all. They glowed with their own light, an icy blue that could not be diminished by the hue of the road flares. He lunged for her again and she kicked him hard in the face.

"Stop!" she shouted, and kicked him again, wondering how he could be here. Her thoughts churned. They hadn't even known him during the Harrison House project, he never stepped inside the psychomanteum, so the dead could not have stolen his reflection. This couldn't be a doppelgänger, but if it was the real Steven, how could he be here?

Tess scrambled backward, started to rise.

"Steven, stop! It's me, Tess! Lili is here." She pointed. "Right there! Look at her!"

Nick and Audrey hung back as Lili approached the pit. She glanced at Tess and then moved toward Steven, searching his face for some sign of recognition.

"Lili?" Steven rasped, his throat rusty and unused,

as if it were a dead thing speaking to them. An ancient thing.

"It's still here," Audrey whispered. "The demon is still here. I don't think you should—"

Lili reached up to touch Steven's face with her left hand, caressing his cheek. The ice blue light in his eyes dimmed just a bit and the stone foundations of the house trembled with that moment of recognition. Deeper in the pit, something spoke, then. To Tess it sounded as if the sound came from the base of her skull, from some primeval bit of her brain, a part where only the deepest, most ancient instincts still lurked.

Steven went rigid. Frost turned his skin a dark blue.

He reached for Lili and Tess, hurled himself from the ground. Tess took Lili's wrist and forced her hand forward . . . forced her to stab him in the abdomen. Together, their two hands plunged that shard of mirror deep into his gut.

"Tess, no!" Nick roared.

But the icy light in Steven's eyes blinked out and the rumble beneath their feet went still. Steven let out a kind of sigh and began to tumble forward into Lili's arms. Tess released her wrist and Lili dropped the shard, and then the two of them caught Steven as he fell. Nick and Audrey rushed forward to help and together they lay Steven on the stone floor just a few feet from the edge of the pit.

Bleeding, but breathing. Eyes clear.

TWENTY

Tess stared at Audrey, trying to read her expression in the fading light of the road flares.

"Is it gone?" she asked. "You could feel it before. Is it still here? Is it still inside him?"

Audrey smiled. "We should go."

She stood and walked to the pit, stared into its darkness a moment, and then tossed in the shard of mirror she'd carried with her from the Nepenthe. Relief flooded through Tess—a relief she did not yet trust.

"Take mine," Lili said. "Get rid of it."

Tess glanced over to where Lili had dropped her fragment of the psychomanteum mirror. It had broken into several pieces, but that wasn't enough as far as Tess was concerned. If somehow the madness and malice of Cornell Berrige lived inside that glass, she wanted to make sure it would never escape. Standing, she stamped on the shards over and over and then used the edge of her shoe to brush as many of the pieces as she could into the pit, and then did the same with her own.

Nick flung his piece into the pit with as much force

as he could muster and they all heard it shatter against the inner wall, fragments showering down into the hole.

Lili knelt by Steven, cradling his head in her lap. When Tess rejoined her, she was surprised to see that his eyes were open. Lili shuddered as she exhaled, and only then did Tess realize that she could no longer see their breath. The icy air had begun to recede and the cellar to warm.

"Steven—" Tess said.

"Call 911," Lili interrupted, glancing up at her, face blank but eyes wide with worry. "We've got to get him to a hospital."

Tess could smell the blood. In the fading, flickering flare light, she saw the way Steven held one hand over the stab wound. She pulled out her cell phone, glanced at it, and swore.

"No signal down here," she said.

Nick moved for the steps. "I'll call from upstairs."

"No," Steven grunted. "You . . . all of you need to go."

"Bullshit," Tess said, heart quickening.

"We're not going to just leave you here," Lili said, glancing around at Audrey and Tess to make sure they were on the same page.

"No," Steven said through gritted teeth. He gave Lili his hand. "Help me up."

"I don't think—" Audrey began.

But Steven was already moving. With or without their help, he was determined to move. Tess and Nick rushed to help Lili and together the three of them eased Steven to his feet. One arm over Nick's shoulder, he shuffled toward the steps.

"We get up there and I'll make the call," he said. "I'll report I saw someone breaking in, came in after them, and got myself stabbed for my trouble. I'll call Lili when they've stitched me up and we can talk then. Maybe you can explain the parts of tonight that—"

"Parts of it confuse the hell out of us, too," Tess said.

"I was gonna say 'scare the shit out of me,' but either way."

When he laughed, it became a grimace of pain and he hissed air in through his teeth. Tess kept silent after that, letting Lili and Nick help him up the stairs. Lili whispered tender encouragements to Steven and Tess knew this night would be a new beginning for them. At least something good would come from the terror they'd endured.

She turned to see Audrey lagging behind, staring at the pit in the cellar as the crimson flickering dimmed.

"He's going to be all right," Audrey said, her voice a soft rasp. "Whatever darkness was in him, that bit of mirror drew it out. Otherwise some of us would be dead now. And it wouldn't be so . . . quiet, down here."

Tess knew without asking that she didn't mean the silence in the cellar, but the quiet she felt inside herself.

"Come on," she said. "The light'll go out soon. You don't want to be down here in the dark."

Audrey stared at the pit for another moment, then nodded slowly. She went to pick up the raggedy man's coat. Tess wanted to shout at her, to stop her from touching the fabric. She remembered the suffering faces peering out from the darkness inside that coat. But Audrey snatched it up off the stone floor before she could say a word, carried it back to the pit, and threw it in.

That only left the blindfold. Tess watched as Audrey used the edge of her shoe, just as she had done with the broken shards of mirror, to drag the blindfold to the pit and scrape it over the side.

They both paused then, and Tess realized they were waiting for the same thing. A sound that didn't belong there. A tremor in the stones beneath their feet.

"It's gone," she said quietly.

Audrey glanced at her. "So now you're the psychic one?"

Tess shuddered. "No, thanks. I don't envy you that."

"You need to get that stitched up," Audrey said, gesturing at the bloody cloth wrapped around Tess's hand. "And start hoping the police don't trace any of the blood down here back to you."

Tess frowned. "Thanks. I needed something else to worry about."

Audrey kept talking after that, a quiet but steady stream of words perhaps meant to comfort them both as they left the cellar behind. Tess barely heard Audrey, her mind racing ahead to the moment when she could be reunited with Maddie. All she wanted was to hold her girl in her arms and let her know that all was well, that they were all safe—daughter, mother, and father.

Whatever happened in the future, whether Nick went to London with Kyrie or not, the bond the three of them shared had been made unbreakable in the past couple of days. Tess had no interest in being married to Nick, but they would do anything to keep their daughter safe, would stand shoulder to shoulder in that battle forever. They were allies, and as far as Tess was concerned, that was more than enough.

"Let's go," Audrey said.

Without another word, as the last crimson light of the road flares guttered out, Tess led the way up out of the darkness.

TWENTY-ONE

Frank Lindbergh sat in a chair in the restaurant at the back of the Nepenthe Hotel, wrists cuffed behind his back. A little bubble of madness kept floating up inside him, making him want to laugh out loud at the fact that he'd been cuffed again, but he kept his expression blank and impassive. A lot depended on it.

Nearly an hour had passed since the police had first arrived. The initial response had been a pair of uniformed cops but that had quickly blossomed into nearly a dozen officers, two detectives, and several crime scene techs who spent their time lifting fingerprints off the weapons the vandals had used to demolish the psychomanteum. There was no point in dusting the rear door for prints, since there would no doubt be hundreds to choose from.

They had already bagged his gun—his father's unregistered gun—which they had found in the wreckage of broken glass, wiped clean of any prints.

In the center of the room, one of the detectives engaged the hotel manager in conversation. Both women looked profoundly disturbed, and the detective kept taking deep breaths and working her jaw in frustration. At a table, the other detective sat speaking to a young blond guy named Spencer, who wiped tears from his eyes. His face was flushed a bright pink and he threw up his hands.

"I already *told* you!" Spencer yelled.

The detective hushed him, but Frank didn't need to hear the words to know what was going on. Of the three hotel employees who had witnessed the events concerning the destruction of the psychomanteum, Spencer was the only one who had told the truth. The kid had fallen apart, terrified and jumping at shadows. The other two—including a security guard named Clyde—had wrestled Frank to the ground as the others had fled to pursue the raggedy man.

"The cops are on the way, asshole," Clyde had said.

Frank had sighed, a headache coming on. "And you're gonna tell them what? I only ask because in your shoes I'd want to still have a job tomorrow morning, and I'd be wondering what hotel management would think of the story you're going to tell being quoted in the media. 'Cops say ghosts vandalize hotel restaurant.' Not the publicity your bosses are hoping for, I'm pretty sure."

Clyde had cussed for a few seconds, and then let him up. His pupils were widely dilated and he seemed unsteady on his feet. No doubt he had a concussion from the way Not-Nick had slammed him into the wall, but he still had enough of his wits about him to know they needed a better story than the truth.

The detective who'd been talking to the manager

broke off suddenly and strode over to the corner where Frank sat in his cuffs. After the past week, he felt more at home with cuffs on than off.

"Mr. Lindbergh," she said, dark skin gleaming in the bright overhead lights.

"Detective Nunnally."

"You're going to stick with the story you've been telling?"

Frank eased back in his chair, ignoring the way the cuffs bit into his wrists. "No simpler story than the truth, detective."

"Tell it again."

Frank shrugged. "I was on my way to meet a friend for a late dinner when I saw three guys waiting around by the door over there." He nodded toward the rear door of the restaurant, the one that opened out onto the sidewalk. "The door popped open and I saw they had, like, golf clubs and stuff. One had a gun. I was maybe thirty feet away when they went inside and I hurried over. I heard glass shattering and their voices—laughing, y'know? I pulled out my phone, figured I'd just call you guys, but then I heard someone else shout and a scuffle and I ran in through the same door. One of the guys was fighting with the security guard over there. I tried to help and got my ass kicked for it. When I shook it off, the guys were gone and all the mirrors were shattered."

Detective Nunnally stared at him. "And you didn't hear any of these men say anything that might suggest why they decided to break in here and vandalize this . . . whatever it is?"

With a sigh, Frank rolled his eyes. "I don't know,

man. Maybe one of them got a bad omelet for breakfast one day or something. Are you going to take these
cuffs off now?"

She sat down in the chair beside him. "You going to
tell me why you've got those abrasions on your wrists?
You're obviously no stranger to handcuffs."

Frank gave her a playful grin. "Come on, detective.
Don't tell me you haven't used your cuffs for extracur-
ricular activities now and then. Why don't you check
the damn surveillance videos and see for yourself what
happened? Then you can go back to work and I can go
and call my date and explain why I stood her up."

Nunnally rubbed tiredly at her eyes, a little smile at
the edges of her mouth. Frank suspected that she
knew that *he* knew there were no cameras in the restaurant. There would be cameras out on the street, of
course, but it would take them time to examine that
footage. He had no idea what it would show. If they
found video of him entering with the others, he would
keep spinning lies until he ran out of breath. At worst,
they would charge him with destruction of property.

What else could they do? Believe the crazy kid
shouting about twins trying to kill each other and people vanishing into mirrors?

Detective Nunnally stood. "You're not going home
yet, Mr. Lindbergh. We're going to have this conversation again, somewhere quieter."

Frank got up and the detective took him by the arm.
He had let his life unravel to the point where it had
ceased to matter to him. When his double had imprisoned him, that had begun to change. Dead bastard or
not, the other Frank had shown him that a better version

of himself was not out of reach. He intended to become that better version.

Just as soon as the police let him go.

Nunnally marched him toward the sidewalk door, right past a hotel employee who had at last been allowed to begin sweeping up the shattered mirror glass from the psychomanteum. The detective pushed open the door and a cold autumn breeze blew in. In the same moment, Frank paused, frowning deeply. For half a second, he thought he'd heard someone calling his name, the voice panicked but muffled, as if it came from far away.

The detective jerked him by the arm. "You gonna give me a hard time now?"

Frank glanced back at the broken shards of mirror lying on the floor. In some of them he glimpsed his own reflection, but there were fragments of other faces there. He cocked his head and bent a little closer, trying to make them out.

Detective Nunnally groaned in aggravation and dragged him forward, propelling him out through the open door and into the fresh air and the darkness.

Frank shivered, but not from the autumn chill.

He didn't look back.

TWENTY-TWO

Trapped inside a pile of razor-sharp slivers of mirrored glass, the faded soul of the real Lili Pillai screamed for someone to save her.

No one heard.

They swept up the glass and threw it away.